I0587271

THE
TRUEST
OF
WORDS

GEORGINA GUTHRIE

OMNIFIC PUBLISHING
LOS ANGELES

Omnific Publishing
1901 Avenue of the Stars, 2nd floor
Los Angeles, CA 90067
www.omnificpublishing.com

First Omnific eBook edition, November 2014
First Omnific trade paperback edition, November 2014

The characters and events in this book are fictitious.
Any similarity to real persons, living or dead,
is coincidental and not intended by the author.

Library of Congress Cataloguing-in-Publication Data

Guthrie, Georgina.
  The Truest of Words / Georgina Guthrie – 1st ed.
  ISBN: 978-1-623420-78-9
  1. Contemporary Romance — Fiction. 2. University — Fiction.
  3. Shakespeare — Fiction. 4. Forbidden Romance — Fiction. I. Title

10 9 8 7 6 5 4 3 2 1

Cover Design by Micha Stone and Amy Brokaw
Interior Book Design by Coreen Montagna

Printed in the United States of America

To my readers, with gratitude.

Let me not to the marriage of true minds
Admit impediments. Love is not love
Which alters when it alteration finds,
Or bends with the remover to remove:
O, no! it is an ever-fixed mark,
That looks on tempests and is never shaken...
(William Shakespeare, *Sonnet 116*)

John William Waterhouse (England, 1849–1917)
Miranda and the Tempest, 1916, oil on canvas
Private collection

Aubrey

CHAPTER 1

Beginning

I will tell you the beginning; and, if it please your
ladyships, you may see the end, for the best is yet to do…
(*As You Like It*, Act 1, Scene 2)

"**M**att, can you hurry the hell up?" I banged on the bathroom door.
Surely he could hear me? I tested the handle. Locked. "Matt!"

Behind me, Matt's bedroom door swung open. He appeared
wearing a holey T-shirt and a pair of gym shorts.

"What are you doing in your PJs?" He yawned and squinted at
me. "Shouldn't you be getting ready?"

"I'm trying. I slept in. I'm supposed to be at work in less than
half an hour…" I looked at the bathroom door. "But if you're out
here and Jo is out running—" I pointed to the Post-it note Joanna
had left for me "—then who the hell is in the shower?"

"It's Sarah. She has a job interview at nine thirty."

"Oh."

I clamped my mouth shut. Everyone's doors had been closed
when I'd returned from the Grant family cottage the night before.
Sarah had stayed over on a Sunday night before a Monday morning
interview? That was serious business.

"Sarah had to move out of residence on Saturday," Matt said. "She might hang out with us for a while—if that's okay with you, of course."

Hang out? Did he mean *live* here?

"I already ran it by Jo. She's cool with it."

So, if I don't like it, I'm uncool?

"Yeah, that's cool. I'm completely cool with it. Absolutely cool."

I needed to stop saying that. The more I said it, the more uncool I felt.

"Only if you're sure."

I bit my tongue hard and nodded.

"Awesome. Thanks." He jiggled the bathroom door handle. "Sorry about this. Maybe you could shower later?" He looked at me hopefully.

Um, yeah, I had sex while showering yesterday morning, followed by afternoon pool table sex, after which I whore-bathed with baby wipes. Shower later? Nuh-uh.

"I really need to shower. Like…*really*."

"Ooooh, gotcha. *Sarah?*" he bellowed through the door. "Can you hurry up?" He raised an eyebrow and leaned against the wall. "So, good weekend, huh?"

Ah, Matt. Quick on the uptake, as usual.

Half an hour later, I texted Daniel as I raced across the quad, not sure if he was awake but compelled to share my misery.

> **We should NOT have talked on the phone until one!**
> **I slept in and now I'm gonna be late for work!! -A**

As it turned out, Daniel was awake and in fine form.

> *Good morning, beautiful! Sorry for bending your ear*
> *until all hours. You should have stayed here!*
> *As for you being late for work,*
> *I'd take that as A SIGN. -D*

> **Haha. How did you sleep? Why are you up so early?**
> **What time are you going to your dad's office**
> **to help him unpack?**
> **(See how I changed the subject there?) -A**

(Yes, kudos. Masterful avoidance, as usual.)
I slept like a baby. Helping my dad at nine.
You busy later? -D

You slept like a baby?
Sucked your thumb and soiled yourself repeatedly?
That's attractive. And I'm not sure.
Who's asking? -A

Your favorite snooker instructor. -D

In that case, my afternoon is wide open. -A

Will anything else be "wide open" this afternoon?
I'm sure he'll ask. What should I tell him? -D

Tell him he's a pervert. -A

You know him well! ;) I'll be in touch later.
Good luck with the Snow Queen. -D

Thanks for the vote of confidence.
Ttyl. Love you, SAILOR. xo -A

I love you too, poppet. You'll do great at work.
Although...never mind. You KNOW what I think.
Miss you already. -D

Though I hadn't risen to the bait, Daniel's not-so-subtle hints that I should quit my job weren't lost on me. He was right about one thing, though — I got so little sleep, I might as well have slept at his place.

Dashing up the stairs to the dean's office, I recalled Daniel's face when he'd given me my own set of condo keys the night before. He'd been so sincere — desperate for me to know I could come and go as I pleased and feel at home. I smiled, rubbing my fingers across the Swarovski keychain in my pocket. But when I reached the top step, my smile withered. On the other side of the office windows, the new dean, Elaine Armstrong, was tapping her fingers on the counter, her eyes aimed at a spot above the door. She was staring at the clock.

I breathed deeply, held my head high, and hefted the door open.

"Wow, what a crazy morning—" I started, but she stopped me with a blistering glare before I'd even reached the counter.

"Eight thirty?"

"I'm sorry?"

"That's what time your shift starts, correct? Eight thirty? You *are* Aubrey Price?"

I peeked at the clock. Five minutes late.

Attempting to take a chip out of her frosty demeanor, I held out my hand. "Yes, of course. Aubrey Price. Nice to meet you."

Whereas my hand was sweaty, hers was cold and dry. *Bony claw* seemed an apt description.

"I'm sorry I'm a few minutes late," I continued, trying to fill the stony silence. "I had the most insane—"

She retrieved her hand and interrupted me again.

"Perhaps David Grant wasn't concerned about things like punctuality, but I have a fondness for reliability. Call me a stickler."

Her blue eyes were humorless and flinty.

A stickler? I can think of a few things I'd call you, but "stickler" doesn't come to mind.

The acid in my empty stomach churned. So, she had no time for apologies or explanations. Fair enough.

"It won't happen again," I said, meeting her eyes and refusing to let her intimidate me.

"I'm glad we understand one another."

I escaped to my desk, wiping my palms on my skirt. She sauntered over and ran a manicured fingernail along the front of the desk. I fought the urge to shudder.

"I came in last week," she said. "If you'd been here, we could have talked about my expectations."

"You must have come in during one of Gisele's shifts. I work in the mornings on Monday, Wednesday, and Friday," I explained.

"I'm aware of your schedule. I came in Monday morning. You weren't here."

"Oh, that's right. Dean Grant let me switch shifts with Gisele to accommodate my exam that day."

"I see."

What do you see, you bitch? I had a fucking exam!

"I'm surprised Dean Grant didn't suggest that you come on Wednesday or—"

She cut me off with a flick of her hand. "Never mind. And please don't forget, David Grant isn't the dean anymore. *I* am."

"Of course."

"You'll get used to the new order. In time."

Lady, there ain't enough time in the world for that to be true.

"I want some coffee," she announced. "Skim milk and one sweetener."

She turned on her stiletto heel and strode into her office.

Okay, Miss Manners. Coffee it is.

I started a pot brewing and returned to my desk to open my email account. After several unsuccessful attempts to log in, I gave up. I poured Elaine a coffee and approached her door.

"Dean Armstrong? Here's your coffee." I perched it on the bookshelf near the door, fearing I'd get zapped by an invisible electric fence if I stepped beyond the threshold. "And we'll need to call the IT department. My email password isn't working."

"I've had the email access protocols changed." She addressed the shelves in front of her as she pulled catalogs from the bookcase and dropped them on the floor. "As a Victoria student, your access to that email account isn't appropriate. I wouldn't have hired a current student for this position if it were up to me. Gisele can deal with emails."

What? Dean Grant had always sought my opinion when he made decisions that would affect the student body. My opinion was no longer valid, apparently.

"I'll get the filing done, then." I grabbed the pile of folders from the outbox tray.

Elaine appeared in the doorway behind me, coffee cup in hand.

"There's no need for you to access the filing cabinet either. I'll take your key."

I dropped the folders and slid the key off my key ring, gritting my teeth as I placed it on her outstretched hand.

"Good grief, what kind of coffee is this?" She put her cup down with a scowl.

David and I had often laughed about the sketchiness of our morning coffee, but we'd always drained our cups anyway. It was a bit of a running joke. Armstrong and I apparently wouldn't have running jokes about the coffee. In fact, jokes of any kind, be they running, walking, or immobile, were improbable.

"It's President's Choice, Great Canadian Coffee," I said.

"There's nothing great about *that*." She retreated to her office and returned with a ten dollar bill. "I'd rather have Starbucks, but for now, go to Wymilwood and get me a cup of Bold Morning Blend. Leave it black. I'll do the rest."

"You want me to go buy you a coffee?"

She took in a sharp breath through her pointy nose, and I half expected her to expel fire as she breathed out.

"Is there a problem?"

"Not at all. That's fine. I thought with everything you need to get done here—"

"Somehow I'll cope for ten minutes." She rolled her eyes and returned to her office.

Well, ten minutes away from her wasn't a bad thing, I reasoned, grabbing my purse. I texted Daniel as I walked outside.

Elaine thinks my coffee tastes gross. -A

He answered as I was waiting in line to pay for the coffee.

What did I tell you?
Condescending, patronizing, superior bitch. Right? -D

Not to mention pompous, arrogant and demeaning. ;)
I'll never mock your use of redundant adjectives again.
Forgive me? -A

Maybe you can make it up to me... -D

I could make you dinner tonight...
How about another massage? Back scratch? :) -A

Yes please, fuck yes, and YES! ;)
You've made my day. Talk to you in a bit. -D

How was Daniel always able to turn my mood around, just like that? I hummed as I strolled back to Northrop Frye Hall, hoping the hot coffee might defrost Armstrong's frigid digits and improve her mood. Wishful thinking. For the next hour and a half, she was as vile as she'd been during the first fifteen minutes of our unfortunate acquaintance. When Daniel waltzed through the front office door at quarter to eleven, my mood lifted instantly.

Short-sleeved T-shirt. No jacket.

Ogling his lovely forearms, I sent up a silent prayer of thanks for springtime. Then I remembered where I was. Elaine was in her office with her door wide open.

Daniel and I had talked about a gradual revelation of our relationship, at least on campus, especially in front of admin types. A personal visit at work three days after the end of term didn't strike me as particularly gradual.

"Daniel," I hissed, my eyes darting to Elaine's door. "What are you doing here?"

He frowned playfully and waved his hand back and forth. "Relax," he whispered. "I've been over at my dad's office," he said, throwing his voice so Elaine would hear. "He misses you already. He *especially* misses the way you make his coffee."

I frowned a warning at him. What the fuck was he trying to do?

"That's nice to hear," I said, my voice laced with sweetness. "I miss him too. How's his morning so far?"

Elaine barged out of her office carrying a collection of old catalogs.

"Oh, hello, Daniel," she snapped. "Forgotten how to find the Provost's Office?"

"No, I was just over there—helping my father unpack," he added, inclining his head toward her deferentially.

"And how is he enjoying things at the Boys' Club?"

"He's got quite a learning curve ahead of him."

"Bitten off more than he can chew?" she asked, lifting a hopeful eyebrow.

"I don't think so. Looking forward to a job that will challenge him, I should imagine."

She looked at him speculatively. Had she caught his insult?

"And what brings you over here?" she asked.

"My dad asked me to drop this off for Aubrey." He winked at me furtively, handing me a white envelope. *Reference Letter* was written on the front, but the handwriting was Daniel's, not David's. "He wanted you to have this for your job search. Later in the summer, of course," Daniel added. "He'll email you an electronic copy as well."

"Thank you. I'll look at it later."

I slid the envelope into my bag. Elaine looked at Daniel as if to say, *Okay, you've done what you came here for. You're dismissed.*

Daniel didn't push his luck.

"I'd best be going. I'm exhausted. I think I'll grab an afternoon nap," he said, a playful glint in his eye. "Nice seeing you again, Aubrey." He tilted his head at Elaine, his smile tightening as his back stiffened. "*Dean* Armstrong."

All that was missing was a heel-click and a *Heil, Hitler*. He breezed out the door, whistling Guns N' Roses' "Patience" as he crossed the lobby. Smartass. The frosty *fraulein* dumped the catalogs on my desk with a thump.

"He's so conceited," she mumbled. "No wonder he gets himself in trouble." She gestured to the catalogs. "Throw these away. We won't be ordering supplies through them."

"But they're the vendors of record."

"Not any more. Order catalogs from these suppliers." She handed me a list of companies I'd never heard of. "Then we can sort this mess out."

This *mess?* What mess? It wasn't easy, but I stifled my hostility with a forced smile.

"I'll get right on it after I use the washroom."

She mumbled something under her breath and returned to her office while I headed to the bathroom with my purse, locking myself in.

Conceited? No wonder he gets himself in trouble? Bitch!

I put my purse on the vanity and pulled out my phone. Daniel had sent me a text.

Don't open that envelope in front of Jack Frost's sister. NSFW. ;) -D

I left the envelope tucked in my purse and dialed his number.

"Hey, there's my glutton for punishment."

"Don't start with me," I said, keeping my voice low.

"I can't help it. How will you put up with her for…how long?"

"I don't know. Seven weeks? Eight?"

"*Eight weeks?* Christ."

"Look, I don't want to talk about it, okay? What was the deal with your visit? Living on the edge, aren't we?"

"Not really," he said. "It's part of my campaign to legitimize our relationship."

I laughed quietly. "You have a campaign?"

"Yep. I've got it all worked out. There're bar graphs and pie charts cross-referenced with outcome-based hypotheses—"

"I'm way too tired to decipher what you're talking about."

"Don't worry. I'm rambling. I'm bagged, too."

"Are you really going to have an afternoon nap?"

"Absolutely. Care to join me?"

I smiled and traced the lines on the bathroom countertop. "Thought you'd never ask."

"I was hoping you'd say that."

I could hear the smile in his voice. While things were complicated on campus, once we were alone, it would be the two of us and our love, plain and simple.

"How about after work, you go to residence and pack an overnight bag. I'll pick you up from Union Station at one thirty."

"Perfect." In the mirror, I noticed two red spots already forming on my cheeks at the thought of being in his bed—in his arms again. "I can't wait."

"I know exactly how you feel." He laughed, and then he lowered his voice. "Maybe that's the problem. I *do* know exactly how you feel and I can't fucking wait to feel you again."

During my first three-hour shift, Elaine Armstrong reduced me to little more than a cleaning lady and coffee gopher. After my chat with Daniel, she deigned to allow me to empty the mailbag, watching me sort the mail from inside her office while I quietly seethed. She gave new meaning to the term *micro-manager*.

I hated women who seemed intent on proving they had virtual testicles. Surely it was possible to be strong and decisive without being a bitch? Well, I'd simply have to grit my teeth and soldier on. It aggravated Elaine to no end when I smiled in the face of her frostiness. I'd continue doing that. Like Shakespeare had said, I'd *kill her with kindness.*

Coming to this decision put an extra bounce in my step as I made my way to Union Station to meet Daniel. On the subway, I remembered the envelope he'd delivered earlier and dug it out of my bag. Was it a love note disguised as a letter of reference? As I started to read, I quickly realized it wasn't love letter, but it was awesome all the same.

Performance Appraisal
Date: Monday May 4th
Employee: Aubrey L. Price
Employer: Daniel G. Grant
Employment commencing Saturday, May 2nd
Anecdotal observations conducted during completion of assigned *jobs*
Saturday, May 2nd through Sunday, May 3rd

LEADERSHIP

Miss Price demonstrates excellent leadership qualities, often taking the initiative in stressful or *hard* situations.

SENSE OF URGENCY

When required, Miss Price seems prepared to put forth whatever effort is needed in order to ensure the swift conclusion of a *mutually satisfying end* to each and every job.

TEAMWORK

Miss Price is extremely *flexible* and cooperative, prepared to bend over backward — or *forward* — if doing so will lead to favorable results. Within moments of being hired, she was responsive to my needs and very supportive when I required extra *encouragement* to meet my...goals.

DEPENDABILITY

Miss Price eagerly takes on her share of the workload, assuming tasks that I'd previously had to complete myself. I look forward to her taking these jobs out of my hands (my right hand in particular) for good!

ORAL COMMUNICATION SKILLS

While *oral skills* are outstanding, oral *communication* skills could be refined. Elocution classes are recommended, particularly where the use of certain...*diction* is required.

INFLUENCE WITHOUT POSITIONAL AUTHORITY

Though positional authority is often frowned upon, I noted that Miss Price uses *certain positions* to great advantage. I am not averse to her use of authority to achieve her own personal goals, and to assist me as I strive to meet mine, for that matter.

RESPONSIBILITY

Miss Price obviously takes great pride in her work. It is a supreme pleasure to have her ~~under me~~ under my *employ*. I would recommend her unfailingly as an exemplar employee. However, you'll have to pry her from my cold, dead hands because, in short, she is simply *unnghh*.

Signed: *Daniel G. Grant*

When Daniel pulled up in front of Union Station, my stomach flip-flopped. Would he kiss me right away, or would he make me wait until we were at the condo? Hoping for option A, I crossed to the car and climbed in.

"Finally." He pulled me close and kissed me, his tongue cool and sweet against mine.

Option A. Thank God.

We settled into our seats, but before Daniel could start the car, I took his hand. "Just a sec. I swung by a bookstore on the way here and got you something."

"You got *me* something?"

"Uh-huh."

I retrieved the journal I'd bought myself before passing him the bookstore bag.

"You didn't have to do this," he said, but he was grinning like a kid who'd just been given a Happy Meal with the best toy ever inside.

"You said you weren't familiar with Rabindranath Tagore's work. I wanted to share it with you."

"*The Gardener*," he said, opening the cover, flipping through the first few pages and scanning the poems. "Thank you. This is very thoughtful." He kissed my cheek. "And *that*, sweetheart, is how you graciously accept a gift from someone you love."

"Okay." I rolled my eyes. "Point made."

He gestured to the book on my lap. "What's that?"

"A notebook. I was thinking about what you said about me bottling things up. Now that I've finished school, I'll have time to write for enjoyment. I thought I'd give it a try."

"Great idea. You can record all my foibles and fuck-ups." He laughed.

"That's not what I meant. But you write about me. Can't I unburden my heart, too?"

"Sure. Just don't forget to tell *me* how you're feeling, okay?"

"I won't," I assured him. "Like, right now I'd love to exert some *positional authority*. Can we go?"

He laughed. "You read the performance appraisal?"

"Yes, you cheeky bastard."

"Come on, it was funny."

"It was." I squeezed his hand. "When did you do that?"

"When I got up this morning."

"Such creativity at such an ungodly hour."

He gave a faux-modest toss of his head. "It's a gift."

As he pulled out of his parking spot, he threaded his fingers through mine. A few moments later, we turned onto the Don Valley Parkway.

"Wait, where are we going?" I asked.

"We have to make a vital pit stop before going home."

"Oh, come on," I groaned. "It's nap time…"

He shook his head. "You'll be glad when you see where we're going."

And as aggravating as it was, because I really wanted to get naked and remind him of my *sense of urgency* and practice my *oral communication skills*, when we reached our destination and I realized what this vital pit stop was all about, I *was* very glad indeed.

CHAPTER 2

Happy Hours

...Now stand you on the top of happy hours...
(*Sonnet 16*)

Daniel brushed his lips across my cheek, his dimpled smile making my heart thrum.

"This is kind of risqué." I dropped the bag of bolster cushions and wrapped my arms around his shoulders. "First we go shopping for linens a mere thirty-five-minute drive off campus, and now we're canoodling in your condo's elevator..."

He coiled his free arm around me.

"And how does this risqué canoodling make you feel?" he asked, kissing my neck in that new-whiskery way that made me tingle.

"Naughty."

"I like the sound of that."

His lips skimmed across mine, and his tongue slid along my lower lip. I pressed my body against his.

"Mr. Grant, is that a bolster in your pocket or are you just happy to see me?" I giggled.

"Call it what you like, Miss Price, but I'm definitely happy to see you. I'll be even happier to see you completely naked, preferably in bed."

The elevator chimed, and he picked up the bags I'd dropped.

"I can take those," I said.

"No, you have to open the door. You have your key, right?" he asked.

I reached into my backpack and pulled out the Swarovski heart. Daniel smiled as I wiggled the key into the lock. The click of the bolt echoed down the empty hallway, and he motioned for me to walk through ahead of him. He kicked the door closed and tossed the bags of sheets and pillows onto the floor before scooping me up. I held onto his shoulders as he spun me around.

"Finally!" he said, rubbing my nose lightly with his. "Permission to be incredibly cheesy?"

"Permission granted."

"Welcome home, my lovely."

"Lord, that *is* cheesy."

"Mock me. I don't care. I'm so happy you're here."

He retrieved the sheets and tore open the packages. In the kitchen, he opened a set of louvered doors.

"Laundry room," he said, reaching for the detergent. "If you ever need to do laundry, help yourself." He stuffed the sheets into the machine and turned to me, his eyes sparkling. "Nothing like christening a new set of clean sheets."

"I think we should have made them worthy of washing first."

"Are you kidding?" He shuddered. "Imagine how many people touched them during manufacturing."

"So, we have to wait for these to finish in the washer and the dryer before we can *nap?*"

"Speed wash and then thirty minutes in the dryer. Think you can make it?"

"I *am* really tired," I said with a sigh.

He smirked as he closed the laundry room doors. Sleeping was the last thing on my mind, but we seemed to be developing our own secret language where *napping* was code for *getting it on in the afternoon.*

"It'll be worth the wait. For now, come with me."

He led me to the bedroom. The bed was bare. I didn't ask what he'd done with the linens his ex, Sabrina, had given him as a housewarming gift. Everything was gone, and that was good enough for me. In the walk-in closet, he pointed to a row of hangers.

"You can hang your things here. I emptied the top drawer of my dresser too."

I smiled. "Don't you think you're getting ahead of yourself, sailor? I brought an overnight bag, and you've already got me putting away clothes and doing laundry."

His face fell. "Too much?"

"I love that you're excited to have me here, and I appreciate that you want to make me feel welcome, but can we slow down a bit?"

"I'm sorry. I am excited. I guess I'm getting carried away."

"I don't want to rain on your parade, it's just…"

"It's all right, poppet. I understand."

I inspected Daniel's closet. "So, on top of alphabetizing, you're also a fan of color-coding, huh?" I ran my hand along a row of shirts arranged by color and hue. The word *organized* didn't do it justice.

"Can I ask you something?" he asked.

"Of course."

"Remember when you were here in March, and you said you thought I was OCD? Were you serious?"

"My first impression was that you're very organized. I hope I didn't offend you."

"Some of my eccentricities must seem odd," he said. "I should probably explain."

We returned to the living room and curled up on the couch together.

"You don't have to, Daniel. This is how you like your home."

"No, I don't want to be like this. Not that I'd rather be a slob, but the excessive attention to detail — the extreme orderliness — it's just a coping mechanism that's become habit." He took my hand. "After Nicola blew my life out of the water last year and the anxiety started, the strangest things would set me off. I'd try to work on my thesis, and if my desk was a mess, my skin would crawl. I couldn't focus until I'd tidied everything up. Or I'd search for something in my closet, and if I couldn't find it, I'd get so exasperated…It's hard to explain unless it's happened to you…"

"I see what you mean. Go on," I said.

"I was living with my parents when I came back to Canada, and they noticed I was overly focused on things being *just so*. It was like I needed to impose order on inconsequential things to compensate for the parts of my life that had spun out of control. My mom said it wasn't bad to have coping strategies as long as I didn't allow them to become compulsions. I was taken aback when you started tossing around terms like OCD when you were here in March. I've done a lot of reading about this stuff. It scares the shit out of me, you know?"

"I'm sorry. I guess I was kind of flippant."

"You didn't know. It must seem strange to a casual observer. My blue shirts don't need to be together. I don't have to wash my car every other day. The world won't come to a halt if my books aren't in alpha order..." He expelled a gusty breath and squeezed my hand. "I'm trying to give up control of trivial things."

"I'll help however I can," I said.

He looked down at our joined hands. "It's funny, in February, when my mother suggested I try not to draw attention to myself by being too concerned with my appearance, I dreaded the thought of walking into Martin's classroom without ironing my shirt or shaving. I've always tried to make a good impression. But, oddly enough, I enjoyed throwing myself together in the morning. It made me feel like I was beating something." He shook his head and frowned. "Fuck, I sound certifiable."

"No you don't," I reassured him.

"You don't think I'm a freak?"

"I didn't say that..." I laughed gently and snuggled into his side. "Thanks for telling me. I'd hate to do something careless while I'm here without realizing it might upset you."

"Please don't worry. One of my favorite things about you is how relaxed you are...how much you embrace having fun. You have no idea how much it's helping me."

I didn't know what to say, so I kissed him instead.

"Have I mentioned today how much I love you?" he whispered.

As he began to kiss his way down my neck, the washing machine buzzed. I dropped my head back, encouraging him to continue.

"Screw the sheets, Daniel. I think we should take a nap on the rug..."

He squeezed my knee and gave me a quick peck. "Just for today, humor me, okay?"

While he tossed the sheets into the dryer, I reclined and crossed my hands behind my head. Humor him? Yeah, I could humor him because, honestly, watching Daniel doing laundry? *That* was foreplay.

"I would have been happy christening the rug, you know," I said, tucking the last corner of the sheet under the mattress, trying to emulate Daniel's "hospital corner" fold. He dragged the duvet across the bed, a look of mock horror on his face.

"Have you any idea how long it's been since I vacuumed out there?" he asked, joining me at the end of the bed.

"Three days?" I guessed.

"Uh-uh," he said, pulling me into his arms. "Longer."

"Four?"

"Longer."

He kissed me softly and unbuttoned my blouse.

"Five?"

"Nope."

He slid the blouse off my shoulders, letting it drop on the floor behind me. I shivered as he ran his fingertips down my arms.

"Surely not six."

"Bingo." He drew my hands up around his neck and kissed me deeply, his tongue sweeping across mine as he unclasped my bra. I was already feeling wobbly from our half hour make-out session on the couch. Now he was simply turning me into goo.

"Six days?" I murmured. "I'm shocked and appalled."

"Tough call, right?" he said between kisses. "I had to ask myself, 'Do I make love to my delicious girlfriend on the Egyptian cotton sheets, or roll her around in the dust mites and bread crumbs?' See my dilemma?"

He slipped my bra off and tossed it onto the dresser. As he circled my nipples with his thumbs, I closed my eyes and held onto his shoulders, afraid my knees might give out any second.

"Yes…" I managed to say.

He slowly unzipped my skirt and inched the fabric down my hips.

"Stop talking and kiss me, Aubrey."

Happy to do as I was told, I offered my lips, and he walked me backward until I sat on the edge of the mattress. I lay down, expecting him to join me, but he didn't. He stood there, looking down at me, his gaze traveling up my legs and then onward, pausing momentarily at my breasts before moving up to my face.

"I knew seeing you naked in my bed would make me perfectly happy," he said. "No, wait." He slipped my panties down my legs and tossed them over his shoulder. "There. Now *that's* perfect."

I reached for his hand, pulling him onto the bed with me. He lay on his side and kissed me, his fingertips lightly skimming across my tummy. I tugged at his T-shirt.

"How did this happen again? The only thing you've taken off is your socks, and I'm completely naked," I said.

"I don't know, Miss Price. I may have to take a look at that performance appraisal and make some revisions. Your initiative seems to be lagging. Would you care to rectify the situation?" He drew my hand down to his zipper.

"How about *you* rectify it for me?"

"You want me to strip for you?" He smiled.

"I hadn't thought of it that way, but hell yes." I pushed myself up onto my elbows. "And I'd like some music, too."

He went to turn on his iPod. Was he seriously going to do this?

"Requests?" he asked.

"That Style Council song? You know, the sexy one?"

"'Paris Match'?"

I nodded, and soon the sultry music started. He looked over his shoulder at me and wiggled his eyebrows. I couldn't help laughing. I didn't know how he straddled the line between adorable and sexy so perfectly, but he had it down to a frigging art.

He pulled off his T-shirt and swung it around his head a couple of times before tossing it at me. I giggled and threw it over the edge of the bed as he lowered his zipper, slowly pushing his jeans and boxers over his hips. They fell to the floor where they were kicked aside. I whistled and hooted, and he smiled, joining me on the bed again, his body warm against mine.

"Nicely done, though next time you might want to spice it up, work in some props—there's plenty of room for a pole over there." I pointed to his reading nook.

"Don't push your luck," he said, pressing himself against my thigh. "I've been thinking about this all day." His hands roamed all over my body, lips following, his tongue darting out to tease me, making me shiver and squirm.

"Me too," I breathed.

"Not sore anymore?" he asked, cupping me gently.

"No." I lifted my hips to meet the light pressure of his fingers.

"This was a good song choice," he whispered grinding against me in time with the music.

All I could manage was a throaty moan. His kisses and caresses were soft and slow, but my responses were frantic and eager. I was *so* done with foreplay. I pushed him onto his back and straddled him. He looked up at me, just breathing. Waiting.

My initiative seems to be lagging? I'd give him lagging initiative.

I placed his hands above his head. "Don't move." I slid my fingertips down his arms.

His Adam's apple bobbed, and he wrapped his fingers around the corners of the pillow above his head. I leaned to kiss him, angling my hips *just so* and sliding against him.

"I can't wait," he groaned, balling his hands into tight fists and arching his hips as I moved. "Don't make me wait…"

I considered doing just that. After all, he'd made me wait for the stupid sheets. But what was the point in punishing myself as well? So, I guided him inside me, sighing as we melted together and shifting my hips to accommodate his movements.

He sucked in a long breath. "Oh, Christ, Aubrey…You're so… *fuck…*"

I rocked, slipping my hand between my thighs, already eager for release.

"You're seriously trying to kill me," he said, watching my fingers, his voice sexy as hell.

I took in his lidded eyes and beautiful lashes, consumed by the way his tongue teased at his lip. His hands clenched and unclenched above his head.

I circled my hips, holding him deeply inside me, anticipating the imminent rush of pleasure. He urged me on, his hands sliding up my legs. Within seconds, my body was buzzing with relief, and I fell forward onto his chest.

"That didn't take long," he said.

I sighed contentedly. "I was *so* ready for that."

Daniel smiled and took my face in his hands, devouring my lips. He grasped my hips, pushing me hard against him over and over again, our bodies perfectly in sync. I leaned in, the heat of his chest intoxicating against the coolness of my breasts.

"I don't want it to be over—" he gasped "—but you feel too good…"

And then he was gone, lost in his own moment of bliss. He held me close, and I stayed still and quiet for a long time, my face nestled in the warmth of his neck. His heart beat steadily under my hand as we lay there, the music and our breathing the only sounds in the room.

"Are you okay?" I whispered at last.

"I'm more than okay. I'm fucking spectacular."

I rested my forehead against his, loving him with every fiber of my being and wishing I could stay folded around him like that forever. Sadly, my thigh muscles were seizing up, making another minute unlikely, never mind forever. I needed to move, but if I rolled onto the bed, I'd make one hell of a mess on the freshly laundered Egyptian-cotton sheets—a dilemma indeed.

And so I did the only thing I could do—I eased myself out of his arms, and quickly performing what felt like a very awkward double toe loop off the bed, I dashed toward the bathroom, certainly a less-than-graceful exit. But really—was there a graceful way to deal with the inevitable post-coital wet spot?

"Where are you going? Canoodle your way back here right now," he said.

"Just a sec. I don't want to splooge on the sheets."

He laughed and mumbled to himself as I closed the bathroom door, cleaned up, and washed my hands before returning to the bedroom. I reclaimed my panties and scooped up his discarded T-shirt, both of which I pulled on as I headed for the front hall.

"Now what are you doing?" he called out. "You're supposed to want to snuggle after sex!"

I grabbed Daniel's copy of *The Gardener* from the front hall and rejoined him in bed where he was now sitting up against the pillows, the top sheet covering him.

"I thought we'd snuggle and read at the same time."

"Oh, I see. In that case…" Daniel handed me a sausage-shaped cushion.

I curled up into his side.

"Can you find me the original of the poem Neruda translated? The one I put to music for you?" he asked.

I flipped to the thirtieth verse and watched his lips move as he read the poem to himself.

"That's it exactly. I can't believe I didn't make the connection between the two poets. I was so fixated on finding a Neruda poem that had something to do with a sunset that I had blinders on. What else would you recommend?" He scanned the index.

"Read the opening dialogue to get context," I suggested. "We should read it out loud. You be the servant, and I'll be the queen."

"There's typecasting."

I slapped his arm. "Don't be an ass. You're ruining the snuggle."

"Sorry. Your humble servant begs your forgiveness. Please go ahead."

"I can't. Your line is first."

"Oh, right, so it is." He closed his eyes and pursed his lips.

"What are you doing?"

"I'm getting into character."

"Oh, forget it." I laughed, moving to sit up.

"No, come back, I'm sorry. I mean it this time. Here goes." He cleared his throat as I settled onto my pillow. "*Have mercy upon your servant, my queen!*"

He angled the book so I could see the page. "*The assembly is over and my servants are all gone. Why do you come at this late hour?*"

"Huh. And here I thought I came too early."

"Daniel, would you focus?" I laughed, redirecting his attention to the page.

He smiled, and we continued reading. When we reached the bottom of the page, I waited for him to continue, but he seemed to be reading ahead, processing the next passage. When he spoke again, his voice was softer.

"*Make me the gardener of your flower garden.*"

"*What will your duties be?*"

"*The service of your idle days. I will keep fresh the grassy path where you walk in the morning, where your feet will be greeted with praise at every step by the flowers eager for death.'"* He turned the page quickly and finished the remainder of the servant's speech.

"'*What will you have for your reward?*'" I read.

He took my hand in his as he spoke the next passage.

"'*To be allowed to hold your little fists like tender lotus-buds and slip flower chains over your wrists; to tinge the soles of your feet with the red juice of ashoka petals and kiss away the speck of dust that may chance to linger there.*'"

"'*Your prayers are granted, my servant, you will be the gardener of my flower garden.*'" I closed the book. "Well?"

"Wow."

"You like it?"

"I love it. The imagery...the emotion...and this servant is my kind of guy. If only you were as accommodating as his queen."

"What's that supposed to mean?"

"He says he wants his duty to be the service of her idle days, and she agrees, just like that." He snapped his fingers. "That's what I want to do for you. If you'll let me."

"Sailor, you can service me any day you please," I said.

"But first I have to wait for you to get home after being tortured by Elaine Armstrong, right?" he whispered against my lips.

I braced myself for another lecture about the futility of hanging onto my job, but it didn't come. Instead, he kissed me and rubbed his nose against mine. "So, what are we going to do for dinner?"

"I said I'd cook for you. Any requests?"

"Would you make me a risotto? It's your specialty, right?"

"I make a kickass risotto, but I doubt you have the right ingredients."

He looked affronted. "Sure I do."

"Arborio rice and porcini mushrooms?"

"Okay, I don't have the right ingredients." He looked at the clock. "I don't feel like shopping now. We could shop in the morning and have risotto tomorrow night. Assuming you'll be here tomorrow night. I guess I shouldn't be presumptuous..."

"I'd love to make you dinner tomorrow."

"Okay, good." He smiled and drew me close. "Why don't we grab dinner out tonight? There's an Oyster House a five minute walk from here. We can find a quiet corner to disappear into."

THE TRUEST OF WORDS

"Or we could order a pizza…"

"That doesn't sound very glamorous," he said.

"I don't need glamor."

"Maybe not, but you *do* seem to be enjoying these Egyptian cotton sheets. You went to great pains to protect them from the…What was it you said earlier?"

"The splooge," I said.

"Right, the *splooge*." He chuckled. "So? Oysters? They are an aphrodisiac, right?" he said, running his finger lightly along my bottom lip. "And the ones at The Oyster House are spectacular…"

"Aphrodisiac. *Right*." I smiled, nipping at his finger playfully. "Get dressed, Daniel. We're going out."

A Thing in Rhyme

When shall you see me write a thing in rime?
(*Love's Labour's Lost,* Act IV, Scene 3)

Julie yawned noisily into the phone. "Are you sure I didn't wake you up?" I asked.

"No, I'm up. I'm…" She yawned again. "Shit, sorry, I'm so wiped. The run of this show is killing me. Hey, are you calling me from work?"

"Sort of. I'm going to Starbucks to get Elaine Armstrong a frigging cup of coffee."

"Can't you make a pot at the office?"

I put on my best officious voice. "You can't be serious. I couldn't posssssibly let that sludge past my teeth."

"Oh no. Total bitch?"

"Epic bitch. I don't think she hates the coffee as much as she hates me."

"How can she hate you? She doesn't know you."

"Whatever. I'm just smiling and nodding, and it's making her crazy. She doesn't know how to react."

She laughed, but then quickly changed the subject. "Soooo…your email yesterday was sadly lacking in details about, *you know*. Spill, woman."

"A lady never kisses and tells…"

"Bullshit, Aubrey. Talk!"

I smiled at the sidewalk. "Well, he's amazing."

"Obviously! How's the cottage?"

"Beautiful. Huge. *Ridiculously* huge, actually."

"Crap, I can't wait to see it! And the shmexy times? How is he?"

"Beautiful," I said, still smiling like a moron.

"And ridiculously huge?" she prompted.

"Julie!"

She giggled insanely. "I'm kidding."

"I should hope so, sicko. But, yeah, he's amazing. And funny and sweet and romantic and sexy—"

"And you're head over heels in love."

"Completely."

She sighed. "Me too."

"Yeah? Things are good with you and Jeremy?"

"Oh, hellz yeah."

"Look at us, eh?"

"I know. Crazy. So, Daniel gave you a key? Are you moving in?"

"No, but he wants me to feel free to go over, even if he's not there. I stayed over the last two nights."

"Is he easy to be around?"

"Totally. We're in this little bubble right now, but we mesh well. Sometimes we sit and read, or he plays guitar for me. He works on his thesis, and I hang out and write. We went out for dinner on Monday, but yesterday we took turns cooking for each other. It's good."

"How was going out for dinner in public? Weird?"

"We'll both be a bit freaked out until convocation. We went to this quiet oyster bar in the Distillery District."

"Oysters, huh? That's disappointing."

"Why? They were great."

"You've only been doing the horizontal hustle for five days, and you're already using performance enhancing foods? That's lame."

I laughed and shook my head.

"Look, wingnut, I've gotta go. I'm at Starbucks. I'll be in residence for a bit later on if you want to give me a buzz. I've got laundry to do and stuff. I hope Daniel doesn't wig out if I decide to stay at Jackman tonight. I want to catch up with Matt and Jo."

"I'm sure he'll understand. If I don't catch you this aft, we'll talk later in the week, okay?"

"No worries. I'm excited to see your show, by the way."

"Aww, thanks. It'll be great to have everyone there."

We said our good-byes, and I joined the ridiculous line for over-priced Starbucks coffee. Then I returned to Vic where I spent the remainder of my mind-numbing shift stuffing hundreds of envelopes with convocation invites.

Elaine didn't stay in one place for longer than five minutes. Through-out the morning, she circled the outer office like a piranha looking to feed, talking into her Bluetooth constantly. Most of the time it looked like she was talking to herself. Watching her yammer away to nothing-ness gave me the willies. I stifled a shudder every time she passed my desk.

Her calls were mainly personal, her gossipy whispers not nearly as discreet as she must have thought. With each trip past me, her eyes swept across the desk as if she was waiting for me to screw up. What could I possibly botch? All I was doing was sliding invitations into addressed envelopes. I took the opportunity during one of her circuits away from my desk to find my own invitation. Seeing the words *Victoria College Convocation* above my own name made graduation real. Feeling remarkably proud of myself, I slipped the invitation into my envelope and popped it into my purse.

At eleven twenty-five, just as I was contemplating leaving, Elaine glanced at the clock. Prepared to be dismissed, I gathered up the re-maining invitations.

"How far did you get?" she asked.

"I finished the Js."

"Would you stay until twelve and try to get the Ls finished? There are more important things for Gisele to do this afternoon."

I thought about refusing, but I smiled sweetly at her instead. "Any-thing to make Gisele's afternoon easier."

"Good. And leave the front door unlocked. I'm expecting someone."

She disappeared into her office and pulled the door halfway closed behind her while I reclaimed the pile of invitations. I didn't want to be here longer than necessary, but I'd be damned if I'd let her think she was inconveniencing me. As I worked, I tried not to keep checking my phone for messages, but it was futile. I'd peek at it every few minutes, and there would inevitably be some random message from Daniel.

Sometimes it would merely be a passing remark:

Remind me to arrange to borrow
Brad's pickup truck to get the boat. -D

Sometimes it would be a random question:

I'm at the grocery store.
Red Rose tea or Tetley? -D

And sometimes his words would make me ache with the need to be with him:

I miss the taste of your tongue.
I can't wait to kiss you again. -D

At eleven forty-five, I was reading one such message when my phone rang in my hand, yanking me from my wayward thoughts.

"Good morning, Victoria College, Dean Armstrong's Office, how can I help you?" I said.

"Aubrey?"

"Yes."

"It's David."

"David! Hi, I wasn't expecting to hear from you."

"Out of sight out of mind?"

"No, of course not. I didn't anticipate your call, that's all."

He laughed. "It's all right, Aubrey. I understand. Do you always make a habit of answering your cell phone so professionally?"

"I'm still at work." I laughed. "Reflex, I guess."

"You're still at work? That's why you sound distracted. Your mind must be elsewhere."

Gee, as a matter of fact, I was just imagining your son's hands running up my thighs to touch my...um...elsewhere...

Through the cracks between the hinges, I saw Elaine standing inside her door. She'd heard me say David's name, and now she was shamelessly eavesdropping. God, I hated her.

"How are things?" I asked him.

"It's busy. But that's to be expected."

"I've been thinking about you. I miss you over here." I made no effort to disguise the warmth in my voice. I wanted Elaine to know how much I preferred my former employer.

"That's nice to hear, especially after the way things have been between us the last couple of months," he said. "I know it hasn't been easy."

"Circumstances beyond our control. These things happen."

"You're very gracious, as always. Listen, I thought you'd have left by now. I didn't intend to call while you're at work. Are you alone?"

"Not exactly."

"Elaine's in the room?"

"Pretty close."

"Well, it's most likely not the best time to talk if she's right there, but it's a rather time-sensitive issue to discuss. You see, I have a proposition."

A proposition? How intriguing.

"It's up to you, David. I could call you later, if you'd prefer," I said.

Elaine was still hovering around her doorway. Nosy bitch.

"I don't think that'll be necessary. I'm sure I'm overreacting, as usual." He laughed lightly. It was nice to hear him trying not to take everything so seriously. "I just got off the phone with Daniel, and he has all the details, but I wanted to extend a personal invitation. Gwen has been talking about having high tea at the King Edward Hotel for a while. I've decided to take her there this Sunday for Mother's Day with the whole family. I have to confirm numbers by one o'clock. Would you be interested in joining us?"

I put my hand over my mouth to contain an elated gasp. At last—a sign that I was welcome to join the family instead of being cast aside as a dirty secret!

"That sounds lovely," I said.

"Excellent. So, I suppose we'll see you on Sunday?"

"Perfect. I can't wait."

"Oh, and this outing is fencepost. We're surprising Gwen. I hope we can keep the cat in the bag for the next few days."

"I'm sure Gwen won't suspect a thing."

"I hope you're right. Maybe you could tell Daniel we'll firm up plans later in the week? Oh, and Aubrey?"

"Yes?"

"Daniel sounds relaxed and very happy—happier than he has in a long time. I know we have you to thank for that."

As I hung up, I could barely contain my euphoria. I was no longer merely being tolerated. I was being *accepted*. I worked methodically, thinking about Mother's Day tea at the King Edward Hotel, imagining how the afternoon would play out. The whole family would be there. Julie wouldn't be able to go, though. Her parents were taking her home on Sunday morning. Did David and Gwen even know about Julie?

While I was pondering this question and finishing off the invitations with the surname "K," a young man walked in. A summer-school student perhaps? I rounded my desk and greeted him as he approached the counter.

"Can I help you?"

He looked at me searchingly. "Wow, you don't remember me. I'm crushed, Aubrey." He put his hand over his heart, regarding me with a puppy dog expression.

I examined his face for a clue—something that would jog my memory. I suppose there was something vaguely familiar about him, but I couldn't place him, and though he knew my name, I *certainly* didn't know his. He smiled and tapped the counter with his hand.

"When you were in first year, you were going out with my best friend, Lyle Kennedy. I was one of his housemates. I helped you roll him into bed after he'd had too much to drink a couple of times…"

My hands rose to my cheeks, a series of vague, uncomfortable memories flooding my mind. "Goodness, you're right. I'm so sorry! Gosh, um, Terry?" I grimaced. I knew as soon as I spoke that his name wasn't Terry.

He shook his head. "Close. Travis."

"Of course! Travis…right…"

I nodded, though frankly, I hadn't devoted any time to reminiscing about Lyle Kennedy or our short-lived relationship since we'd broken up, and I certainly hadn't given Travis or any of Lyle's other roommates a second thought.

"It's been ages since I thought about those days. How've you been?"

"Not bad. I graduated last year. Bumming around, to be honest," he said. "It's not easy to get a job. I'm getting desperate."

"I feel your pain. What about Lyle?"

"Lyle? He dropped out after first year. Only got two credits. He was put on academic probation so his folks yanked him. He went home to Halifax so they could keep an eye on him. Last I heard he was at Dalhousie University."

"Hopefully he pulled everything together at home. He was a decent guy."

"He was an awesome guy—when he wasn't wasted."

"Very true." I laughed. "So, what brings you over here? You taking summer courses?"

"No, I'm here to see Elaine. She suggested I drop by."

"Oh. Sure." I resisted asking what business he could possibly have with Elaine. As long as I wasn't the one dealing with her, I didn't care. "She's in her office."

As Travis made his way around the counter, Elaine pushed the door open wide.

"There you are," she said, taking both of his hands in hers. Having never witnessed anything even remotely warm in her demeanor, I almost fell over. "I was expecting you at eleven fifteen. I was wondering what happened to you."

"Sorry, traffic was terrible."

"Don't worry. That can't be helped."

Don't worry? That can't be helped? He was thirty-five minutes late for a scheduled meeting! I'd been four-and-a-half minutes late for work on Monday, and you'd have thought I'd committed a federal offense.

"Please, come in." She ushered Travis into her office and turned to me. "Aubrey you can go. Lock the door on your way out."

"But you wanted me to finish the Ls. I've almost—"

"Don't concern yourself." She shooed me with her hand. "Gisele can finish it."

I gritted my teeth. "Right. Of course. See you on Friday." I turned to her guest. "Travis, it was nice seeing you again. Sorry I didn't recognize you at first."

"Don't give it a second thought, Aubrey. Not everyone has a photographic memory," he said, tapping the side of his head with a sly wink.

Elaine flashed a smug smile and closed the door in my face. I stared at the knots in the wood in front of me. The woman was a freak show.

Two hours later I was in my room at Jackman, folding laundry. I hated folding laundry. Daniel probably loved it. Would he organize the laundered clothes according to color or genre? Maybe both?

I smiled as I thought about his efforts to seem relaxed in the face of my carefree attitude. I'd caught him staring sadly at the chair beside the bed—the "clothes chair" as I was fond of calling it—where I tossed semi-clean clothes. As soon as I was out the door, he probably went into tidy mode, finding a home for all my stray items.

I returned to my laundry, planning to call him as a reward once I'd finished. This plan was thwarted by an incoming text message.

> *Hey, crazy legs! Finished your laundry yet?*
> *I miss you. -D*

I sat down among the bras and polka-dotted panties.

> **Hi, sugar. Folding right now.**
> **What exactly do you miss? -A**

> *Lots of things. Canoodling, for example. Smooching.*
> *Splooges! I REALLY miss splooges. -D*

> **LOL! Wow, there's a lot of Os in those words, sailor. -A**

> *So there are. Multiple Os.*
> *Tell me, how do you feel about multiple Os? -D*

> **I find them VERY enjoyable. -A**

> *I bet you do. Pfft, what am I saying? I KNOW you do.*
> *May I offer you some enjoyment tonight? -D*

I'd been dreading this moment. I'd wanted to stay at the condo, but Jo had been so excited to see me when I'd swung by after work. She'd made me lunch, helped me lug my laundry downstairs, and immediately started planning what we'd have for dinner. When she beseechingly suggested a movie night, I'd agreed without hesitating. Instead of replying to Daniel with another text, I dialed his number, continuing to fold with my free hand.

"Hi, my lovely. That's better. How was work?"

"Verging on tolerable."

"And Elaine?"

"Completely *in*tolerable. She had her hair pulled into such a tight bun, I swear it was doubling as a facelift. And she threw away Archie, the hanging plant. She said it made the office look sloppy. I'm sad. I loved Archie."

"Plants need to be nurtured. I'm guessing she gets along better with inanimate objects. I hear she has a fabulous rapport with Stan."

"Who's Stan?"

"The front counter."

I laughed. He was in a strange mood. "She particularly likes Stan after he's been Swiffered. By me, of course."

"That goes without saying. What else is new? Anything good?"

"I had nice chat with your dad. He called to ask about Sunday."

"Good. I didn't want to say anything. He told me not to talk to you about Mother's Day until he'd invited you himself."

"I never dreamed he'd buckle this soon."

"He must have taken it as a good sign that the earth didn't careen off its axis when we went away for the weekend. Plus, I don't think he likes the idea of you not spending time with your own mom on Mother's Day."

"That's sweet."

"He cares about you, you know that, right?"

"I know." I flopped onto my pillow and closed my eyes. "Will everyone be tense with me there? I don't want to ruin your mother's afternoon."

"This is what we've wanted for weeks—to be a normal couple. I'm thrilled that you'll be there with my family. So, what's the plan? Are you coming over later?"

I hesitated. "Would you be upset if I declined?"

"I'd be disappointed, but I'll survive. Mind if I ask why?"

"Stephen's gone home, and Jo's lonely. She's starting a course next week, but she's at loose ends right now."

"Can we make plans for tomorrow, then? I'd like to take you shopping for an outfit for Sunday."

"Daniel, you're impossible."

"And the sooner you accept it, the happier everyone will be."

"What's in it for you?"

"Ah, poppet, you know me well." His voice dropped a register, as if he were telling me something top-secret. "There's a lingerie store at Bayview Village I think we should check out."

"More polka-dots?" I looked down at the sea of dotted panties surrounding me.

"Hmm, maybe we should consider branching out…"

I laughed. "Meaning?"

"I don't know. How do you feel about…stripes?"

After talking to Daniel, I wandered out to the kitchen. Matt and Sarah were watching a movie. He was staring at the screen, but her eyes were fixed on a spot on the wall about four feet away from the TV. She looked completely detached. It gave me a vague, uneasy feeling.

"Can I get you guys anything?" I asked.

Matt paused the movie. "No thanks, Aubs. How about you, Sarah?"

She snapped to attention as if Matt had clapped his hands in front of her face.

"Huh? Oh, I'll grab some water." She joined me in the kitchen, talking to Matt over her shoulder. "Don't pause it on my account."

Matt shrugged and restarted the movie.

"I could've gotten it for you," I said, handing Sarah a bottle of water.

"That's okay. It's great of you guys to let me stay. I don't want you to feel like you have to serve me, too."

She leaned against the counter. "So, Matt said you've got a new boyfriend, but you don't talk about him much? Something about jinxing it?"

"Things are great, but you know Murphy's Law," I said, improvising as I went. "When you start telling the world about the guy and bragging about how great everything is, things start to fall apart."

"That's so true," she said, staring vacantly at the cereal cupboard.

"Is everything okay?" I whispered, bobbing my head toward the other room. "You know…"

A smile ghosted across her face, and she lowered her voice. "Things are fine. It's just…You're lucky you have this place to escape to when you need a break. Matt's great, but I guess I wish there was some place I could go sometimes. It's nothing. Please don't tell him, okay?"

"Of course." I patted her arm and returned to my room. Matt was still sitting on the couch, entranced by his movie, oblivious to his girlfriend's need for space.

While I waited for Jo to return from the grocery store, I logged onto my email to send my mom a message about the timing for convocation. I was on the verge of logging off when an email from Daniel arrived in my inbox. I laughed as I looked at the subject line. What on earth was he up to now?

From: Jung Willman
To: Miss_V
Sent: Wed, May 6, 3:26:05 PM
Subject: When shall you see me write a thing in rhyme?

Hey gorgeous,

Let me explain what happens when I miss you. After we hung up, I reorganized my sock drawer and ironed some towels. Then, after rereading our texts from earlier, I was struck with inspiration and had to write the masterpiece below. In lieu of the type of multiple Os I'd prefer to see you enjoy, I hope these suffice this evening…

Multiple Os

I know you will most likely think I'm a stooge,
But I love you so much, oh yes, even your splooge.
I'm sitting here useless, just lost in my doodles;
I miss you like crazy, I need some canoodles.
You're gorgeous and hot, (but with feet like Nanook);
Your risotto's delicious, I love how you cook.
Your smooches are perfect, "you kiss by the book,"
And the thought of your boobs, well, I'd kill for a look.
My mind is so dirty; I'm thinking 'bout spooning,
(This poem is epic, I bet that you're swooning.)
I must go and tidy, and vacuum some too.
I like the place clean when I'm planning to woo.
I imagine you're laughing and thinking "Oh dooood,"
*But I know in my heart that you're **sooo** in the mood…*

See the levels of brilliance you inspire? You're no doubt packing an overnight bag. Poor Joanna! How can she compete? ;) I'm kidding, of course. (Shakespeare is turning in his grave…I can't believe I couched his glorious words among all those ridiculous ones!)

Have a nice evening and call me before you go to bed. I love you, crazy legs.

-D

xoxoxo

P.S. I didn't really reorganize my sock drawer. Just so you know…

Faithful

You are there follow'd by a faithful shepherd:
Look upon him, love him; he worships you.
(*As You Like It*, Act v, Scene 2)

I strode into the office on Friday morning feeling powerful, confident, and comfortable in my skin. It's strange how clothes can entirely alter one's mindset. Elaine was at the counter, flipping through papers. She glanced at the clock. I knew I was five minutes early, so I swept past her, grinning my stupid face off.

"Good morning. Beautiful day, isn't it? What's on the slate for today?" I stowed my purse under my desk, smiling at her expectantly.

She narrowed her eyes. She was far too easy to aggravate.

"That dress is a little short, isn't it?" she said, assessing my legs with a critical eye.

"Do you think? Huh, I was sure it was the same length as the one you were wearing on Wednesday," I said. "And it's a hard to imagine a dress from Judith and Charles being considered trashy, don't you think?"

She gave me another suspicious once-over. "Judith and Charles?"

"Uh-huh." I reached for the notes Gisele had left me.

Elaine's nostrils flared in annoyance. "Don't get too comfortable." She disappeared into her office and returned with ten dollars. "Extra bold, venti."

Thank God! I'd been hoping she'd send me out again today.

I took the money, humming as I left. Half an hour of freedom! I practically kicked up my heels as I dashed outside, taking a giant breath of fresh spring air. Was there any better feeling than enjoying a sunny morning, knowing that in a few hours you'd be off to spend a fabulous few days with the man of your dreams? The weekend lay before me like an undiscovered country I couldn't wait to explore. All I had to do was get through the next few hours.

I peered down at my lovely new dress. Daniel had suggested I wear it to work. After telling me how beautiful and self-assured I looked as I stepped out of the dressing room, he'd insisted on buying me both this dress and another one for Sunday's tea at the King Eddy. I'd hesitated, but in the end, I'd closed my eyes and repeated my new mantra:

Let Daniel spoil you, let Daniel spoil you…

And so, at the clothing store, the shoe store, and the lingerie shop, I'd let Daniel spoil the hell out of me. I pondered how I'd show my gratitude. It would involve stripes. Lots and lots of stripes. I would start tonight, and I would show him my gratitude repeatedly.

Sometimes payback ain't a bitch.

Foliage. That's what greeted me when I arrived back at the office. A giant plant sat on the counter, tendrils hanging everywhere.

I handed Elaine her coffee. "What's with the shrub?"

"There's a card. Feel free to read it."

She glowered at the plant while I rooted around in the leaves for the card.

Elaine, I hope your first week as dean has gone well. With Aubrey and Gisele at your side, you can't go wrong. This is something to brighten a stuffy corner. Enjoy!

Regards, David

Too frigging funny. First a dig about what great employees Gisele and I were, and then a slam about the tone in the office. She'd have to strap the damn plant to her head if it were to brighten a stuffy corner, since every part of the office was stuffy when she was in it.

"The man doesn't know me at all. What a ridiculous gift," she said snidely.

Oh, he knows you.

I almost wanted to call David to thank him for having a bit of fun at her expense. Daniel must have told him about the demise of Archie.

"You'll have to water it. I don't do plants," she snipped.

"I'm not sure I'll be able to," I said, running my finger along one of the plant's leafy fronds. "At least not for much longer…"

"Oh?" She lifted an eyebrow. "Why?"

Because I'm not the fucking plant whisperer.

That's not what I said. What did I say?

"I'm giving my two weeks' notice. I've decided to take some down time before I start looking for a job. A *real* job."

That's what I said. And I had no earthly clue where the hell the words had come from.

"Really?" She smiled, leaning against the counter and crossing her arms. "I'm surprised David didn't mention this to me."

"It's a recent decision."

I made it a minute ago.

"I've done some thinking."

About what an odious bitch you are.

I breathed deeply to prevent what felt like impending heart failure.

She tapped her nails on the counter. "I'd better make some phone calls to line up a replacement."

"I could ask around, see if there's anyone looking for—"

"Oh, that won't be necessary." Her nose wrinkled as if she'd suddenly encountered an offensive smell. "I can think of several people who'd be qualified."

"I'll stay on to train whomever you hire."

"I'm sure I won't need you for the whole two weeks. Unless you insist…"

I can't imagine making it through the next two hours, never mind the next two weeks!

"Whatever's easiest. I'm just trying to be accommodating."

"Oh, yes, you're very *accommodating*," she said, looking at me archly.

What was that supposed to mean? I plastered my tongue to the roof of the mouth, a move which, according to Daniel, made it impossible to reveal how annoyed you are. He was right. I had the sudden urge to giggle.

"Thanks for being so understanding."

"Understanding?" She looked me up and down. "Oh, I understand, believe me."

She continued to appraise me while I tried to figure out what the hell she was getting at.

"Anyway, I should get to work. Shall I try to find a spot for Archie Junior?"

"I beg your pardon?"

"Archie Junior." I gestured to the plant. "Shall I try to find him a home?"

She dismissed my comment with a wave of her hand. "Do whatever you want with it. Don't interrupt me unless there's an emergency."

She slammed her office door, and I smiled as I pulled a chair over to the bookshelf, climbing up to rest the plant where his predecessor had sat.

"AJ, I hope you have a long and happy life here," I said, arranging the leaves along the shelves. "But I wouldn't hold your breath."

I looked at the plant sadly because, let's be honest, as soon as I was gone, AJ would be toast. Maybe I'd try to smuggle him out with me on my last day. Archie Junior would come and live with me, a souvenir of the day I'd finally agreed to Daniel's wishes. He wanted to catch me? Well, this was it. I was about to start a free fall with absolutely no safety net.

Buying me pretty dresses and striped panties was one thing, but truly being there to break my fall? That was something else entirely.

Euphoria? Panic? I couldn't decide which emotion was winning. As I rode the subway, I imagined the look of surprise on Daniel's face when I told him I'd quit. The thought made me smile, but then a wave of anxiety washed over me, and the next moment, I was wringing my hands together.

Fuckity fuck, what have I done?

I must have repeated the cycle at least five times, trying to convince myself everything would be okay, only to realize a few moments later I had absolutely no way of earning money and would have to start dipping into the spending money I'd saved for my trip.

Inside Daniel's condo, I closed my eyes and took several deep breaths. I had to get a grip before he came home from his meeting with Martin.

This was the first time I'd been there alone. It was quiet. Too quiet. I turned on some music and made my way into the bedroom where I undressed and stood in the closet in my underwear, admiring the other dress Daniel had bought me. Then I spent a few minutes going through the top drawer of the dresser where all of my new bras and panties were neatly folded, picking them up one at a time to touch the soft fabrics.

"I think I've died and gone to heaven."

I whirled around, my hand over my heart. "Daniel! You scared the shit out of me."

"Sorry." He laughed. "I thought you'd have heard me come in. Look at you." He whistled through his teeth as he crossed the room to pull me into his arms. "What a sight to come home to."

His lips sought mine, and as our lips parted, I felt a sudden pang in my chest. The sharp pain worked its way up into my throat where it became a dull ache. Tears welled up in my eyes, and a small sob escaped my lips. He looked at me worriedly as the tears spilled onto my cheeks.

"What the hell? Are you okay? What is it?"

I laughed through my tears. "I don't even know."

I clasped my hands around his neck and held onto him, letting him rub my back and comfort me. Finally, he pushed me away gently so he could see my face.

"Aubrey, what's going on?"

I shook my head and smiled weakly. "There's nothing to worry about. I'm fine. It's just—well, I quit."

"You quit?"

"My job. I quit my job."

"You're serious?"

I shrugged self-consciously. "I gave two weeks' notice."

"Holy fuck, that's amazing!"

He swung me around, kissing me with complete abandon while I alternated between laughing and crying.

"I can't believe it. This is—What happened? Did she upset you? What did she say? Tell me everything—no, wait. Hang on. You stay here. I'll…Just give me a minute, all right?"

He was grinning as he babbled, surprised but obviously thrilled with my news. He dashed out of the room, and I took the opportunity to blow my nose and dab my eyes. I pulled on my silk wrap and flopped onto the bed, propping the pillows behind me. Daniel returned with a bottle of champagne and two flute glasses.

"Champagne?" I laughed. "It's one thirty in the afternoon."

"I don't give a flying fuck what time it is. This is cause for celebration."

With a hand towel, he caught the cork and the frothy overflow. Then he poured two full glasses and joined me on the bed.

"A toast," he said, narrowing his eyes in thought. "To idle days?"

"Huh, I guess so, eh?" I tapped my glass against the edge of his and took a sip.

"No, wait. I'd like to revise that. To the *service* of your idle days."

"You, of course, being the one to provide this service?"

"Mm hmm. You'd better believe it, my queen." He kissed me, teasing my tongue with his. As he pulled away, he looked at me meditatively. "Have another sip…"

I did as he'd requested, and he kissed me again, smiling against my lips.

"What?"

"Champagne. You taste like our first kiss. That was the best first kiss ever."

"If you do say so yourself?"

"I was talking about *you*."

He smiled and put our glasses on the night stand, and then he pulled me into his arms and reclined on the pillow, angling himself so he could see my face.

"So, tell me how hell came to freeze over. I'm thrilled that you quit, but I must admit, I'm a little surprised."

"I don't even know. One minute we were talking about watering plants, and the next thing I knew, I was quitting. I have no clue what came over me."

"A blinding flash of good sense?"

"Hey, zip it, bucko."

"I'd rather unzip it." He pressed himself against my thigh.

"I thought we were discussing my epic morning."

"You're right. I got distracted by the zebra stripes," he said, inching aside my robe and peeking at my black-and-white striped bra. "Please, carry on. What were you saying? It was an impulse?"

"I guess my decision can be summed up in five words: *Elaine Armstrong is a fucking bitch.*"

"That's six words, sweetheart."

"I know. The adjective was an essential last minute addition."

"So. are you relieved?"

"Yes and no. I'm glad my days there are numbered, but I'm kind of scared."

"Of what?"

"Of not having money. Of owing you…"

He pushed himself up on his elbow and frowned.

"Aubrey, you'll never owe me anything. I wish you wouldn't say things like that."

I shook my head. "I don't know what's going to happen now. My summer residence is paid for, but I need spending money for England, and I still have expenses…"

"Like what?"

"Like my cell phone and toiletries and contributing to the cable bill and the groceries at Jackman…"

"I can think of one way to eliminate two of those expenses like *that.*" He snapped his fingers.

I was *so* not ready to go down that road. "Daniel…"

He rolled over and stood up, holding his hand out and then leading me to the armchairs beside the bed.

"In case this gets heated," he said. "No arguing in bed, remember?"

I sat and tucked my feet under me. "I don't want to argue about this."

He reached for my hand. "You probably don't even want to *talk* about this."

"Not really, no."

"Is it so horrible imagining moving in here?"

"It's not horrible at all." I huffed with exasperation.

"Can you at least consider it, then?"

I stared at our joined hands, Sarah's words rattling around in my head. *You're lucky you have this place to escape to when you need a break.* Daniel sat, observing my quiet contemplation, but when I didn't say anything, he finally spoke up.

"Is it your parents? Would they be upset because we've only known each other a few months?"

I avoided his eyes, trying to think of a suitable answer.

"What? Is that it? Would your dad give you a hard time?"

I shook my head. "No, I don't think so. Although…The thing is…I haven't *exactly* told them about you. Or us."

"Are you kidding?"

I shook my head.

He slumped into his chair as if I'd just punched me in the stomach. "Wow. I didn't see that coming."

"I'm sorry, but unless there's a special occasion or something, we mostly email each other, and the way I feel about you isn't something I'd want to gloss over in an email. Plus, I wanted to wait until things were on surer footing before telling them. Now the semester's over and things are calmer, I'll tell them."

I stood and tugged on his hand, and he allowed me to guide him to the bed.

"You promise?" he asked, lying down beside me.

"I promise."

"You'll call your mom for Mother's Day, right? You can tell her then?"

"Sounds like a plan."

"Good," he said, kissing me.

"Good."

I'd managed to derail the moving-in discussion, and I wasn't looking to re-open it. Further evasive maneuvers were essential. I popped his jeans button and lowered his zipper, sliding my hand inside his boxers.

"Gosh, I'm feeling awfully idle. I think I need some service," I whispered.

I smiled as he moaned and moved against my hand. He let me stroke him for a few minutes before taking my hand in his and rolling me onto my back.

"If you need service, shouldn't I be the one doing the work?"

He lowered his lips to my cleavage and nudged my robe out of the way with his nose.

"I suppose you're right." I stretched out beside him as his hand slid between us, slowly inching downward and under the frilly pink elastic on my zebra-striped panties.

And, Lord, the services he provided—first with his fingers and then with his tongue, and then with his fingers and tongue at the same time. Not until I was begging him to stop, my legs shaking with exhaustion, did he finally make love to me, taking his time, holding me close, and telling me how much he loved me.

Generally speaking, the events of the afternoon allowed me to conclude that idle days were extraordinarily underrated.

"So, how was your meeting? We've been talking about me all afternoon. How'd things go with Professor Brown?"

Daniel and I were standing side by side at the kitchen counter, making Moroccan chicken. I was in my element. Daniel's kitchen accoutrements were amazing.

"It was good," he said, lining up a collection of spices on the counter. "He wants me to be assigned to his Intro to Shakespeare class in the fall. He thinks I need to see the other end of the spectrum—to check out what freshmen are capable of."

"How do you feel about that?"

"I learned a lot in the three months I worked with Martin. A full-year course would be great. I have to get the okay from Aaron O'Connor, but I don't see that being a problem."

"I don't know how you can think of being in the same room with that man. He's so creepy."

"He's a weasel. I didn't like the way he was looking at me at my dad's party. He was talking to Elaine at one point, and they both looked at me with disgust. I suppose my false reputation precedes me. Unfortunately for O'Connor, he has no choice but to associate with me, at least occasionally."

"Unfortunate for *you*, I'd say. He seemed keen on getting some dirt on you."

"True. I assume he came up empty, but he did tell me he wants to discuss those class evaluations. I should set something up soon and get it over with."

I watched Daniel chop the dried apricots.

"I didn't know he and Elaine knew each other."

"Apparently." Daniel grimaced.

I wasn't a fan of either of them individually, and the thought of them together was particularly distasteful.

"Hey, did you and Professor Brown discuss grades, by any chance?" I asked.

He glanced at me and smiled. "Yes."

"Any idea when final marks are being sent out?"

"End of May, I think."

"You think?"

He paused for a moment and then resumed chopping. "I'm ninety-four-percent sure that's when they'll be sent out, yes."

"Ninety-four percent?"

"I can't be one-hundred-percent sure. Nobody's perfect, after all." He winked.

"True." I stole a piece of apricot and nibbled on it. "I can't believe I got ninety-four percent," I whispered.

He grinned at the cutting board. "I don't know what you're talking about, Miss Price."

"Right, of course not. Should we change the subject?"

"Yes, please."

I stirred the apricots into the pan. "Let me see…How about this? Who do you like better, Dr. Seuss or Shel Silverstein?"

He blinked at me. "Have I mentioned how much I love it out here in left field?"

"You know there's always a rational explanation for the things I say, sunshine."

"Right. How moronic of me. Um, I can't say I was attached to either of them."

"You came out of the womb clutching *Shakespeare's Complete Works*, I suppose?"

"That's not what I mean. My mom read us books she'd read when she was a girl—Beatrix Potter, Alfred Bestall, Enid Blyton. I loved Paddington Bear. He was my favorite."

"Interesting." I tapped my chin thoughtfully. "Paddington Bear was notoriously messy. I think I might be onto something."

"Very funny, Dr. Freud," he said. "Now back up. Why the sudden interest in my childhood reading habits?"

"I was thinking about the poem you wrote me and wondering who your influences were. You know, what inspired you as a writer."

He laughed. "I believe my influence was a couple of glasses of Guinness, and my inspiration was a dreadful case of missing you. I waited so long to be able to spend time with you, it makes me crazy when you're not here. The poem was a disastrous side effect. Maybe all the sex we're having is turning my brain to mush. I wish I could channel this energy into my thesis."

"I happen to love the poem, but if you're really worried about your brain, we can dial it down. All you have to do is say the word."

"Whoa, that's crazy talk. I'm quite enjoying having mush for brains." He stole a kiss. "I'm glad you liked the poem."

"*Loved*, Daniel. I loved it. What was it anyway? A sonnet?"

"Hmm. It can't have been a sonnet. It was fourteen lines, but the rhyme scheme and meter were all wrong."

"Oh, horribly wrong." I smiled and added lemon juice to the pan.

"I'm going to say it was an ode." He nodded confidently. "Yes, it was definitely an ode."

"An ode to multiple orgasms?"

"Yes…and to splooge."

"Perfect. *An Ode to Splooge*," I said.

He stood behind me, resting his chin on my head and sliding his hands around my waist. I set the pan to simmer and popped the lid on top. Then I spun around in his arms. "Okay, that's good to go for half an hour or so."

"Why don't we sit on the balcony?" He grabbed the bottle of wine and two glasses and waited for me to get settled on the loveseat before joining me.

"I was going to ask Brad to borrow his truck on Monday to go get the boat. I assumed you'd be working, but now I'm not sure," he said. "What's the plan?"

I groaned at the thought of returning to the office. "Elaine's going to need at least a week to post the job and do interviews."

"So, you'll be at work anyway. Brad and I can swap vehicles on Sunday after Mother's Day tea. I'll go to the cottage first thing Monday morning." He sipped his wine. "On Sunday, I might ask my mom if she can pull some strings—get you a meeting with the editor of *The Globe and Mail*. He's a friend of hers."

"Why would I want to meet him?"

"Maybe you could try some freelance work. I'm sure he'd be happy to take a look at your writing."

"I don't have any training. What if I suck?"

"You're a fantastic writer."

"Of essays, Daniel. That doesn't make me a journalist."

"Good writing is good writing. I thought you'd leap at the chance."

"As much as I need the money, I was hoping I wouldn't have to worry about job hunting until after my trip."

"You *don't* have to worry about it. Don't even give it another thought until August."

I shook my head and sighed. "You make it sound so easy."

"You think I don't understand," he said, tracing circles on the top of my hand.

I shrugged, but that's exactly what I was thinking. How could he possibly understand how much I hated feeling dependent?

He turned my face. "'*With playful carelessness you avoid my gifts. I know your art, You never will take what you would.*'"

Jesus.

"Was that Shakespeare?"

"Nope. Verse thirty-five of Tagore's *The Gardener*. I thought of you as soon as I read it."

"I knew I shouldn't have given you that damn book."

"And *this* is the point where you make jokes and change the subject. Don't tell me I don't know you, Aubrey."

"I should check on the chicken," I said, pretending to sit up.

He laughed and pulled me into his side. "Look, I don't want to ruin the evening quibbling. We'll have to talk about the future eventually, though."

"I know. I'm sorry. I must drive you crazy."

"Yes, you do. But oddly enough, I still love you."

I smiled and kissed him tenderly. Maybe I wasn't giving him enough credit. He was doing his best to figure out where I was coming from, just as I was trying to understand his quirks and habits.

As Daniel returned my kisses, caressing my cheek with his fingertips, I realized with blinding clarity that our feelings for one another were deepening with every passing day, despite our imperfections. This was not a case of opposites attracting. This was two people wholeheartedly accepting one another, despite the unique failings that each possessed.

Quite simply, this was unconditional love.

Present Mirth

What is love? 'tis not hereafter;
Present mirth hath present laughter...
(*Twelfth Night*, Act II, Scene 3)

Saturday afternoon, I was at Jackman, packing a knapsack full of clothes, when Matt appeared in my doorway.

"Hey, you!" He crossed the room and pulled me into a hug. "I miss you."

"I miss you too."

"I feel like we haven't talked in ages." He sat on the edge of my bed while I squeezed a hoodie into my bag. "How are things with Prince Charming?"

"Things are good. Mr. Charming has been wonderful," I assured him. "You don't need to worry about him anymore. Seriously."

"Fair enough. No more worrying."

"I do have big news, though. I quit my job yesterday."

"Get out! You quit?"

"I had to. I couldn't take another second. Once I train my replacement, I'm out."

"Can't say I blame you. If Armstrong wasn't such a bitch, I'd tell Sarah to apply for the job."

"Dude, I wouldn't wish that job on my worst enemy. Where is Sarah, anyway?"

"She went out. Something about window shopping. She still hasn't heard about that job she applied for. Maybe she needed to burn off some stress."

Or maybe she needed to escape for a couple of hours. I kept this hypothesis to myself, and Matt went off to shower while I ran through a checklist in my head, making sure I had everything I'd need to get through tonight, Sunday afternoon tea at the King Eddy, and Monday's shift at work.

I glanced at the clock. Daniel was picking me up in a taxi at five thirty, and then we were meeting Penny and Brad for a quick drink and a snack before Julie's show. I grabbed my phone to send him a quick text.

Almost done here. How is it possible that we've been apart for four hours and I already miss you? xo -A

He texted me back straight away.

I miss you, too, and you KNOW what happens when I miss you. Watch for an email in a couple of minutes, my lovely. -D

I chuckled as I finished zipping several last-minute items into my bag, taking a second to scan my room again. A few moments later, my phone chimed. I sat on the edge of the bed to eagerly read Daniel's email, hoping it contained what I suspected it did. I wasn't disappointed.

From: Jung Willman
To: Miss_V
Sent: Sat, May, 9, 4:34:38 PM
Subject: Dr. Seuss can kiss my ass...

Hey, beautiful,
I got my hair cut this afternoon, and as I sat in the barber's chair, I was struck with more inspiration. I had to rush home to write this down. You humbly requested another poem and since I am your servant, I had no choice but to comply, right? ;)

I'm not sure if this is an ode. It's definitely not a sonnet. Perhaps I've invented a new poetic form. Enjoy. I mean every word—especially the last seven...

Dots and Stripes Forever

You know I love your polka-dots,
But stripes? I also love them lots.
I must confess, I never thought
Such things could make me overwrought.
Those zebra panties made me "schwing,"
Your ass looks sweet in everything.
I say we hit another store—
There's dots and stripes, but I want more!
I'm thinking satin, silk and lace...
(Good God, I'm in my happy place!)
But want to know what I love best?
What makes me say, "Hell, fuck the rest"?
Some sweet, soft velvet, yes it's true,
So bring yours here, so we can screw.

There you go. This is what goes through my mind when Gino is cutting my hair. That's an alarming confession. (Trust me, he's happily married...)

-D

"Right, then," Penny said. "The food's in the oven, so while we wait for Jeremy and Julie to get here, I'll try to make these mojito things."

I joined her at the counter. "You're making mojitos? That's dangerous, Penny."

"I know you and Julie like them. I hunted out this recipe last night."

"Can I help?"

"No, sit, really. Brad and I can do this."

I joined Daniel at the table. Brad handed him a glass of Guinness. Daniel took a sip then threw his arm around my shoulders, tilting my chin up and kissing me.

Warm tongue Guinness kisses, how I love thee.

"Look at you two. I think I might bloody cry," Penny said.

"And I think I might vomit." Brad made gagging noises, and Penny slapped his arm.

"Brad, stop being a ponce. Why don't you set the table?" she suggested, opening the fridge and rifling through the crisper.

"Yes, ma'am," Brad said, staring at her thong creeping over the top of her jeans as she bent to retrieve a bag of limes. "Hey, beauty, you want a pipe to go with that crack?"

Penny hiked up her jeans and tugged her top down. "Better?" she asked, sticking her tongue out at him.

He pulled her into his arms. "Don't stick that out unless you plan to use it." The door opening in the front hall interrupted their smooching.

"Hello?" Jeremy's voice rang down the hall.

Penny bobbed her head at the door, and Brad dutifully made his way out to meet Julie and Jeremy. Julie's face was flushed. She'd had a lot of excitement for one evening.

"Julie, you were amazing, tonight," I said.

She beamed and curtsied extravagantly in the kitchen doorway.

Penny tapped her lips with a long red fingernail. "And the verdict is in, dolly. You're *definitely* bendy."

I nodded. "Are you ever! You can touch your head with your foot! How the hell do you do that?"

"Years and years of practice." She laughed.

"Can you try practicing that?" Brad asked Penny. "If you start now, maybe by our wedding night…" She shot him a warning look, and he zipped his lip.

Beside me, Daniel opened his mouth and then closed it again. Smart man.

"Thanks so much for doing this, guys," Julie said as she grabbed a chair. "I'm gonna eat my own weight in nachos."

"I'll believe that when I see it," Jeremy said, draping his arm along her chair.

"I hope you're *all* hungry because there's a shite-load of food," Penny said. "We ordered nachos and cheese, beef tacos, chicken quesadillas. Oh, and I also got flatitos."

Brad looked at her lecherously. "Baby, you ain't never gonna have *flat titos*. Not without a ton of cosmetic surgery."

"Can we please get through at least one night without discussing my boobs non-stop?" she said.

Brad laughed as he loaded the table with platters of food. He and Penny finally joined us at the table, and some serious chowing down and drinking began. After about five minutes of voracious eating, accompanied by moans of satisfaction, mostly from Julie, Daniel lifted his glass.

"Penny, Brad, thanks for having us. And since this is the first time we've all been together here, happy new house."

"And happy closing night, Julie," Jeremy added.

"And happy end of semester, you two," Julie said, waggling her eyebrows at us.

"I'll drink to that," Daniel said, stealing a kiss before taking several large gulps of his beer. Julie caught my eye, her eyebrows darting up. I hadn't thought about it before, but this was the first time she'd seen us openly affectionate with each other.

"Me too. I'll drink to it twice," Brad said. "Your whining was getting old."

"Thanks for your support," Daniel said dryly.

"Any time, bro."

"Such a loving family I'm marrying into." Penny laughed, helping herself to another quesadilla.

"Are you guys getting nervous about the wedding?" I asked.

Penny dabbed at her mouth with a napkin. "It's nerve-racking being here while all the plans are being made there. My dad's going a bit off his nut with all the bills."

"My folks will settle up when we get over there, don't worry," Brad assured her, crossing to the counter to grab another round of beers.

"Hmm, we'll see."

Brad's hand stopped in midair. "Are you saying my parents are cheapskates?"

"Your dad's family is Scottish, right?"

"What's that got to do with anything?" I asked.

"Scotsmen aren't traditionally known for their deep pockets," Daniel explained.

"Oh, that's not really the problem," Penny clarified. "It's the fact that they have really short arms that poses difficulties." As she said this she held her hands up beside her boobs, miming stubby arms. Julie found this particularly amusing, giggling into her mojito glass.

The banter continued, and I got a pain in my side from laughing. In fact, I spent most of the night laughing my ass off. We all did. We ate, we drank, we talked and listened to music, occasionally dancing around the kitchen as we took turns playing bartender. When Brad crossed to the counter to make Penny what had to be her fourth *very* strong mojito, she put up her hands in protest.

"I think I should slow down. Make me a virgin, will you love?"

Daniel laughed shortly. "Ha, that I'd like to see."

"You're right, D," his brother said. "I'm not even gonna try…"

Penny crossed her arms. "Excuse me?"

"Oh, come on, you stepped right in that one, Penn," Daniel said.

She sighed. "I did, didn't I?" She rolled her eyes and turned to Brad. "As for you, you had your fair share of tumbles. You can't begrudge me sowing my oats."

"But you should have seen the size of that bag of oats," Daniel said, smiling as he took a swig of his beer. Penny narrowed her eyes at him.

"That was the real reason for your insomnia, right, bro?" Brad piped up. "Couldn't sleep because of the shrieking from the bedroom next door?"

Penny cleared a couple of plates, clobbering him with an oven mitt in the process. "Right, shut your gob, you. You're pushing your bloody luck."

"Oh, don't be like that," he said, stepping up behind her and putting his arms around her waist. She spun in his arms and kissed him passionately, pressing her chest hard against him. Out of the blue, he scooped her up in his arms and carried her out of the kitchen toward the stairs, ignoring her kicking feet and laughing protests.

"No, really, don't concern yourselves!" Jeremy called after them. "We'll be fine!"

"Don't worry, we'll only be two minutes!" Penny called back.

"Oh-ho, you little…" Brad said.

But we couldn't hear the rest. Penny's screams of laughter and Brad's footsteps as he bounded up the stairs with her drowned out the rest of his complaint.

I shook my head at Daniel. "They're insane." Daniel smiled and gazed out at the hallway. "The squabbling's bravado. Neither one of them is all that sentimental. They prefer actions to words."

"I can see that." I gestured to the doorway they'd just disappeared through.

Daniel turned to Jeremy. "Has Brad shown you a speech yet? He's already stressing about it. I guess Penny's nagging him. She's panicking about the first dance, too. Can't blame her. He's not exactly light on his toes."

Julie looked into the hallway for a moment, lost in thought. "I should try to teach them something. Yes! That's such a great idea! Maybe they'll let me choreograph their first dance."

"That's a noble proposition, Julie, but you haven't seen him dance," Daniel said.

"Ever seen a bear with a burr stuck on his ass and tar paper on his feet?" Jeremy asked.

Julie laughed and squinted at the ceiling. "Can't say that I have."

"Well, try to get a visual of that, and then you're close."

"You know, that's a frighteningly accurate description, J," Daniel said.

"I think your idea is awesome, Jul," I said. "And if it works out, I promise to get video and tons of pictures at the wedding."

Jeremy grabbed Julie's hand. "Actually that might not be necessary."

I took in their conspiratorial smiles. "What? What's going on?"

"If we can work out timing, Julie's gonna try to come to the wedding," Jeremy said.

"Penny told Jeremy she'd love it if I could try to swing it. I only have a few days after my European showcase is done, but there's nothing saying I have to stay in Germany once we've performed," Julie added. "I might even try to extend my trip. It's not confirmed yet, so we're not mentioning anything in front of Penny."

She and Jeremy smiled at each other again. Julie was positively glowing. They were so freaking sweet together.

"Do Mom and Dad know about you two yet?" Daniel asked.

"I thought I might mention something tomorrow," Jeremy said, his eyes betraying his apprehension. "Maybe it'll be easier with everyone else there, I don't know…"

"We'll support you if things get tense," Daniel said.

"Thanks, man."

Daniel patted my leg. "Since everyone's sharing their big news, did you tell Julie the highlight of your week?"

"Not yet."

"What?" Julie said, sitting up in her seat. "What happened?"

"Um, I gave my two weeks' notice at work."

Her mouth dropped open. "I thought you said you weren't going to give her the satisfaction of breaking you?"

"I was punishing myself more than her. And she was giving me strange looks and saying weird shit. I'll do my last two weeks, and then I'll go on welfare, I guess."

"You're not going on welfare, Aubrey." Daniel frowned.

I poked him in the side. "I was joking, sailor."

"So, what are you going to do? Bum around until you go to England?" Julie asked.

"I don't know. I don't do the 'bumming around' thing too well."

"What are you interested in doing, anyway?" Jeremy asked.

"I've considered something to do with writing."

"Like journalism?"

"Maybe, but I don't have journalistic training."

"She's an excellent writer," Daniel said.

Jeremy narrowed his eyes. "Have you thought of freelance writing? Not a huge commitment, but you could start getting experience."

"I wouldn't know where to begin," I said.

"That's not true," Daniel said, miffed. "I told Aubrey about Mom's connections with Ralph Davidson from *The Globe and Mail*. She wasn't interested."

"I said it sounded *intimidating*."

Daniel didn't say anything. He polished off the last of his beer.

"You know, this might be a long shot, but I have a friend I could hook you up with," Jeremy said. "He started an indie arts magazine called *Sidelines*. Really low-key."

"Who's that?" Daniel asked.

"Eli Cantor."

Daniel's eyebrows shot up. "What? You talk to him?"

"Why? What's wrong with Eli Cantor?" I asked.

"There's *nothing* wrong with him," Jeremy assured me. "He loves working with new writers. From what I can tell, it's on-the-job training. I'll call him for you."

"Thanks, Jeremy. That would be great."

"No problem."

Daniel frowned and stood, heading to the fridge for another round. I joined him at the counter, running my hand across his shoulders. "Hey, you okay?"

"What? Oh, yeah. I'm fine."

"Do you think they'll come back down, or should we leave?" Jeremy asked as Daniel passed him another beer.

"They won't be long," Daniel said. "Penny's probably got Brad folding laundry or something while she lectures him about making jokes about her boobs."

We laughed, but then a thumping sound started overhead. All eyes moved to the ceiling.

"Full contact laundry folding," Jeremy observed.

"The best kind," Daniel said, smiling as he took another drink.

"So, did you have a good time?" Daniel asked as we snuggled in bed later that night. Tipsy Daniel was particularly cuddly.

"I had a lot of fun."

"Me too."

I sighed and nestled against him. He made a purring sound and moved closer. "You know what?" I mumbled into his neck. "I'm so excited that Julie might be able to come to Brad and Penny's wedding. I love Penny. I can see why you two are so close."

"She's very special, that's for sure," he said. "Not as special as you, though." He pushed himself up on his elbow. "You're the specialest of all."

"Specialest? I don't think that's a word, sunshine."

"I'm borderline drunk. I always make up words when I'm borderline drunk. I also get very horny."

"So, you've been borderline drunk since we met?"

"Mmm, probably."

He showered me with hot, wet kisses.

"You could at least *try* to stay inside the lines." I laughed, wiping my chin.

"Quit smothering my creativity." He snuck his hand under the covers, hooking his finger under the edge of my panties and tugging them down my legs.

"On second thought, I guess staying in the lines is good sometimes," he whispered. "But it depends what lines we're talking about…" He kicked off his boxers and rolled on top of me, clasping my hands above my head. "And how far apart they are," he added, pushing my legs open with his knee before sliding inside me with a quick thrust. "Mmm…these lines, for example?"

"Uh-huh?" I said, gazing up at his face as I lifted my hips.

"Fuck, I could stay inside *these* lines forever."

Hopeful Expectations

I leave it to your honourable survey, and your honour to your
heart's content; which I wish may always answer your own wish
and the world's hopeful expectation.
(*Venus and Adonis,* Dedication)

"Hi, Mom," I said, watching Daniel pretend fascination with his
newspaper.

"Aubrey? What a surprise. I didn't recognize the phone number.
Did I know you were calling today?"

"I wanted to wish you a happy Mother's Day."

"Thank you, sweetie. I got your card on Thursday. Only a few
weeks now and I'll be on a plane heading home to see you graduate.
How are things? Any job prospects?"

"Not yet. I'm working on it."

I decided against informing her that I'd just abandoned the secure
source of income I'd intended to rely on until the end of July. No
point worrying her. Daniel peeked over the top of his newspaper as if
to say, *Well, get on with it.* I slid onto one of the breakfast bar stools.

"Look, Mom, there's another reason why I'm calling."

"Is everything okay? You sound strange."

"I'm fine, really. I just wanted to tell you that when you come home, there's someone I want you to meet."

"Someone you want me to meet?"

"Yeah, you see, there's this guy…" I looked over my shoulder. Daniel had abandoned all pretense of reading the paper and was leaning on his hand, smiling at me.

Daniel pressed a kiss to my lips. "You look beautiful."

"It's a beautiful dress."

"I'm not talking about the dress, Aubrey. I'm talking about *you*." He pushed the elevator button while appraising my legs. "The shoes on the other hand? I can't wait to see you in *just* the shoes later on."

His eyes sparkled as he grinned at me. I snuck my fingers inside the collar of his shirt.

"I like it when you wear your collar open. Very shmexy."

"That's exactly the look I was going for. Gotta look shmexy for Mother's Day, I always say." He kissed me again, smiling against my lips. "I'm glad you're here."

"Me too."

When the elevator doors opened to reveal the hotel lobby, Daniel casually dropped my hand. His father's one request had been that we behave discreetly until we were inside the private dining room he'd booked.

"I can't believe I'm at the King Edward Hotel," I whispered as we crossed the grand lobby.

Daniel led me down a hallway and pushed open a door, revealing a room with lightly painted walls, ornate sconces every few feet, and a coffered ceiling. There were eight place settings on the table, each with a delicate china cup and saucer and folded white napkin. The centerpiece was a beautiful arrangement of white flowers. Tasteful and elegant. Brad, Penny, and Jeremy were lounging in a sitting area in the corner of the room.

"I'm glad we're not late," Daniel said, placing our gifts on a table inside the door.

"You're cutting it close," Penny said as she joined us. "Your dad just texted Brad. They're in the parking garage downstairs."

"Mom's gonna be stoked to have everyone here," Brad said through a mouthful of food.

I peered at him around Daniel's shoulder. "What's he eating?"

"Roast beef on a Kaiser." Penny rolled her eyes. "He's afraid he'll languish and die, being forced to eat cucumber sandwiches. Bloody gannet."

"Penn, try to speak English," Daniel said, gesturing to my confused expression.

"I *am* speaking English, you daft prat."

"Don't worry. I'm getting every fourth word." I laughed.

"Am I that bad?" Penny asked.

"I'm kidding. You're fine." I gestured at Jeremy, who was glumly staring at his phone. "Is he okay?"

"He was talking to Julie. She's on her way home to Windsor. Poor sod misses her already."

The door opened behind us, and we all turned to watch David enter, his wife and mother-in-law on either side of him. Gwen drew her hands over her mouth, her eyes widening in delight.

"Surprise!" Brad said, abandoning his roll on the table and crossing the room to give her and Patty a hug. Jeremy and Daniel followed.

Gwen swatted Jeremy's arm. "You lied to me. You told me you had a business meeting."

"Gwendolyn, it was a surprise," Patty said. "It's not lying when you're trying to surprise someone."

"I suppose not," Gwen said, hugging Daniel and Jeremy in turn, then spinning around and surveying the room. "Thank you for doing this, David, but did we really need a private dining room?"

The boys moved on to fuss over Patty, and David put his arm around Gwen's waist. "I wanted Aubrey to join us. I thought the privacy would make us all more comfortable."

More likely the arrangement made *him* more comfortable, but I wasn't about to split hairs.

"How lovely." Gwen reached for my hand, smiling warmly. "Thank you for coming."

"My pleasure. Happy Mother's Day."

Penny echoed my greetings, hugging her future mother-in-law.

"Ladies," David interrupted. "Shall we sit?"

"Of course," Gwen said.

Two waitresses wheeled a tea trolley into the room. On the top, pots of coffee and tea and four three-tiered trays with sandwiches and assorted sweets were arranged. David suggested a seating arrangement and everyone sat accordingly. I had Daniel on one side of me and Jeremy on the other. The waitresses moved around the table, serving coffee and tea, and then they encouraged us to help ourselves to food before exiting the room.

"May I say something before we start?" Gwen said.

"Of course," David said. "It's your day."

"I just wanted to say thank you to everyone for giving up your afternoon to be here. You know how important it is to me to have the family together. I feel very blessed."

Jeremy wagged his finger at her. "Don't get all weepy."

"I'm sorry. I'm a terrible sap, aren't I?"

I caught David winking at her, and she smiled coquettishly. I had a sudden vision of their courtship. He must have swept her off her feet. There was no denying that Daniel had learned a few tricks from his father.

Quiet conversations broke out around the table as everyone filled their plates and passed the milk, cream, and sugar. Brad struggled to hold the dainty tea cup. He was all thumbs.

"So, Aubrey," Gwen said, once we were all settled. "You're just a few weeks away from convocation. You must be pleased to be finished."

"It's wonderful," I said.

David sighed heavily. "Please don't start counting down the days until convocations begin, Gwen. Do you realize how much I have to prepare in the next few weeks?"

"You'll do brilliantly, dear," Gwen assured him. "You still have plenty of time to get everything ready for the ceremonies, and you always shine, regardless of what you turn your hand to. Tell me, Aubrey," she said, looking over at me. "I've been meaning to ask Daniel, what is it that your father does?"

"He's a consultant for a new mining company in Calgary."

"That sounds interesting."

"I suppose. I don't completely understand what his job entails. He travels a lot. He's up in Fort McMurray right now on a three-month contract. Turns out he won't be able to come to convocation. I just found out on Thursday."

"That's unfortunate. Will your mother be coming?"

"She's coming for a few days, yes."

"Only a few days?"

"I'm sure we'll make the most of our time together."

Daniel smiled at me reassuringly. We'd discussed my mother's visit, and he'd promised to give me lots of space while she was here. He'd even proposed that I sleep at Jackman during her stay, since the hotel she'd booked was on Bloor, five minutes from campus.

Gwen turned her attention to Jeremy, allowing me to work my way through a couple of sandwiches.

"Before I forget, Jeremy, have you sorted out your schedule for the assemblies?" she asked. "I meant to bring it up this morning, but you were out the door like a shot, and it completely slipped my mind."

"Yeah, I should be good for both."

"What's that about?" Daniel asked.

"Jeremy is addressing the spring prom assemblies at UCC and Havergal," Gwen explained. "It's a Mothers Against Drunk Drivers initiative to discourage drinking and driving on prom night. I've been asking him for a couple of years now, and he's finally agreed to help."

Jeremy shrugged uncomfortably. Had his mother worn him down, or was this something he genuinely wanted to do?

"Good for you for taking it on, J," Daniel said.

Jeremy waved off his brother's compliment. "No biggie."

"Your father and I are proud of you for doing this," Gwen said. "It's an important step, being able to talk about everything openly. If only one person remembers your story and makes a wise decision as a result, then it's worthwhile, don't you think?"

He smiled grimly and rubbed the back of his neck. "I suppose so. Can we talk about something else?"

Patty quickly filled the uncomfortable silence, moving the attention away from Jeremy.

"I'm curious to hear about your paper, Daniel. How's the writing coming along?"

"Daniel's been writing quite a bit this week, actually," I said.

I didn't think dirty poems were quite what Patty was referring to, but I couldn't resist making him squirm. He tapped my foot with his before saying, "Yes, that's true. Aubrey is very…motivating. I'm sure I'll be able to make a lot of headway now that life is settling down."

"That's marvelous," Patty said. "I wish your grandfather could be here to read your work. Gwen, won't it be lovely to have another professor in the family?"

"Patty," Daniel protested quietly.

"Goodness, you boys need to stop withering under the slightest compliment," Patty observed.

"Don't lump me in with them," Brad chimed in. "I know I'm awesome."

"Of course you are, dear," Patty said. "You've got your grandfather's business sense, that's for certain."

"Thanks, Patty," he said, jamming another sandwich into his mouth.

"Not to mention his superior taste in women," Penny added.

"You're absolutely right," Patty said. "Bradley and Daniel have chosen very wisely."

Daniel squeezed my hand under the table, and my face warmed with pleasure.

"Now we just need to find a lovely girl for our Jeremy," Gwen said, looking at him affectionately.

"Um, yeah, about that…" Jeremy fidgeted in his seat.

Uh-oh. The moment of truth.

"I actually *am* seeing someone," he added.

I felt Daniel tensing beside me.

"You are?" Gwen seemed both surprised and thrilled. "That's wonderful. Tell us about her."

Jeremy cleared his throat. "Her name is Julie," he said, looking down at his coffee. For a second, I thought that's all he was going to say, but then he blurted, "She's a dancer."

David's eyebrows shot up.

"Wait, not *that* kind of dancer," Jeremy said, shaking his head. "Ballet, tap, modern dance. That sort of thing. She's taken dance lessons since she was a kid. While she's been at university, she's been dancing with a Toronto-based company, but she still dances with a studio in Windsor. That's where she's from."

"She *does* have a degree, then?" David clarified.

"She's graduating from Trinity at U of T. Don't worry, she's very intelligent, Dad."

"What did she major in?" Gwen asked.

"Art history and English," Jeremy said, relaxing. Now that the topic of their relationship was open for discussion, he seemed relieved to be talking about it.

"Art history, how lovely." Gwen smiled at her husband. "I wish we'd known. She could have joined us today."

"She's heading home with her parents today," Jeremy said.

"Oh, I see," Gwen said.

"You'll meet her soon. I'm sure you'll like her."

"What's not to like?" Brad said. "She's cute, she's feisty, she's smart, and she puts up with your brutal driving. All win."

David's eyes flickered over to Brad. "You've met her?"

Brad nodded, unable to say more, having just closed his mouth around a whole strawberry tart.

"She's delightful, David," Penny said. "They make a lovely couple."

Daniel nodded, and David looked at him. "You've met her as well?"

Daniel smiled grimly. "Yep."

David's glance darted to me. I grimaced. "Guilty. She's actually one of my best friends."

And she was in Professor Brown's class, too! Surprise!

I didn't share that tidbit.

Patty was grinning, clearly amused by the goings-on.

"Surely you haven't met her, Mother?" Gwen said.

Patty laughed. "Of course I haven't met her. And don't get your britches in a knot. Jeremy's been testing the waters. Surely you remember how difficult it is bringing someone home to meet your parents."

She looked pointedly at David who cleared his throat and smirked at his mother-in-law. Gwen ignored her mother's comment.

"Long distance relationships are difficult, Jeremy. What will you do?" she asked.

"She's coming back to Toronto before convocation," Jeremy explained. "Actually, we're, uh, thinking of getting a place together. A two-bedroom apartment or something."

David's mouth stopped mid-chew, and Daniel turned to me, as if to inquire if I'd known about this. I was just as surprised as everyone else. Why hadn't they mentioned it the night before?

"How wonderful," Patty said, perhaps hoping to prevent any unfavorable reaction from Gwen and David. "It's lovely to see everyone starting their lives." She reached across to pat his hand. "I'm thrilled for you, dear."

"Thanks, Patty." Jeremy smiled at her.

"It would seem that my sons are masters of secrecy," David said.

"You know what they say about apples and trees." Patty took a sip of her tea and gazed impassively at her son-in-law over the edge of her cup.

Yeah, he couldn't deny that one.

"I completely understand his desire to keep his young lady under wraps for a while," Patty said. "I've been a keeping a certain gentleman to myself for a few months, as well."

Daniel expelled a quiet hissing breath, and we both braced ourselves for Patty to break the news about Gerald. Yet another fencepost was about to be reduced to wood shavings before our eyes.

"What do you mean, Mother?" Gwen said.

"I've been spending time with a gentleman named Gerald," Patty said matter-of-factly. "We've been courting for about six months."

Patty took another sip of tea, blinking serenely at her daughter across the table.

"Gerald?" Gwen said. "Where did he come from? How did you meet him?"

"He's perfectly lovely. I met him at Florence's house at Christmas. And before you get all worked up, Gwendolyn, Gerald will never take your father's place in my heart. He's a companion—a wonderful friend—and a dear man."

"No, I wasn't…" Gwen looked at her husband for some sort of assistance. "I'm happy for you, Mother. I'd…we'd…like to meet him."

"In due time." Patty dabbed her mouth and folded her napkin beside her plate. "I need to visit the ladies room," she announced. "Aubrey, would you accompany me, please?"

"Oh, yes, of course. I should…p-powder my nose," I stammered.

I was relieved to have the opportunity to escape for a few minutes. I followed Patty to the washroom where she dropped her handbag on the counter and smiled roguishly.

"Having fun yet?" she said, uncapping a tube of coral lipstick and applying it liberally before using a tissue to dab off the excess.

"Never a dull moment, that's for sure."

"Not with this family." She drew a compact from her purse and proceeded to pat her face with powder. "I hadn't planned to say anything about Gerald today. I think I took myself by surprise. I need to collect my thoughts. Thank you for joining me. I have this irrational fear of dying alone in a public washroom."

"It's all right, Patty. A breather is good. I need to deal with this blister, anyway. New shoes," I explained, rustling in my purse for a Band-Aid and wrapping it around my heel. "I'm glad you told everyone about Gerald. It's too bad he couldn't have come today."

I reclined against the counter as she fanned herself with a hanky.

"You know, I briefly considered inviting him. He's lost two wives, you know. Both of them to breast cancer. He was alone for a long time. He has his children, of course, but they have busy lives."

"Mother's Day must be difficult for him. There are probably lots of bittersweet memories."

"Undoubtedly. Breast cancer is a terrible disease. Make sure you do regular breast exams, Aubrey." She wagged her finger at me. "Get Daniel's help. That makes the process far more enjoyable. Take my advice and learn about each other's bodies," she said. "Memorize each other. One day, you'll know his body almost as well as your own. That's how it was with my Bradford. There comes a point, after you've loved someone long enough, that you can't even tell where you end and where he begins, both in body and soul." Her eyes twinkled. "That probably sounds quaint and old-fashioned to you."

"Not at all. I understand perfectly." I thought about the way I felt when Daniel and I made love. The bond between us surpassed a mere physical connection.

Patty crossed to the stalls. "I suppose while we're here, I ought to use the washroom. Run the water for me, will you, dear? And don't you leave me in here alone."

I turned on the tap and smiled. "I won't abandon you, don't worry."

While Patty was in a stall, Penny burst into the washroom. "Daniel sent me to make sure you're all right."

"We're fine. Patty's just using the washroom."

"You know Daniel. Worry wart."

"How are things?" I bobbed my head toward the dining room.

"The usual Grant hysteria. I'm quite happy to leave the boys to it for a few minutes."

Patty emerged from the stall and bustled over to the sinks to wash her hands. "And how are you coping, Penny?" she said. "Wedding plans sorting themselves out?"

"I think so. I can't wait to be married. Silly isn't it?"

"It's not silly at all," Patty said. "But try to enjoy this time as well. The wedding day will be here soon enough."

"I'm trying, Patty."

"I'm sure you are. You've got a good head on your shoulders. So do you, young lady," she said, patting my hand. She gazed at us pensively. "You know, while I've got you both here, perhaps you'll let me give you a piece of advice my mother gave me. It's one of the most valuable things she ever told me."

We looked at her expectantly.

"Whatever you do—in your relationship, raising children, around the house, no matter what, *start* as you plan to *continue*," she said seriously. "Whatever habits and behaviors you establish now, be prepared to maintain them."

She turned to Penny. "If you have no desire to spend your life—oh, I don't know—ironing and starching Bradley's shirts, for example, then, for the love of God, don't do it now. He'll expect you to continue, and then you'll be resentful if you feel you have to. If you one day stop ironing his shirts, he'll wonder what happened to the woman he once knew. You're neither a maid nor a cook. Of course, you'll have to compromise from time to time, but demand balance and equality right from the outset. It's not nineteen fifty-five anymore, thank heavens."

Penny and I smiled, and Patty took our hands, lowering her voice.

"And I suppose this is as good a time as any to give you a piece of advice best not shared in mixed company. Never, *ever,* fake an orgasm."

I almost fell over, but Penny didn't even flinch, responding as if Patty had just advised her not to let Brad leave the toilet seat up.

"You don't know your grandson, Patty," she said, smiling wickedly.

"Grand*sons*," I added, reasoning that if Penny could be blasé, hell, so could I.

"Good. Selfish men aren't to be endured." Patty looked at me. "So, I gather the oil is being changed now?"

"Regularly."

"Excellent. And the engine?"

"Running beautifully."

"I'm happy to hear it. I must say, he appears quite relaxed. Amazing what releasing pent up sexual tension can do for a person." She squeezed our hands. "Well? Shall we?"

We retrieved our purses and returned to the private dining room where the Grants awaited our return, looking at us with interest as we crossed the room. Daniel held my chair out for me, and as I sat down, I surveyed the table. Brad had been busy in our absence.

There wasn't a single crumb of food left.

"Julie, you should have been there."

"I'm so pissed that I missed it. Was Gwen surprised?"

"Definitely," I said, switching my phone to the other ear as Daniel passed me a glass of Perrier. He sat beside me, pulling my legs onto his lap. "Not as surprised as we all were to hear about you moving in with Jeremy, though. What the hell? Why didn't you tell us last night?"

"We didn't know. We were up for hours talking on the phone. I was in tears thinking about how much I was going to miss him, and we sort of decided out of nowhere to look for a place in Toronto when I get back. He was so nervous about telling everyone. How'd the news go over?"

"His dad looked peeved at first. He doesn't like being out of the loop. But other than that, I think it was cool. Patty and I went to the washroom, and I missed the rest of the convo."

"I can't believe I haven't met her," Julie said.

"Jesus, she was on fire today. In the washroom, she told Penny and me to make sure we never fake an orgasm."

"No way!" Julie shrieked.

Daniel shook his head and snickered.

"I'm serious. If you'd been there, she would have said the same to you, so you keep that under advisement, you big faker."

"Holy shit, Aubrey, I'm dying."

"She's unreal. You've got to meet her."

"I can't freaking wait, seriously." Julie yawned loudly. "I'm sorry to do this, but I'm gonna bail. I'm fried. I have to crash early."

"Yeah, I think we'll be doing that too," I said, jumping as Daniel's roaming fingers reached the ticklish spot behind my knee.

"I bet," Julie said suggestively.

"That's not what I meant," I said, watching his hand creep up my thigh.

Hmm. Maybe that *was* what I meant...

"Look, keep in touch, okay?" Julie said. "I'm gonna go crazy alone here for two weeks."

"I'll call you every day. Twice a day. And I'll text you and email you and send smoke signals every morning."

"Perfect."

"Night, Julie. Sleep well."

"You too. Give Daniel a smooch for me."

I laughed as I hung up, and then I scooted down the couch, giving Daniel a long, hot kiss.

"Wow," he breathed. "What was that for?"

"That was from Julie," I said, smiling against his lips.

"Julie's quite a kisser. Can I have another one?"

I rubbed my nose against his and gave him a little peck. "Watch it, bucko."

"So, let me get this straight," he said. "Patty told you outright to never fake an orgasm?"

"Yep."

"Huh."

"What?"

"Have you?"

"Have I what?"

"Ever faked it?"

"Are you seriously asking me that?"

"Sure. Of the twenty-odd orgasms I've witnessed, any of them fake?"

"Daniel Grant, you know I'm a terrible liar and an even worse actress."

"This is true."

"Besides, when a woman fakes it, she must want to get it over with." I leaned into him again, breathing hotly in his ear. "I never *want to get it over with* when we're together."

"Oh yeah?" He relieved me of my glass and helped me onto his lap.

"Oh yeah." I wrapped my arms around his neck, and he kissed me softly.

"Can you do me a favor?" he asked.

"Maybe."

"Can you put those new shoes on, take everything else off, and meet me in the bedroom?"

"Gosh, I don't know. What's in it for me?"

"How about several very real orgasms? Sound interesting?"

"Sounds like business as usual to me," I said, smiling playfully and heading to the front hall to retrieve my shoes.

Blisters be damned.

Mad Slanderers

Now this ill-wresting world is grown so bad,
Mad slanderers by mad ears believed be.
(*Sonnet 140*)

D aniel pulled up in front of the Starbucks and turned on the truck's hazard lights. He took my hand.

"Look, I don't know how long I'll be. It'll take a couple of hours to get to the cottage, then I have to hitch the boat, drive back, and sort out docking."

"Take your time. I'll swing by Jackman after work, but I'll be at the condo by the time you get home, okay?"

"Sounds perfect. How're the blisters?"

"The Band-Aids will hold out until I get to Vic."

"I can't believe she makes you come down here to get her a coffee every day."

"It's just a way to get rid of me. She doesn't even care if I stay on for two weeks to train my replacement."

"Which begs the question," he said, trailing off as he examined my face.

"I'm staying on because I know she doesn't want me to." I rubbed my hands together with an evil laugh and then gathered up my things.

"Try not to kill her. Homicide doesn't look good on a résumé."

"Excellent advice, thank you. So, you'll stay in touch today?"

His hand flew to his forehead. "Oh, shit. I left my Bluetooth in my car."

"Check in with me when you're not driving. No texting and driving."

"Yes, dear."

"I'm serious. You're not accustomed to handling this truck."

He turned off his phone and stashed it in the glove compartment. "Happy?"

"Yes, thank you. Good luck with the boat. I'll see you tonight."

I reluctantly tore myself away and watched him drive off before making my way into Starbucks and joining the line. As I rifled through my purse for my wallet, I heard an indiscreet voice from somewhere up ahead. I'd know that officious tone anywhere. I peeked over the shoulder of the redhead in front of me. Yep, that was Elaine's carefully coiffed bun, all right. She was getting her own coffee which meant she wouldn't have even sent me out to get it! Damn.

"How do you think I feel?" she was saying. "I have to spend time with the tart."

Typical. She was gossiping again, yammering away into her Blue-tooth. Was there any point in staying? Should I grab myself a coffee anyway? She continued chirping shrilly as I nibbled my thumbnail, trying to decide what to do.

"Like I told you, it's just a feeling. After what I witnessed last week, there's got to be more between them than meets the eye. Did I tell you about the dress she was wearing on Friday? Judith and Charles? There's no way the twerp could afford to buy that, but *he* could..."

My head snapped up. What the hell? Judith and Charles? She was talking about *me!* Me and some man who could afford to buy me expensive clothes. Holy fuck...*Daniel*. Was there something she'd witnessed? I knew he shouldn't have dropped by the office! She'd sensed the chemistry between us. Maybe she even saw him wink at me.

I was rooted to the spot, listening with morbid fascination.

"You can say 'I told you so,' but I didn't see the way he was look-ing at her at the party, did I? She was gone by the time I got there. If you say he looked guilty, then I'm *sure* he looked guilty..."

Oh, crap! The person she was talking to had seen Daniel looking at me guiltily at his father's party, just as David had feared. I probably should have fled from the coffee shop at that point, but I didn't. In fact, I stepped closer to the redhead, desperate to hear the rest of the conversation.

"I'm sorry I doubted you," she said. "It all adds up. I wish they'd done something more damning when she got out of his car in February. Travis said there was affection between them, but if he'd seen them kissing, there'd be no doubt, right?"

Travis? That weasel had seen me getting out of Daniel's car in February? What the hell was she talking about? And how did Travis even know Daniel? None of this made sense…

"You can't go public with this sort of information without proof," Elaine continued. "I'll watch her carefully. I wish we'd known about this earlier, Aaron, when it could have helped you get the Provost position. They think they can behave however they please, buying their way out of their problems, but don't worry, darling. They'll get their comeuppance."

Oh. My. God.

Aaron? Not O'Connor! No, surely…not the eyebrow. The Teaching Assistant Coordinator for the English department! And she called him *darling*. Were they involved? Could this get any worse? They knew everything, and they were conspiring to bring Daniel down! And poor David. They seemed intent on ruining him in the process!

Aaron had jokingly said he'd been looking for some sort of dirt on David when they'd been competing for the position of Provost. Clearly, he hadn't been joking. But they had no proof that Daniel and I had been romantically involved all semester. Surely there was nothing they could do now…

I spun around, my pulse throbbing in my temples as I tumbled onto the street. I needed to talk to Daniel. He would help me make sense of all of this. I crossed the road and dialed his cell, but then I remembered his phone was in the glove compartment. Shit.

I put my phone away and hurried back to campus, the blister on my foot screaming with every step. The closer I got to Northrop Frye Hall and the more I thought about Elaine's treatment of me since day one, the more convinced I was that that I hadn't misheard. I'd heard *exactly* right.

She'd been perfectly clear about her feelings for Daniel last week. *So conceited. No wonder he's always getting himself into trouble.* What was I going to do? I couldn't keep working for her. She was determined to prove that Daniel and I were an item and had been for a long time. The last place I should be was under her nose.

When I reached Northrop Frye Hall, it was twenty past eight. I moved around the office by rote, panic truly beginning to set in as I wondered how I'd be able to maintain my composure.

Calm down. She has no proof. It's all hearsay. There's nothing she can do.

But did she have proof? How had Travis become involved? And what had he even seen? Me getting out of Daniel's car in February? I'd been in Daniel's car the night of the Hart House play, but he'd been terrified of being seen with me in his car, never mind touching me. The only affection that night had been between me and Matt when he'd arrived to help take me upstairs. This wasn't adding up.

I was still puzzling through the rest of Elaine's one-sided conversation when she pushed the door open and strode imperiously around the counter.

"What a surprise," she said. "You're early."

"I suppose I am." It took every ounce of my self-control not to clock her on the nose.

She frowned at me over her shoulder as she fiddled with her key. "Everything all right?"

She was actually concerned about my welfare?

"Yep," I said, my hands leaving sweaty smudges on the desk blotter. "Dandy."

"Good. It wouldn't be the best day to be feeling under the weather. The person who's taking over for you will be here any minute. I'd like to get this training over and done with."

So much for her being concerned about me. She went into her office and closed the door before I had a chance to say anything. Probably for the best. I needed to think. So, she'd already found a replacement. She wasn't messing around.

I rested my head on my sweaty hands, hoping for a few moments of calm. No such luck. Within seconds, it seemed, the door swung open. I lifted my head and pushed myself out of my desk, preparing to deal with the poor sap whose fate was to spend God knows how long as Elaine's new part-time employee.

And what do you know? It was *him*. Travis. The bastard who'd reported me getting out of Daniel's car. I wanted to leap across the counter and claw his eyes out.

You rat fink. Why the hell did you have to open your big trap?

"Good morning, Aubrey." He strolled around the counter. "I'm sure you're surprised to see me again so soon."

I regarded him coolly. "Remarkably surprised. I hadn't taken you for a sadist."

He raised an eyebrow and smiled. Arrogant prick. I knew there was a reason I'd wiped him from my memory. At that moment, Elaine came barging out of her office, jabbering into her earpiece.

"Yes, he's here, right on time." She smiled at Travis. "Aaron, please stop worrying. I'll talk to you later."

O'Connor again? And why was he asking about Travis? Elaine rolled her eyes, and Travis frowned.

"Give him a break, Elaine."

"Your dad is like a mother hen."

"He's concerned, that's all."

They kept talking, but their voices merely echoed in my ears — or was that my blood rushing through my veins?

Your dad is like a mother hen.

She'd been talking to Aaron. *He was Travis's father?* Travis O'Connor. Of course! Holy hell.

I snapped back to reality as Elaine asked me a question.

"Pardon?" I said stupidly.

"Hmm." She narrowed her eyes. "You know what? Perhaps while I get Travis acquainted with the space, you could dash to Starbucks. You know I can't function until I've had my morning coffee."

What. The. Fuck?

Was this her game? Had she been sending me for coffee every morning unnecessarily? I'd have to hit her. The lying bitch!

"Once you get back, you can start showing Travis the ropes," she said, holding out a ten dollar bill.

Oh, I'd show him the ropes, all right. Then I'd take one, wrap it around his neck, tie it to a rafter at the top of Old Vic, and give him a push. Bastard. Forget the old adage to keep your friends close and your enemies closer. I was done. I stood, ignoring her outstretched hand.

"You know what? You want me to show Travis the ropes? I'd be happy to."

I grabbed the Swiffer from under the front counter and handed it to him. Then I jammed the watering can into his other hand. He looked at me like I'd sprouted a third ear in the middle of my forehead.

"Ready?"

He nodded dumbly, his eyes sliding over to Elaine. I didn't follow his gaze. I couldn't care less what Armstrong was doing.

"Try to follow along, Travis." I adopted a falsely sincere tone. "It's critical that you Swiffer on Mondays, and don't forget to water the plants on Wednesdays. Oh, and *this* is crucial…" I grabbed a piece of paper and scribbled a map on it. "Northrop Frye Hall is here." I jabbed my finger on a big square on the left side of the page and drew a dotted line down the middle of the map, my hand shaking with restrained fury. "*This* is Starbucks. Venti, extra bold, with a splash of low-fat milk." I pushed the piece of paper down the counter. "I think that covers it. Knock yourself out."

I dusted off my hands, grabbed my purse, and tossed my office key on the desk before heading for the door, turning as I pushed it open. Travis was staring at me idiotically, but Elaine was fuming, her facing starting to turn purple. She was a vision of apoplexy.

"Oh, and don't worry. I won't need a letter of reference," I said through gritted teeth.

I couldn't be sure, but I think smoke came out of her ears.

A Vulgar Comment

A vulgar comment will be made of it…
…And dwell upon your grave when you are dead;
For slander lives upon succession,
For ever housed where it gets possession.
(*Comedy of Errors*, Act III, Scene 1)

How foolish of me to think Armstrong would let me leave without giving me a piece of her mind. Before I'd reached the stairs, she was behind me and grabbing my arm to stop my descent.

"Take your hand off me," I said as calmly as I could.

"Trust me, I have no desire to touch you, you little tramp," she hissed.

Tramp?

"What is your problem?"

"*My* problem? Ha! You're quite the actress. Sweet as pie last week, when it was obvious you had no desire to be here once David had left. Your true colors are showing now, though, so run along, Aubrey. Go crying to your sugar daddy. He'll take care of you. But I think what you're doing is disgusting. A married man, twice your age? Not to mention the Provost of one of the most prestigious universities in the country. You *both* make me sick," she spat.

She turned and stormed back into the office, slamming the door and making a big production of locking it. "*Don't even think of coming back in here,*" her flashing eyes said. As if I could move, even if I'd wanted to.

The floor seemed to be listing beneath my feet as I processed what she'd said. I was so stunned, it was a wonder I didn't faint.

How could I have been so stupid? She had no idea about my relationship with Daniel. But the momentary relief I felt was quickly quashed by another horrid realization: she thought I was having an affair with David!

If her accusation wasn't so shocking, I might have laughed. Holy shit. Was she on drugs?

David was going to have a cow. I needed to talk to him. Now.

Somehow I made it down the stairs without keeling over. I regained my wits as I reached the sidewalk between Old Vic and Northrop Frye and quickly formulated a plan.

First, I ran to Jackman to change my shoes, grateful that everyone was asleep so I didn't have to explain my newest bizarre life-crisis.

Then I trekked to David's office.

"Provost Grant will see you now."

I crossed the waiting room where I'd sat for fifteen minutes, trying to figure out how best to break the disgusting news. His secretary ushered me into his office. David took off his glasses and tossed them on his daybook, standing as I approached his desk.

"This is a surprise, Aubrey. You didn't hint yesterday that you'd be coming by this morning."

"I didn't actually know…" I turned, watching the secretary pull the door closed behind her.

"I'm so glad you were able to join us for tea," David said.

"I had a nice time. Thank you for including me."

"It was our pleasure. Patty certainly enjoyed having you there. She might be your biggest fan."

I smiled unconvincingly, and he examined my face.

"Is everything all right?" He frowned at his watch. "It's nine thirty. Shouldn't you be at work?"

"You're right. I should be. I was just there, in fact. That's why I'm here…" He looked confused. I couldn't blame him. I wasn't making any sense. "David, I think you should sit down."

He sat, his face draining of color. "Is Daniel okay? I've been worrying about him ever since you two drove off in Brad's truck yesterday—"

"Daniel's fine. He's on his way to the cottage. I'm sure everything's fine. I've heard nothing to suggest otherwise."

"So, what is it, then? Something's obviously wrong."

I clenched my hands in my lap. "I have something to tell you. You're not going to be happy…"

"Aubrey?" he prompted. "You're not…You and Daniel haven't… You're being careful, right?" He looked at my stomach meaningfully.

"Oh, no." I waved my hands in the air. "It's not that. Nothing like that." His shoulders slumped, a relieved expression crossing his face. "No," I continued, "it's…well, it's Elaine Armstrong."

"Elaine? What about her?"

"She hasn't liked me since day one. I couldn't understand what her problem was, but I found out today."

"I don't understand. What could she possibly have against you?"

"It's actually against you, too," I said, biting my lip anxiously. "You see, she thinks we're having an affair."

"She *what?*"

I nodded. "She thinks we're involved."

He put his glasses on, as if clearer vision might facilitate his understanding of what I was saying.

"This is absurd. Why would she make such a ludicrous claim?"

I sighed and recapped the episode at Starbucks, and how I'd wrongly assumed she'd been talking to Aaron O'Connor about Daniel and me. Then I attempted to explain her reasoning, applying her accusations to David instead.

"She thinks you've been buying me clothes. She called you my *sugar daddy*," I said, squirming. The connotation of the term was heinous.

He shook his head again. "Why would she jump to the conclusion that I've been buying you clothes? That makes no sense."

"I suppose she finds it strange that we're in touch even though our employee-employer relationship is over."

"Again, that's no basis for assuming we're having an *affair!*" His face reddened as the implications of what I was saying started to sink in.

"It sounds like she and Aaron have been seeing what they *want* to see. He did admit to trying to dig up dirt on you. During the phone call I overhead, she mentioned the evening of your reception at Old Vic..I thought she was talking about Daniel looking at me strangely, but she must have been referring to you."

"I was anxious that night about you and Daniel hiding your feelings. I found myself watching both of you," he admitted.

"Aaron O'Connor misinterpreted those looks. He thought you looked guilty and self-conscious."

"It's still an enormous leap to make based on a few uncomfortable glances," David said. "How did the idea even occur to him?"

"I think I know the answer to that too. Aaron has a son—"

"Yes, I'm acquainted with Travis. He was a student at Vic. I had a run-in with him and one of his roommates a few years ago. They'd urinated in the stacks at the library. They were so drunk, they didn't even realize where they were. Some books and flooring needed to be replaced. Aaron wasn't too impressed with that incident."

I blushed. I remembered the night in question. I'd broken up with Lyle a few days before it had happened. Smartest move of my life.

"The roommate was Lyle Kennedy, right?"

"You knew him?"

"Uh…we sort of dated for a while. It didn't last long. He was a bit of a mess."

"Not your finest hour?" David asked.

"Definitely not."

"I suppose that's neither here nor there. What's Travis got to do with this?"

"Apparently, Travis saw me getting out of your car one night. He must have told his father what he saw. Or what he *thought* he saw."

David shook his head. "I'm not following. When did you get out of my car?"

"You drove me home after dinner at your house in February," I reminded him. "It was around ten o'clock? Daniel was asleep in the back seat."

"Oh, of course." His eyes drifted as he remembered the evening in question.

"According to Travis, we were *affectionate*."

"Affectionate?" David asked, his eyebrows shooting up in surprise.

"You clasped me by the shoulders when you were saying good night. I only remember it because afterward I felt so horrible about not having told you that Daniel was my TA, but then you squeezed my shoulders, and it was kind of like you were saying, '*No harm done*.' I felt so much better."

"Good grief, Aubrey. Squeezing someone's shoulders is hardly adultery!" he exclaimed.

"*I* know that, and *you* know that," I said. "But when you're grasping at straws? Aaron was trying to find something—anything—and when he came up empty, Travis might have piped up and told him what he'd seen. You brought me home late at night, you caressed my arm—or whatever they thought that was. What if he and Elaine started watching you…watching us…and drew whatever conclusions suited them?"

He rubbed his face with one hand. "This is just…I can't even…"

"I know. It's crazy. And you know what? When you called last week, she listened to our whole conversation. I knew she was there, and I didn't disguise how happy I was to hear from you. I wanted her to know I missed working for you. My side of the conversation might have sounded incriminating. I was kind of pouring it on."

He expelled a giant breath and fell back in his seat. "I won't stand by and let them sully my name, not to mention yours. They've got to be stopped."

"Do you want to talk to them now? I'll come with you if you want…"

"No, when I talk to Elaine, I want Gwen there. And Travis as well." He pinched the bridge of his nose, sighing heavily. "I can't believe this…"

"She hired him, you know. Travis? He's my replacement."

"That smacks of nepotism. He's essentially her stepson."

"I gathered from the phone call I overheard this morning that she and Aaron are involved."

"For a couple of years, now," David confirmed. "Well, if Travis is your replacement, he'll be at Vic on Wednesday morning. I'll clear my schedule and make sure Gwen's available. Can you join us for a meeting?"

"Of course. What about Daniel?"

"Daniel doesn't need to be involved. In fact, I don't want him anywhere near there. Can I leave it to you to explain this mess to him?"

"Do you think he'll take it all right? It won't upset him, will it?"

"He cares for you a great deal, and Elaine is being unusually cruel and slanderous. He's bound to be upset. That doesn't necessarily mean he'll have an anxiety attack, if that's what you're concerned about. Tell him to give me a call if you'd rather, but given how close you two are becoming, it's best you learn how to deal with his… emotional tendencies."

"You're probably right."

As my thoughts drifted to Daniel, I realized history was repeating itself. A false accusation was again being leveled, only this time it wasn't Daniel being accused: it was his father.

Daniel didn't get home until early evening, by which time I was fast asleep on his living room couch. He woke me with a gentle kiss on the forehead.

"Hey there, sleepyhead."

I sat up and snuggled into his arms. "Hi, I'm glad you're home. What time is it?"

"Five thirty." He pushed himself off the couch and headed for the kitchen. "I think I deserve a beer after the day I've had. Can I get you something?"

"Vodka and soda?" I asked.

"Wow, straight for the big guns."

A few minutes later, he returned with our drinks, mine with a twist of lemon and lime perched on the rim of the glass. He flopped on the couch beside me and tapped his glass against mine.

"Cheers."

"Cheers, sunshine."

"Any particular reason why you feel the need to drink vodka on a Monday evening?"

"My day wasn't exactly a walk in the park."

"Stressful shift? Did you get a cramp from Swiffering? Or did one of the plants take a turn for the worse?"

"You think you're pretty funny, don't you?"

He shrugged and smiled, resting his beer on his thigh. "I have my moments."

"If you must know, I've handed the Swiffering duties to someone else," I said, taking his hand and squeezing it gently. "For good." He sat up. Now I had his attention. "Elaine hired a replacement. I'm not staying on to train him."

"Really? That's amazing. Wait, how come you're not training him? Did she tell you she didn't want you to come back?"

"Not exactly."

"Okay…"

I took a deep breath and explained the whole story. I concluded with my panicky trip to visit his father. He listened without interrupting, his eyes widening and his fingers tightening around mine as the story unfolded.

"So, your dad figures he'll take your mom with him to confront Elaine on Wednesday, along with that shithead, Travis."

"Wow." He brought his hand to his mouth in disbelief. "I can't… This is just…Holy shit."

"I think that's exactly what your father said. Except for the 'holy shit' part."

He moved his hand over his eyes, his fingers sort of squeezing at his temples. I let him be for a minute, allowing him to absorb everything I'd told him. When his shoulders started to shake, I felt a flutter of panic in my stomach.

"Daniel?" I gently rubbed his back.

He moved his hand away from his face and looked at me, and then he started to laugh uncontrollably.

"You shit!" I exclaimed, shoving his shoulder. "I thought you were having an anxiety attack!"

"I'm sorry…I'm sorry," he said as he gasped. "Holy fuck, this is too funny."

I crossed my arms while he giggled his ass off. When he'd run out of steam, he reached for my hand.

"I'm sorry, it's just that this is—"

"Absurd?"

"Totally. She's certifiable. You and my dad? Jesus."

"Yep."

"I'm sure it was awful for you, but, fuck, I wish I'd been a fly on the wall. You lost it, eh?"

"Pretty much. I hate confrontations like that, but I was so angry. It's fair to say I snapped."

"When you talked to my dad, how was he?"

"He kind of wigged out. He's livid, but he didn't make me feel bad or anything."

"Wow," he whispered. "This is perfect—poetic justice, plain and simple. Now he'll know *exactly* how I felt when Nicola falsely accused me."

"I don't blame you for getting some satisfaction from this, but don't forget, I'm stuck right in the middle of it."

"I'm sorry. I don't mean to be insensitive. Forgive me?"

"I'll think about it."

I was trying to keep things light, but he should have been more concerned about my welfare. He examined my face.

"So, I was passed out in the car when we drove you home that night in February. I missed all the action. Exactly *how affectionate* were you?"

"Daniel!" I smacked his arm. "Your father's reputation is on the line. As is mine."

"Ouch!" He laughed and rubbed his arm. Then he composed himself, trying his best to appear contrite. "Okay, I'm sorry. No more jokes. I promise."

"Thank you." I was beginning to wonder if a panic attack might have been a preferable reaction.

"I can't believe Elaine and Aaron have been so focused on my dad, they've been oblivious to what was going on right under their noses between us. We couldn't have planned it better if we'd tried."

"I don't think I would have planned *this*. This is a serious accusation."

"You're right." He patted my leg. "The whole fucked up scenario must appeal to my love of dark humor. I guess I should call him."

He crossed to the breakfast bar, blowing me an air kiss as he waited for his dad to answer the phone.

"Hi, Dad, it's me. How are things there?" he asked. "Yes, she just told me the whole story. It's preposterous. It's almost laughable."

He winked at me. *Almost* laughable. Right.

"How's Mom?" he said, joining me on the couch again. "Huh, that's understandable."

He took my hand and squeezed it.

"I'm sure...Yes, it must be very frustrating, you know, being accused of something you didn't do."

His lip twitched. He was trying his damnedest not to break out laughing again, I was sure of it.

"No, of course I do. This concerns Aubrey, too. I'd love nothing more than to throttle Armstrong with my bare hands, not to mention this Travis. I'd happily kick *his* ass. And don't even get me started on Aaron. I have a meeting with him soon to discuss class evaluations and my placement for September."

He rolled his eyes, retrieving his hand and holding it up to make a chirping gesture. His father was ranting.

"I'm sure you will, but just remember, Dad, if you rip her head off, she'll probably grow two new ones..."

Full of Ire

The accuser and the accused freely speak:
High-stomach'd are they both, and full of ire...
(*Richard II*, Act I, Scene I)

"Are you okay?" Daniel asked, peering into my eyes.

"I'm nervous. I'm looking forward to your dad tearing a strip off Armstrong, but it could get ugly."

"Luckily, you're not going into this alone. And I'll be right here when you're done. Okay?"

I melted into his arms. "Okay."

"I wish I could come in with you," he whispered.

"I'll be fine."

"I'm sure you will. I just really wish I could watch. I suppose it wouldn't be appropriate of you to take video..."

I pushed him away. "You're awful."

"I know. I should be flogged."

I smiled grudgingly. I couldn't fault him for trying to lighten my mood.

"I should go. Your dad said ten thirty, right?"

"He said he'd meet you outside Northrop Frye." He tipped my chin up. "Go kick some ass. And get a few kicks in for me."

"Deal."

I stepped away reluctantly, leaving him alone in the writing lab. David was waiting for me on the front step of Northrop Frye Hall, staring at his watch every few seconds.

"There you are," he said as I joined him.

"Where's Gwen?"

"She had a meeting at nine with some of the women from MADD. It's not easy to find a mutually convenient time. She was reluctant to cancel." David cleared his throat. "She'll be here any minute."

I looked around uneasily. Damn that idiotic Elaine Armstrong. David and I had just started getting back to normal after my missteps with Daniel, and now she'd screwed everything up again.

"How've you been the last couple of days? You haven't been worrying, I hope?" he asked.

"No, I've been fine."

"Good. And Daniel?"

"He's fine too. He's waiting for me downstairs in Old Vic."

He nodded, and we stood there awkwardly, neither one of us bothering to pursue more small talk. I was running out of things I could describe as being "fine." He tugged at his tie, as if the collar of his shirt was cutting off his circulation.

"Did you want to go inside?" I asked.

"Why don't we?" He opened the door and let me pass through ahead of him.

We stopped in the lobby. I perused the flyers on the bulletin board while David paced at the top of the staircase. After about five minutes, he looked at his watch for the millionth time.

"Maybe we should go in. I have no idea what's keeping Gwen. I'd say let's postpone, but I need to resolve the situation."

"It's up to you."

If I were Gwen, I'd want to be here, but it wasn't my call.

"I'll text her and let her know we've gone in." He quickly punched a message into his phone, and then he took me by the elbow and led me to the office. "Let me do the talking."

"Of course."

As much as I wanted to give Elaine a piece of my mind, who knows what kind of vitriol would spew from my mouth if I was afforded the opportunity to speak. That wouldn't help our cause.

When we rounded the counter, Travis stood up at the desk and managed to say, "Can I help..." before realizing what was going on. He snatched the phone, presumably to warn Elaine.

David took the phone from him and replaced it on the receiver, smiling blithely at Travis.

"Hold Dean Armstrong's calls, would you?" He turned to look at me. "Aubrey?"

He pushed the office door open and ushered me inside, closing the door behind him. Elaine looked up, startled for an instant, but then a satisfied smile spread across her face.

"Won't you come in?" she said dryly.

"Thank you. Don't mind if we do."

David motioned for me sit in one of the chairs across from Elaine's desk. He sat beside me, unbuttoning his jacket. I tried to mimic his unruffled exterior. It wasn't easy.

Elaine appraised us across the desk. "I can't say I'm surprised to see you. I'm shocked you didn't come sooner."

"What are you playing at, Elaine?"

"Playing? Oh, I'm not playing, David."

She was virtually purring. I longed to reach out and slap the smug smirk off her face. She regarded me with mock interest.

"How about you, Aubrey? Are you playing? You don't understand what's going on here, do you? I'd have thought with your GPA you'd be brighter, but I suppose you've been blinded by the glamor of it all. Think about it, though. Can you imagine what would happen if Gwen knew what was going on? Your sons are older than Aubrey, if I'm not mistaken, David. But then, I suppose that's what makes this so stimulating. Is that it?"

I gasped and had to clench my teeth together to avoid calling her a stupid bitch. David's hand flew to my wrist.

"Don't answer that, Aubrey. Don't even dignify the question with a—"

David didn't finish because at that moment, Gwen's voice rang out on the other side of the door, telling Travis not to trouble himself because she didn't need to be announced. The door flew open, and Gwen appeared. She closed the door and crossed decisively to the desk. I was kind of glad Gwen had been late. Her entrance was amazing, and the look on Elaine's face was priceless.

"Gwen! What a surprise," she choked out, standing up shakily.

David offered his wife his chair, and Gwen looked at Elaine serenely.

"Elaine, please sit, won't you?"

Nothing like treating someone as a guest in their own office. Elaine slowly resumed her seat, and Gwen smiled at me.

"Hello, Aubrey. How are you, dear?"

"I'm as well as can be expected under the circumstances, Gwen. Thank you."

David pulled one of the chairs from the round table over to the desk. He placed it between Gwen and me and sat down, crossing his legs comfortably while Elaine tried to regain her composure, her eyes darting between the three of us.

Gwen smoothed her skirt over her knees. "I'm a busy woman, Elaine," she said. "I don't have all day to waste dealing with nonsense. I'd like to get to the bottom of these ridiculous allegations you've made against my husband and Aubrey."

Her self-possession regained, Elaine lifted her eyebrow, her mouth twisted into wry smile.

"I must say I never imagined you'd come clean. How admirable, Provost Grant." She turned her attention to Gwen. "And so noble of you to stand by your man, regardless of his impropriety. I never took you for the self-sacrificing type."

Gwen sighed heavily. "I'm not interested in your faux-sycophantic drivel, Elaine. Let's get down to brass tacks, shall we?"

Faux-sycophantic drivel? Wowza. No vacuous charity wife here, folks.

"Fair enough," Elaine said, tapping one of her fingernails on the mahogany desk. "David's behavior with *this girl* is a disgrace to the university. Perhaps you can put up with his philandering, but having someone in such an important and ethically demanding position behaving so immorally is unconscionable. I simply can't stand by and let it go—"

David waved his hands and grimaced.

"Okay, enough of this nonsense. When Aubrey told me about these claims of yours, I thought she was joking. The whole thing is preposterous. You can't seriously be prepared to stand by your accusations?"

"I most certainly do. Everything adds up, David."

"You must be using one hell of a calculator, because you have nothing—absolutely nothing—to base your claims on."

"That's not true. I have a witness—someone who saw a late night tryst between—"

"Don't start with the business of me dropping Aubrey off at residence in February," David said. "Gwen and I had Aubrey over for a family dinner during Reading Week, and I was merely seeing her home safely. Travis should get his facts straight before running around spreading half-truths."

The blood drained from Elaine's face, and she glared at me.

"You snoop. Have you been reading my emails?"

The gall of the woman! She was calling *me* a snoop?

"You do realize that would require a password, Dean Armstrong," I said calmly. "I don't even have a password to access my *own* email anymore."

She expelled a sharp breath through her nose. David looked at me in confusion.

"You haven't been able to get into the email account?" he asked.

"Dean Armstrong changed the access protocols," I explained, matter-of-factly.

Gwen leaned forward. "David, could we discuss email accounts later? I'd like to return to the topic at hand."

"Of course." He turned to Elaine. "Suffice it to say that we're well aware of the so-called proof you think you have, but trust me, Aubrey didn't discover that information nefariously. You might want to consider your own indiscretions. I can't control what absurd scenarios you cook up in your head, but when you publicly spout lies about me, lies that affect my reputation, my marriage, and my relationship with people who are dear to me and my family—" he glanced at me briefly "—that's when the gloves come off."

"I'm not the only one who's noticed what's going on," she said. "It suits you to believe I've concocted this, but you made quite a spectacle of yourself the week before your party. Running from office to office demanding an extra invitation be printed for Aubrey…"

David sighed and pinched the bridge of his nose. Gwen put her hand on his sleeve and leaned forward, speaking on his behalf.

"As an employee and close family friend, Aubrey had every right to be on that guest list, Elaine, and you know it. David had a lot on his mind the week before his tenure came to an end. He made an oversight, forgot to put Aubrey on the list, and was merely trying to rectify an error. Surely there are more important things to concern yourself with. You're supposed to an officer at a university!"

Elaine narrowed her eyes at Gwen. "You've thought this through carefully. You have an answer for everything. Tell me, David, does Gwen know about this secret that you and Aubrey were discussing on the phone last week?" Elaine looked at me. "*Don't worry, Gwen won't suspect a thing?*' Isn't that what you said?"

Gwen turned to me. I sighed wearily.

"Mother's Day tea. When David called to invite me, apparently Dean Armstrong was eavesdropping." I shot an incredulous look at Elaine, as if I hadn't known she'd been standing there absorbing every word. I was right to suspect she'd twisted everything I'd said to suit her own purposes.

"Honestly, Elaine," Gwen exclaimed. "This is what you're basing accusations of adultery on? You must see how ridiculous you're being?"

"I don't think people will find this ridiculous at all," Elaine said. "And stories like these have a way of spreading without it even being clear how they began."

David was instantly on his feet and looming over her desk.

"If I catch a *whiff* of this business beyond this office, I'll sue you for defamation before you've had a chance to blink."

My own heart was thundering, so I can only imagine how David felt. How he wasn't strangling her was beyond me. Gwen was sitting with her hands clasped together in her lap, the very picture of poise. I did my best to follow suit.

"We seem to have reached an impasse," Elaine said, her voice restrained. Even so, a flicker of doubt danced behind her gaze.

"Aubrey, would you excuse us for a moment?" David asked, not once breaking eye contact with Elaine. "We'll be out shortly."

Gwen reached across the empty chair to squeeze my hand.

"Um, yes, of course." I pushed myself out of my chair.

They hadn't reached an impasse. Elaine was trying to save face, and David wasn't having any of it. Perhaps he thought he'd get further with her if I wasn't there. He was probably right. By the same token, I wanted to stay. I knew I was about to miss the good stuff.

"Fun times?" Travis asked as I closed the office door. He was staring out the window.

"Best time I've had in months."

"Look, don't bitchface me. You brought this on yourself."

"I beg your pardon?" I crossed to the window. "I brought this on *myself*? Are you mental?"

"You think someone else is responsible for you fucking the Provost of the university?"

I wanted to be calm and dignified like Gwen. But, hell, let's call a spade a spade. I'd never be like Gwen.

So what did I do?

I slapped Travis.

I slapped him really frigging hard, my palm stinging on impact. He recoiled in disbelief, his hand flying to his cheek to cover the red mark.

"You *bitch*," he said, his back hitting the windowsill. "I can't believe you hit me!"

"You're lucky I didn't punch you in the junk, asshole," I hissed. "It's all lies. I'm no more having an affair with David than you're having tea with the Queen every afternoon."

He rubbed his cheek again, giving me a smug sideways look before turning to gaze out the window. I put my hands on my hips, trying to contain my fury.

"What?" He shrugged nonchalantly.

"You know, don't you! You know there's nothing going on between David and me. You're playing this all up. You bastard."

He didn't reply, instead turning his spiteful smile out the window again.

"Why would you do something like this?"

He gave me another quick glance. "David had it coming to him. He's a pompous prick. Embarrassed the shit out of me a few years ago after the episode at the library. It was all Lyle's fault, and I got dragged down with him. We ended up paying all this money to replace old books that should have been tossed in the garbage years ago anyway—"

I crossed my arms, fuming. "Travis, you *urinated* on books…in the library! What the hell did you think David's reaction would be? It's called restitution for destroyed property. He was doing his job."

"Whatever. He didn't have to be such a dick about it."

"*Whatever?* This isn't a frat boy prank. This is the kind of shit that makes people toss around words like *slander, libel…lawsuit.* Don't you get it? And what about me? I'm stuck right in the middle of it!"

He glanced at me indifferently. "Collateral damage."

I shook my head in disbelief. "You're such an asshole."

"And you're a superior bitch. You were a bitch then, and you're a bitch now. Lyle was going off the rails, and you blew him off. He wasn't good enough for you so you bolted. I was the one who ended up trying to drag him through the rest of the year."

Wait, he was blaming *me* for Lyle's academic failure?

"I can't believe you—I can't even…"

I had to walk away. If I didn't, I wouldn't be able to control my desire to grab the stapler and sink a bunch of metal clips into his forehead. I crossed my arms and moved to the front of the office, breathing deeply to slow the flow of adrenaline pumping through my body. The door of the inner office flew open, and I spun around to see David stride out, steering Gwen by the elbow. Elaine appeared behind them, her face a fabulous shade of gray.

"We'll just leave you to your apple polishing, Elaine. Have a lovely day. Aubrey?" Gwen joined me at the door. "We're leaving now."

I nodded and shot a final death glare at Travis who'd reclaimed his seat at the desk.

"I almost forgot," David said, producing a small white envelope from his inside pocket and placing it in Gisele's inbox tray. "Elaine, please let Gisele know there's a posting across campus for a senior secretary. With her qualifications, she's a solid contender for advancement. The necessary information is in that envelope. I'll call tomorrow to follow up."

Elaine crossed her arms and raised her chin haughtily. David leaned over the desk, and Travis glared up at him.

"As for *you,* I'll be meeting with your father at my office tomorrow morning. I suggest you make yourself available."

Travis swallowed hard.

"Oh, and I want that," David said, pointing to the plant atop the bookshelf. "Get it for me. Now."

Travis's gaze flickered over to Elaine. She closed her eyes and nodded once. I got the distinct impression that if she let her control slip, even for a second, her face would crack open and a hundred snakes would burst out of her head. Travis stood on a chair and retrieved Archie Junior.

"Thank you," David said with exaggerated graciousness as he took the plant in both hands. "*Now* we're leaving."

In the writing lab, Daniel was pacing like an expectant father. As I pulled the door shut, he closed the distance between us, taking me into his arms and examining my face.

"Is everyone okay? Where's my mom and dad?"

"Everyone's fine. Your dad said he'll call you later. He's taking your mom home. She was pretty shaken."

"What happened?"

"Do we have to talk here? I'd rather not."

"Of course not. You said you wanted to swing by Jackman and grab a few things. Why don't we go now? You head over, and I'll join you in a few minutes."

I dashed to Jackman Hall, let myself in, and looked around. Matt's door was closed, but Jo's was wide open. Even so, she didn't appear to be home. I slipped off my shoes, adding them to the pile of footwear in the hallway. Before I had a chance to contemplate giving my room a quick tidy, the buzzer sounded. I let Daniel in, and he leapt through the stairwell door a moment later, walking briskly down the corridor.

"Hey," he said, putting his arm around me. "Are you sure you're okay? Your cheeks are flushed."

"I'm fine," I assured him.

Satisfied that I was none the worse for wear, he scanned the apartment. "This is it, huh?"

"This is it."

"Let's go in your room, and you can tell me everything."

We started down the hallway when Matt opened his door.

"Hey, this is a surprise," he said.

Under normal circumstances, he'd have reached out for a hug. Instead, he held out his hand for Daniel to shake. Daniel took his hand warily, as if he thought Matt might be about to press one of those practical joke buzzers into his palm.

Hand-shaking. No practical joke buzzers. This is progress.

A strange look passed between them, and Matt nodded.

Silent communication?

"What brings you by?" Matt asked.

"This is sort of an impulse visit. Is Sarah here?" I asked, compelled to remind Daniel that Matt was happily planting his flag elsewhere.

"She's at the gym."

"How come you're not with her?"

"She says I distract her. It's understandable. You can't blame her, right?" he said with a self-satisfied smirk.

Daniel looked at me meaningfully. He didn't want to chat with Matt. He wanted to hear about how things had gone with Elaine.

"I just need to grab a few things," I said, tugging on Daniel's hand.

Matt took the hint and bobbed his head. I walked backward as I opened my door.

"Now, be nice. This is just a residence room."

"I don't care about your room, poppet."

He closed the door and took my hands in his, not even letting me move beyond the doorway before pressing me for the details of the meeting. I explained the whole sordid story, describing his mother's composure and his father's quiet rage. His eyes almost popped out of his head when I related the face-slapping incident.

"Your dad said not to worry and that everything was going to be okay. Apparently, he's planning to see O'Connor tomorrow."

"I couldn't care less about O'Connor. I'm worried about you. What if Travis had hit you back?"

I shook my head. "I couldn't help it. What he said about me and your dad was so crude. I don't think he would've hit me. He doesn't have the balls."

Daniel drew me into his arms. "He messed with the wrong lady, huh?"

"You know it."

"I was right to suspect you'd need cheering up."

He spun me around slowly and on my desk was a vase with the most breathtaking purple flowers. I freed myself from Daniel's clasped hands, eager to take a closer look.

"They're orchids," he explained. "My mom suggested them. Apparently orchids symbolize rare beauty—something to make up for the ugliness of the morning."

"Thank you. They're exquisite. You're so thoughtful, Daniel."

"I called Matt. He agreed to be here when they were delivered." Daniel squeezed my shoulder gently. "There's something else."

He pointed to the closet. There was a garment bag hanging inside. "What's that?"

"Remember yesterday when I said I was going to the Metro Reference Library to get a book? That wasn't exactly true. I went to Bayview Village." He gave me a little push, propelling me toward the closet. "Open it."

I opened the garment bag, finding a beautiful violet dress inside—one of several dresses I'd tried on at Judith and Charles but resolutely refused to allow him to buy, reasoning that two was plenty. I'd thought about the dress a few times since that day. Daniel had practically salivated when I'd emerged from the dressing room to model it for him.

"You shouldn't have," I said, gently rubbing the fabric between my fingers.

"But I did. We're going out for dinner tonight, and you have to look extra special." He kissed me tenderly. "After all, it's our three month anniversary, and I'm taking you to Auberge du Pommier."

My hand flew to my mouth. The thirteenth. It was May thirteenth.

"I completely forgot. I'm so sorry. I'll make it up to you," I promised.

"I'm counting on it."

He cradled my face and kissed me. I allowed myself to get swept away in his passionate embrace, grateful for the reprieve from the angst and tension of the last few days. Dropping a soft kiss on my forehead, he brushed my hair out of my eyes, his expression fierce.

"You've been incredible this week," he said. "So strong and brave."

"Looks like my acting skills are improving."

"Whatever you say." He winked and then rubbed his hands to-gether. "How about while we're here we pack everything up and bring it to the condo?"

"*Daniel.*" I didn't need to say more. My tone spoke volumes.

"Hey, it was worth a try."

"Don't forget I'm staying here when my mom comes. I have to leave some stuff here."

"*Some,*" he emphasized. "You don't need all this." He gestured around him.

I shrugged and looked around forlornly. He held up his hands, admitting quick defeat.

"Fine, but at least bring some books. I need to work on my paper before the weekend. I don't want you to be bored. You should prob-ably pack a different pair of shoes for tonight as well—give your blisters a chance to heal."

"I feel like I should wear the new ones anyway, or I'll never break them in."

"You know, you don't have to wear them in public to break them in, right?" he said, a devilish glint in his eye.

A few hours later, I stood in Daniel's shower, trying to wash away Elaine's horrid accusations and Travis's snide personal attacks. The situation was in David's hands now, and I'd never have to deal with Elaine Armstrong in a professional capacity ever again.

Unfortunately, if I'd managed to secure a spot on the dean's list, she'd be the one handing me the award. Talk about sucking the joy out of the experience. The thought made me shudder. I forced myself to wipe her from my mind. Daniel and I were going out for a lovely dinner, and I had a sexy new dress to wear. I needed to put the week's nastiness behind me.

Eyes closed, I was vigorously working shampoo into my scalp when a tapping on the shower door interrupted my scrubbing. I rinsed my face as Daniel slid the door open and popped his head inside the stall.

"I don't think we have time, sailor."

He smiled as he scanned my body. "I know. It's devastating. But strange as it sounds, I haven't come in here to maul you. I thought I'd better give you fair warning. My dad just called from the lobby. He's on his way up for a quick visit."

I rubbed my eyes again. "Shit, what should I do?"

"Well," he said, a look of contemplation on his face. "Whatever you do, don't come sauntering into the living room in ten minutes wearing a towel." He winked. "People will talk."

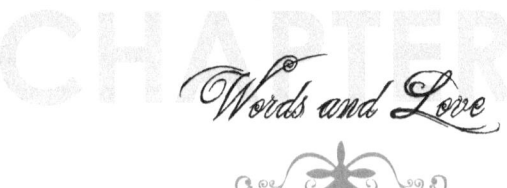

Words and Love

...I love you more than words can wield the matter...
...A love that makes breath poor and speech unable...
(*King Lear,* Act 1, Scene 1)

By the time I emerged from Daniel's room, dressed and almost ready to go, David had left. I found Daniel in the kitchen, recapping his bottle of scotch.

I touched his shoulder lightly. "Sorry I missed your dad. Is he okay?"

He tilted his head as he appraised me. "You expect me to think about my dad with you looking like that?" He swept a stray curl away from my face.

"No, seriously, what happened? Why'd he stop by?"

"He just wanted to reassure us that everything's going to be all right."

I gestured to the scotch bottle. "You had a drink together?"

"I took a pass, but he definitely needed something. He looked wrecked. This has been a tough couple of days for him."

"Of course. For your mother, too. Did he tell you what happened after I left the office?"

"He said he called Elaine out on the way she'd hired Travis—circumventing hiring protocols, skipping the tiered posting system. She claimed she got special dispensation to expedite the hiring process because of your sudden decision to quit."

"I gave her two weeks' notice."

"Elaine was lying. My dad knew that. He also mentioned the nepotism thing. He told her if she posts the job properly and gets rid of Travis, he won't report her."

"I can't believe he gave her a chance to put things right."

"I think he's trying to be conciliatory because he knows so much is at stake. He's worried about my future on campus as well as his own. He doesn't want to be too heavy-handed."

"Do you think she played the 'you report me and I'll spread rumors about you' card?"

"I'm not sure, but if she were to do something like that, my dad would sue her for defamation in a heartbeat. He's sure they won't go forward with things. There's no proof. They don't have a leg to stand on."

"That's almost beside the point. Whether they can prove their claims or not, all it takes is a seed of doubt in people's minds, and it's out there. Forever."

Daniel nodded, his eyes drifting over my shoulder. "I know all about that."

"Of course you do." I wrapped my arms around his waist. "Is that how you feel about what happened in England? Like it'll never go away?"

"I've felt that way from time to time. Everyone who reads that letter in my file knows what happened at Oxford. How can I put it behind me? It's bad enough dealing with admin on campus, but when I wonder if my dad still has doubts?" He rubbed his cheek against my hair and sighed. "I'm not *celebrating* his discomfort, but I can't help feeling somewhat vindicated that he's being forced to walk around the block in my shoes."

"I suppose you can't be blamed for that."

"Look, I don't want to talk about that stuff anymore tonight. Let's enjoy our evening—starting with this dress," he said. "Let me see?"

I spun around slowly. The dress was backless. Daniel approved.

"You're not wearing a bra, are you?" he said.

"I don't have one of those fancy halter-dress bras."

"Hey, I'm not complaining. I'd say this is my anniversary gift right here," he whispered, gently tickling my bare sides.

"I told you I'd make it up to you," I said.

"Yes, you did." As he kissed me, he skimmed his fingertips across the thin fabric covering my breasts. I breathed out quietly, holding his shoulders to steady myself. "You might want to bring a sweater to the restaurant," he said, still caressing me. "You seem a little chilly."

The morning after our three-month anniversary celebration, I slept until nine thirty. When I opened my eyes, I saw my new dress draped across the chair beside the bed. I smiled, remembering the night before.

We'd had an amazing dinner at Auberge du Pommier, one which I'd capped off with the most delectable serving of crème brûlée. Daniel had urged me to eat quickly, eager to return home to continue the celebration. He'd barely closed the condo door before he was trying to peel me out of the dress, virtually taking scissors to it after grappling with the complicated wraparound design for a couple of frustrating minutes.

Once he had me undressed, he'd carried me to the dining room where he made me recline on the mahogany table and proceeded to *have me for dessert*, as he put it. I'd suggested whipped cream. He'd scoffed at the suggestion.

"*I prefer my pussy the way I take my scotch. Neat.*"

Not surprisingly, the events that followed were the highlight of the evening — hell, they might have been the highlight of the *month*.

I sighed and rolled over, hoping to cuddle up to Daniel's warm chest, but he wasn't there. Why he got up at the butt-crack of dawn regardless of whatever ungodly hour we'd gone to bed was a mystery to me. I needed a good seven hours of sleep to function properly. Daniel seemed capable of running on fumes.

I crawled out of bed, threw on a T-shirt and some panties, and stole a pair of his white sweat socks. I collected an armful of laundry and found Daniel sitting on the sofa in the living room, reading the newspaper.

"Hey, there you are. Sleep okay?" he asked.

"Morning, sunshine. I slept great." I gave him a quick kiss before taking the pile of clothes to the kitchen where I dropped it on the floor to sort it.

When I turned around, Daniel was peeking around the corner of the paper, watching me. "How do you do that?" he asked.

"Do what?"

"How do you make white cotton panties and sweat socks sexy?" He tossed the paper on the coffee table and held out his hands, beckoning me to join him.

"If that's what I'm doing, it's purely accidental." I sat beside him, draping my legs across his lap. "I'm surprised you're not in the office writing."

"I wrote for a bit. I had to step away. Hamlet's not cooperating."

"In what way?"

"He keeps fenceposting me." He smiled.

"Secretive characters. They're the worst."

"It's true. Plus I was thinking about my dad's eight thirty meeting with O'Connor. I can't help wondering what's going on."

"You need a distraction." I straddled his lap and nipped playfully at his ear.

He chuckled, cupping my breast as I wiggled against him. He traced circles around my nipple with his thumb, smiling as I squirmed.

"This shirt is ridiculous, you know that, right?"

"I think it's clever," I protested, looking down at the decal of Shakespeare with the crossbones behind his head.

"'*Bard to the bone*'?" he said, reading the words beneath Shakespeare's face.

"That's me."

He grasped my hips, directing my movements. "I'd say you're rather *good* to the bone."

He tangled his hand in my hair, tilting my head and showering my neck with soft, tickly kisses. On the coffee table, Daniel's phone vibrated. He glanced over my shoulder.

"Go ahead and check," I said. "It might your dad."

"Sorry, poppet. I'll only be a second." I watched him read the message. "It's not my dad, but listen to this," he said, pulling me close. "It's an email from O'Connor's secretary: '*Please be advised that your meeting with Mr. O'Connor has been canceled due to unforeseen circumstances. You will be contacted as soon as possible to reschedule the meeting. We apologize for any inconvenience this may cause.*'"

"Was that the meeting where you were supposed to talk about plans for the fall?"

"Yes, and look over the class evaluations."

"What do you think these unforeseen circumstances are?"

"No clue. I wonder if it's got anything to do with his meeting with my dad."

"Why don't you call your father and see?"

Daniel pursed his lips, his eyes sliding down my legs. He got up, tugging me to my feet. "I'll call him after I shower. Care to join me? Can you be Bard to the bone in the shower?"

"You have to ask? Don't you remember?" I dropped my eyes to the front of his pajama bottoms and raised a cheeky eyebrow. "Looks like *someone* remembers."

When I emerged from the bedroom after blow-drying my hair, I found Daniel on the balcony, sitting on the lounge chair and frowning at his phone. I pushed the patio door open, and he smiled up at me. It was the smile of someone who's chewing something distasteful at a dinner party while telling the host how delicious the food is.

I gestured to his phone. "You talked to your dad?"

"Yes."

"And?"

"Aaron and Elaine have backed off. My dad said they won't cause any more problems."

"Does he know anything about the postponed meeting with O'Connor?"

"No, but he said it's not something I should worry about."

"That's reassuring." I sat beside him and squeezed his thigh. "So, why don't you seem happy?"

He shook his head, doing his best to smile again and patting my hand.

"I am. I'm very relieved." He stood and stretched, moving to the railing and gazing southward. "By the way, I just heard from Jeremy," he said. "He set up a meeting for you with his friend Eli—the one with the magazine. He wants you to go to his place at noon on Wednesday for an interview."

Daniel had his eyes trained on the lake, but I didn't need to see his face to know that he still looked as if he were chewing something he'd rather spit out than swallow.

Welcome and Unwelcome Things

Such welcome and unwelcome things at once
'Tis hard to reconcile.
(*Macbeth*, Act IV, Scene 3)

Knowing I wouldn't have someone to run interference during my first meeting with Eli made me feel as if I were embarking on a blind date. Would our meeting be awkward? Had Jeremy exaggerated Eli's interest in taking on new writers? Was I talented, or were Daniel's feelings for me coloring his ability to judge my writing objectively? I spent much of the night before our designated meeting imagining the questions he'd ask and planning answers. Sleep was elusive, at best. Beside me, Daniel tossed and turned as well.

I needn't have worried. Eli was everything Jeremy had described: warm and outgoing, vaguely eccentric-looking—a cardigan and corduroy-wearing Johnny Depp, perhaps—but enthusiastic and eager to share his knowledge and expertise and help me "hone my craft" as he put it. He was generous with both his time and encouragement, and at the end of our two-hour meeting, we had a plan in place that would allow me to start my freelance career that weekend.

I returned to the condo brimming with excitement, eager to tell Daniel all about the meeting. I dashed through the door, quickly dropping my bag and keys. Daniel was gazing out the living room window, but he turned to greet me as I skipped across the room.

"You look chipper."

"I had the best afternoon," I gushed, slipping my arms around him. "Jeremy was right. Eli's great. He's so creative and smart. He's going to give me a shot at writing for the magazine. He wants me to do reviews of new music, like going to local concerts. He said he wants to try a 'girl on the street' approach with me. Isn't that cool? You know how much I love indie music. I'm so stoked. Anyway, Eli said he'll take me to The National concert on Saturday and talk me through it, you know, show me what to watch for, how to take notes. Then I can write a review, and he'll look at it. We talked about my playlists, and he said he thinks I have great taste in music, but he's not sure about the writing yet…"

I trailed off and stepped back. Daniel was looking at me with a strange glint in his eyes. He crossed his arms and quirked an eyebrow.

"Did he say anything else?" he asked. There was a snide, falsely curious undertone to his voice.

I felt the air rush out of me as my bubble burst. He might as well have punched me in the stomach.

"What's that supposed to mean?"

He shrugged and turned to look out the window again. "Nothing. Never mind."

"If you have something you want to say, say it."

He shook his head, refusing to look at me.

"That's not fair. This whole thing—me trying my hand at writing—it was all your idea. Now I'm excited about Eli giving me a chance, and you're pissed off?" He closed his eyes and pressed his forehead to the window. "Fine. Forget it." I stormed out of the living room and into the office, slamming the door.

I paced like a caged animal, muttering about how unfair he was being. He'd gone on and on about me quitting the job at Vic and finding a passion, a vocation—and now someone was inspiring me to take a chance, and he was angry because I was enthusiastic about connecting with that person? How infantile!

A quiet tapping on the door interrupted my angry monologue. I made a few more laps of the room, fuming quietly. He knocked again, louder this time.

"Aubrey? Can I come in?"

I gritted my teeth and opened the door. "It's your condo. You can come and go wherever you please, Daniel."

"And right now you'd be happy if I went to hell, I'm guessing?"

"What you said out there wasn't fair. You made me feel guilty for being excited."

He shook his head and sighed. "It was your face, as you were talking. Something inside you was lit up. And that's great. I want that for you. I was just wishing…well, I wish I'd done that for you, and not Eli Cantor."

His lip curled as the said Eli's name. What the hell?

"Daniel, you can't colonize every part of my life. You have to let other people help me too."

"I know. It's just, if it was anyone but *him*…Fuck…" His hands rose, his fingers knotting above his head.

"What's this about? Do you have a history with him? Some sort of grudge? You've been weird about this since Jeremy mentioned Eli's name at Penny and Brad's place, and you weren't happy when you told me Jeremy had set up today's meeting. Now that I think of it, you were miserable before I left this morning, too. What's going on?"

He shook his head. "It's nothing."

"Don't do that! I know something's wrong. You all went to UCC together. Did he steal your grade nine girlfriend or something?"

My tone had crept into spiteful territory. Daniel narrowed his eyes. I was pushing the envelope. I should have stopped, but I couldn't seem to control my temper.

"That's it, isn't it? He got the girl you wanted, and you're afraid he's going to steal me, too?"

He shook his head. "No, Aubrey, you're wrong."

"I don't think I am. I think I'm right on the fucking money, and you're afraid to admit you're jealous because we've been down this road and you said you wouldn't do this again."

He made his way to the door, where he turned and looked at me steadily.

"He didn't steal my girlfriend," he said. "He stole Jeremy's."

He walked out, pulling the door closed behind him with a soft click.

"Oh shit." I brought my fingers to my temples and shook my head as my pulse beat in my ears.

Blindsided, I dropped onto the couch. I tried to imagine Eli—cardigan-and-corduroy-wearing Eli—as a ruthless lothario who went around stealing other guys' girlfriends. And not just any guy either. Lovely, sweet Jeremy. But he'd been a perfect gentleman with me.

I stared at the closed door, contemplating my next move. I could stomp out and demand to know why Daniel hadn't explained this story sooner, but I didn't need to do that. The reason was clear. He hadn't wanted to color my perception of Eli. He'd kept his feelings to himself, but today the dam had burst. Then I'd jabbed at his underbelly spitefully until he'd buckled.

It had been a while since we'd argued, but the ache in my heart was familiar—not a feeling one easily forgets. I crossed the room, passing through to the hallway.

"Daniel?" I called out.

He was at the front door, jamming his keys into his jacket pocket. He had a baseball cap pulled down over his eyes.

Bleakness bloomed like a hideous weed in my heart. "Where are you going?"

"I need to take a break and cool off."

He left without looking back. No slamming. No shouting. It was the kind of quiet anger I'd frequently witnessed after my parents had fought—an anger that had evolved into resentment over the passing years.

He needed a break from me.

Sarah's words returned with a vengeance.

"You're lucky you have this place to escape to when you need a break."

What about Daniel? I was in his space. Where was he supposed to go? I decided I'd make things easier for him. I'd give him tons of space. I grabbed a pen and a message pad and scrawled a quick note:

Daniel,

Take however long you need. I'll be at Jackman.

Call if you want.

Aubrey

I gathered a few things, grabbed my own keys, and left. All the way to Jackman, I clutched the Swarovski keychain, my face burning with shame and tears pricking at my eyes.

Someone knocked gently on my bedroom door. Then a muffled voice called my name.

"Aubrey?"

I sat up on my bed. "Come in, Jo."

"Hey." She popped her head in then came to sit beside me. "I saw your shoes in the front hall when I got back from my run. I hoped that meant you were here. I miss you. How are you?"

"I've been better, I guess." I tucked my knees to my chest. "Daniel and I had a fight."

"Oh, no. What happened?"

I explained the events of the afternoon, trying to present as unbiased a version of what had happened as I could.

"I didn't know what else to do, so I came here," I said.

Joanna looked at me quizzically. "Mind if I play devil's advocate?"

"I guess not."

"You said you didn't know what else to do. Couldn't you have waited for him to come home?"

"He said he needed a break. I'm in his condo, and he feels like he has to leave if he wants a breather. That hardly seems fair. He's been out of sorts the last few days. Maybe I'm getting on his nerves."

She thought for a minute. "He's probably home by now. When he read the note you left, what do you think went through his mind?"

I frowned. "I told him to call me when he was ready. That was over two hours ago. He hasn't called. What does that tell you?"

"Any number of things. Maybe he thinks you're so ticked that you don't want to be with him anymore. Or he's feeling bad and wishing you guys could sort this out, but he's too proud to make the first move. Or he's drunk himself into a stupor…"

"Or maybe he's not ready to talk yet."

"Maybe," she mused. "You were leaving the ball in his court with your note, but why not swallow your pride and open the door? You guys got yourselves into a nasty mess in March by not communicating properly. Don't let history repeat itself."

I glumly stared at the wall. Jo leaned over, pulling a silk ribbon from a basket on the corner of my desk.

"This is something my mom told me once," she said, stretching the ribbon out between her hands and then tying a loose knot on one end. "Imagine this is your relationship with Daniel." She handed me the ribbon and pointed at the knot. "This is where you are right now. Untie it."

I slipped the knot free.

"Pretty easy, right?" she said. "There's a small bump on the fabric, but you can smooth it down. If I'd pulled the knot really tight, it'd be harder to untie, and there'd be a big dent left behind."

I flattened the ribbon across my leg. "Meaning the more you drag out conflicts the harder they are to recover from, and the more damage they leave behind?"

"Precisely."

"How'd you get to be so smart?" I smiled at her gratefully.

Jo patted my hand. "Sounds to me like you both overreacted. You need to talk everything through." She made her way to the door, turning before leaving. "It's great to see you, and I'd beg you to stay and hang out with me, but I think there's somewhere else you should be."

She slipped out of my room, closing the door behind her.

Jo was right. It was time to untie a knot.

Tongue-Tied Sorrows

Those gracious words revive my drooping thoughts,
And give my tongue-tied sorrows leave to speak.
(*Henry VI, Part III*, Act III, Scene 3)

I stood outside Daniel's condo for ages, repeatedly reaching for the doorknob, only to drop my hand and step back each time. I could hear music through the door. Like our stubbornness, this tendency to listen to emotionally wrenching music as we wallowed in misery was a predisposition we shared.

I reached for the doorknob one last time and slowly twisted it open. Daniel was in the living room, but he didn't register my arrival. He was staring out the window, his back to me, just as he'd been when I'd returned from my meeting with Eli earlier. I lowered my bag to the floor and set my keys on top. Then I crossed the room and stood behind him. When the song finished, I opened my mouth to speak, but he beat me to it.

"Hi," he said quietly, not turning to look at me.

"How did you know I was here?"

"Blind hope, I guess." He slowly spun around and looked at me mournfully. "Every time I turned around this afternoon, I hoped you'd be standing there. This time I got lucky."

I'd barely managed to breathe the words, "I'm sorry," before he pulled me into his arms, his hand stroking my cheek, our foreheads touching, then noses, then lips. I knew we needed to talk, but in that moment, I had absolutely no desire to speak. I just wanted this — this holding and touching and clasping — this desperate breathing and kissing which became a fumbling of buttons and frantic tearing at clothes. Irrational as it was, this was somehow all I wanted.

We stumbled toward the dining room table, and he spun me around, bending me across the surface, lifting my skirt, and hastily slipping my panties off. A rush of desire flooded through me as Daniel fumbled with his jeans and then pushed my legs apart with his knee, sinking into me with a hissing breath. With his chest flush with my back and his hands tangling in my hair, he bit the fleshy part of my shoulder. I winced, but didn't tell him to stop. I needed his urgency, his lust, his raw desire. Our movements were determined and focused — purely carnal. Release was the goal, and neither of us pretended otherwise.

With his movements, my hips crashed repeatedly against the edge of the table, and I reached up to pull his hair, a rebuttal of sorts, an homage to what I'd done earlier with words after he'd hurt me with his indifference. When he bit my shoulder again, I dug my nails into the back of his neck, making him curse and slam into me harder. He said my name, and I answered with his until we were both panting, urging each other on.

"Faster," I gasped.

He drove against me relentlessly, and I closed my eyes, lost amid waves of pleasure.

"Open your eyes," he begged. "Look at me, Aubrey…"

I blinked up at him, riding out the deep, shuddering throes of my orgasm. His gaze didn't falter, remaining locked on mine as he sucked in breath after breath through clenched teeth. At last, he collapsed across my back, one hand twisted in my hair, the other gently stroking between my legs. After a few moments he withdrew, kissed my cheek, and carefully pulled my skirt down. I adjusted my shirt while he hiked his jeans up.

"Take my hand," he whispered.

He led me to the washroom where he undressed me with infinite care. I shivered as he kissed the tender spot on my shoulder, feeling not just naked, but completely exposed. He helped me slip my robe on and gently gathered my hair up. This gesture, so reminiscent of our earliest encounters, made my heart sting with its sweet simplicity.

"Daniel…"

The soft touch of his fingers against my lips stopped my words. "Shh. We'll talk in a minute."

He perched on the edge of the tub and turned the taps on full blast. I stood by his side, gripping his hand tightly. Once the bath was filled, he undressed and stepped into the tub. Leaving my wrap on the floor, I climbed in and settled between his outstretched legs, swallowing thickly as he hugged me.

"I'm sorry I hurt you," he whispered against my temple.

I shook my head, my fingers unconsciously tracing the spot where he'd bitten me. "I would have said something if you were really hurting me."

"I was actually talking about earlier," he said.

"Oh. Right."

"I didn't share your enthusiasm. That was wrong."

"I couldn't wait to tell you about my meeting with Eli. I thought you'd be happy for me."

"I'm so sorry."

"Me too. I said some awful things about you being jealous. From the way you were reacting, it seemed like you assumed I was into him. I lashed out. I shouldn't have said what I did. I felt wretched afterward."

"We're quite a pair."

"Yes we are."

He rested his chin on my head and ran his fingers gently across the swell of my breasts. I closed my eyes and relaxed into his touch.

"Tell me something, honestly, Daniel. Were you mad as soon as Jeremy brought up Eli's name at Penny and Brad's that night?"

He sighed heavily. "I hadn't heard his name in years. Just the mention of him made me want to hit something."

"I knew you were pissed off."

"Then when Jer told me he'd set something up, I tried not to let it bother me that you were meeting with him, you know? I tried to dismiss how aggravated I was. In the end, I couldn't pretend I wasn't annoyed anymore."

"Why do you hate Eli so much? So he stole Jeremy's girlfriend, or however you want to put it, but Jeremy's forgiven him. They're even friends. Why are you holding a grudge?"

"Jeremy has an amazing capacity for forgiveness. If he wasn't that way, he'd be eaten alive with anger over what happened to his parents. I don't mean to condescend, but you don't have siblings. You might not understand the protectiveness a brother can feel. I didn't go through that breakup, but witnessing it? I swear it was almost as bad."

"What happened?"

"You know how I told you Jeremy was a unique character in high school? He was kind of eccentric, but to a bunch of high school kids, he was just a weirdo. He used to drag this sketchpad around with him—always drawing. Similar to me and writing, I guess. Anyway, most people thought he was a freak."

"Kids are so cruel."

"It was awful watching all the assholes at school judging him. But then he met Naomi at an arts camp in the summer after eleventh grade, and she saw him for what he really was—a sensitive guy trying to come to terms with the baggage he'd been forced to carry around. She gave him a chance. He really came out of his shell thanks to her. He adored her."

"How did Eli fit into all that?"

"Naomi went on a bit of a religious kick in twelfth grade—she's Jewish. She got immersed in activities at the synagogue where she met Eli, and he convinced her that staying with Jeremy would be a bad idea because her parents wouldn't permit a long-term relationship. After being with Jeremy for a little over a year, she broke up with him and took up with Eli. Jer was devastated. He totally withdrew again."

I thought about Jeremy, imagining him being abandoned by his first love. "That's sad, but it was years ago. I'm sorry for Jeremy's broken heart. But he has Julie now, and they're in love. Can't you let it go? It's not healthy to carry grudges for so long."

"You're right. And if I'm really honest, I think my anger at him was mixed in with my aggravation that you were prepared to accept his help so quickly after casting aside my attempts without so much as a second thought—"

"I'm sorry, Daniel, it's just—"

"Let me finish, Aubrey, please?"

"Okay." I settled back against him.

"You know I'm not jealous, right? At least not in the way you think. I know you're not going to run away with him or something."

"Of course I know that. What I said earlier was stupid."

"I'm glad to hear you say that. I have to admit, though, I am jealous that he gets to be the one who opens a door for you. Why does it have to be him, of all people?"

"When Jeremy described him to me, he seemed accessible — way less imposing than meeting the editor of *The Globe and Mail.*"

"You don't give yourself enough credit."

"Maybe not, but it's not fair to invalidate my feelings. Besides, look at it this way — Jeremy asked for a favor, and Eli agreed to help him…to help *me*. It's like Eli's getting a chance to do something to make amends. Even if that's not why he's helping me, does it help to look at the situation that way?"

"I suppose." He sighed. "So, if I promise to try to get past my aversion to Eli Cantor, will you let me help too, if I can?"

"Of course. I'd love that."

"You really liked him, huh?"

"He was very kind and encouraging."

"Then I'll do my best to get along with him." He shifted his position so he could see my eyes. "Can I ask you something? I was thinking about what you said about me trying to colonize your life. You don't think I'm one of those obsessive guys who tries to control his girlfriend's every move, do you?"

I sat up, the water swishing as I moved. "That's not what I meant."

His expression was pained. "After you said that, I worried that maybe I'm too overbearing and that's why you're reluctant to commit."

"Reluctant to commit? What do you mean? I'm all yours, Daniel. You know that."

He leaned forward, bringing his mouth close to my ear.

"Then why won't you bring all your stuff here and have done with it?"

I should have known he wouldn't let this go. I closed my eyes and breathed deeply.

"Don't shut down on me, Aubrey." He traced a circle on my temple. "I feel like there's this part of you parceled away behind a wall, and I can't get at it. I keep crashing into the wall, so I back off. Then when I try again, I find another layer of bricks. It's very frustrating."

I shrugged uncomfortably. "I didn't think I was that bad. You're not an open book all the time."

"This isn't a competition to see who's got the most hang-ups." He rested his lips against my cheek. "I know we agreed you'd stay at Jackman when your mom's here, but that's just for a few days. You don't need to leave all your stuff there. Is there something you're not telling me? Some reason why you don't want to make a clean break? You have to trust that I can handle whatever's going on with you, Aubrey."

I closed my eyes trying to bring my feelings into focus.

"You know how you said I wouldn't understand your feelings about Jeremy because I don't have siblings? Maybe you don't understand what it's like to be an only child who's gone through what I have."

"Do you need more space? We can find another place—a bigger condo, or a house, so you can have a room to go to if you're feeling crowded."

"It's not that."

"What is it, then? Help me understand."

I held his hand above the water, tracing the veins crisscrossing his skin. How could I help him understand what I could barely comprehend myself?

"How would you describe your house when you were a kid, Daniel?"

"What do you mean?"

"The atmosphere. What was it like growing up in your family?"

"I don't know. Busy. Loud. There was always music, people playing instruments. My folks had lots of dinner parties. We had friends over a lot. Is that what you mean?"

"I suppose. Did you sit around the table every night to have dinner together? Stuff like that?"

"We tried. Our routines were crazy, but we tried..." He trailed off. "I'm not sure where you're going with this, sweetheart."

"Well, try to imagine a different kind of noise—two parents constantly shouting at each other. Then picture the quietness after the argument when they gave each other the silent treatment for days. And think about what it must have been like for the only other person in the house—me—to walk around on eggshells, trying to be perfect, trying not to be another reason for them to fight, and not having a single person to share that burden with…"

I wanted to continue talking—wanted to help Daniel understand where I was coming from, but all of a sudden I broke down into body-racking sobs, my hands flying wetly to cover my eyes. After years of never discussing my feelings about my parents' relationship and divorce, after keeping everything buried under layers of casual jokes and stoicism, the gates opened, and all of my wretchedness burst forth.

"Oh, Jesus, Aubrey, come here."

Daniel wrapped his arms around me while I cried uncontrollably.

"I can't," I sobbed. "I'm sorry, I can't…"

"Fuck, what have I done? Shh…"

He rocked me, the water sloshing up the sides of the tub as he tried to soothe me. After a minute, the rocking and sloshing began to make me feel seasick.

"I need to get out," I blubbered.

"Of course, of course." We climbed out, and he wrapped a towel around me, knotting his own towel at his waist. "I don't know what I was thinking." He gestured to the bathtub. "This was a stupid idea."

I shook my head and protested quietly as he held me.

"Wasn't stupid," I assured him through my tears and hiccoughing. "It was sweet."

"Sweet. Pfft. I'm sorry." He handed me a Kleenex. "I don't know how I could have been so obtuse."

"You're not obtuse." I sniffed, wiping my nose and streaming eyes. "How were you supposed to know? I didn't even know."

"I should have guessed. You're afraid things won't work and we'll end up fighting like your parents—if you move in here and we break up, you'll have nowhere to go because your parents are so far away. Is that it?"

"I don't know if I've thought it out that clearly. I just feel this trepidation."

"It's okay. I think I understand."

"Thank you." I smiled up at him feebly. "For trying."

"Is there anything I can do?" he asked, his plaintive expression making my chin wobble.

I shook my head and sniffed again. "You're doing all the right things. Talking is good. My parents didn't talk. They yelled and then shut down. I'm afraid I'm doing the same thing. I don't want to repeat their mistakes, but I don't know what's worse in those situations, fight or flight."

"I guess the question is — what's more dangerous, the ugly words or the silence?"

"We've mastered both. Earlier we said things we regretted."

"And then we ran away. I guess we have some work to do." He stroked my hair and cradled my head on his shoulder. "All I know is I want you here with me. Not just you, but all your stuff as well. Is it okay for me to hope for that?"

"Don't give up on me. I need time, that's all."

"Good." He kissed my forehead. "Listen, can I ask you another question?"

"Okay."

"What did your parents fight about?"

"Lots of things. Everything."

"What did they fight about the most?" he asked gently.

"Honestly? Money."

"Lack of it?"

"Sort of. My father earning it, my mother spending it and never having any of her own...Having to lie about things she'd bought, hiding stuff in the closet..."

He nodded. "That explains so much, poppet. Knowing all this weeks ago would have saved me hours of worrying. Isn't it amazing how our parents can screw up our psyches? It's a wonder we aren't all in therapy." I did my best to smile, and he tweaked my chin. "You look wiped."

"I didn't sleep last night worrying about my interview with Eli. Would you mind if I took a nap?"

"Of course not."

We dried off and hung our towels, then we went into the bedroom. Daniel waited until I'd crawled in and settled on my side before curling around me.

"I love you, Daniel."

"I love you too."

"Promise?"

"Aubrey, I love you so much. I'd do anything for you, you know that. A silly squabble won't change that." He kissed my hair and drew me closer. "You sleep, my lovely," he whispered.

And cocooned in the warmth of Daniel's embrace, at last, I did.

CHAPTER 13

Bonds

...I have scanted all
Wherein I should your great deserts repay,
Forgot upon your dearest love to call,
Whereto all bonds do tie me day by day...
(*Sonnet 117*)

Sometimes you have to hide away from the world and focus inward. For Daniel and me, learning to communicate without relying on the words of our favorite authors and forcing ourselves not to retreat into sullen silence when things got tense became top priorities.

After unburdening our souls on Wednesday, we spent the rest of the week concentrating on our relationship. We didn't think about his parents, we didn't worry about O'Connor and what was happening at U of T, we didn't talk about Eli or my writing, and Daniel put away his thesis paper. We focused on each other. It was therapeutic and incredibly romantic.

Holed away in the condo, we ordered in everything from pizza to Thai food, drinking red wine like it was going out of style. We spent an inordinate amount of time in bed, making love, cuddling, and talking. We'd shower and then climb into bed again. We gave those new sheets a run for their money.

When we'd exhausted our words and our libidos, we loafed around, watching movies, playing Scrabble, doing crosswords, and challenging each other to numerous games of "would you rather," laughing hysterically and grossing each other out.

As much as I loved spending all that time with Daniel, by Saturday I was getting cabin fever. I tried to curb my excitement about my evening trip to see The National with Eli. Daniel was still coming to terms with me spending time alone with Eli doing something new. I certainly didn't want to rub his nose in my enthusiasm.

Late Saturday afternoon, I was writing in my journal on the balcony when Daniel joined me. He handed me an iced tea and sat beside me on the loveseat.

"So, I'm driving you over to the concert tonight, right?" he asked.

I flipped my journal closed and snuggled into his side. "You feel up to meeting Eli after all these years?"

"I want to, poppet. This is important to you."

"Am I allowed to tell him about us?" I asked.

"We need to work on coming out in public. Maybe this is a good first step. The only person I'm worried about at this point is Martin. I have to think of a way to bring our relationship up so it'll seem like the innocent progression of what started as an in-class friendship. I'd rather he didn't find out from someone else and jump to conclusions."

He patted my thigh, essentially bringing the subject to a close. "Hey, am I losing my mind or were you wearing different pants before I got in the shower?"

"You're not losing your mind. I remembered it's nearly that time of the month down in the netherlands. Those pants were too light."

"The Netherlands, huh? I've recently become a big fan of the Netherlands."

"You've been a regular visitor lately. I hope you collect frequent flyer points."

He grinned. "I have to admit, I was wondering about the timing of your period."

"Any day now, I guess. I'm not excusing my behavior on Wednesday, but I do tend to get feisty a couple of days beforehand. Distant early warning."

He rubbed his scruff and looked at me quizzically. "Do you think I should keep track on a calendar so I know when it's time to duck and weave?"

I laughed, but knowing Daniel, he probably wasn't joking in the slightest.

My mind wandered as Daniel and I made our way down Queen's Quay a few hours later. We'd been out of touch with the outside world for the better part of the week. I couldn't help wondering how everyone else was doing.

"When was the last time you talked to Jeremy?" I asked him.

"Earlier, when you were showering. Why?"

"I was wondering how that prom assembly went—the one about drinking and driving."

"I think it went well."

"Cool. Hey, tonight's the night, you know? For him and Julie? He's picking her up from Windsor, and they're grabbing a hotel room downtown for the night."

"Yes, I did know that."

"Is he nervous?"

"*Desperate* might be a better word." He smiled broadly.

"Julie too. She's jonesing big time."

"Not surprising. These days, it's almost unheard of for couples to delay having sex."

"I think it's awesome."

"I agree," he said, bringing my hand to his lips.

A few moments later, we pulled into the Kool Haus parking lot.

"So, how do you feel?" he asked.

"I'm nervous, but excited to see The National." I squeezed his hand. "I wish I were seeing them with you."

He smiled wistfully. "Another time. Don't worry about me tonight, okay? Promise me you'll have fun?"

"I'll try. What are you gonna do?"

"I'm swinging by Penny and Brad's for a bit and then heading home. I'll be fine. I'll chill and play guitar or something. Text me when you're done, and I'll pick you up."

"Okay." I looked at him for a moment, weighing how best to broach a topic I'd been thinking about for a while. "You know what,

sunshine? You spend too much time alone. You should try to recon-
nect with some of your old friends."

He nodded, pensively gazing out the front window.

"Calling people out of the blue that you haven't seen or talked
to for years is kind of daunting."

My heart ached for him. He looked so lost.

"Why don't you reactivate your Facebook account and try to
track some people down? You can keep your privacy controls high."

"I'll give it some thought." He leaned over to kiss me, and then he
pressed his forehead to mine. "We should go. I don't want to make
you late. You've got the set list?"

"Yep. And a notebook, a pen, and my phone."

"All right, let's get this show on the road."

As I climbed out of the car, my mouth went dry. Sure I was
stressed about Eli and Daniel meeting, but I was also jittery about
spending a whole evening with someone I didn't know but was trying to impress. I'd probably go all fan-girly as soon as The National
hit the stage and make an ass of myself. Most of all, I was worried
Eli would discover I was a fraud who wasn't up to the task of writing
for publication. Daniel met me on my side of the car.

"Where are you meeting him?" he asked.

"Outside the front doors. You don't have to do this, you know."

"I want to," he said, his lips pressed into a grim line.

"And you say *my* poker face needs work."

When Eli offered to drive me home after the concert to save Daniel
the trip, I couldn't think of a good reason not to agree. After quickly
texting Daniel to let him know I was on my way home, I found
myself in the passenger seat of Eli's car, directing him to the condo
as I replayed the concert, trying to remember all of the important
things I should mention in my review.

"I don't want to pressure you," Eli said as we neared the Distillery
District, "but I'd like to squeak your review into the June issue. Think
you could send me something tomorrow night?"

Uh, yeah, no pressure...

"I'll do my best."

"I know it sounds like a tight timeline, but it's best to write as much as you can while the show is fresh in your memory."

"I'll set aside some time tomorrow. Daniel will be glad for the chance to get some writing done as well."

"It was good to see him. I heard he had a tough go of things in the UK."

"He had a difficult year." I thought about how ambiguous Daniel had been earlier during his reunion with Eli and mimicked his vagueness, not wanting to lend any credence to the gossipy tales Eli might have heard. "That's the condo up there," I said, anxious to escape further questioning.

Eli pulled up to the curb. "Email me as soon as you have something fleshed out. I'll give you feedback, and we'll go from there."

"Sounds good." I clambered out of the car, waving as he drove off into the night.

Riding the elevator, I scrolled through the alerts I'd missed over the course of the evening. Daniel hadn't sent a response to my text, but he had sent a Facebook friend request. I smiled as I accepted it, pleased that he'd taken my advice and reactivated his account.

All was quiet in the condo. I quickly saw why. Daniel was fast asleep, his laptop and phone beside him on the bed. As much as I hated to wake him, I had to. He was still dressed. I perched on the edge of the bed, reaching over to ruffle his hair. I expected him to snuffle and blink at me as he regained awareness, but instead he lurched up, grabbing my wrist.

"Let me go!" he shouted.

"Ouch, Daniel, it's me." I wrenched my wrist free of his grasp.

"What?" Gradually his eyes came into focus. "Shit, I fell asleep. Sorry. How did you get home?"

"Eli drove me. Are you okay?"

"Yeah. Weird dream." He shook his head. "I'm fine. How was the concert?"

"It was good. I'll have some writing to do tomorrow." I rubbed my wrist where he'd grabbed me.

"Did I hurt you? I'm sorry, I don't know…" He trailed off, confused.

"I'm fine, Daniel." I gestured to the laptop beside him. "I guess I don't have to ask what you've been up to. I see I have a new Facebook friend."

"What do you think?"

"I'm glad you took the plunge. Did you catch up with anyone?"

"No, I snooped around on people's profiles for a bit. It was interesting checking out what everyone's been up to overseas."

I assumed he was talking about old school friends. If I'd truly understood what he meant, I might have kicked myself for suggesting he revive his Facebook profile.

Open Hand, Open Heart

His heart and hand both open and both free;
For what he has he gives, what thinks he shows…
(*Troilus and Cressida*, Act IV, Scene 5)

Late the following afternoon, I gave my review a final read-through and decided to call it quits. It would need editing, but I'd leave that to Eli and his trained eye. I emailed him the draft and turned my attention to Facebook, eager to log on and take a peek at Daniel's profile.

I scanned his wall quickly. There wasn't anything recent, so I clicked on a couple of his photo albums. No wonder he missed his social life in England. In most of the pictures, he was in the middle of a group of people, in a pub or at a party. And, wowza, he had so many good-looking friends. Not surprisingly, there were lots of shots of Penny in the mix, too. My favorite photos were the candid ones where Daniel was laughing—the beloved Guinness-giggle in full force. It was amazing to see him so carefree and happy.

I shut down the laptop and piled everything on the corner of the table, then I tiptoed down the hall to poke my head into the office. Daniel was leaning on his hand, staring at his laptop screen. I loved his intense furrowed-brow expression. I dared not interrupt when he was that lost in his thesis. I was about to step away when he muttered, "Jesus, what the hell is she doing?"

He turned his chair, his elbows on his knees as he rubbed his eyes and looked outside.

"You okay, sailor?"

He spun and smiled, snapping his laptop closed. "Oh, I'm fine. You know, just want to flog several of Shakespeare's characters with a rusty toilet brush as usual."

I flopped onto the couch, and he joined me, taking my hand and pressing a kiss on my wrist.

"Any long-term damage?"

"Daniel, you didn't mean to hurt me. You were asleep."

"I still feel awful. We have to take care of these precious commodities. Looks like you'll be doing a lot of typing in the near future." He threaded his fingers through mine. "How's your review?"

"First draft's done and sent. I left my stuff on the table, though, in case I have editing to do later."

"I was thinking—we should get you a desk. We can move my guitar stand and fit a workspace in the corner here—if you want," he added hastily. "I thought you'd like to leave your things set up instead of having to keep cleaning up the dining room table..."

He rubbed the back of his neck. I leaned into his side.

"That sounds wonderful."

He expelled a big breath. "Really? I wanted to mention something when we were having lunch, but I thought I was being overbearing again."

"Not at all. It's a great idea."

"Don't worry about the cost. I want to buy it for you."

"My final Vic pay check went into my account yesterday. I'll get a check from Eli as well. I'd like to help pay for it."

"You should save your Vic check for spending money for your trip." He paused for a moment. "Mind if I ask how much the check from Eli will be?"

"Thirty dollars. Ten cents a word to start."

It was a laughable amount, but it didn't matter. It hardly seemed possible to get paid for doing something fun. I looked at him smugly, almost daring him to mock me. He didn't. Instead, he cradled my cheek in his hand.

"You're going to be published. How cool is that?"

My false bravado dissolved, genuine self-satisfaction taking its place. "I still can't believe it."

"You can do anything you put your mind to."

"Like help pay for a desk," I said.

"I'm not going to let you give me your first check as a writer to pay for part of a desk. You should get something personal. Something meaningful."

His earnest expression crushed my resolve.

"Okay," I said, hugging him fiercely.

"Huh, that was easy," he mumbled into my neck. "Are you going soft on me, Miss Price?"

"Nope, just picking my fights more carefully."

He laughed. "That's a relief. I like it when you're feisty."

"You know what they say about leopards and spots. I'm not about to roll over and give up yet."

"Good. Hey, speaking of picking fights, I got another email from O'Connor's office."

"Jesus, what do they want with you now?"

"Aaron's back next week. I'm meeting him first thing Monday morning."

"How do you feel about that?"

"It'll be uncomfortable, but I'm looking forward to putting everything behind me so I can focus on more important things. Like you…"

He smiled and nuzzled my neck, feathering kisses along my jaw.

"You know my period could start any time," I murmured as his lips moved lower.

"Then we should make hay while the sun shines." He stood, dragging my shirt off as he walked me toward the hall. He was fiddling with the button on my jeans and trying to simultaneously kiss me when the buzzer sounded from the lobby.

"Are you expecting someone?" I breathed.

"Nope."

He peeled off his own shirt and tossed it behind him. The buzzer went again, and once more we ignored it. At the bedroom door, my jeans started their descent to the floor. Daniel's phone chimed on the dresser. Then mine rang out in the front hall. We both groaned at the same time. He pressed his forehead against mine.

"What if there's some sort of emergency?" I said.

"I was just thinking the same thing. Fuck."

He retrieved his phone, scrolling through his messages.

"Huh, it's Jeremy. He's downstairs with Julie." He gestured to my jeans, which were currently halfway down my legs. "You should…"

I held up my hands. "I'm on it." I hurriedly put myself back together, and we retraced our steps, retrieving our shirts on the way.

While Daniel attended to letting Jeremy and Julie in, I snuck into the powder room to check my hair. Then I dashed out to the living room and sat down, casually thumbing through a magazine. Daniel opened the door and stuck his head out into the hall. He looked at me over his shoulder and smiled conspiratorially.

"Rain check?" he whispered.

Julie hugged me, but it wasn't one of her customary ebullient hugs. She looked wiped. So did Jeremy, the bleariness in his usually sparkling eyes betraying his fatigue. They'd stayed in a hotel the night before, finally consummating their relationship, but this wasn't the exhaustion of the over-sexed. They both seemed entirely dispirited.

"Can I get you something?" Daniel said. "We have beer, wine, pop…"

"A couple of beers would be great," Jeremy said, dropping onto the couch. Then he looked at Julie. "What'll you have, Jul?"

Daniel laughed and shot me a nervous look. "Bad day at the office, Jer?"

"You could say that."

Julie reached for his hand. "I'll just have a soda water if you've got it, thanks. I'll drive so Jer can have a drink. Jeremy added me to his car insurance," she explained.

"Remind me to do that, Aubrey," Daniel called from the kitchen. "It's a good idea, in case there's an emergency."

"Sounds like a plan." I flushed with pleasure at the thought of Daniel trusting me enough to let me drive his car—his pride and joy.

He returned with the drinks, and Jeremy took several long gulps of his beer, closing his eyes and breathing deeply.

"You okay?" Julie asked, scooting close to his side.

He took her hand. "I'm fine."

I'd have mocked their sentimentality if it weren't obvious that he was upset about something and she was at a loss for how to comfort him.

Daniel leaned forward in his chair. "So, this is an unexpected visit," he said.

"Yeah, sorry to barge in. Hope we're not interrupting." Jeremy looked back and forth between us.

"Not at all," Daniel assured him. "We were just hanging out."

Half naked.

"So, what's up, J? The apartment hunt going okay?" Daniel asked.

"Done," Jeremy said. "We'll be signing off on a townhouse this afternoon."

"You guys, that's amazing!" I said.

"You're not wasting any time," Daniel said.

"Are you kidding?" Jeremy snorted. "I'm so ready to get out of Mom and Dad's house, you have no idea."

"It'll be nice for you to have your own space, for sure. Especially *now...*"

Daniel gave them both a meaningful look.

Especially now...what? I wanted to ask, just to stir the shit, but the vibe in the room didn't seem conducive to me being a total dink.

"No, you're right on the money." Jeremy looked at Daniel seriously. "We'll be moving in as quickly as possible."

"Is everything okay?" Daniel asked, his expression transforming to one of concern.

Julie placed her other hand over top of Jeremy's, and he took a deep breath. "We went to the house for brunch this morning so Mom and Dad could meet Julie."

"Things didn't go well?" Daniel prompted.

"They liked Julie. That wasn't the issue. Dad showed me something — something he should have shared with me months ago. They got a letter in the mail in March. It was from the drunk driver...the one who...you know..."

"*What?*" Daniel's eyes widened, and he pushed himself to the edge of his chair.

"Turns out it was a woman," Jeremy continued. "Her name is Anita. She lives in Spain. She was writing to find out about me. Apparently she's been trying to track us down for a long time—"

"Wait," Daniel said. "They got the letter in *March?* And they're just telling you *now?*"

Jeremy nodded and sighed, glancing uncomfortably in my direction. "Um, Aubrey, would you and Julie mind…Can we just have a second?"

"Of course," I said, quickly crossing to stand behind Daniel's chair. "We'll be in the office."

"Sorry," Jeremy said sheepishly.

"It's okay, Jer," Julie assured him.

Daniel cast a grim look at me over his shoulder, obviously wishing he didn't have to deal with this crisis alone, but what could I do? I led Julie into the office and closed the door. We flopped onto the couch.

"Fuck, Julie. Is he okay?"

She shook her head. "I don't know. He gets so quiet sometimes and disappears into himself. It's like he has to think stuff through without interruption. It's hard to gauge his emotions."

"Daniel does that too. They're sensitive, that's all."

"Doing these MADD assemblies and then getting the letter on top of that…I guess it's stirred up a lot of confusion."

"That's understandable."

"Between you and me, I think that's why his folks didn't tell him about the letter before now. I think they wanted to see how he coped with the assemblies. Since he handled everything okay, they decided to tell him." She sighed and pursed her lips. "Gwen's so overprotective. Jer is the most patient person I've ever met, but this drives him mental. He's sick of being treated like a child."

"I can't imagine how it must feel to be in his shoes."

"He blows my mind sometimes. He's so…I don't know…*pragmatic* about everything. He doesn't blame anyone or feel sorry for himself. I hate to see him hurting."

She sighed, and I squeezed her hand.

"Hey, how'd last night go?" I said, thinking a new topic might be a good idea.

"Honestly?" Her face lit up a little. "It was perfect. He's incredible. Too bad this shit happened today; it kind of took the shine off what went down last night."

"I wasn't really asking for details about who went down on whom." I was rewarded with a dirty snicker, and I shoved her shoulder lightly. "Hey, we can help you move—" I started to say, but then there were two quick knocks, and Jeremy's head poked through the door.

"Come on, Jul," he said. "We should jet. We have a ton of shit to do."

Julie looked at me warily. "Okay." She joined him in the hallway.

"You'll let us know if you need anything, right?" I said, following Daniel as he walked them to the door.

"Sure thing." Jeremy dropped his car keys onto Julie's outstretched hand. "Take it easy, Aubrey."

"You, too. Bye, guys."

Daniel's shoulders slumped as he closed the door. I put my hand on his back. "That didn't sound good. Is he okay?"

He turned from the door, coiling his arm around me, pulling me hard against him as he kissed me. At last he released me, and I searched his stormy expression.

"Everything's fine," he said. "I promise we'll talk about it later. Can we pick up where we left off before they got here, please?" He brushed his lips against mine. "I just need a few minutes. Wait for me in bed?"

I nodded and stepped back, but he tugged at my hand again, his eyes traveling down to my breasts. "Naked…"

"Don't be long," I whispered.

I undressed and slipped into bed to wait for him. Was he really okay? He'd always felt an overwhelming protective instinct where Jeremy was concerned. Maybe this latest wrinkle in Jeremy's life had knocked him for a loop.

I was considering throwing on my wrap and going out to find him—to tell him that he didn't have to sneak away to pull himself together—when he appeared at the bedroom door. He certainly didn't seem upset. In fact, he was grinning cheekily.

"You got anything on under there?" he asked, crawling up the bed to join me.

"Uh-uh. Naked as a jaybird."

He tugged the cover, lifting an eyebrow as he peeked underneath.

"Hmm. Almost perfect." He lowered the blanket and gently pushed a strand of hair away from my face. "But would you object to wearing something for me?"

Here I was expecting him to be morose, and instead he was being playful, seemingly on the verge of requesting that I put on stockings or high heels.

"I didn't think you'd be in a kinky mood this afternoon, Mr. Grant," I said, smiling coyly and sliding my hand under the hem of his T-shirt.

"Is that a yes or a no?"

"Tell me what you want me to wear, and I'll think about it."

He reached into his pocket and retrieved a small box. A small *blue* box. He opened my hand and rested the box on my palm.

Tiffany & Co.

"Daniel, what's this all about?"

"This is about me buying you a graduation present way too early and not being able to wait to give it to you because I love you so much, that's what it's about."

"What am I going to do with you?"

"We'll discuss what you're going to do with me in *detail* in a few minutes. Right now, will you please open your gift?"

I smiled at him shyly and opened the box. The most beautiful necklace was inside. The pendant was the outline of a heart. It had a pinkish hue. It was like nothing I'd ever seen. Even the chain was unique, a black cord contrasting strikingly with the pink of the heart.

"You agreed to the desk earlier. Maybe I'm pushing my luck, but I hope you'll accept this without kicking up a fuss," he said, gently moving the pendant on the velvet padding. "It's rose gold. Those are diamonds." He pointed to the semi-circle of jewels embedded in the heart. "Do you like it?"

"Daniel, it's beautiful. I've never seen anything like it. I don't know what to say."

"Say thank you and then say you'd like me to help you put it on."

I pressed my hand to his cheek, and he kissed my palm.

"I love it," I whispered. "And I love you. Thank you."

"I love you too."

"So, this is what you want me to wear?" I asked, freeing the chain from the velvet backing and setting aside the box.

"Yes. Just that. Here, let me help you."

He secured the clasp as I held up my hair.

"What do you think?" I asked, touching the pendant.

"It looks perfect."

"I'm trying not to worry about how much it cost. I've never even window shopped at Tiffany's."

He rolled his eyes. "I wasn't paying attention to price tags. I was more focused on the name of the pendant. It's called an *open heart*."

"Really?"

He nodded. "That seems especially appropriate now, after you opened up and shared your past with me last week. I know it wasn't easy for you to talk about, but you can tell me anything, any time, and I won't judge you. I hope you know that."

"Same goes for you." I rested my hand on his chest. "I don't want to pressure you, but you *are* going to tell me what happened with Jeremy, right?"

He lay back on the pillows, and I moved beside him, resting my cheek on his chest.

"He's frustrated with my parents for holding out on him. He talked to them for a long time about disclosure. He's tired of being treated with kid gloves."

"That's what Julie said."

"As much as we'd like to help him with the move, I think he needs to do this himself."

"I totally get that. You'd call it martyrdom, but sometimes it's just a need to prove to yourself and others that you can do something."

"I'm starting to understand that," he said, pressing his lips to my temple. "Anyway, Jeremy and I made a deal. He wants to put an end to the cycle of secrecy that my dad's been perpetuating for years. No more family drama. It's ridiculous."

"I couldn't agree more. So, what's Jeremy going to do about this woman and the letter?"

"He's going to write to her."

"Wow."

"He's convinced there's a reason why she's been looking for him, and he won't feel right until he communicates with her."

"He's one in a million."

"I know. I'm so proud to be his brother. I'll support him and help him, but I'm going to do my best not to worry about him. Besides, why expend energy worrying when the woman I love is here, naked and warm, waiting in our bed?"

He kissed the tip of my nose, and I snuggled against him. "In that case, I don't see any reason for you to worry about anything again, sunshine."

Kissing me softly, he gently traced his finger around the pendant, then ran his hand lightly across my collarbone to my breast, circling my nipple with this thumb. "Lovely. And the necklace looks pretty good, too."

My laugh turned to a sigh as his lips took the place of his thumb.

"Now," he said, his face lighting up, "I believe you owe me a rain check…"

Daniel

CHAPTER 15

Did ever raven sing so like a lark,
That gives sweet tidings of the sun's uprise?…
…I'll send the emperor my hand:
Good Aaron, wilt thou help to chop it off?
(*Titus Andronicus,* Act iii, Scene i)

"**G**ood morning, lovely."

"Hey! Morning, sunshine."

Aubrey yawned, and I pictured the accompanying cat stretch. More often than not when she'd stretch like that, pressing her body against mine in the morning, I'd find her impossible to resist, and the day would get off to a resounding start. I was the luckiest bastard in the world. Unfortunately, she'd spent the weekend at Jackman. After being kept at arms' length all week because of her period, I was champing at the bit.

"Sorry I'm calling so early," I said. "I'm about to head off to U of T. Did you have a nice evening with Jo?"

"I did. She appreciated the company."

"And how did you sleep?"

"I don't like my bed. It's too soft. I like yours better."

"You like how hard mine is?"

"I had no idea something so hard could feel so good until I met you."
I chuckled.

"How are you feeling about your meeting with Aaron?" she asked.

"It's like walking into a dark room. I have no clue what'll be waiting for me when the light goes on," I said. "But I'm meeting with
Martin after I leave O'Connor's office, so that's good. He's hoping
to finalize things for the fall before he leaves for vacation." I sifted
through some papers, trying to decide what to bring with me. "Have
you made plans for the day, poppet?"

Regardless of how my meetings played out, I wanted to see her.

"I'll head out around ten thirty, grab a coffee at the Arbor Room,
and spend some time writing in the Hart House library."

"Do you want to go out for lunch together? We could meet somewhere and eat on campus."

"Do you think that's a good idea?"

"It's June first. Convocation is around the corner. It's about time
we started casually dating, don't you think?"

"Maybe we should wait until your meeting with Aaron is over
before we start planning this big reveal—"

"Aubrey, unless Aaron has somehow miraculously found out about
us, I don't see the point in waiting."

"Are you sure?"

"I am. How's twelve? The Gallery Restaurant at Hart House?" I
suggested.

"Okay…it's a date," she said, after a moment's hesitation.

"Do you suppose it's our *first* date?"

"I thought we already had our first date." She laughed. "A couple
of times."

"This is different, though."

"Our first on-campus date?"

"Pretty exciting, sweetheart."

"It is. Gosh, what will I wear?" she asked. "I have to make a
good impression."

"Wear a dress. You've got great legs. It's best to play up your assets
in situations like this."

"A dress it is. And what should I wear underneath? In case one thing leads to another..."

"Miss Price, are you implying that I might get lucky after our first date?"

"After a glass of wine, I might not be able to control my impulses."

I smiled, imagining Aubrey lying in bed, twirling her hair around her finger, her lip tucked coyly under her teeth.

"I'm not sure if I've mentioned this before, but one of my favorite things about you is your appalling lack of impulse control."

As I drove toward U of T, I couldn't help feeling hopeful despite this impending meeting with Aaron O'Connor. It was a brand new month. Surely June would be less turbulent than May.

June first also meant moving day for Jeremy and Julie. It was taking every ounce of self-control I could muster to refrain from calling him. He was intent on proving he was capable of running his life, and he wouldn't prove anything with all of us meddling.

I was reminded of Aubrey's willful insistence on doing things her way and using her own resources. She was still stubborn as hell, but she was mellowing. She'd accepted the Tiffany necklace without a single eye roll or uncomfortable grimace, and even let me buy her a desk without any issues. I'd shown incredible restraint for weeks, but all bets were officially off.

And now her convocation was only a couple of weeks away, an exciting event in and of itself, but once it was behind us, we could *really* move forward. What I wanted more than anything was for her to officially move in. With her mother in town over convocation we'd be spending five days apart, but perhaps after that I'd be able to persuade her to gradually pack up her things and bring them to the condo.

I arrived on campus in good time, abandoning my meandering thoughts and locking up the car. At the graduate studies office, I took a deep breath before opening the doors to find O'Connor's personal office. His secretary was sipping her morning coffee while flipping through a pile of papers.

"Good morning, I'm Daniel Grant. I'm here to see Mr. O'Connor."

"Of course," she said, appraising me quickly as she picked up the phone. She announced my arrival, and his door opened a few seconds later. As he beckoned me over, I steeled myself for what was sure to be an uncomfortable meeting. He didn't shake my hand, simply motioning for me to enter. I sat in the chair in front of the desk and crossed my leg, aiming for nonchalance.

"How are you?" he asked, sitting across from me.

"Well, thank you."

He shuffled through the file folders on his desk.

"And your parents?"

Was he really going to pretend my father hadn't been on the verge of suing him for slander no more than two weeks ago?

"My parents are wonderful. How was your vacation?"

His eyes snapped up to meet mine. I regarded him with casual interest.

"My vacation was fine," he said. "Thank you for asking."

I bit back my desire to ask for details about how he'd spent his time off, particularly interested to hear about Elaine.

He opened a file folder—a file about me, apparently. On top of the sheaf of papers sat the letter that had made its way here from England, the Oxford crest stamped at the top. I longed to grab that page and rip it into a billion pieces. That single piece of paper perpetuated my tainted reputation. A black mark caused by a foolish girl's reckless lie.

"So, let's talk about the semester. I read the course evaluations at the end of the term. A few responses raised flags, so I brought some students in to chat to get a better handle on what they meant."

I almost laughed in his face. *Liar.* Those interviews had been a desperate bid to ferret out dirt on me which he could use to hurt my father.

"And?" I clasped my hands in my lap.

"One of the evaluations struck me as interesting. A young lady…"

He trailed off as he leafed through the sheets.

A young lady? Fuck, what now?

"Yes, here it is," he said, pulling a page free from the pile.

My heart rate spiked. Was it Aubrey's course evaluation? He peered at me across the desk.

"Tell me about Cara Switzer," he said.

Cara Switzer? Oh no, what had she done?

"Cara was…She struggled. She required significant help, I suppose you'd say."

He started to read from the page, looking at me occasionally across the top of the sheet. "*Daniel was the best TA ever. He was super helpful and never made you feel like you were taking up his valuable time, and believe me, I know, because I took up a lot of Daniel's time.*"

Although he was obviously trying to make a point, I had to suppress a laugh. Cara's words sounded silly coming from her mouth, but coming from his, they were utterly absurd.

"*He helped me with all of my papers and was really great all semester long. I know I wouldn't have the mark I do if it wasn't for Daniel.*" He lowered the page. "High praise."

I shrugged. What else could I do? His eyes traveled down the page, and he continued to read Cara's comments. "*Daniel's an awesome TA. Sometimes I understood Daniel way better than Professor Brown. I always looked forward to his amazing tutorials. Keep up the great job, Daniel.*"

O'Connor narrowed his eyes again. "You struck a chord with this girl. During my meeting with her, she was even *more* enthused, if that's possible." As he spoke these words, he flipped to the beginning of the file, placing Cara's evaluation beside the letter from Oxford. A symbolic gesture? Prick.

I gestured to the folder, trying to corral my frenzied thoughts. "I did my best to help her. I thought I was doing my job. Perhaps you'd correct me if I'm wrong, but isn't it a TA's responsibility to help students with course content and class assignments?"

He tossed his glasses on the desk and tapped the letter from Oxford. "I'd be interested to hear a more about what happened over there, Daniel."

Ah, here we go.

Our eyes met, and I smiled, allowing my gaze to drift across his shoulder to a framed photograph of the Coliseum. How fucking appropriate, considering I felt as if he were trying to throw me to the lions.

"It's pretty straight-forward. Apparently, I screwed up."

His eyebrows shot up. "I was led to believe you'd denied her allegations." He bridged his hands and gazed at me, his interest piqued.

"I *did* deny them."

He narrowed his eyes at me. "But now you're saying the accusations were true?"

"I didn't say that," I replied calmly.

"You just claim to have 'screwed up.'"

"When I look back at what happened, that's sometimes how I feel," I explained. "Maybe I allowed that girl to get too close. I let down my guard—failed to maintain an appropriate distance. Either she got the wrong idea, or she saw my desire to help her as leverage she could use when she had no other recourse. Regardless, I was too generous with my efforts. I sincerely wanted her to succeed. She used my sincerity against me."

"I see. And how does that differ from what happened with Miss Switzer here, who seems to believe you bent over backward for her as well?"

I paused to gather my thoughts. "I suppose it doesn't differ at all, with one notable exception. Cara didn't falsely accuse me of molesting her to get back at me for not compromising my principles."

I spoke quietly, but vehemently. I'd done everything possible to help Cara. I wouldn't let this asshole take that away from me.

"So, assuming what you say is true, and this young lady at Oxford was lying, are you saying you fell into a similar relationship with this Cara Switzer? What was to stop her from accusing you of impropriety? Did you learn nothing from your experiences overseas?"

Assuming? I itched to take a swing at him, but if I wanted to make my point, I'd have to rely on the one weapon that had rarely failed me: words.

"With all due respect, I think it would be impossible to go through an experience like that and not learn something. At first I blamed myself for being too naïve, but the more I thought, the more I realized I'd been taken advantage of. When you do the right thing and someone treats you so abysmally, you inevitably conclude that some people prefer to trample on others to achieve their goals instead of working hard and using their own talents."

I spoke these last words hoping he'd realize I was referring to his behavior as well as Nicola's. Explicitly referring to his appalling treatment of my father would be tantamount to falling on my own sword, but I wasn't about to sit there and let him browbeat me without getting in a few subtle digs.

He looked at me pensively while I struggled to remain composed. He had the most piercing gaze. I had a vision of Aubrey sitting in this very seat in April, squirming under his scrutiny. I wondered if he'd still been bent on finding out dirt about me by that point, or if he'd merely wanted to see her with his own eyes before pursuing those ridiculous accusations against my father. Again, I had to stifle the desire to throttle him.

He didn't comment on my veiled insult, preferring to bring the conversation back to my failings.

"I suppose it's a moot point because, as you say, Miss Switzer didn't follow in the footsteps of this young woman at Oxford. Even so, you must be careful—"

"For the record, I *was* extremely careful," I said. "I never once met with a student behind closed doors. I avoided treating students as friends. I scrupulously avoided developing bonds with them beyond the classroom."

Fair enough, this was a bold-faced lie, but given my relationship with Aubrey, there was no getting though this meeting without telling a few untruths. Aaron wagged his finger at me as if he'd suddenly been reminded of something.

"Now, it's interesting you've said that. You do need to be aware of the way you're perceived by students in that regard too."

"I'm not sure what you mean…"

Reclaiming his glasses, he flipped through the pile of papers in the file.

"In your attempt to distance yourself, you have to be careful not to appear arrogant or supercilious. There were a number of comments about you seeming condescending at times, treating people with an overly superior attitude, and even being argumentative during tutorials."

I felt my spine stiffen. "Are you serious?"

"Now, most of those comments came with the caveat that you softened as the semester progressed, but even so…" He looked down at the page in his hand. "Yes, this is what I was looking for. According to a couple of young men in your Friday tutorial, you spent a fair bit of time challenging a particular student in that group, calling into question many of her arguments and claims in what they called a *confrontational* way."

Oh Christ. Friday tutorial? A female student? Well, that was a no-brainer.

"Did they mention the name of this student?"

He looked at me over the top of his glasses. "Yes. They did."

There was no doubt in my mind that he was referring to Aubrey. Sure, we'd often held genuinely conflicting beliefs about things and sincerely enjoyed debating, but there were other times when our arguments were incited by our personal crises. As I'd feared, our hostility hadn't escaped the notice of the others in the room. Well, if Aaron was going to bring the conversation around to Aubrey, then I was going to turn it to my advantage.

"If it's Aubrey Price you're talking about," I said, "you're right. I do need to work harder to rein in my feelings if I don't get along with someone."

"You admit you didn't get along with her?"

"I didn't particularly like her at first, to be honest," I said — or more accurately, *lied.*

"Really? How so?"

"She challenged virtually everything I said from day one. I was nervous at the beginning of the semester. She seemed to enjoy making tutorials difficult for me."

Say what you like, there wasn't anything false in that last claim. She *had* made my life a living hell. Every look, every innocent smile, every hair twirl, and every lip bite had been pure torture.

"Why do you suppose she was so keen to engage you in conflict?"

"In hindsight, I suppose she might have been trying to be playful, thinking her pre-existing relationship with my parents afforded her that luxury. As I've mentioned, I had no desire to cultivate friendships, so I didn't rise to the bait. This might have annoyed her."

Good God, where had that come from? I was on a fucking roll!

"I see. So, did your feelings influence your ability to assess her work impartially?"

Absolutely, but not in the way you're thinking, dick wad.

"I admit to being particularly picky on one of her tests. Martin and I discussed it as being an area of growth for me. Martin overruled my assessment and assigned her a perfect grade. I learned a lot from the experience."

He nodded. "I met with her, and we discussed the incident you're referring to. She said you were open to seeing where you had gone wrong."

"Absolutely."

"And there were no other major conflicts with her, then?"

I shook my head and smiled at him wryly.

"Things are quite amicable now. I've been forced to get along with her out of necessity. I've run into her a few times at family events over the last few weeks, like the party at Victoria College to celebrate my father's promotion. I'm sure our paths will continue to cross." I paused for effect. "As you know, Aubrey is close to my father *and* my mother."

He pursed his lips and tapped his pen on the pile of papers in front of him.

"I suppose I deserved that," he said, weary all of a sudden.

I clasped my hands and leaned my elbows on my knees.

"Look, I'm not here to rehash what happened between you and my father. He led me to believe you've come to an understanding. That's fine. It's between the two of you." O'Connor looked at me steadily, saying nothing, so I continued. "All I want to do is work on my paper and gain more classroom experience. I have a meeting with Martin after I leave here. He's keen to have me assigned to his Intro to Shakespeare class."

I gestured to the folder on the desk.

"If everything you've gathered here indicates that I'm not a complete moron and might actually be of some use to a group of first-year students, I'd like to tell him things are settled."

He tossed his glasses on the desk, pinching the bridge of his nose. Our talk seemed to have sucked the life out of him. I wasn't particularly distressed by this fact, nor could I summon up any guilt about my lack of empathy. He closed the folder. After pondering for a moment, he nodded.

"Martin is an excellent mentor. I see no problem with you working with him again. Consider it done."

He walked over to the door and opened it. Just like that, we were finished. I could only imagine he wanted me out of there as badly as I wanted to leave.

"Someone will be in touch with you in late August to finalize details," he said. "And please, remember what we talked about."

I nodded as I escaped through the doorway. "I will. Thanks."

I turned, almost knocking over a stack of boxes piled outside his door in my haste to get the hell out of there. I didn't look back as I strode down the hall, pushing my way through the doors and walking steadily until I reached the archway to the UC quad. I turned, dropped my bag, and bent double, resting my hands on my knees and breathing deeply.

My heart pounded in my ears, but this was not anxiety. No, this was something else. Maybe euphoria. I wanted to hoot with laughter. In a secret corner of my mind, I'd feared something horrible would happen at that meeting with Aaron—that today he'd reveal his knowledge of my relationship with Aubrey. But by some fluke, O'Connor believed that we'd been nursing ill-will toward each other all semester long. It was almost impossible to believe.

I had to tell her. She'd seemed blasé about my meeting, but she must have been worried, too. I called her, but she didn't answer. Rather than leaving a message, I hung up and opted to text her instead, smiling as I typed.

I am fucking brilliant, poppet.
You really should bow down before my brilliance.
Oh, and while you're down there... ;) -D

CHAPTER 16

Thought and Action

…the native hue of resolution
Is sicklied o'er with the pale cast of thought,
And enterprises of great pith and moment
With this regard their currents turn awry,
And lose the name of action.
(*Hamlet,* Act III, Scene 1)

Cutting through the pathways leading to the University College courtyard, I looked for somewhere to stop and gather my thoughts while I waited for Aubrey to respond to my message. I surveyed the quad before sitting on a bench facing the classrooms on the other side of the square.

How many times had I sat in the room on the end, staring out the window so I wouldn't betray my feelings for Aubrey? There were days when I'd believed I might not make it through the semester in one piece, and now here I was, on this side of those windows, liberated from the constraints of that damn classroom. Was it crazy of me to think myself truly free?

I don't know how long I sat there, gazing blindly across the courtyard, before my phone finally rang.

"Hello there, beautiful."

"Hello yourself, handsome. I just got your text. To what do we owe your brilliance this time, and when and where do I get to bow before it?"

I explained my meeting with Aaron. She groaned when I told her how he'd taunted me about my experiences at Oxford, but when I related the part of the conversation in which we'd discussed my arrogance and reported distaste for her and her in-class opinions, she guffawed.

"No way!"

"Apparently, we hated each other. However, we're getting along better these days. My parents insist on me playing nice because they think highly of you, of course."

"Daniel, you didn't tell him that!"

"Sure I did. It stopped him in his tracks. You should have heard me in there, Aubrey. I could hardly believe half the things coming out of my mouth."

"Maybe that's because half the things coming out of your mouth weren't true." She laughed.

"Good point. Anyway, it couldn't have gone better if I'd scripted it."

"I hope your ill-will isn't too deep-seated. Why would you want to date someone you've despised for months?"

"I think I'll put it down to the changing seasons. One look at your legs in a short dress, and I'm sure any distaste I may have felt for you in the past will immediately seem unwarranted and highly illogical."

"How shallow of you, Mr. Grant."

"That's me. I'm not just arrogant, but completely superficial as well."

She sighed dramatically. "I'm kind of ashamed of myself. I usually have more refined taste in men."

"You can't be held responsible for your attraction to me. I have the sweetest knees in town."

"Can't argue with that," she said without missing a beat.

"So, are you still planning to grab a coffee at ten thirty and head to the Hart House library to write?"

"Yep."

"And you're still good to meet in the lobby of the Gallery Restaurant at twelve?"

"Sounds perfect. Hey, sunshine?"

"Yes?"

"I was afraid to let myself think about it earlier, but we might actually have this locked up."

"I was thinking the same thing before you called."

"Really?"

"Absolutely. I can't wait to walk across campus holding your hand. I want everyone to know you're my girl."

"That sounds divine. Oh, and good luck with Professor Brown."

"I don't need luck with him."

"You don't?"

"Not at all. This'll be child's play compared to meeting with Aaron. I think I'll save that good luck wish for after our first date."

"I don't think you'll need it then, either." I could practically hear the wink in her voice.

Martin finally joined me, sliding a cup of coffee across the table.

"Thanks. Are you sure you're okay staying here?" I asked him. "I don't mind going to your office, if you'd prefer—"

"No, no." He settled into the chair across from me. "It's a relief to get out of the cave once in a while."

"I suppose it is." I took a quick look at my phone. If Aubrey was going to grab a coffee before heading upstairs, she'd be arriving any time now.

"You know, I received a phone call from Aaron about half an hour ago," Martin said.

My stomach lurched. "He called you?"

"He said you two had quite a heart-to-heart this morning."

"Frankly, he raked me over the coals. It was kind of unpleasant."

"He was being thorough, Daniel."

I grimaced. "Oh, he was thorough. He went through those evaluations with a fine-toothed comb."

Martin leaned across the table. "I read those evaluations, son. There was nothing surprising in there. You've got some work ahead of you, but that's to be expected. Treating everyone equitably, making yourself approachable but not breeding familiarity, trying to over-come personality conflicts, maintaining authority without excessive superiority—you must know that all goes with the territory."

"I guess. The good news is he agreed to assign me to your first year Shakespeare course."

"I confess, I wheedled that out of him." Martin smiled slyly. "I'm thrilled. I hope you are too."

"Absolutely."

"Good." He tapped the table beside my hand. "Now, how are things going with your paper? The last time we talked, you were feeling unfocussed. Any movement?"

My thesis was proving to be a constant source of frustration. I'd hit a wall and couldn't seem to forge ahead.

"Life's been turbulent. It's difficult to concentrate when everything's upside down. I find myself getting too lost in my thoughts sometimes."

"I don't mean to pry, Daniel, but you aren't still suffering the fallout of the nasty episode at Oxford?"

"Occasionally I catch myself thinking people are looking at me and wondering about what happened. Aaron even brought it up this morning."

"The way I see it, you had a successful semester. Try to put your past behind you."

"Easier said than done, sir. I wish I could turn back time. If only I'd never met that girl."

"That sort of thinking is a waste of energy. Focus your efforts on the here and now. Work on your paper in earnest. Try to get some-thing accomplished. You'll feel much better."

"I've been trying to work through *Hamlet*. I'm not getting very far."

"Ahh. And what's *your* difficulty with the young prince?"

"I keep thinking I should be able to do something with his con-stant inner examination—all his talk of dreams and death and the references to shadows and mirrors. Unfortunately, I get sidetracked and start thinking about my own life."

Martin mulled this over.

"Introspection in and of itself isn't enough. We can look inward until the cows come home, but if a man fails to integrate the differ-ent experiences he's had, then he's nowhere. The hand wringing and the 'why me' mentality won't get Hamlet anywhere as far as Jung is concerned. Inaction is crippling. *The less you do, the less you find yourself able to get done*, if that makes sense."

"Martin, are you really talking about Hamlet?"

He took a quiet sip of his coffee, a playful smile tugging at the corner of his mouth. "I believe you just answered that question yourself."

I smirked and stared down at my cup.

"Keep plugging away. Explore something else and revisit *Hamlet* when you're in a better frame of mind."

I'd have explained that I'd already abandoned *Hamlet* for the better part of a year and was just now coming back to it, but I was sidetracked by Aubrey's arrival in the coffee shop. Finally! And she looked gorgeous in a short flowery sundress with thin straps. Her hair hung loose and curly around her face. Martin obviously noticed my zoned out expression and looked over his shoulder to see what I was staring at.

"Look at that," he said, clearly pleased to see her. "Miss Price. Lovely young lady, and so bright." He paused. "Pretty girl, too, wouldn't you say?"

We watched her order a coffee, and when Martin turned around again, I tried to set my face in a neutral expression.

"I suppose so. Strong-minded, though," I said. "We got into quite a few debates during seminars. She's got firm opinions. Doesn't like to be challenged."

"Sounds like you two had an interesting semester."

"You could say that." I shook my head and worked on my second Academy Award-winning performance of the day. "I started to wonder if she was contradicting me just to get a rise out of me. I have to give her credit—she started some great tutorial debates."

Professor Brown drained the rest of his coffee and smiled knowingly.

"Sounds like my Marianne. Always playing the devil's advocate. Loves to get my goat." He raised an eyebrow. "Delightful spending time with people who are your intellectual equal, wouldn't you say? Wishy-washy people are so tiresome."

"That sounds like something my grandmother would say."

"Your grandmother is a wise woman."

I smiled, watching Aubrey at the cash register. Her legs looked amazing in that dress, to say nothing of her cleavage. I forced myself to stop imagining what she *wasn't* wearing underneath.

As she crossed to the exit leading to the Hart House corridor, Martin held up his hand and called her name. Her eyes widened, and she stopped in her tracks. Panic. But panic that might have appeared like surprise to the casual observer.

Perfect.

"Miss Price," Martin said, beckoning her over. "How lovely to see you."

"Professor Brown. Good to see you." She pulled her backpack higher on her shoulder and smiled at me cautiously. "Daniel, how are you?"

I returned her smile, trying to radiate calm vibes.

"I'm well, thanks."

"What brings you here?" Martin asked her.

"I needed a break from residence. I thought I'd go up to the library and get some writing done. I'm doing some freelance work for a local magazine," she said.

"Isn't that marvelous!" Martin said. "I told you she was a brilliant writer, Daniel. You were far too hard on her."

I cleared my throat, feigning embarrassment.

Aubrey shrugged. "I think Daniel's high expectations made me try harder."

"With excellent results, wouldn't you say? Your final grade was impressive," Martin said.

She reddened and glanced at me self-consciously again. I congratulated myself for not warning her that Martin and I would be here this morning. Her reactions were entirely genuine.

She shifted her weight from one foot to the other. "Well, I should go…"

"Of course, don't let us keep you. It was lovely seeing you. Best of luck with the writing."

She gave me a sheepish wave and headed for the door. As she disappeared through it, Martin shook his head.

"Wonderful young lady."

"Yes."

I pretended to think for a second and then leapt out of my chair. "Actually, Martin, would you excuse me for a second?"

"Certainly."

I bolted out the door, catching Aubrey as she was heading up the stairs at the end of the corridor.

"Miss Price?" I called out.

She turned and rolled her eyes. "Daniel, I almost had heart failure in there!"

"I'm sorry. I kind of contrived it that we'd bump into you."

"Kind of?"

"Relax, you were perfect. I'm going back in and telling him we're having lunch."

She examined my face. "Are you sure?"

"Listen, Martin's in there singing your praises, and you look gorgeous. I believe I just saw you as a beautiful young woman for the first time, right before Martin's eyes. I simply had to run out here and ask you to join me for lunch." I leaned in a little closer. "After all, we have to mend some fences, right? Overcome this extreme dislike we have for one another..."

She sighed and looked over my shoulder.

"Trust me? I'll see you upstairs at noon," I said.

"You're a little too good at this scheming, you know that?"

"All for a good cause." I winked and returned to the coffee shop where I reclaimed my seat.

"Everything all right?" Martin asked.

"Yes, fine. Great, actually. I'm...Well, I just asked Miss Price if she'd join me for lunch today." I rubbed my whiskers, trying my best to look shell-shocked, as if I couldn't believe what I'd just done.

"That's splendid."

"Not inappropriate?"

"Really, Daniel?" he asked, his eyebrows shooting up in surprise.

"Given everything...You know..."

"Don't be ridiculous."

He waved off my concern with a flick of his hand — a small but significant gesture that ultimately endorsed my "pursuit" of his former student.

"Might I make one small suggestion?" he added.

"Of course."

He smiled. "I think I'd use her *first name*, if I were you."

At five minutes past twelve, I was pacing in the Gallery Restaurant lobby. How could Aubrey be late when she was already in the building? When she arrived, her hair freshly brushed and her lips glossy, my annoyance evaporated instantly. I smiled, admiring the Tiffany necklace resting above her cleavage.

"Sorry I'm late," she said. "I wanted to freshen up, and I needed a few minutes to breathe."

The hostess checked the reservation book and led us to a table overlooking the Great Hall. The restaurant was busy and wide open; there was nowhere to hide. It didn't matter, though, because we didn't *have* to hide. I thought my heart might burst from the sheer relief of it all.

I held Aubrey's gaze across the table. "This is it."

"It's nice," she said, peering out the windows at the Great Hall below.

"I'm not talking about the restaurant."

Her eyes flickered across mine before sweeping over the surrounding tables again.

"I know, I'm just trying not to freak out," she said quietly. "My heart is pounding."

"Mine too."

She looked at me worriedly. "Are you okay?"

"Don't worry. It's the good kind of pounding."

"The good kind of pounding, huh?"

I laughed. I hadn't meant to be suggestive.

"Not the *best* kind of pounding, but a good kind all the same." She shifted uneasily. We were so accustomed to being on high alert on campus, we didn't even know how to let our guards down. "Let's both try to relax and enjoy this. We're officially not doing anything wrong," I said.

"Okay, I'll try."

She scanned the menu while I perused the wine list. As far as I was concerned, we were celebrating. It had to be done. "Would you prefer white or red, poppet?"

"You know wine goes to my head," she said. "Somehow, I feel like I ought to keep my wits about me today."

"Wits?" I waved my hand dismissively. "Can't stand wits. Never have had any use for them."

"Well, then, wine it is," she said, twirling her hair around her finger and looking up at me from under her lashes.

I groaned and shifted in my seat. It had been a week since we'd made love. Did she realize she was torturing me?

"You're gorgeous, you know that? I can't believe how lucky I am to have found a woman who's beautiful *and* brilliant."

"I don't know about beautiful, but I do feel kind of brilliant." She smiled shyly. "I got my marks this morning, Daniel. I did well."

"How well?"

"A ninety-three-percent average." She took a deep breath. "I made the dean's list. I received an invitation to a reception at Old Vic before the graduation ceremony."

"I'm so proud of you. I guess it wouldn't be appropriate to leap across the table and give you a giant congratulatory kiss?"

"Probably not."

I reached over to squeeze her hand. "You realize I don't know a single person in here, and no one's paying us an iota of attention anyway."

"I know. But I'm enjoying this first date thing. Role playing appeals to my kinky side."

I leaned across the table and lowered my voice. "Wait…You have a *kinky side?*"

She laughed, but as her eyes drifted over my shoulder, her smile rapidly faded and the color drained from her face.

The Blood Burns

When the blood burns, how prodigal the soul
Lends the tongue vows…
(*Hamlet*, Act 1, Scene 3)

followed her anxious gaze, and wouldn't you know it—there, stand-ing at the hostess stand, was my father.

He absently scanned the room as the hostess led him through the restaurant, but inevitably his eyes landed on us. He stopped, said a few quiet words to the hostess, and made his way over. Aubrey gave him a rueful look as he stepped up beside my chair.

"This is a surprise," he said, incapable of hiding the grimness behind his smile. He lowered his voice. "I thought we'd agreed you'd wait until after Aubrey's convocation to do this publicly."

"I know, Dad, but we—"

"And it had to be here and today of all days? Do you have any idea who I'm meeting for lunch?"

Aubrey and I looked at each other blankly.

"Aaron O'Connor, that's who," he said.

I couldn't conceal my shock. "What? Why the hell—?"

"I don't have time to explain. He'll be here any minute."

"Speak of the devil," Aubrey murmured, her eyes trained on the door.

"Let me handle this." I looked at my dad calmly. "Trust me, it's all good."

He sighed and adopted his best genial smile, turning to the door and holding up a hand. O'Connor sauntered over.

"Well, Daniel, twice in one day," he said.

"Mr. O'Connor, you know Aubrey Price, of course?" I gestured across the table to her, and she gave him a tight-lipped smile.

"We've met on a couple of occasions now. Nice to see you, Aubrey." He raised an eyebrow at me. "So? Making nice with the enemy?"

I laughed abruptly, taking in my father's confused expression.

"I guess you could say that. Martin and I ran into Aubrey in the Arbor Room earlier. I felt bad about those evaluations you showed me this morning, so I invited her to join me for a coffee — an effort to bury the hatchet properly, I suppose you could say."

Aubrey nodded her agreement, and O'Connor looked at her with interest. My father followed suit.

"And?" Aaron said, cocking his head.

"Daniel has been most apologetic. I'd say the hatchet is duly buried."

"That's excellent news." O'Connor looked at my father. "You must be happy to hear this, David?"

"I'm thrilled, of course." My father smiled, playing along before turning his attention back to O'Connor. "Well, shall we?"

"We were just finishing up." I pushed my chair back and flashed a quick glance at Aubrey.

My father squeezed my shoulder. "Enjoy your day, son. Aubrey, I'll see you next week at convocation. Have a nice visit with your mother."

"Thank you, sir. See you then."

Aubrey wrapped her hand around the strap of her bag as they walked away.

"Do you think he bought that?" she whispered.

"I sure hope so. Let's get the hell out of here."

She nodded, almost vaulting out of her chair, and we made a speedy departure.

"Holy shit," she muttered through clenched teeth as we dashed toward the exit. "I've never taken to scotch, but today could be the day."

On the drive home, Aubrey trained her eyes out the window, her hand clasped in mine. I was interested to know what she was thinking, but I let her be. If her scattered thoughts were anything like mine, coherent conversation would be nearly impossible. I mean, what the fuck was my dad doing having lunch with Aaron O'Connor? Was he certifiable?

As I drove, I cursed pedestrians and sighed with exasperation at red light after red light. By the time we were back at my building, my nerves were frayed. Inside at last, we dropped our bags, slumped against the door, and sighed with relief.

"Safe?" she asked, her hand gripping mine tightly.

"I'd say so."

"Scotch?"

"Fuck, yes."

I went straight to the liquor cabinet, pouring us both a healthy shot. Though Aubrey wrinkled her nose as she brought the glass to her mouth, she drank it in one gulp. I followed suit, chuckling as she grimaced and shuddered.

"How do you drink this stuff?" She wiped her mouth with the back of her hand.

"Another?"

"Absolutely."

Aubrey knocked back a second shot, this time expelling a loud satisfied sigh to stave off the shudder. I downed mine and held the bottle aloft.

"I'm out." She put the bottle and my glass on the shelf, then stepped into my arms and dissolved against me, all soft and vulnerable and sweet. "Hey, sailor."

"Hey. You okay?"

She nodded into my neck. "Getting there. How are you doing?"

"I'm a bit of a wreck."

Clasping my face, she searched my eyes. "What can I do?"

"It's sensory overload. I don't want to think any more today. Let's forget about the world for a while." I kissed her. "Can you help me with that?"

She nodded, wrapping her arms around me and fitting her body against mine in all the right places.

"I think I know the precise remedy for sensory overload." She stood on her tiptoes and brought her lips to my ear. "You need to be fucked *senseless*," she whispered, looking up at me as if she couldn't believe what she'd said.

I just about lost my shit, a surge of raw lust igniting every nerve in my body. I lifted her, almost ripping her dress as she circled my waist with her legs and pressed her hot little panties against my stomach. We kissed feverishly while I half-walked, half-stumbled down the hall, stopping occasionally to push her to the wall to regain my balance. Somehow she managed to tear my T-shirt over my head and was fumbling with the button on my jeans as we passed through to the bedroom.

I lowered her onto the bed, and she pushed down my jeans and boxers. Before I knew it, her beautiful lips were around me, drawing me deeply into her mouth. She moaned and sighed as if there was nothing in the world she'd rather be doing, and I sent up a silent prayer of thanks for having Aubrey in my life.

All I could do was slide my hands through her silky hair. A door slammed shut in my brain, as if the chaos of the day had been left in a room at the end of a long hallway.

"Aubrey…that feels…*so* fucking amazing…"

It actually felt *too* fucking good. After a week of celibacy, I was ready to explode. I gently pushed her away.

"I need to pace myself." My voice tight was tight with the effort of holding back. "Come here."

Kissing her shoulders, I tugged at the dress's zipper, trailing my fingers down her back. Inch by inch, her creamy skin was exposed. She slid the straps over her shoulders, and the dress fell to the floor. I devoured her body with my eyes.

"God, you're sexy."

She pressed against me, and I captured her lips, teasing her scotch-laced tongue with mine. Instead of dipping my fingers inside her panties, I tickled my way across the small triangle of fabric. She squirmed and whimpered against my lips, her eyes reflecting raw desire.

I'd wanted to draw things out, to touch her and tease her first, but who was I kidding? She was soft and warm, and impossibly wet.

A fucking oasis is what she was, and I needed her—*now*. I tugged at her panties, and she slipped them off, nudging me toward the bed and waiting for me to lie back before crawling up to join me.

"Where do you want me?" she asked, trailing wet heat along my thigh as she moved against me.

"Where *don't* I want you?"

I held her eyes with mine as I lost myself inside her. She moaned with seductive abandon, allowing me to turn her this way and that, happily contorting herself into every conceivable position while I slowed every few minutes to kiss and caress her, coaxing several orgasms from her and willing myself to delay my own climax for as long as possible.

When I thought my head might implode from the sheer effort of holding back, I finally acknowledged my body's frantic need for release. After a few decisive thrusts, she pressed her hands to my chest.

"Daniel, stop…"

"Am I hurting you?"

She shook her head and pushed my shoulder, urging me onto my back before climbing atop me.

"I thought I was supposed to be fucking *you* senseless."

Jesus Christ.

She rocked and circled her hips, her hair falling wildly across her face. She was incredible. No bells and whistles, no fucking gizmos required. Just watching the movements of her gorgeous body as we made love was pure bliss. I sat up, wrapping my arms around her. I was probably squeezing her too hard, but I was lost, slick heat and friction taking away all sense and logic.

"Oh God, I can't," I gasped out.

She brought her lips to my ear and whispered, "Come on, Daniel. Come for me." Her words swept me away, and a searing wave of relief flooded my body. I clung to her, breathless, my eyes watering from the intensity of my orgasm, and then I collapsed against the pillows.

With her cheek on my chest, she curled around me, making sweet little purring sounds while I waited for the world to come back into focus. At last she stretched her legs out and buried her face in my neck.

"Aubrey?"

"Mmm?"

"That was hot as hell."

"Yeah?" she said shyly.

"Um…yeah." I chuckled. "Seriously."

She smiled and tickled my scruff with her fingers.

"I wanted to help you forget your stressful morning—that awful meeting with Aaron."

"Meeting?" I sighed. "What meeting?"

"I'm glad you're feeling better."

"That's an understatement."

"Wait till you see what I'll do after a second date," she said, giving me a dirty grin.

CHAPTER 18

A Convenient Courtship

Be merry, and employ your chiefest thoughts
To courtship and such fair ostents of love
As shall conveniently become you there…
(*The Merchant of Venice*, Act II, Scene 8)

After a late lunch of pizza and chicken wings, Daniel retreated to the office to call his father while I paced, waiting for him to finish. I couldn't bring myself to believe that the lunch date was a sign of impending doom. Daniel's meetings with Aaron and Professor Brown had gone well. Was I foolish to think we were finally free to share our love with the world beyond the confines of the condo?

Not that I don't enjoy the times we share here…

I smiled, picturing the disbelief on Daniel's face as I'd slung my leg over his shoulder in bed earlier. I suppose the scotch had loosened up my limbs *and* my tongue. I was still grinning like a smitten school-girl when Daniel emerged from the office.

"Well?" I said.

"Guess who's no longer in a relationship with Elaine Armstrong."

"Get out! Aaron and Elaine broke up?"

Daniel joined me, leaning his elbows on the breakfast bar.

"*And* he's moving to the Mississauga campus. It's a lateral move from what my dad could gather. He doesn't want to work down here anymore in case he runs into her."

"That's crazy. He's seen the light, I guess."

"Seems like it."

"So he won't be your TA advisor anymore."

"Apparently not."

"Huh. So, what was the lunch meeting with your dad all about?"

Daniel frowned. "'Unfinished business,' my dad called it. He said he'll tell me more later—something about not wanting to get my hopes up. He assured me there's absolutely nothing for us to worry about."

"Your dad loves being cryptic, doesn't he?"

"I think he's trying to help me with something. I'm just not sure what it is. They talked about us, and my dad told him he was pleased to see us putting our petty disagreements behind us because the family thinks so highly of you, of course."

"Your dad's quite the storyteller, just like his son."

Daniel shrugged. "I'm beyond worrying about who had to lie to whom."

"Then everything's okay? We're good to go?"

He took my hands in his, eyes twinkling. "I think it's full steam ahead."

"I can't believe it."

He nodded. "It's about time something went our way."

I'll say.

With the arrival of the North by Northwest music festival, June promised to be a busy concert month. I told Eli I'd be out of commission while my mom was in town, in addition to being unavailable two of the festival days because of Daniel's birthday. Gwen was planning a small get-together at their house the night before his birthday, leaving the next day open so Daniel and I could celebrate alone.

To compensate for my lack of availability later in the month, I was covering four concerts in the next six days—a grueling schedule for a newbie, but I needed to learn how to write under pressure. I was reading an email from Eli and jotting the concert dates on my calendar when Daniel wandered into the office. I drew his attention to the email, and he peered over my shoulder to read it.

"Is Eli going with you to these shows?"

"No, this is all me."

"We'll have a busy week, then," he said, stepping back and looking at me levelly.

I knew that look. He was bracing himself for a fight.

"What do you mean *we'll* have a busy week?"

"The Mod Club, Lee's Palace, Sneaky Dee's — *Tattoo Rock Parlour?* You think you're going to these clubs by yourself while I stay home folding laundry?"

"Daniel, I think you're —"

He pinched my lips shut with his finger and thumb and shook his head. "No arguments."

I mumbled a muffled protest against his fingers.

"Sorry, this isn't open for discussion. If I let go, promise me you won't argue?"

I rolled my eyes and nodded. He released my lips.

"Sunshine, I think you're overrea —"

Again, he cut off my words, resuming the clamp.

"When you took this job, you promised to let me help. I'm buying tickets for these shows. They're all general admission, right?"

I nodded again, feeling like a moron with him holding my lips like that.

"So, I'll come along to make sure you don't get trampled or accosted. Deal?"

I pulled his fingers away from my mouth. "Okay. Deal."

I considered pointing out the foolishness of him spending money to facilitate me having a job, but he'd just brush off that concern with a flippant wave of his hand. Something about my expression must have told him I wasn't finished pleading my case because he put his hands on his hips and sighed.

"You can't be angry with me for wanting you to be safe. I won't interfere with what you're doing. I'll take pictures or something. But I'll be there in case you need me." He tipped my chin up. "Besides, this will give us an excuse to spend more time together in public. Think of this week as a pre-convocation whirlwind courtship. We'll roll with the punches if we see anyone we know."

There was no point disagreeing with him. He wasn't budging.

"All right." I stood and curled into his embrace. "I suppose I will feel better having you there. Thanks."

"Don't thank me. Just stop being so goddamn stubborn."

"I can't," I mumbled against his chest. "It's in my genes."

"And to whom do I owe thanks for this genetic obstinacy, your mother or your father?"

"Both."

"Super. Double DNA stubbornness. The *worst* kind."

"Whirlwind courtship" was an interesting term, one I'd always thought of in the context of a royal couple—the prince sweeping his future princess off her feet, jet-setting off to Paris, dazzling her with diamonds, and maybe surprising her with a holiday on a secluded island.

My pre-convocation whirlwind courtship with Daniel took place in restaurants and noisy bars along College, Queen, and Bloor Streets—not exactly the royal treatment. We had a great time, but by the end of the week, I considered starting a spreadsheet to record which Toronto clubs were least likely to have toilet paper in the women's washrooms.

Though I'd griped about Daniel joining me at the concerts, we ended having a hell of a lot of fun. Seedy-dive-bar-Daniel was slightly unkempt and reluctant to shave. Dr. Hobo came back to town with a sexy vengeance, and I couldn't help seeing the bright side of him tagging along when tattered jeans and threadbare concert T-shirts were part of the deal.

As promised, he took pictures, documenting our horrendous meals and snapping shots of the venues and the bands. We cajoled some friendly patrons into taking some photos of us, and soon we had a scrapbook of dive-bar memories stored on a memory card.

On the nights of the concerts, we stayed out late, showered together when we got home, made love in the middle of the night, and woke whenever our eyes grudgingly opened. Every afternoon, we'd write at our desks, Daniel working on his *Hamlet* analysis while I sat on the other side of the room, frantically penning reviews. By seven o'clock in the evening, we'd start all over again—another restaurant and another venue.

By week's end, we were wiped, and though I loved the writing and the concerts, not to mention my dates with Daniel, I couldn't deny my exhaustion. On the Monday morning after the last of the four concerts, I woke up with a terrible case of cottonmouth and a curious vibrating sensation in my ears.

I dragged my ass out of bed and found Daniel on the couch in the living room, his laptop open in front of him, listening to music through ear buds as he typed. When he saw me, he closed his laptop and pulled the ear buds out.

"How long have you been up?" I asked, crossing to give him a good morning kiss.

"A few hours. I couldn't sleep any more. No clue why."

"It's not like you to work out here. And I can't believe you were listening to music. My ears are ringing like crazy."

He shrugged. "I wasn't really working. Just goofing off. I've been Facebook chatting with an old friend from UCC. We're trying to set up a game of golf."

"That's great news, sunshine."

He pushed his laptop aside, gathering me in his arms.

"Why don't you seem more excited?" I asked him.

"I am. I guess I'm worried about Jeremy. I've texted him a few times since he and Julie moved into their new place, but I haven't heard anything back."

"Daniel, I've spoken to Julie three times this week. They're fine."

"I know. It's just…" He sighed, staring over my shoulder.

"Do you want me to call her again?"

He looked at me hopefully. "Would you?"

I gave him a quick kiss and headed to the bedroom to retrieve my phone. Julie answered on the first ring.

"Wow, are you sitting on your phone?" I said.

"Babe, my phone's on vibrate. If I was sitting on it, I guarantee I would have let it ring more than once."

"That sounds desperate. Jeremy leaving you high and dry?"

"Not at all. I'm actually kind of sore," she whispered. "And, holy shit, my jaw —"

"Whoa! TMI. Glad you're getting your freak on, but don't wanna know the painful details."

"You asked!"

"Consider this me officially un-asking." I snickered as I thought of Jeremy and Julie christening their new place. Daniel and I had been there, done that, and bought not just the T-shirt, but the whole wardrobe — which, of course, he'd then organized according to color and sleeve length.

"So, what's going on?" Julie asked. "Everything went okay with the concert rounds?"

"Yeah, we hit Lee's Palace last night."

"And did you end up seeing anyone you knew?"

"Nope. Not a single person. Daniel and I might as well have been going out all semester. So annoying. But that's not why I called. Jer hasn't responded to any of Daniel's texts in the last couple of days. Is he okay?"

Julie sighed. "He's dealing with something and kind of in his own head space right now, but he's fine. Tell Daniel not to worry. He'll be in touch when he's ready."

We talked for a few more minutes, but as always, Julie was on the fly. After she'd wished me good luck at my convocation, we hung up, and I re-joined Daniel in the living room.

"Jeremy's fine," I said, dropping my phone on the coffee table and sinking onto the couch. "Julie said he's distracted and dealing with something, but you don't need to worry about him."

"Wow, that's as cryptic as something my dad would say."

I gave him best stern face. "Cryptic or not, *stop worrying*."

"Yes, ma'am."

I smiled wistfully, and he raised an eyebrow.

"You okay?"

"Is it weird that I'm nervous about telling my mom about my new job? I'm sure it's not what she or my dad imagined me doing after getting a four-year degree. I'm the only child, so there's just me to make them proud, you know?"

"All children want to please their parents. I can't imagine your mom and dad being anything less than a hundred percent proud of you. When that issue of *Sidelines* is published with your first article in there for them to see, they'll be thrilled. Plus you're about to graduate with distinction. How could they be disappointed? You're amazing."

"In your completely *unbiased* opinion?"

"I'm well-versed in being completely unbiased when assessing your achievements, Aubrey," he said. "Three months of practice, remember?"

No, Time, thou shalt not boast that I do change...
...This I do vow and this shall ever be;
I will be true...
(*Sonnet 123*)

aiting for my mother at the arrivals gate, I second-guessed my decision not to let Daniel come with me to pick her up. But no, this was better. I wanted to see my mom first and spend some time with her before introducing her to Daniel.

I peered over the heads of the people in front of me, watching families and loved ones reuniting. Airports were great places to people-watch. When my mother finally breezed through the doors, pushing her luggage cart with one hand while holding her straw hat to her head with the other, I was caught off-guard by the emotional heft of seeing her.

Mom.

I squeezed through the crowd, waving to catch her attention. She smiled and waved back.

"Aubrey! Hi!"

I tried to speak, but a sudden tightness closed my throat, so I just laughed through my tears as she rushed down the exit ramp, wrestling with the cart whose wheels clearly wanted to go a different way. She hugged me fiercely, and my knees almost gave way as the familiar scent of perfume and peppermint chewing gum washed over me.

"Mom…"

"Oh, Aubrey. I missed you, honey." She laughed, rocking me from side to side.

"I missed you too."

I held onto her for a long time and then finally let go, rifling through my pockets for a Kleenex as she smiled and licked her thumbs, gently rubbing them under my eyes.

"Aw, sweetie. Come on, let's get out of here. Which is the best way to go to get a taxi?" she asked. I relieved her of the meandering cart, and we headed for the exit.

I sniffed, recovering from my silly outburst and trying to regain my bearings. "Um, we don't need to get a taxi. Daniel ordered a car service."

"Daniel. That's your new boyfriend?"

"He really wanted to drive me here to pick you up himself, but I wanted some time with you first. He booked us a car."

"How thoughtful," she said.

"He's *definitely* thoughtful, Mom." I pushed the cart down the sidewalk toward the waiting car.

The driver hopped out, popping the trunk and greeting my mother with a welcoming smile. My mom grinned at me as he held the door open for her and we clambered into the back seat while he dealt with her suitcase. She ran her hands over the leather seats.

"A Cadillac Escalade? Aubrey, there's thoughtful, and then there's saint-like."

My mom picked aimlessly at the remnants of her tandoori chicken. Good thing I'd waited until she'd almost finished eating before I'd dropped the bomb. She seemed to lose her appetite the minute I revealed my news.

"So, let me get this straight. You quit a perfectly good job to go to concerts and write for a magazine. And you're dating a boy who —"

I cringed. "He's really not a boy, Mom."

"Okay, you're dating a *man* who has a condo in the Distillery District and a boat docked at Centre Island. His family has a house in Forest Hill and a million dollar cottage up north. He takes you places like Auberge du Pommier and buys Tiffany jewelry…" She gestured to the pendant at my neck, sighing extravagantly. "I don't know. This doesn't sound like you."

I groaned and slumped back in the booth. She took a long drink of her margarita, gazing at me across the table. I wished I hadn't told her so much about Daniel and his family.

"You're making him sound snooty and pretentious. He's not," I said defensively.

"Auberge du Pommier? Tiffany's? I don't think I'm reading into this, Aubrey."

I placed my hands palm-down on the table, trying to collect my thoughts.

"I know it *sounds* like he's ostentatious, but he isn't. He and his family are down-to-earth. They live in a big house and eat in nice restaurants, but Daniel feels just as comfortable in ripped jeans and a concert T-shirt, ordering takeout pizza. He likes to spoil me once in a while, that's all."

"And how do you feel about all this?" she asked, pushing her plate away and poking at her drink with her straw.

"At first I was overwhelmed. I forced him to stop buying me gifts because I was uncomfortable."

"And how did he react to that?"

I smiled wistfully. "He got creative. He made me a CD and picked flowers from a friend's garden. He doesn't use his money as a crutch. At first I thought that's what he was doing as well, but now I know that's not true. Sometimes I even forget about the money."

As I made this admission, I recognized the truth behind it. What at first might have been a desperate attempt to defend Daniel to my mother was actually the plain truth. It *was* easy to forget about Daniel's money. The misgivings I'd had all those weeks ago about conspicuous consumption and pretensions were unfounded. He *was* just as happy eating nachos and beer and then heading to Lee's Palace for a concert as he was getting dressed up and dining at Auberge du Pommier.

"He's the real deal, Mom. He treats me well because he loves me."

"And you?" She squeezed my hand. "How do you feel about him?"

"Honestly? I love him too. He's amazing." Mom pursed her lips. "He's not perfect. I'm not blind to his flaws," I said. "He can be broody and overprotective sometimes. He has a hard time letting things go when he's upset, and he has…anxiety issues…but he's working through all that. I'm not idealizing him. We recognize each other's imperfections. We complement each other."

"You sound happy."

"I am, Mom. So happy. Really."

"That's all your dad and I have ever wanted for you. And as far as this writing business goes, you can do whatever you want, as long as you're being true to yourself and you enjoy doing it."

"You mean that?"

"Aubrey, come on, really? I'm upset that you didn't tell me earlier, but I don't care what you pursue as a career." She gestured to herself. "Look at me — making candles, selling handmade jewelry at craft shows — I do it because I enjoy it. Luckily, I have Rick to help with the bills. That's the tricky part. How does the writing pay?"

I grimaced. "Freelance writers for small magazines get paid about ten to fifteen cents a word."

"And you're not writing two-thousand-word articles, I bet."

"No." I chuckled.

"That would be my only concern. It's nice to throw yourself into something you love, but you do need a roof over your head and meals on the table, not to mention some money of your own. Your room at residence is paid for until the end of July, right?"

"That's right. I haven't been staying there much lately. Matt's girlfriend moved in, and it's a bit cramped. I've kind of been staying at Daniel's here and there…"

Mom raised an inquisitive eyebrow.

"I haven't moved in with him or anything. Almost all of my stuff is still at Jackman." I looked at her uneasily. "Daniel wants me to move in…"

"But you're not sure?"

I shook my head.

"And why's that?" she asked gently.

"What if it doesn't work out? I feel so young. Look at you and Dad…"

"When I was twenty-three, you were already four years old. Now, *that* was too young. Your dad and I didn't grow apart, we just…grew *up*. We were kids. We didn't understand ourselves. How could we possibly understand each other?" She smiled sadly. "But just because we screwed up doesn't mean you will. You can't let my history with your dad dictate your decisions and actions."

"I don't mean to. I guess I'm just trying to learn from it."

"There's nothing wrong with that." She patted my hand. "You're so much more grounded than I've ever been. Your dad and I are so proud of you. You know he's crushed that he can't be here, right?"

"I know. He sent me a long email."

"I'd be lying if I said there wasn't a part of me that's happy I'll get to have you to myself for the next few days. I can't believe how much you've grown up this year. I feel like I've missed so much."

I shrugged. What could I say? She *had* missed a lot.

"Maybe I'll get the Facebook," she said.

"It's just called Facebook, Mom. Not *the* Facebook."

"Whatever it's called, if I can look at your updates, maybe I won't feel so out of the loop."

Maybe you should have thought about the loop before you moved thirteen-hundred miles away, I thought. It would have been harsh to say out loud. I felt cruel just thinking it.

I flew through the door at Jackman at exactly quarter past ten the next morning. Matt was sprawled on the couch watching *SpongeBob SquarePants*. He smiled broadly as I snapped the bolt closed, kicked my shoes off, and dropped my bag on the floor.

"Whoa, Aubrey where's the fire?"

"Most people don't run *in* to a burning apartment, cowboy."

"This is true. Unless you're here to rescue me, of course." He pushed himself up off the couch.

"Don't trouble yourself." I motioned to the TV. "Looks like you're getting caught up on some quality programming there."

He snorted and gave me a hug.

"It's about time I got up, anyway," he said. "Starting to get a square ass from sitting too long."

"You could always ask your pal SpongeBob if you can borrow some of his pants," I said as I extricated myself from his arms.

He wagged a finger at me. "See? *That's* what I miss."

"My fabulous wit?"

"Exactly." A wistful smile played on his lips. "Among other things…"

"Sorry, dude. Wish I could entertain you all day, but I need to get ready."

Matt headed back to the couch to resume his date with his square-trousered friend. As I walked past Jo's room on the way to my own, her door swung open and she beckoned me inside.

"Hey, Jo, what's up?"

"Did Matt say anything about Sarah?" she whispered.

"No. Why? What's going on?"

"She's gone to a cottage with a girlfriend until Trinity's convocation."

"What the hell? It's his graduation day. I'd be pissed if Daniel wasn't interested in seeing me graduate."

She tapped the side of her forehead. "That girl's not all there, I'm telling you."

"Poor Matt."

"I'm counting the days until I head overseas. She's getting on my nerves."

I patted her shoulder sympathetically before leaving to get ready in my own room. I leaned against my door with my eyes closed, and my sadness for Matt turned into apprehension as I contemplated my imminent meeting with Elaine Armstrong. I pictured myself shaking her bony claw as she congratulated me *so sincerely* for making the dean's list. If she ruined my moment, I'd have to clock her.

I rifled through my pockets for my phone, thinking I'd give Daniel a quick call. He'd calm me down. As usual, he'd anticipated my needs, sending me a soothing text message.

> **I'm running a little late, but I'll be there in time
> for the ceremony. Can't wait to see you shine.
> Breathe, my lovely. -D xoxoxo…**

I took Daniel's advice. I breathed. Then I ran around my room like a maniac.

The lobby of Old Vic had been transformed for the ceremony. The leather club chairs and sofas were gone, replaced by rows of folding chairs facing a podium. A banquet table set up along the side wall held several trays of cookies as well as urns of tea and coffee and a pyramid of cups and saucers. My mother's eyes lit up, and she quickly fixed herself a coffee.

We surveyed the room, watching as honorees and their parents took their seats, everyone chattering excitedly and taking photographs while they waited for the ceremony to begin. But where was Daniel?

"I'm so excited," my mother said. "Make sure you stay up there long enough for me to get a couple of good pictures of you and the dean. I promised your dad I'd email him."

A couple of good pictures of me and my pal, Dean Armstrong. Ha! I decided against telling my mother the story that had led to me abandoning my job. No point ruining her perception of the day's events.

The unfortunate arrival of the dragon lady herself underscored my feelings of dread. She walked haughtily down one of the rows of chairs, intent on her destination — not surprisingly, the coffee table. I felt a shiver of dread at the sight of her. She was jabbering away to someone on the ever-present Bluetooth, so focused on her phone call and her need for caffeine that she didn't even notice me.

"Where are you?" she snapped, pausing to listen as she poured milk into her cup. "Good. Just hurry up."

She ended the call and turned around, stirring her coffee as she gazed furiously across the crowded room. When her eyes landed on me, she pulled herself up to her full height with an icy glare.

"Good morning, Dean Armstrong," I said, oozing sweetness. "Lovely day, don't you think?"

Her cup hit her saucer with a loud clink, and she clamped her teeth together, her eyes flitting to my mother who had moved closer, perhaps expecting to be introduced. I didn't have an opportunity to make introductions. Armstrong's eyes moved over my right shoulder, and she abandoned her coffee on the table and disappeared without another word.

I turned to see what had made her flee and saw David crossing the room, stopping to speak to students as he moved through the crowd. What was he doing here? Shouldn't he be at Convocation Hall preparing for this afternoon's graduation?

"Who was that woman?" my mother said, but then David was before us, smiling graciously and reaching for my mother's hand.

I beat back the adrenaline my brief exchange with Elaine had stirred up. "Mom, this is David Grant, my former boss — and Daniel's father."

"Linda," my mom said, forgoing formality as she shook his hand.

"It's a pleasure to meet you," David said. "I'm so glad you were able to make the trip home to help your daughter celebrate her accomplishments. She's had a banner year."

He smiled warmly, but before I had a chance to ask him what had brought him all the way over to Vic, he pointed at the first three rows of chairs, directing me to find my spot. My mother gave my hand a quick squeeze and moved to the rows reserved for parents. I took my seat, steeling myself for the ceremony.

That's when I spotted Daniel on the other side of the room, camera at the ready. He was flanked by several other people holding their cameras aloft. I waved at him and smiled. He winked and bobbed his head at the podium. His father was standing behind the lectern, putting on his glasses. After tapping the microphone lightly, he cleared his throat and scanned the crowd. What was he doing?

"Good morning, ladies and gentlemen, and thank you for joining us today to celebrate these select hard-working students whose efforts have earned them the much-deserved honor of a place on the dean's list," David said.

A polite smattering of applause interrupted him briefly.

"My name is David Grant, and I am the Provost at the University of Toronto. However, up until six weeks ago, I was the Dean of Students here at Vic." His eyes scanned the crowd until he found mine. "I felt compelled to return today to bestow this honor on the students I was lucky enough to have witnessed working so hard to achieve the distinction they're being recognized for today…"

From that point on, the ceremony was a blur as I struggled to contain the emotions roused by David's gesture. He must have known that if Elaine had presented me my award today, the honor being conferred would have been tainted by her insincerity. He'd come all the way here despite being incredibly busy to make sure that wouldn't happen. Never in a million years would I be able to articulate my gratitude.

When my name was called, my legs somehow carried me to the podium where David stood, waiting to give me my plaque and shake my hand. After he'd patted me on the shoulder and congratulated me, I took a quick moment to look out at the sea of faces. My mother was holding up her camera, madly snapping pictures while Daniel watched from his spot at the side of the hall, his eyes shining with pride.

After the ceremony, the heat chased everyone outside. My mother hugged me and examined my plaque with a contented smile before slipping it into her purse for safe keeping.

"I'm so proud of you, sweetie. I can't tell you how great it felt seeing you up there getting that award."

"Hey, that was just the beginning. Now we head over to Convocation Hall so you can watch me and hundreds of other people get our diplomas. Doesn't that sound awesome?"

My mother laughed while I hunted around for Daniel, biting my thumbnail as I contemplated the impending introductions.

"So, Daniel's father is an important man on campus, I gather?" my mother said.

"He's pretty high up there."

"And who do you suppose that man is? The one who's shaking his hand," my mother whispered, gesturing behind me. "He seems too old to be a student. Not old enough to be a professor, though. And profs aren't generally that good-looking, either, are they?"

When I turned around and saw who she was talking about, I suppressed a guffaw.

"Mom, that's Daniel."

"*That's* Daniel?" She flushed and covered her mouth. "Oh. Oops…"

I tried to view Daniel as my mother might be seeing him — a young man in a beautifully-cut suit, earnestly shaking his dad's hand and listening attentively to what his father was saying. He and David stood out like sore thumbs, a veritable father-son spread from *GQ*.

"He's very handsome and well-put-together," my mother said, recovering quickly from her blunder. "A little serious, maybe."

Daniel, perhaps sensing he was being watched, turned away from his father and smiled in our direction. His love swept me up like a warm, soothing wave.

"He's not always serious," I pointed out.

"Well, yes…that's…quite a smile," my mother said, breathlessly.

Ah, yes—the dimple. Capable of making grown women lose the feeling in their kneecaps.

As Daniel wrapped up with his father and walked toward us, I felt a flurry of panic. My smile faltered as he greeted us. I shifted my weight and swallowed, demonstrating the social graces of a tree stump. Daniel took over, his hand outstretched as he addressed my mother.

"I'm Daniel Grant. It's a pleasure to meet you, Mrs. —"

"Please, call me Linda," my mother insisted. "It's nice to meet you too, Daniel."

"My father said to congratulate you again, Aubrey," Daniel said. "He's on his way to Convocation Hall to run over his speech for later. He's nervous."

"He certainly did a lovely job here. It was a nice ceremony," Mom said. "Oh, and thank you so much for ordering that car service from the airport yesterday. That was kind of you."

"It was no trouble at all." He slipped one hand in his pocket while the other brushed against mine.

I turned my hand slightly, my fingertips skimming his knuckles.

"Um, Mom, could you excuse us for a second? We need to sort out some plans for later and whatnot."

"Take your time," my mom said. "I'll use the washroom and catch up with you in a few minutes."

I nodded and allowed Daniel to deliver his "*It was nice to meet you*" speech before I dragged him to the shade of a maple tree.

"I'm sorry I was late," he said. "I had to swing by Patty's to pick up her graduation gift for you. My dad told me they have something for you, too."

"They didn't have to do that. After what your dad just did, I'd say I owe *him* a gift. Did you know he was running the ceremony instead of Elaine?"

"Not until about ten o'clock, right after I texted you. Just think—you will never have to see Elaine Armstrong ever again."

"I'm thrilled, believe me."

He smiled, his eyes drifting to my lips. I could almost taste his mouth, almost feel his tongue against mine. I wanted to step into his arms and press my lips to his, but I didn't have the courage.

"Fuck, is there any chance of getting you alone today? *Really* alone," he murmured, his lips almost brushing my cheek.

"Are you getting fresh with me right in the middle of the Vic quad, Mr. Grant?"

"Honestly, Miss Price? Probably." He straightened and rubbed at his scruff, smiling cheekily. "That dress does amazing things for your ass."

"I'm sorry to disappoint you, but I think my ass might be out of commission for the day."

"So, it's going to be 'look but don't touch'?"

"Don't worry. When I put on my black gown, you won't be able to see a thing."

"I suppose that'll lessen the temptation." He chuckled. "What about tonight? Will you have some free time?"

"My mom and I are going to see *The Sound of Music*. The tickets were a surprise gift from my dad. I won't be done until close to midnight. The next two days look pretty busy too."

His face fell.

"We'll figure out something, sailor."

I reached for his hand without thinking and squeezed it lightly. He raised his eyebrows, and we looked down at our joined fingers before dropping our hands. I glanced over my shoulder self-consciously. This *coming out* business was going to take some practice.

"Um, I should probably head over and get my gown," I said.

"I'll wait for you here?"

"Okay."

I weaved through the crowd, reaching the long row of tables on the other side of the quad where I waited my turn before locating my gown, hood, and processional card. I slipped the gown around my shoulders and folded the white fur hood across my arm. This was it. In approximately three hours, I would be a graduate of U of T. Wowza.

Daniel watched from near the maple tree as I soaked in the moment. As we smiled across the quad at each other, hundreds of memories merged in my mind, the ones from recent months standing out in sharp relief against the rest. I had no idea what to expect in the future, but whatever changes were in store for me, I'd handle them. Daniel was always telling me I could do anything I put my mind to, and after what I'd achieved over the last four years, I had to admit, he was right.

I read the card in my hand, the words written in elegant script under the Victoria College crest.

Aubrey Lynn Price
Bachelor of Arts
Honors Graduate

You kicked some ass, Miss Price, I added quietly.

Truth and Beauty

But from thine eyes my knowledge I derive,
And, constant stars, in them I read such art
As 'Truth and beauty shall together thrive...'
(*Sonnet 14*)

I closed the apartment door, slipping my shoes off with a grateful sigh. Longest. Day. Ever.

Padding quietly to my bedroom, I chuckled at the thunderous snores coming from behind Matt's closed door. Hopefully I'd be sleeping just as deeply very soon. First, though, I had to call Daniel. I hadn't spoken to him since I'd left the post-convocation reception to go for dinner with my mom. He'd made me promise to call him as soon as I got home, regardless of the hour.

I cringed, imagining I was waking him. On the contrary, when he answered, he sounded remarkably awake.

"There's my favorite graduate. How was your evening?"

"Nice, but *very* long. I'm dragging my ass."

"That's too bad. I've been thinking about that ass of yours, and I was hoping you could come out and play."

"What do you mean?"

"I'm downstairs. I've been waiting for you."

"Are you serious?"

"Yep."

"Then get the hell up here!"

"I'd rather you came down."

"Daniel, it's almost midnight."

"I know, but I have a surprise for you. I can't bring it up there."

"Okay, I'll be right down."

I made my way back to the door and slipped on my shoes, trying to ignore the protests of my toes which had wrongly assumed the torture was over. Daniel wasn't in the Jackman lobby. I pushed open the front doors, thinking he'd be right outside. He wasn't.

I peered up and down the street, and then I heard a low whistle coming from the gatehouse. Daniel stepped into the glow of a street-light. Although he was still wearing his dress shirt and trousers, he'd abandoned the jacket and tie. He propped himself against the lamp-post, slipping his hands into his pockets. Sex on legs. I rushed straight into his arms, sighing contentedly. He held me close with one hand, but the other slid down my back until he was cupping my ass cheek.

"Fuck, I've been wanting to do that all day."

"Let me understand this," I said. "I was receiving my honors plaque and my diploma, and all you were thinking about was feeling my ass?"

"That wasn't all I was thinking about, but you looked so gorgeous today. You can't blame my imagination for working overtime. Listen, it won't be your graduation day for much longer. You'd better come with me."

"What's going on?"

"You'll see." He took my hand and guided me through the gate-house and down the steps toward the lower residence houses.

"We're holding hands in the quad," I whispered.

"Feels pretty good, huh?"

"Feels awesome, sailor."

"I wish this was happening in broad daylight instead of midnight, but I'm not about to split hairs," he said.

At the bottom of the stairs, he motioned around the corner. There, nestled in the middle of the Peace Garden, was a row of tea lights glowing on the stone wall around the pond. He'd thrown a blanket on another section of the surrounding ledge. A collection of gift bags was arranged on the ground in front of it.

"Daniel, this is beautiful."

"You think so?" We sat down on the blanket.

"This garden is lovely. I'd forgotten it was here."

"I've only recently discovered it myself. Once I realized we wouldn't get any time alone today, I came up with Plan B." He took my hand in his. "I wanted to carve out some time on your day, just for us, without any interruptions. I know there's no one around, but I wanted to do this out in the open, here at Vic."

"Just because we can?"

"Exactly."

"So, is this our *coming out* party?" I asked.

"I don't know if it's a party, but there are presents." He pointed at the collection of gift bags on the ground. "That's from Patty, and that one's from my mom and dad, but you can open those later. The only one I'd like you to open tonight is mine."

"I thought the necklace was my graduation present."

"Meh. That was just a warm-up. You'll like this. At least I hope so."

As usual, his sincerity disarmed me. Instead of protesting, I rested my head on his shoulder. "I can't imagine not liking a gift from you, sunshine. You're always so thoughtful."

"This might be the best one yet. Are you familiar with Shakespeare's *Sonnet 14*?"

"You know the sonnets aren't my specialty."

"Trust me, you'll like it. I've always thought it was a beautiful poem, but now the words mean something tangible. They make me think of you." He gave me a sly smile. "Would you like me to recite it for you?"

I sat up. "Are you kidding me? Of course!" I almost clapped my hands with excitement.

"All right, here goes."

He took a deep breath and then cradled my cheek as he looked into my eyes. I could feel myself quivering and he hadn't even started yet.

"Aubrey…

'Not from the stars do I my judgment pluck;
And yet methinks I have astronomy,
But not to tell of good or evil luck,
Of plagues, of dearths, or seasons' quality;
Nor can I fortune to brief minutes tell,
Pointing to each his thunder, rain and wind,
Or say with princes if it shall go well,
By oft predict that I in heaven find…'"

He ran his thumb gently under my eye before continuing, his voice softening.

"'But from thine eyes my knowledge I derive,
And, constant stars, in them I read such art
As truth and beauty shall together thrive,
If from thyself to store thou wouldst convert;
Or else of thee this I prognosticate:
Thy end is truth's and beauty's doom and date.'"

He lifted his eyebrows inquisitively as if to say, *How'd I do?*

I hugged him tightly. "Daniel, that's the most beautiful gift anyone's ever given me."

"Oh, *that's* not the gift." He extricated himself from my embrace and reached into his pocket, withdrawing a small blue bag. It was another gift from Tiffany & Co. "Consider the sonnet the gift tag. *This* is the gift."

He tugged the drawstring and held the bag open for me. I lowered my fingers inside the velvet and pulled out a gorgeous bangle. It twinkled with a pinkish cast and three diamonds inlaid near the clasp glittered in the moonlight.

"It's stunning," I breathed. "Rose gold?"

"To go with your necklace."

The roman numerals one to twelve were etched into the outer surface of the bracelet. I traced them with my fingertip. "I love it. What's the significance of the numbers?"

He frowned. "It reminded me of a clock — *time*. That's all we've known for months. Always waiting. Always counting down…"

"Not anymore."

"I know." He gazed down at me thoughtfully. "I suppose it signifies more than just where we've come from. It's a reminder to cherish our time together, to try to be present in every moment."

I pressed my lips together, the emotional peaks of my day finally crashing together.

"I don't know what to say," I whispered, not trusting my voice to make it through the tightness in my throat.

"Don't say anything—at least, not yet. You see, there's more. I had it engraved."

He tilted the bracelet, attempting to show me the words etched inside the band, but it was too dark. I squinted and shook my head.

"Shall I tell you what it says?" he asked.

I nodded, and he tipped my quivering chin up.

"I'm not sure if you believe the words engraved over on Old Vic's south entrance—" his eyes flickered across the quad "—but if the truth *can* make you free, there's something I know." As he spoke, he unclasped the bracelet, held my wrist steady and snapped the clasp closed.

"'*Aubrey, your love is my truth; all my love is yours, in return.*'" He took both of my hands in his. "That's what it says."

Words failed me. There was nothing to do but kiss him, which I did with unrestrained passion.

"Does the invitation to go upstairs with you still stand?" he asked, once I'd given him a chance to come up for air.

"You'd better believe it."

"Good, because kissing you in the Peace Garden is one thing. Making love to you here would be another thing entirely."

And then we were kissing again, but this time he took the lead, his lips gentle and sweet, his tongue slow and deliberate.

"I could live to be a hundred years old and never get tired of kissing you," he said thickly.

"Do you have any idea how much I love you, Daniel?"

He lowered his eyelids and grinned. It was the smile of the victorious, as if winning my love was the most glorious achievement in the world.

"Why don't we go up to your room?" he suggested. "You can tell me all about it—or better yet, show me."

"I have a single bed. There won't be a lot of space."

"Then we'll have to lie *really* close together," he said.

"How do you feel about doing the walk of shame back to your car, sailor?"

I giggled as I put on a pair of pajama bottoms and an oversized T-shirt, ready to take a shower.

"It's only the walk of shame if you're hoping no one sees you." Daniel kicked off the sheets and reached for his boxers. "I'll be doing the epic stride of pride. I intend to walk you all the way to your mom's hotel, holding your hand the entire time and kissing you every twenty feet. I hope I see everyone I know."

He stole a quick kiss and then pinched my ass playfully. "Okay, crazy legs. Your mom's expecting you. You should shower. I'll entertain myself by snooping through your underwear drawer."

I laughed and went to the bathroom. Matt was sitting on his bed pulling on some socks, apparently about to go for a morning run.

"Good morning, cowboy."

"Speak for yourself," he said. "Or maybe I should say *shriek* for yourself. Good times last night?"

"You know it," I said, smiling saucily before locking myself in the bathroom.

When I returned to my room fifteen minutes later, Daniel was dressed and crouched in front of my closet, his head tilted as he scanned the labelled boxes piled inside.

"What are you doing?"

"*High school junk and yearbooks*," he said, reading from one of the taped-up boxes. "Why would you drag all of this stuff with you to university?"

"Where else would I put it?"

He shook his head and blinked at me.

"Daniel, when my mom moved to Vegas, I had to go home and decide what I wanted to keep and what I wanted to toss. This is everything I own."

He stood and spun around, taking in the piles of stuff everywhere. "Of course. Jesus, I'm such a dumbass. Sorry."

"That's okay. Make my bed, and I'll forgive you."

He smiled sheepishly and did as I'd asked while I dressed and quickly blow-dried my hair, my breakfast date with my mom spurring us out the door. In the living room, Matt cast a knowing look in our direction from the couch as he scrolled through his phone messages. Daniel smiled smugly, holding my hand and not letting go, even when we'd reached the street.

This is it. We're out.

When we reached the gatehouse, I tugged his hand.

"Hey. We've walked more than twenty feet, and you haven't kissed me yet. Were you joking upstairs?"

"Hardly. You know I'd kiss you all day long if you'd let me."

"And now you can. Even here in the quad."

He tipped my chin up and kissed me. Smiling, I flung my arms around his shoulders, showering his lips, then his jaw, then his neck with kisses.

"When will I see you again?" he murmured.

"I'm not sure. Sunday afternoon?"

"Sunday afternoon? That's a lifetime away."

"It's two days. You'll live."

"Barely. You know, I don't mind driving you and your mom to the airport," he said. "I can play golf with Bryce another time."

"No, you need this time with your friend. Let's stick with the car service. I'd rather say good-bye to my mom at the hotel. I hate airport good-byes."

"Whatever works best for you."

"Thanks, sunshine. I love you."

"I'm sorry, what was that?" He leaned back and narrowed his eyes. "Did you just say you love me, Aubrey Price?" he yelled. "Because I love you, too!"

"Daniel, what are you doing?"

"Pretending I'm on a rooftop," he said. "I'm desperately in love with you, and I don't care who knows."

Comfort and Despair

Two loves I have, of comfort and despair,
That like two spirits do suggest me still...
(*The Passionate Pilgrim*, Poem II)

Sunday morning, a white Escalade pulled away from the curb with my mother waving madly from the back seat. A whirling sea of emotions battled in my heart. After a great visit, she was returning to pick up where she'd left off in Vegas. And oddly enough, I was okay watching her go. I was making my own way in the world, seeking happiness in things that were important to me. My mother deserved the same consideration. I smiled, comforted by my epiphany, as the car disappeared into Bloor Street traffic.

With my mom safely on her way, I was free to return to Jackman, collect my things, and head back to the condo where I'd wait for Daniel to return from his morning golf game. I texted him as I made the short trip back to residence, though he was only an hour into his round of golf and I knew he probably wouldn't reply.

Morning, sunshine. Mom just left.
On my way back to Jackman to grab my stuff.
Hope you're having fun. -A

I pocketed my phone, but it vibrated almost immediately. I perched on the steps in front of the museum to read his response.

"Fun" might not be the best word... -D

Uh-oh. I'm afraid to ask... -A

Wish I'd hit the driving range this week.
I'm so rusty I'm considering getting
a tetanus shot on the way home. -D

Sorry to hear that. Are you having fun anyway? -A

I am. Trying not to get frustrated,
but sand is not my friend today.
Water? Apparently not my friend either. -D

Oh no... -A

And have I mentioned holes?
Also not my friend. -D

I snorted as I considered the dirty implications of what he'd just written.

I can't believe you just said that. -A

There are certain exceptions to that last claim. ;)
Sorry, I have to go, poppet. Further humiliation awaits.
See you later. I miss you. -D

I miss you too, sunshine.
I'll be waiting at the condo when you're done.
Hope the sand, water, and...um...
"holes" get friendlier... xo -A

I put my phone in my pocket once again and resumed my trek back to residence. I'm not sure what I expected to find when I walked through the door, but it certainly wasn't the piles of clothes, backpacks, and boxes stacked inside the doorway.

I dropped my bag and went in search of answers. Jo dragged me into her room, telling me she was so glad I was back.

"What's going on?" I asked.

"I wish you'd been here last night. It was awful."

"What was?" I dropped onto the bed beside her. "What's all that stuff in the front hall?"

"It's Sarah's."

"Is she moving out?"

"*Moved*," Jo clarified. "Actually, more like *turfed*. Matt and Sarah are finished."

"What?"

I didn't know why I sounded so surprised to hear that Sarah and Matt had broken up. I'd be lying if I said I hadn't seen this coming, but I'd been holding out hope that I was misreading the writing on the wall, for Matt's sake.

"What happened? Did she do something? Did they have a fight?"

"It's not that she suddenly did something. It's more what she's been doing for weeks."

"Meaning?"

"The whole time Sarah was living here, she was using Matt so she'd have a place to crash while she looked for a job. She didn't want to spend money on an apartment if she ended up not being able to find work in Toronto. Getting back together with Matt was all an act."

"Oh, *no*." I put my hand over my mouth. Matt — the kindest, most loyal boyfriend a girl could ask for, and she'd taken advantage of his generosity. "What a bitch."

"Totally." Jo nodded earnestly. "Even her best friend thought so. She called Matt to tip him off. She couldn't stand to watch anymore."

"Shit. So, he confronted her?"

"Last night."

"Where were you?"

"In here. At first I didn't know anything was going on. But then Matt started taking her stuff and piling it by the door. She was shrieking, asking him what he was doing and where he expected her to go. He said he didn't give a you-know-what where she went and if she didn't get out, he'd throw all her stuff out the window."

"Oh, Jesus. Poor Matt. And poor *you*. Were you mortified?"

"I didn't know what to do. Sarah took some of her stuff, and Matt told her she'd better get the rest of it quickly or she'd be buying it back from Goodwill. I tried to comfort him, but I know he wished you were here."

"I would've come back if I'd known. My mom and I stayed up late talking, but I could've easily come back here to sleep."

"It was your mom's last night in town. Matt knew that. I said I'd call you, but he wouldn't let me. He'll be happy to see you this morning, though."

"Is he around?"

"He went out for a run earlier, but he's already back and showered. He might be in his room."

That was a good sign. Better than consuming vast quantities of edible oil product and drinking beer in front of the TV like last time. Jo stopped me as I reached for the doorknob.

"Go easy on him, Aubrey. I know you guys are good friends and you try to make light of stuff, but he was a mess last night."

I nodded and headed out to the hallway. Matt's door was ajar, and his room was empty. I found him in the kitchen, slumped against the counter and staring vacantly at a spot on the cupboard. Dark circles under his eyes betrayed his lack of sleep.

"Hey, cowboy?"

I put my hand on his shoulder, and he shook his head and blinked.

"Hey, sorry. I was zoned out I guess."

"You're reeling, huh?"

"Jo told you what happened?"

I nodded. "You okay?"

"Don't worry, Aubs. I'll be fine."

"Do you want to talk?" I offered, aimlessly picking up flecks of sugar from the counter with my finger and dropping them into the sink.

"I don't know." He dropped his head, dragging his hands through his hair.

"Hey," I said, trying to peer into his eyes. He responded by stepping into my arms. I rubbed his back and listened to his unsteady breathing. We stood like that for a long time, but eventually he pulled away and averted his face, rinsing out a coffee cup and a small plate and placing them in the dish rack. As he dried his hands, he stared into the sink as if some words of wisdom might come whispering out of the drain if he concentrated hard enough. Finally, he turned to look at me.

"Would you come for a walk with me? I need to get out of here."

"Of course."

Together we went to Charles Street where I put my hands on my hips and squinted up at the late morning sun.

"Where to?"

He bobbed his head toward Bay Street. "Doesn't matter."

We fell in step and headed east. I waited for him to speak, not sure if he felt like talking at all. Somehow, I seemed to have forgotten how to navigate the subtleties of our complicated friendship.

"This isn't the end of the world. I know that," he said at last, jamming his hands into his pockets, a gesture that seemed to belie the confidence behind his words.

"Breaking up isn't easy, Matt. It's okay to be sad."

"Honestly, I've been preparing myself for this for a while. Sarah's not the same. The way we've been together for the last month and a half…She was different. I *knew* something wasn't right, but I kept trying to convince myself I was imagining things, that if I kept trying, things would get better."

I sighed and shook my head. Stupid Sarah. I hated her for what she'd done. This was the second time I'd watched Matt deal with the aftermath of a breakup with her, and I wanted nothing more than to kick her ass.

"Don't blame yourself. Maybe she couldn't handle the living-together thing. Or maybe you've grown apart. That's not all that strange at our age."

I was grasping. Jo had made it clear that Sarah had been using Matt, but I didn't know what else to say. He'd loved her. As much as I wanted to curse her name and rake her over the coals, I couldn't bring myself to be that insensitive. He shrugged noncommittally, and I found myself rambling.

"Hey, we've gone from partying, to realizing we needed to get good grades, to graduating, and now looking for jobs. We're growing up. I guess some people change more than others during that process. There's not much you can do. It's kind of futile to compare who she is now with who she used to be."

He stopped and looked directly up at the sky, taking a giant cleansing breath before looking at me, his eyes heavy with emotion.

"I'm not comparing her with who she used to be, Aubs. I'm comparing her with who I wish she could be." He took one of my hands in his. "I'm comparing her with *you*."

Daniel

CHAPTER 22

Pursuit and Possession

Mad in pursuit, and in possession so;
Had, having, and in quest to have, extreme;
A bliss in proof, —and prov'd, a very woe;
Before, a joy propos'd; behind, a dream.
(*Sonnet 129*)

"Holy shit, Jer, I was wondering if I'd ever talk to you again." I pinched my phone between my shoulder and my ear as I heaved my golf bag out of the trunk. "Everyone's been worried."

"Sorry," he said. "I've had a lot going on. Now that everything's set, I can tell you about it."

"I'm listening."

"When we go over to the UK for the wedding, I've arranged to meet Anita…the driver, you know, the one who wrote the letter."

I leaned against the car, allowing his words to sink in. "Why the hell would you do that?"

"See, this is why I kept it to myself. I knew everyone would try to talk me out of it. The ticket's booked, though. It's a done deal. I'm flying down to meet her in the south of France. She's driving up from Spain."

I sighed and rubbed my temple. "What are you hoping to accomplish, Jer? The whole thing sounds traumatic."

"I need to do this. Think of it as closure."

"Can't you get closure some other way? Write her a letter? Talk to her on the phone?"

"I've already done both."

"And?"

"I felt good about things, but I could tell she didn't. She's lived with the guilt of what she's done her whole life."

Was he for real? Rather than focusing on the implications of the accident on *his* life, he was concerned about *her*. Jesus.

"So, this trip isn't about closure for you at all, is it?"

"It's about forgiveness, bro."

"Fuck, Jer." I shook my head, baffled by his ability to bestow kindness on this woman who'd taken his birth parents from him. "Have you told Mom and Dad?"

"I called them last night. Mom's freaked out. She wants to come with me."

"Which you didn't agree to."

"I don't need anyone holding my hand. Look, I have to do this. What's the point of being a forgiving person if you don't actually forgive people? I need to put things right."

How could I argue with that? His generosity was mind-boggling.

"Will you go before or after the wedding?"

"I've booked a connecting flight as soon as we arrive in the UK. You guys are all going to be busy—"

"Too busy to insist on joining you."

"I'm not trying to be difficult, Daniel," he said firmly, "but I'm not a kid anymore. I know what I'm doing. Once I deal with this, I can truly move on."

"What about Julie? You're going while she's at her dance showcase in Germany. Don't you want her there with you?"

"I love Julie, but this is about who I am as a person, not who we are as a couple."

His words were emphatic. This was not a whim. He'd given this a lot of thought.

"I admire you for what you're doing. If there's anything at all I can —"

"You'll be the first to know. Look, I need to jet."

"Fair enough. Thanks for keeping me in the loop."

After we hung up, I rubbed my aching shoulder and went upstairs. Dropping my golf bag in the front hall closet, I had two goals in mind: first, I needed a beer; next, I needed a massage. Perhaps I could convince Aubrey to give me a back rub. Within a minute of being in the condo, the first goal was addressed. Within two, I realized the massage would have to wait. Aubrey wasn't back. Surely she had to be on her way. Her mother had left hours ago.

When I called her, I discovered that not only was she *not* on her way, but she hadn't even left Jackman.

"Why are you still there?" I said. "Is everything all right?"

"Everything's fine. Hang on a sec, okay?" There was some rustling and then a door closing. "Hey, sorry I haven't called. Things are crazy here. Matt and Sarah broke up. Turns out she was using him so she'd have a place to crash. He's a mess."

"Shit, you're kidding."

I felt bad for him, but also a twinge of annoyance. A happily-in-love Matt was a busy Matt. A single Matt was the last thing I needed.

"The bottom fell out last night when I was with my mom. I missed the fireworks, but I made it back in time for cleanup duties."

"So, he's upset?"

"I wouldn't say upset as much as angry. The last time they broke up, he was as useful as a house plant for a few days. I think he's bypassed the gloomy stage this time."

"So, how do *you* fit into all this?"

"I want to be here for him."

"What does that mean?"

I waited for her answer, wishing I didn't feel so aggravated. Wishing Sarah hadn't been an opportunistic bitch. Wishing I wasn't an egocentric prick.

"I don't know for sure," she said. "Sarah could come by any time to pick up her stuff. I want to be here when she does."

"And if you're not?"

She paused. "He was there for me, Daniel. When I needed him, he was a rock—when your parents took you to the cottage, through all that shit with Cara. Don't forget how he went out on a limb for us after our fight. He brought us back together. I owe him...*He needs me.*"

I stopped short of telling her I needed her too—that it wasn't the same here without her—that I needed her in my bed to chase off my bad dreams. That would be playing dirty. She was intent on helping Matt because she thought she owed him, but I owed him as well, so I surrendered.

"Does this mean you won't be coming back tonight?"

"I'll stay here until Sarah's grabbed the rest of her stuff," she said. "Could be tonight, could be tomorrow, I don't know. You understand, right?"

"Of course. At least I'm trying to." I pounded my forehead with my fist. "I just...Fuck, this sucks. I miss you being here."

"I miss being there too, sweet-knees."

Her soft voice and that crazy nickname knocked the wind out of my sails.

"You'll keep me posted?"

"Of course I will. You'll get tired of hearing from me."

"I doubt that."

After we'd hung up, I stared into space, recalling the nights I'd spent alone at the condo while she'd been immersed in her life at Vic. The thought of more solitary nights was not appealing. But if there was one thing I'd learned about Aubrey in the time we'd been together, it was that she would *always* put herself out to try to make others happy. If I was going to love her for her selflessness, I had to accept that I wouldn't be the only person benefitting from her generous spirit.

In the end, I did the only thing I could do—I gave myself a virtual slap on the side of the head and finished my beer. Then I took a long, hot shower.

Aubrey kept in touch during her stay at Jackman. Unfortunately, Sarah was being noncommittal about picking up her belongings. I was tempted to tell Aubrey I'd jam Sarah's crap into the back of my car and deliver it to her personally, but I didn't articulate this selfish offer. I gave Aubrey the space she needed to be a compassionate friend. I didn't insist on dropping by to see her, I didn't beg her to join me for lunch or to sneak away to spend the night. I was the epitome of the supportive boyfriend.

In the meantime, I caught up with my family. I swung by to see my parents on Monday night, and I played the dutiful grandson on Tuesday, taking Patty out for dinner. I saw her safely home afterward, declining her offer of a cup of tea, claiming I needed to get back to the condo to work on my paper. Not one to mince words, Patty plugged in the kettle and asked me pointedly if that meant I needed to get back to sulking.

"I'm not sulking, Patty." I settled into a kitchen chair, watching her drop a spoonful of sugar into her teacup.

"Yes, you are. Your grandfather used to get that same woebegone look when I'd leave to play bridge. *'Don't you worry about me, Henny,'* he'd say. *'I'll manage just fine here...alone.'* Made me feel horrid for leaving him, but I knew as soon as I was gone, he'd be into the scotch and watching *Jeopardy,* quite happy not to have me prattling in his ear."

I laughed. "I admit it's nice to have some time alone occasionally, but there's a difference between popping out for a few hours and being gone for days at a time—"

"You know perfectly well she'd rather be with you. She's doing a kindness for a friend. Don't sully that with jealousy."

"I know." I rubbed my eyes in frustration. "I don't begrudge her the time with Matt and Joanna. I just wish—"

"You wish what? That you didn't have to share her? Or that she'd run to you every five minutes to reassure you of her feelings?"

"You make me sound like a petulant child."

Patty sat across from me and clasped my hand. "That's not my intention."

I looked at her skeptically, and she narrowed her eyes. Now I was in for it.

"You know how fond your grandfather was of kite analogies, Daniel."

"I know the quotation you had engraved on his bench was a favorite," I said.

"I'm thinking more about what he used to say about kite flying and relationships. '*A kite is beautiful and pretty to hold,*' he'd say. '*But a kite is meant to fly. It's most lovely when it's up in the sky. When everyone stops to watch, you'll feel proud knowing it's your kite they're admiring. But while everyone's eyes are cast skyward in admiration, that string is wrapped securely around your fingers, regardless of how high the kite soars. When the wind dies, you'll draw the string in, and then you'll be the sole witness to its beauty.*'"

I squeezed her fingers. "Thanks, Patty."

"Don't thank *me*. Thank your grandfather," she said.

I nodded and smiled, glancing at the ceiling.

"What are you looking up there for?" Patty asked, frowning play-fully. "He's not sitting on the roof." She placed her hand over my heart. "He's right there, silly boy."

I stared at my laptop screen later that night, thinking about Patty's words. The kite flying analogy was right, but she'd misunderstood. I wasn't questioning Aubrey's feelings for me, and I wasn't angry with her for spending time with her friends. I wasn't even worried that she was allowing Matt to monopolize her time. I knew she loved me, and I trusted her unequivocally. I was frustrated. It was as simple as that.

With Aubrey's graduation behind us, we were free to be together, but instead of moving forward, we were still apart. We'd shared a couple of kisses in the Vic quad the morning after her convocation, and then everything had come to a grinding standstill.

It was like being in a bad dream where you feel like you're run-ning but never actually going anywhere. I was tired of spinning my wheels. Now with my anxiety rearing its ugly head again and recur-ring dreams disturbing my sleep, a blanket of unease had settled around my shoulders.

I logged onto Facebook, catching up with a few friends overseas but stopping myself from checking Nicola's profile. I'd foolishly found myself returning to her page several times over the past couple of weeks, and the things I'd learned from perusing her wall had left me feeling wretched. If only her privacy controls had been higher, I never would have discovered the abysmal state of her life. I certainly wasn't in the right frame of mind to visit her page now. There was no point in torturing myself.

Instead, I clicked on Aubrey's profile to find she'd added a new album dedicated to her convocation day. Her mom had taken numerous pictures of Aubrey posing with her diploma and several group pictures of her with Matt and Jo and her other friends from Vic.

Then, in the mix, there was a candid photo of the two of us at the reception in the Hart House quad. I remembered the moment. I'd been telling her how proud I was. She was smiling, her chin turned up in that half-shy, half-confident way she had.

While the casual observer wouldn't notice anything overtly romantic about the picture, to me, it spoke volumes. After all, we'd shared these types of intimate moments for endless weeks, always surrounded by crowds of people. I stared at the photo for a long time, and then with a couple of clicks, I tagged us both, bringing the picture onto my own profile in the process.

I waited for a sensation of impending doom to wash over me, my hand on the mouse as I waffled over whether to remove the tags, but instead of panicking about my decision or feeling anxious about the potential repercussions, I felt completely at ease. When my phone rang beside me, I smiled as I answered.

"There's my beautiful girl. I was just thinking about you."

"I know. I just received an interesting Facebook alert. Thought I'd better make sure you haven't been drinking."

"I'm jober as a sudge, Ossifer."

She laughed, but I could hear the wariness in her tone.

"You think tagging it was a bad idea?" I asked.

"As long as you're okay with it being on your profile, I'm thrilled."

"I feel great about it. It's a big step forward."

"It is pretty huge."

Frankly, the size of the step was irrelevant. As long as we were moving forward, I was happy.

In my dream, I was a spectator, surrounded by others who'd come to watch. Sadistic voyeurs, they shouted obscenities at the girl whose

head had been placed sideways on the large stone. I didn't shout. I was confused.

What did she do?

I asked the man standing beside me what the girl's crime had been. He shrugged in answer and continued yelling at the accused who was now sobbing, her whole body shaking as she scanned the crowd.

Then her eyes found mine, and she mouthed my name. She knew me? How?

She needed to talk to me.

I tried to shove my way through the crowd, but unyielding bodies pushed back.

"Let me through," I pleaded. "She needs to speak to me. Let me by!"

I struggled and wrestled with the barricade of people, but my passage was blocked at every turn. The executioner shouldered a large axe and flattened his boot to the side of her face as she screamed my name.

I shouted back, "I can't get through! They won't let me through!"

Large black birds flew at my head. I pushed and pushed, batting at the birds helplessly. My frustration turned to panic when my wrists were bound and a hood dropped over my head. I was immobilized. Blind. Was I to meet the executioner's blade as well?

"Let me go!" I shouted into the darkness, trying to wrench myself free. "Let me go!"

"Shh, Daniel — it's okay. It's me. It's Aubrey."

Aubrey?

Confused, I wrestled with the sheets, and then I felt hands taking mine, fingers prying the material from my closed fists, gentle lips at my ear.

"Calm down. You're okay. It was just a dream."

"Aubrey?"

"Yes, it's me."

"But you're not here."

"Daniel, I'm *right here.*"

She took one of my hands, bringing it to rest on her warm cheek. Was this real?

"You're here…"

"Yes, it's me, I'm right here."

Her lips and her soft hands moving across my body were *very* real. I fell against the pillow, keeping her close, not wanting to break away from her kiss, needing to stay joined to her as if she were my only connection to the world beyond my dreams.

"Thank God." I moved with her as she rolled onto her back.

"Are you okay?" she whispered into the darkness.

"I am now."

I dissolved into her kisses again, slipping my hand between her silky thighs. She moaned, but the tension in her body didn't dissipate.

"Daniel, are you sure you're all right?" she breathed.

"I need you."

She didn't answer, instead relaxing against the pillows as she wrapped her legs around me and angled her hips to meet mine.

We made love in the darkness, peaceful and unhurried, my left hand clutching her right hand as we moved. My fingers slipped between our bodies to caress her. She urgently responded to my touch as I increased the speed of my fingers.

At last, her mouth opened against my lips and she gasped. "Come with me," she pleaded. Her nails dug into my shoulder blade, and she clenched and trembled beneath me. The world dissolved with my own release, and I thought I might cry with relief. Aubrey was back. I rested my head on her shoulder and expelled a long, shaky breath.

"You had a nightmare," she said.

"It was nothing. I'm fine."

"It didn't sound like nothing," she persisted.

I propped myself up on my elbow, glad she couldn't see my face in the darkness.

"Sometimes when you're not here, I have bad dreams," I admitted. "It's not a big deal. If I'd known you were coming back tonight, I would've stayed up and waited. I'm glad you're here now."

"I thought Sarah would've come by today. I waited up with Matt until ten, but then he crashed. I missed you so much after we talked on the phone earlier that I couldn't stay away. I'll head back over in the morning."

"I'll drive you."

"That would be nice, thanks."

She yawned, and I felt the rise and fall of her chest beneath me. I kissed her forehead and rolled beside her. "You sound tired."

"I'm bagged. I'll be right back, okay?"

She crossed the room and flicked on the bathroom light, hesitating in the doorway for a moment, worry etched in her brow. I smiled back, an attempt to convince her I was fine. She sighed as she closed the bathroom door behind her.

Was I fine?

Lying back on the pillow, I rubbed my wrists to erase the lingering effects of my dream. The face of the girl from my nightmare took shape in the darkness, her features twisted as she screamed my name.

Nicola.

No, I decided. I *wasn't.*

Two nights later, I was alone again. I folded laundry, focusing my attention on the task as if finding the center fold of every T-shirt was integral to the continued existence of man. It was alarming how comforting I found these mundane chores. When my phone rang, I leapt on it, grateful for the escape from my dark thoughts.

"Hey, D-man, it's Brad."

"Brad, what's going on? I've been trying to reach you."

"Sorry about that. I just got your messages. You know how it is. Busy, busy, same bullshit, different day."

"I hear ya. So, what do you think? Do you want to head over to Mom and Dad's with us tomorrow night? Maybe grab a taxi together or something?"

"Normally I'd say sure, but we have all this stuff to do before we head over. We'll probably catch up with you there."

"Sure, that's cool. No worries."

"You looking forward to the birthday bash?"

"Fuck, please tell me Mom and Dad don't have anything crazy planned."

"Nah, I'm just playin'. Far as I know, it's just family."

"Good. I don't think I could deal with more than that right now."

"You okay? You sound tense."

"It's all this shit with Aubrey and her out-of-control loyalty to Matt. It's making me batshit crazy."

"You don't think he's giving her the wheels, do you? She wouldn't stick around if that was the case."

I contemplated his question and shook my head resolutely. "No, if he was making moves, she'd split. If only he'd get over this girl who dumped him and let Aubrey and I get on with our lives. I have half a mind to go over there right now and talk to him myself—"

"I wouldn't do that if I were you, bro."

"I wouldn't really do it. I'm just venting."

"He'll get his shit together soon and everything'll be back to normal. Look, sorry, dude, but I'm on the fly. We'll see you tomorrow?"

"Yeah, see you then."

I hung up and lugged the laundry to the bedroom, Brad's question ringing in my ears.

You don't think he's giving her the wheels...?

I had to believe Matt knew Aubrey was out of bounds. I also had to trust that she'd tell me if he'd crossed a line, or at least get the hell out of there so he wouldn't interpret her good will as something more than a friend's concern.

As I put my T-shirts away, I glanced at the bed. I didn't relish the thought of another restless night. Might Aubrey consider coming back to the condo tonight as she had on Tuesday? I'd stayed out of her way all week. It wouldn't hurt to ask, would it? Abandoning the laundry, I strode back out to the kitchen and grabbed my phone. She answered on the fifth ring.

"Hi, sunshine, I was about to call you."

"Are you all right? You sound out of breath."

"Yeah, I'm fine. Sarah's stuff is gone, sailor. I know it's almost ten, but can you come and get me? I think I'm good to go."

I had my shoes on and my keys in my hand before she'd even finished speaking.

"Give me twenty minutes."

In the end, I was parked at the curb on Charles Street within fourteen minutes, racing through the front doors to press the buzzer. Aubrey's voice echoed around the lobby.

"Is that you already?"

"Yep. Let me in?"

"I'm coming down. Be right there."

I wandered outside and leaned against the hood of my car. When she emerged, she smiled brightly and hurried down the path, sliding her bag onto the ground and leaping into my arms.

"Hi," she said, burrowing into my neck. "Thanks for getting here so quickly."

I took her face in my hands and gave her a long, slow kiss, relieved to have her back. When I dropped a soft kiss on her forehead and tried to pull away, she wrapped her arms around my shoulders again, squeezing tightly. Was I mistaken, or was she crying?

"Hey, are you okay?"

She nodded against my neck and then stepped back, running her fingers under her eyes.

"I'm fine. Hormones, I guess. Sorry."

"Don't apologize. You've had quite a week. I would've come upstairs to say hi to Matt—to lend my support. We still could—" I gestured to the building.

"No, it's okay," she said hurriedly, trying to smile as she brushed off my offer. "Anyway, he's not there. He went out."

She picked up her bag and turned toward the car, purposely avoiding my gaze. I sighed as I held the door open for her, worried about her tearful outburst, but even more concerned about what was going on with Matt and why she was lying about it.

As soon as we got home, Aubrey fell into bed. I was happy to turn in early too. We crawled under the sheets, both of us sighing contentedly. I smoothed her hair and pulled her back to my chest, listening to her gentle breathing as she gripped my hand and tucked it under her chin.

I hadn't questioned her during the car ride home, but something wasn't right. Something had happened at Jackman, and she was keeping it from me.

"Aubrey?" I whispered into the darkness.

"Mmm?"

"Is everything okay?"

"Everything's fine," she murmured.

"Are you sure?"

She shifted onto her back, still clinging to my hand.

"I'm sorry, sunshine. I'm just really tired."

"I don't mean 'why aren't we having sex.' You just don't seem yourself. When you got in the car earlier, it seemed like something had happened."

"I'm exhausted. I just need a good sleep." She reached up, finding my lips and kissing me tenderly. "You need a good sleep too. Tomorrow'll be a long day."

"You're right." I waited for her to shift back into position, wrapping myself snugly around her.

"I love you," she said.

"I love you. I'm glad you're back."

"Me, too."

I could feel her smiling against my hand which she was now holding tightly against her cheek. I squeezed her fingers in return, thinking about Patty's advice—my grandfather's kite metaphor. Aubrey was back in my arms, and right now, she was all mine.

I examined my reflection in the mirror. It seemed impossible that I was turning twenty-seven. In my head, I'd always be seventeen years old and eager to please my father, as if that was the only way I could achieve true happiness. The sooner I rid myself of that notion the better. Here I was, closer to thirty than twenty, and still feeling the weight of his expectations on my shoulders. As I'd done so many times over the years, I wondered why I couldn't be like Brad—comfortable in my skin and oblivious to paternal disapproval. Life would be so much fucking easier.

The lines around my eyes spoke volumes. This past year hadn't been kind—my own fault, of course, for allowing everything to get to me. I made a birthday resolution: I would work harder at relaxing and re-centering myself.

The last few days had been a reality check. As much as I loved having Aubrey in my life, I had to give her space. I couldn't merely endure our time apart; I needed to accept it — maybe even try to enjoy it. Now that she was back, all I wanted to do was revel in our time together. As far as I was concerned, the sooner we put this birthday dinner behind us, the sooner we'd be home enjoying some private festivities.

Aubrey perched on the edge of the bed, fastening the buckle on one of her shoes, an incredibly sexy high-heeled sandal with thin straps.

Please, God, I thought as I watched her uncross and re-cross her bare legs to attend to the other shoe, *make the night be over quickly.*

Aubrey

CHAPTER 23

Merriment

…frame your mind to mirth and merriment,
Which bars a thousand harms and lengthens life.
(*The Taming of the Shrew*, Introduction, Scene 2)

D aniel stopped me on the pathway leading to his parents' backyard. "Promise me there's nothing crazy waiting back there. This isn't some outlandish surprise party, right?"

"It's just family," I assured him. "No outlandish surprises, I promise."

Well, maybe one, but I wasn't about to tip my hand.

In the backyard, we were met by a chorus of greetings. Daniel received kisses and handshakes from his family, thoroughly relieved to see that his mother hadn't organized a spectacular event in his honor. Julie sprang up and gave me a hug. I squeezed her back just as hard. Lord, I'd missed her.

When Daniel leaned over to kiss her rather formally on the cheek, she blushed and caught my eye. I could only imagine what she must have been thinking.

Mr. Shmexy just planted a wet one on me.

David took drink orders, and we wandered over to the patio to sit down. That's when I realized someone was missing.

"Hey, where's Patty?"

"She's taken Gerald up to the cottage with his daughter and grandchildren," Gwen said. "She feels bad about not being here for your birthday, Daniel, but she told me you two had dinner on Tuesday night?"

"We had a good visit. I'm glad she's spending time with Gerald and his family."

Gwen smiled tartly and summoned David to join her in the house. I wondered if she was equally as amenable to her mother's absence and the reason for it.

"Don't let me eat any more of these samosas," Julie said, slapping her own hand. "I'll never fit into my showcase costume if I keep pigging out."

"Tell me about it," Penny moaned. "Why does stress always make me eat? I had a fitting for my wedding dress yesterday. Bloody stupid thing. I should have picked one with an elastic waist."

Brad sighed as he slung his arm around his bride-to-be.

"Ah, babe, ya gotta love planning weddings. Invitations and dresses and speeches and first dances — it's enough to drive anyone to frigging drink."

"Yeah, how is the speech coming along, Brad?" Daniel asked.

Brad rolled his eyes. "I've got about five words written. Good — eve-ning — ladies — and — gentlemen," he said, counting on his fingers.

Daniel laughed, but before he could harass his brother further, Gwen appeared at the patio doors, her hands full of gift bags. David followed with a large parcel.

"We thought we'd get presents out of the way before dinner," Gwen announced.

Daniel rubbed his hands together eagerly. How adorable was he? A fluttering in my stomach alerted me to my own excitement. Daniel would have a coronary when he saw my gift — we'd decided to save it for last.

Daniel opened his grandmother's present first. "Apparently, this is from Gramps too," he said, briefly scanning the card.

"Dude, is that a kite?" Jeremy asked, peering over the arm of his chair as Daniel tore open the package.

"Patty told me you'd understand what it was about," David said.

THE TRUEST OF WORDS

Daniel smiled wistfully. "Yes, I do." He handed me the red heart-shaped kite. "I'll explain later."

"Give him the big one next," Brad suggested.

David carefully maneuvered a large gift in front of Daniel. It was obviously a picture or painting of some sort, one of those gifts that can't be disguised, even when wrapped.

"There's no card," Jeremy explained. "It's from all of us."

"Do you know what this is?" Daniel asked me.

"Nope. I'm just as curious as you are. Hurry up."

Daniel stuck his finger into the middle of the paper and ripped.

"Wow, you guys, that's beautiful," I said, not even taking in Daniel's reaction, too wrapped up in my own assessment of the piece.

Jeremy crouched in front of the painting. "We bought it at the gallery in the Distillery District. It's from a collection called *Weightlessness*. The title of this piece is *Free*. I thought it was appropriate."

Daniel nodded, still staring at the painting. "I love it. It'll look great in the living room. Thank you, everyone."

David hopped up and moved the painting out of the way, and Daniel held up a small striped bag.

"That's from us," Julie said. "I picked it out."

Daniel smiled as he waded through the tissue and pulled the gift free.

"Hold them up," Julie requested.

"Boxers?" Daniel laughed. "That's cheeky."

"Read the words written on them," Jeremy said.

"'*Thou reedy-wheeling ripe coxcomb*,'" Daniel read. Flipping them around, he tilted his head. "'*Thou art a ragged wart.*' Perfect! Shakespearean insults. These will come in handy in the fall. When students say something stupid, I'll just refer them to my underwear."

He looked over at his dad, who was smiling wryly.

"Or not," Daniel amended, clearing his throat. "Thanks, guys. Okay, last one."

"That one's from us," Brad said. "Aubrey tipped us off."

Daniel stuck his hand inside the bag, pulling out a book.

"'*Eyewitness Travel Guides: The Netherlands*,'" he read. "What…?"

He shook his head, confused. This had Penny written all over it. There was no telling her anything in confidence. She was such a shit.

GEORGINA GUTHRIE

"Aubrey and I were chatting on the phone, and she mentioned you'd developed this sudden fascination with the Netherlands," she said. "We thought maybe a travel book would be interesting, since you seem so keen on visiting."

How is she keeping a straight face?

Daniel chuckled. "I have developed an avid interest in the place," he said. "I promise to dive right in as soon as I get home. Very thoughtful, thank you." He winked at Penny. "And thanks, everyone. This was all great—"

"Wait, there's one more," Brad said, leaning forward in his chair.

"That's right. You still have to open mine," I reminded him.

"I figured you were saving that until tomorrow," he said, squeezing my hand.

"I'd kind of like to give it to you tonight. You can open it now—if we have time before dinner." I looked at Gwen for confirmation.

"Plenty of time," she assured me. "Go ahead."

Brad fished his car keys from his pocket, and I grabbed Daniel's hand. "We have to go out front."

He looked at me curiously. "Okay."

I peeked over my shoulder as we followed Brad to the gate. Everyone smiled expectantly. Julie was tapping her feet excitedly.

My sentiments exactly, bun-head.

Out on the driveway, there was nothing noteworthy going on. Daniel frowned.

"What are you up to, poppet?"

"Patience, sailor." I nodded at Brad, who'd been waiting for my signal to open the garage door.

"Hey, close your eyes, bro," Brad suggested.

Daniel complied, crossing his arms uncomfortably. "You two are freaking me out."

"You're going to like this," I told him.

I hope.

Five days of planning, organizing, and hard work had gone into this surprise, not to mention a few fibs and a crap-load of soul searching. He'd better like it. Brad climbed into his truck. The engine roared to life, and he slowly backed out of the garage.

I slipped my hand around Daniel's forearm. His eyes were scrunched closed, brows furrowed together.

"Okay, sunshine," I whispered. "Open your eyes."

His eyes flickered open, and I held my breath as he looked at the back of Brad's pickup truck, his expression shifting from confusion to stunned understanding. He took two steps forward and stopped, slowly turning to glance at me and then at Brad, who had cut the engine and climbed out of the truck.

Brad flashed me a dimpled smile, but Daniel seemed dumbstruck. He moved to the back of the truck, touching the large red bow and unhooking the tarp to run his hands across the row of boxes, each one labelled clearly in permanent marker. He stopped at one with the words *"High school junk/Yearbooks"* written across the side and froze, his hands flat on the box and his head bowed. Brad bobbed his head at his brother.

"I think he's in shock," he whispered.

I touched his back. "Daniel?"

He spun around, hugging me and burying his face in my neck. Over Daniel's shoulder, I watched Brad back away, holding up his hands as if to say, *I'll just give you guys a minute.* I rubbed my hand across Daniel's shoulders, waiting for him to say something. Finally, he took a deep breath and stepped back.

"Is this what I think it is? These are all of your things?"

"Everything," I confirmed, my smile hesitant. "Brad's going to bring the truck to the condo tomorrow and help us unpack it. What do you think?"

"What do I think? What do I *think?* Are you kidding me?"

He laughed as he hugged me again, lifting me off the ground and spinning me around. I giggled, caught up in his elation. When he finally set me back on my feet, he held my face in his hands.

"I don't know what to say. I can't believe it. How the hell did this happen?"

"I was stumped. Your birthday was coming, and I couldn't help wondering, *what do you get the guy who has everything?"*

"A pickup truck full of boxes, garment bags, and suitcases?" he suggested, bending to kiss me softly.

"Along with the girl who owns it all," I added. "Happy birthday, sweet-knees."

He held my hands against his chest, regarding me solemnly.

"Okay…don't get me wrong, I'm ecstatic, but this is more than a gift for the guy who's hard to buy for. This is huge for you." He propped himself against the truck, drawing me against him. "Where's this coming from all of a sudden?"

"I don't know. My mom and I talked about us and our relationship when she was here. Initially, she's the one who got me thinking, but what sealed the deal was something Matt said last Sunday when we were talking about his breakup. He was complaining about how he wished Sarah could be like *me*."

Daniel's eyes flickered across mine nervously. "Wait, he didn't try—"

I put my fingers to his lips before he could give words to his fears. "I thought the same thing at first. But then he explained what he meant. He said he was amazed by how steadfast we've been in our feelings for each other despite all the crap we've gone through. He wished Sarah could have been half as committed to him as I was to you. As soon as he said that, my heart fell because I wasn't completely committed to you, was I? I was holding back."

I wrapped my arms around him.

"I wanted to do something that would show you how much I love you and prove that I have faith in you—in us. With your birthday coming up, this seemed perfect."

Daniel swiftly captured my lips and then turned to survey the truck again, hands on his hips.

"This is a lot of stuff."

"It would have been more if Matt and Jo hadn't helped me go through everything this week. Matt and I took a ton of donations to Goodwill on Thursday morning."

"And Brad? When did he come by to get everything?"

"Thursday night."

Daniel smirked and shook his head, slipping his arm around my shoulders. "I had a hard time reaching him on Thursday night."

"He was at Jackman when he called you back. He was great, sunshine. He was so excited. Your whole family was thrilled. Keeping the secret was killing me. I almost told you everything on Tuesday night. After that nightmare you had, it was so hard not to tell you."

"I'm glad you didn't tell me. This is one of the best surprises I've ever had. So, all week, I thought you were helping Matt, but really he was helping you."

"We were helping each other. I did want to be there for him when Sarah came to get her stuff. She finally came over Wednesday afternoon, and I would've headed to the condo on Wednesday night, but it was my last night with Matt and Jo. It was kind of emotional," I admitted, remembering the feeling of finality that had descended when I'd crawled into bed at Jackman that night, for what I knew would be the last time. "Then, before I left on Thursday, Matt told me he's heading back to British Columbia at the end of July."

"Hey, wait." Daniel gazed down at me curiously. "That must have been why you were crying when I picked you up." He pulled me into his arms again. "I'm sorry, poppet."

"It's okay," I whispered, putting on my best brave face. "I'll miss Matt, but it's the best decision for him. I know that."

In the midst of Daniel's comforting embrace, I pushed back my feelings of sadness about Matt's eventual departure. Right now, it was time to help the man I loved celebrate his birthday.

CHAPTER 24

True Friendship

…ceremony was but devis'd at first
To set a gloss on faint deeds, hollow welcomes,
Recanting goodness, sorry ere 'tis shown;
But where there is true friendship, there needs none.
(*Timon of Athens*, Act 1, Scene 2)

Once Daniel and I were living together, it would have been easy for me to take our time together for granted, breezing through our days like a spoiled kid surrounded by a mountain of gifts on Christmas morning. I didn't want to do that. I wanted to savor every detail of our time together.

Some days were incredible and I'd pinch myself, amazed that sailing around Toronto's harbor for an afternoon in Daniel's boat or spending a weekend with his family at their luxurious cottage was standard fare.

Of course, not every moment was exotic. I was back on the concert circuit and madly writing reviews while Daniel worked at his thesis, but I'd sometimes catch myself pausing to drink in a moment we were sharing, even if it was as simple as drying dishes together. Sure, we had our fair share of squabbles and misunderstandings. Some of the fights were silly, but even if they weren't epic, the makeup sex always was. Walls, counters, tables, doors — there were no sacred cows.

Many of our daily spats were about the same thing: Daniel's tidiness, and my proclivity for clutter. I'd go looking for something, and Daniel would have "put it away" for me. If he wasn't home, I'd end up on a solo search and rescue mission, looking for the earrings I was *positive* I'd left on the dresser, or hunting down the most recent issue of *Spin* magazine which had been on the coffee table the last time I'd checked.

One day in late July, I was wandering around in a T-shirt and panties looking for my gray shorts. I knew I'd left them on the chair beside the bed after unpacking from a couple of days away at the cottage. Rather than searching blindly, I solicited help.

"Daniel!" He strolled in from the hall, looking at me distractedly. I gestured to the package of felt tacks in his hand. "What are you doing?"

"The felt is coming off the bottom of one of the armchairs. I don't want it to scratch the hardwood. Did you call me?"

"Yeah, I'm looking for my gray shorts. I left them on the chair. Have you seen them?"

"Oh, I put them in the laundry."

"*Daniel.*" I went to fish them out of the hamper. "I wore those for half an hour after my shower at the cottage the other day. That's why they were on the clothes chair."

He followed me into the closet. "You won't find them," he said. "They're in the wash."

I stood up, my hands on my hips.

"Sorry." He shrugged and backed out of the closet.

"It's okay. I'm sure you were trying to help."

"Actually, I was trying to tidy up a bit." He gestured to the books I'd piled on my nightstand and the assorted collection of jewelry and hair accessories on the dresser. "I'm trying to ignore it, poppet," he assured me.

I wrapped my arms around his waist. "I know you are. I'm the one who's sorry." I reached up to kiss his cheek. "You must feel like you're bashing your head against a wall. I clean up one mess, and then I move somewhere else and make another one."

"It's taking some getting used to." He smiled.

I reached for the package in his hand and peeled the backing from one of the felt tacks, sticking it in the middle of his forehead. He looked at me like I was certifiable.

"What are you doing?" he asked.

"I don't want you to hurt your head when you're bashing it against the wall." I giggled.

"You're a lunatic." He peeled the sticker off. "Ouch, I think I just waxed between my eyebrows."

I laughed harder at the red spot the sticker had left behind. "Now you have a bindi."

He tossed the package on the dresser and tackled me onto the bed. "You're going to be the death of me, you know that?"

I sucked on his earlobe and slid open his zipper, then snuck my fingers inside his pants.

He moaned, moving against my hand. "As our friend Romeo once said, '*Come, death, and welcome...*'"

I'd known his departure was fast approaching, but the arrival of Matt's final day in Toronto still took me by surprise. We spent the day together, and after dinner I returned with him to Jackman to say good-bye.

"The apartment's like a ghost town," I said.

"Kinda surreal," Matt agreed, bending to zip up one of the cases. "It hasn't been the same since you left. Without Jo here as well, it's been downright spooky."

Matt's face was hidden, but the sadness in his voice was unmistakable. I sat on the edge of his bed. "I heard from Jo this morning. She and Stephen arrived in Taiwan safely, but it sounds like she's already got culture shock. She misses her stuff."

"Yeah, she sent me a quick message. I know how she feels. Since I shipped my things home, it's felt creepy around here. I can't imagine not having everything for a year."

He interlaced his fingers and tapped his thumbs together.

"So, uh, what time's your flight out?" I asked.

"Ugly early. Seven."

"Yuck, that is gross."

"In a way I'm glad. It's not like there's much I can do around here..." He gestured around his empty room.

I nodded and then took the plunge. "I still can't believe you're going."

There. I'd said it. The proverbial ball was rolling. Almost as soon as I'd spoken the words, I felt the very same ball slide down my throat where it proceeded to get stuck, creating an unpleasant achy feeling that I couldn't dislodge.

"I'm gonna miss you, Aubs," Matt whispered.

I swallowed hard, and when he grabbed my hand and squeezed it, I clamped my eyes shut. Shit, what was the point in pretending? I relaxed my throat and let the tears flow, sniffing as he pulled me into the crook of his neck and patted my back.

"Please don't cry," he said.

I tore myself away, dashing to the bathroom. "This is why I can't do airport good-byes," I called back over my shoulder.

Thinking about airport good-byes made my stomach clench. In a week, I'd be jetting to England alone and spending ten days without Daniel, surrounded by relatives I barely knew. I'd had no luck convincing Daniel that it would be best to hire a car service to take me to the airport and get the good-bye over with at the condo. He'd dug in his heels, and I was sensing the futility of fighting about it.

I blew my nose and surveyed the splotches on my face. What a mess. I returned to Matt's room, dabbing my eyes with toilet paper.

"I'm such a loser." I flopped down beside him.

"You're not a loser, Aubrey. Good-byes are hard. I'm a little numb. It's like we've had this long good-bye going on for months. This is just the last phase."

"Wow, I didn't know you felt that way. That makes me feel like crap."

"I'm not trying to make you feel bad. It hasn't been the same around here without you, that's all."

"I've missed you too. I'm sick at the thought of you leaving. You know that, right?"

He smiled. "It feels good to know you're gonna miss me. I'm gonna miss you a hell of a lot, so I'd feel shitty if you didn't care that I was leaving."

"I was about to tell you not to let the door hit your ass on the way out, but then I lost my train of thought." I smiled at him ruefully. "I can't believe you'd think I wouldn't miss you."

He shrugged, examining a distant spot on the wall. "Things are different now."

"I hope you don't mean *I'm* different."

"It's not that. Your life is full. You've got a lot going on."

"That doesn't mean I don't miss my friends when they're not around."

"I know." He thought for a second. "You *are* different, though."

I drew back defensively. "I don't know what you mean."

"It's not a bad thing. It's like…there used to be this little part of you that seemed sad. Even when you were putting on a brave face, that sad part of you was always under the surface." He shook his head. "I don't see that part anymore."

I opened my mouth to speak, and he held up his hand.

"And I'm not suggesting you need a guy to make you happy. I know that's not true. But maybe Daniel being in your life has filled a void you didn't know was there. He's grounded you…given you a sense of family."

"Wow," I said with false admiration. "Have you considered writing screenplays or something? 'Cause that was really good."

"Don't be a smartass. You know what I mean."

"Yeah, I guess I do."

"It's not easy to accept that you needed someone, which is why you're making jokes."

"Have you and Daniel been comparing notes?"

"No need to," he said. "You're an open book. You just like to *think* you're inscrutable."

I laughed, trying to curtail the cynical tone that threatened to creep into my voice.

"There's nothing wrong with being unguarded. It's not a character flaw, Aubrey. Daniel's good for you. You guys have something special," he said, his eyes losing focus for a few seconds. When he turned back to me, he had that look on his face, the one that said *we really need to wrap this up.*

"I should go and let you sleep," I said.

"I don't mean to chase you out, but I should crash or I'll be useless in the morning."

"No, I get it."

He followed me into the hall, stopping as I paused in my bedroom doorway to survey the barren space.

"You know what this reminds me of?" Matt asked as we made our way to the living room. "That last episode of *Friends*."

"Oh, don't. Every time I watch that episode I bawl my eyes out."

He laughed and hugged me. I could have told myself I was crying for Monica, Chandler, and the rest of the gang, and the pile of keys they'd left on the counter in that final episode of *Friends*, but that wasn't true. I was crying because my best friend was leaving and I was going to miss him and his wonderful hugs in the worst way.

By the time I was back at the condo, I had my feelings in check. I'd barely turned my key in the lock before Daniel was there, arms open, ready to comfort me.

"How was your day?"

"It was fine." I dropped my purse on the bench and kicked off my shoes.

"You've had some tears," he said.

"A few. I'm okay now."

"Are you sure? You don't have to be stoic. I understand."

"I'm fine, honestly. Tell me about *your* day."

"I've been keeping myself busy," he said, taking my hand and leading me to the bedroom. He pointed to his bookshelves. He'd moved some of his own things to fit my paperbacks on a couple of the shelves. I crossed the room and surveyed the rows of books.

"Wow, how difficult was it to throw these up here in no particular order?" I asked, turning to smirk at him.

"Aha, you may *think* they're arbitrarily organized, but a great deal of thought went into that arrangement. I've had the whole day to myself, don't forget."

I examined the two books he'd just pointed to. "Alexander Pope and Margaret Atwood?"

"Two sharp-tongued social commentators. I think Pope would find Atwood delightful company."

"Hmm. I'll give you that one on creative grounds. What about Jeanette Winterson and Sarah Waters? Both British, female novelists?"

He shook his head. "Both lesbians." I laughed, and he linked his hands around my waist. "I wanted to cheer you up. Mission accomplished?"

I led him to the bed. "Mission *almost* accomplished."

"Don't you mean *missionary* almost accomplished?" he whispered, settling between my legs with a sly smile.

CHAPTER 25

Tempered Ink

Never durst poet touch a pen to write
Until his ink were temper'd with Love's sighs…
(*Love's Labour's Lost*, Act IV, Scene 3)

As Daniel and I waited for our turn to check my luggage, he put his arm around me, holding me close while I wondered for the millionth time how we were going to manage ten full days apart without losing our minds.

"Remember, don't worry about data costs on your phone," Daniel said. "I need to know I can reach you when I land next week. Your aunt and uncle have wireless, right?"

"I'll email you every night. I promise."

He turned to kiss me, and we became those annoying people in the check-in line who are so self-absorbed that the line moves twenty feet before they realize *they're* the reason for the throat clearing around them. I finally had to push Daniel away, mumbling apologies to the people behind us. Daniel snickered, dragging my suitcase around a bend in the meandering line which was moving a little too quickly for my liking. The sooner we got to the front counter, the sooner I'd be heading for the departure lounge. Alone.

This will be fun, I told myself. *The time apart will be good for us.*

When our turn came, the woman behind the ticketing desk stamped my passport and tagged my suitcase. She handed me my boarding pass, smiling brightly.

"Have a nice trip."

I nodded dumbly while Daniel gathered my things, steering me toward a wall near the security gate. I leaned into him, resting my hands on his chest.

"This sucks." I sighed.

"I wanted to see you here safely. You can't begrudge me that."

"I hate saying good-bye publicly, that's all. I'll be fine once I'm through the gates." I gestured to his shoulder. "I'm gonna need my knapsack."

He set the bag on the ground between us and cupped my face, kissing me softly.

I blinked up at him. "I'm going to miss you, sunshine."

"I'm going to miss you. Horribly."

Daniel's eyes flickered over my shoulder. I had to go. I jiggled my leg, squeezing his fingers, reluctant to break away. He stuck his hand into his pocket, and with an expression that defied my protests, he pressed a wad of folded bills into my palm.

"Put this in your wallet."

"Daniel, I *have* spending money."

"Humor me? If you won't buy yourself something, get me something. Or get yourself something you know I'll like. Please?"

Defeated, I jammed the money into my pocket.

"I'll keep it for an emergency." I smiled reluctantly. "Like if I run out of undies or something."

"I love you, Aubrey." He hugged me tightly. "I put a letter in the side pocket of your backpack. Read it later, okay?"

I nodded but couldn't speak—I didn't dare. I squeezed him hard, my cheek pressed against the warmth of his neck.

"Daniel?" I finally managed to say. "I'm going to get in line. Don't stand and wait, okay?"

"Okay, poppet."

He kissed me, his tongue warm and sweet against mine. I kept my eyes shut, trying to stop my lips from quivering.

Whatever you do, don't make a scene.

I managed to tear myself away and grab my bag without completely falling apart, doing my best to smile convincingly before making my way to the security line. I shouldn't have turned around, but I did. Daniel was already halfway across the terminal, hands jammed in his pockets, head down as he strode toward the exit.

That's when I fell apart.

After taking the time to stow everything I'd need for an overnight flight in my seat pocket, I dragged the airplane blanket over my lap and tried to get comfortable. What I really wanted was the man beside me to quit clearing his throat and humming mindlessly.

Shortly after takeoff, the cabin lights dimmed. Hummy McCougherson pulled his own blanket up to his chin and proceeded to snore gently into his balled-up sweatshirt.

Thank you.

I squeezed my eyes shut, imagining Daniel returning to the condo alone. Regardless of how busy he kept himself during the days we were apart, he'd be alone at night, which worried me more than anything else.

When I'd returned home late from an evening out with Julie on Saturday, I'd found him asleep, twisted up in the blankets, calling out to this person who tormented him in his dreams. Would he have a nightmare every night while I was away, waking each time to find himself alone? I shook off the horrible thought and reached for the note Daniel had slipped into my bag. His handwritten words filled a whole page.

Sweetheart,

This is it. I'm standing on the brink of ten days without you. As always, when I imagine us being apart, I try to think of ways to bridge the distance between us. So, what have I done this time? Well, I hope you don't mind, but when you asked me to load those new books onto your Kindle, I added a couple of PDF files as well — both of them written by me. The first one is called The Joys of Trying to Cover Your Ass When You're Falling in Love With a Student and Don't Know It. The second one is titled Uncovering Your Ass and Learning to Enjoy It.

If you're confused, cast your mind back to early March. Remember that flash drive you accidentally opened? I told you I'd been writing about you since the beginning of the semester, and despite my better judgment, I've decided to share some of those thoughts with you now.

Reading these files will give you some insight into what I was going through in February — I was a mess. The second file is less frightening, though no less revealing. Read the one with the long title first. You might want to have a stiff drink on hand, just in case.

I hope you enjoy your time with your family, poppet. You know I'll miss you, but I'm so glad you're doing this, and we'll be together soon. Hopefully I'll see you tonight, in my dreams.

Lovingly yours,
Daniel

I grabbed my Kindle, excited to read Daniel's words, but a little wary of what I might find in those documents. I propped the pillow beside my head and opened the file with the ridiculously long title, reading voraciously at first but then slowing and forcing myself to consider his words.

The entries documented our first exchanges, with bracketed insertions added by Daniel later — apologetic explanations to me. I could see why he'd felt the need to editorialize what he'd originally written. His daily documentations revealed that he'd viewed me as a threat, the potential second-coming of Nicola. Paranoia underscored virtually every word he'd recorded. While I might have been insulted by those early suspicions, I wasn't. They merely made me want to find this Nicola girl, wrap my hands around her throat, and squeeze. Really damn hard.

At the end of the fifth page, an entry describing our night at the Hart House theater—the night I'd been ill and Daniel had been forced to take me home—the document stopped, with neither conclusion, nor further comment. I closed my eyes, going over everything he'd written. He'd been so tormented, feeling the need to account for *every* look, *every* conversation, even our most innocent exchanges, lest he have to defend his actions later. No wonder his behavior in those first couple of weeks had been so erratic and his moods so unpredictable.

I opened the other PDF file, seeing the reason for the sudden termination of the first document. This new file— *Uncovering Your Ass and Learning to Enjoy It*—started on the same date that the first one had finished, but the tone was vastly different. There were no parenthetical notes apologizing to me. They weren't necessary. In this document, Daniel was bearing his soul entirely.

> Friday February 13th
> 10:15 p.m.
> I've been in denial, completely and utterly disregarding my interest in Aubrey Price. I was so cool, so professional and detached. Ha! How superior I've been, "fearing" she might be attracted to me, worried she might be harboring some sort of crush on me-Daniel Grant, the handsome, young TA.
> I can't deny the truth any longer. The only thing I've feared is that she might not give me more than a second glance because I've certainly given her several glances, and they've virtually ALL been inappropriate...

Here, at last was Daniel. *My Daniel.*

In the aftermath of that crazy night at the theater, Daniel had been at home alone, pouring his soul out on paper. He'd been thinking of me while, back in Jackman, I'd been in bed, tearfully agonizing over what I'd thought were my unrequited feelings for him.

Even then, despite the distance and obstacles between us, we were already connected, secretly meeting one another in the quiet safety of our thoughts.

Daniel

Thoughts of Love

O absence! what a torment wouldst thou prove,
Were it not thy sour leisure gave sweet leave
To entertain the time with thoughts of love…
(*Sonnet 39*)

When I got home from the airport, I went through the motions of getting ready for bed, though I knew sleep wouldn't come easy. Pulling the comforter back, I found the black nightie Aubrey had worn to bed the night before peeking out from under my pillow.

Had she left it there to be cheeky, knowing her lingerie would torment me with thoughts of the previous night's lovemaking, or was it a sweet gesture intended to console me? I buried my nose in the silky fabric, comforted by her scent.

I imagined her sitting in a dimly lit airplane cabin. Was she reading those files, or was she curled up against the window, too tired to read? When she did look at them, what would she think? Surely she'd see past the idiocy of those first two weeks of February and understand that, after everything I'd gone through at Oxford, I simply wasn't thinking straight. At least I hoped she would.

God, I missed her already. It was going to be a long ten days.

The next morning, I woke up with Aubrey's nightie twisted around my arm. As I untangled it, I noticed I'd ripped one of the seams. A vision of Nicola's face contorting with anguish played behind my eyes. I'd had a bad dream, but it hadn't woken me. I slid the silky garment under my pillow. A nightie, a talisman against the ill-effects of bad dreams? Ridiculous, but hey, whatever worked.

Yawning as I made my way down the hall, I had the strangest sensation that something was off. Obviously the place was quiet without Aubrey there, but it was more than that. The condo *felt* different.

It wasn't until I was about to make coffee that I realized what was wrong. Aubrey had tidied up. The toaster and coffeemaker which she preferred to keep on the counter were tucked in a cupboard, the way I'd stored them before she moved in.

Temporarily abandoning thoughts of coffee, I retraced my steps. There were no shoes scattered by the door, no bags piled on the parson's bench. In the living room, there wasn't a single magazine lying around, no stray earrings or hair clips left on shelves or side tables. In the office, Aubrey's desk was neat. In the bedroom, her favorite "clothes chair" was empty. There wasn't a single stray item of Aubrey's anywhere. The place was spotless.

And it was all wrong.

I sprang into action. First, I draped one of Aubrey's hoodies and a T-shirt over the chair beside the bed, piled a couple of books on her nightstand, and retrieved some of her toiletries from the bathroom drawer and set them on the vanity. Next, I dropped a couple of *Spin* magazines on the coffee table and placed the TV and stereo remotes beside the magazines. Last stop was the kitchen, where I moved the coffee maker and toaster to the counter and plugged them in.

Much better.

I whistled as I resumed making coffee, but the tune died on my lips when I opened the cupboard to retrieve the coffee. Aubrey had carefully arranged the bottom shelf. The soup cans sat in a neat line, not a single foreign item interrupting the outward facing row of red labels.

I grabbed the chicken noodle soup, opened the adjacent cupboard and slid the soup between the tinned salmon and a can of diced tomatoes. Standing back, I assessed the results. Maybe not the most logical organizational approach, but what was the big deal?

Things don't have to be identical to belong together.

I never thought I'd say it, but once I sat down to email Aubrey, I felt a pang of nostalgia for those emails we'd shared during the endless weeks in the spring. I logged onto my Jung Willman account to write to her, figuring she'd get a kick out of seeing the return of my secret persona.

From: Jung Willman
To: Miss_V
Date: Tues, Jul 28,10:17:39 AM
Subject: Thoughts of Love (and other things...)

Hi, sweetheart,

I've been awake for almost three and a half hours. I think I deserve a medal for waiting this long to email you! I hope your flight was good. I'm not sure if you've read the PDF files yet, but if you have, hopefully you don't think I'm a prick for the entries I wrote in February. Aside from the period following Nicola's bombshell last year, those weeks at the beginning of the semester were probably two of the most confusing weeks of my life.

Walking away from you last night at the airport, I wondered what the hell I'd been thinking, sharing those files with you when I wouldn't be sitting beside you to explain everything, but perhaps it's best to let you digest my words without my interference. Besides, all that matters is that I love you now, and if I could have told you then that I wanted to love you, I would have.

Thank you for the treat you left under my pillow. I woke up with it wrapped around my left arm. I can only assume its proximity to my heart kept me safe in my dreams. I trust you found the T-shirts I snuck in with your clothes. I selfishly want you to wear them to bed so you'll think of me before you go to sleep.

It goes without saying that I miss you already, but I'll say it anyway. The condo isn't the same without you (although I've done my best to make it feel like you're still here...don't ask). I hope your family shows you a good time. If you find yourself in a pub, surrounded by drunken lads, keep your wits about you. They're not to be trusted. Believe me, I was one of them. ;)

Since I've revived my Jung Willman persona, allow me to remind you of the man whose words helped JW woo you months ago. These few lines are from Sonnet 39:

"O absence, what a torment wouldst thou prove,
Were it not thy sour leisure gave sweet leave
To entertain the time with thoughts of love..."

And a few thoughts of a certain person's very fine ass...

Yours,
Daniel

From: Miss_V
To: Jung Willman
Date: Tues, Jul 28, 3:48:16 PM
Subject: The torment of absence...

Hey, JW! I miss you too! I'm glad you didn't wait any longer to email me. I read those files, Daniel. Every. Last. Word. How could you think I'd judge you for the way you acted in February? At the time, I thought you were a pompous, potentially bi-polar asshat, but once I knew what was going on, I understood.

But seriously, reading your words from those early days, I wasn't angry with you—I was angry with NICOLA! I'm not sure how I can hate her so passionately when I haven't met her, but getting a glimpse at how paranoid you were made me want to hunt her down. I wish there was some sort of magical potion you could take that would obliterate her from your memory. I'd be quite happy never to hear her name ever again.

Reading the next document made me feel better. Your words in that second file reminded me of so many special moments from those first few weeks we spent together. I love you and I'm grateful for your beautiful gesture—truly the most thoughtful gift you've given me.

As for last night, I'm glad the nightie helped you sleep. When I slipped it under your pillow, all I could think about was you whispering, "Take it off...slowly" the other night. How will I get through all these nights without you? (And who'll warm my feet?)

FYI, I don't need to be wearing one of your T-shirts to think of you in bed, and I've already started planning my wardrobe for our reunion—short skirt, sexy panties, and of course, you'll wear your holey jeans and you'll be unshaven...*sigh*

On that note, I must wrap up. I'll write again tonight.

All my love,

Aubrey

xo

P.S. What do you mean you've tried to make the condo feel like I'm there? Did you buy a blow-up doll?

I'd thought my week without Aubrey would drag, but somehow my days filled with numerous pre-vacation errands. I capped off the week with an impromptu meeting with Martin, who wanted to discuss plans for September before I left for England. Our meeting energized me, and I actually found myself excited for the upcoming school year.

As we were parting, he surprised me by asking how things were proceeding with Aubrey. I told him we were getting along so well that she was sneaking away from a family holiday to join me in Somerset to attend my brother's wedding. He congratulated me for securing the affections of "such a lovely young lady." I wanted to tell him he didn't know the half of it.

On the evening of our flight, my family and I settled into our first class seats at midnight. My father had lucked out, securing two seats to himself while my grandmother and my mother sat in front of him, both of them washing down motion-sickness pills with orange juice.

As for Penny and Brad, they were snuggled together in a little love cocoon. I tried not to dwell on how much I wished Aubrey was beside me instead of Jeremy. I reclined my seat, yawning as we sped along the runway and took to the air.

Jeremey leaned over the armrests between us. "You don't think Penny's upset that I'm not arriving at the estate until Thursday night, do you?"

"Not at all. As long as you're cool with your tuxedo pants not fitting right—"

"Penny said the seamstress is gonna swing by on Friday. She'll be able to do any minor adjustments on the fly."

"It's not the fly I was worrying about," I said, purposely misinterpreting his words. "I was more concerned about your backside. Ill-fitting tuxedo pants can give you a serious wedgie."

He shook his head and peered out at the dark abyss below before turning back to me with a chuckle.

"You're happy to be heading over, I guess?"

"Yes and no. I'll be happy to be in the same country as Aubrey again."

"So what's the bad part?"

"I don't know, Jer." I sighed. "Going back after all this time. I'm a little anxious."

"Try not to think about you-know-who. Focus on the wedding—the family spending time together."

"The wedding will be amazing, and I'm looking forward to having some down time in Somerset this week. I'm more concerned about the week *after* the wedding. Aubrey wants to do some sightseeing." I shrugged. "I don't know…"

"Just stay away from Oxford. You'll be fine."

"It wouldn't matter if we went to Oxford. Nicola's not there."

"How do you know that?"

I shook my head ruefully. "Facebook."

"What the fuck? You're *Facebook friends?*"

"Keep your voice down," I hissed, sneaking a look at my father, who was already snoring against his propped-up hand. "Of course we're not Facebook friends. She's one of those people who leaves her whole profile open for everyone to see."

"Why would you look for her there?" he asked, his voice now hushed like mine.

"Morbid curiosity?"

"Jesus Christ, Daniel, I thought you were supposed to be smart."

I grimaced. He didn't need to say it; I was already feeling plenty stupid. "I only glanced at it the first time—in June—but then something kept drawing me back."

"And that's how you know she's not at Oxford?"

"I'll never understand why people air their lives in their wall posts like that. Anyway, she didn't go back to school this year. She's working in a souvenir shop in London, and she's moved out of her parents' house. Sounds like her life has fallen apart."

"And how do you feel about that?"

"You wouldn't believe me if I told you."

He crossed his arms and gave me a look that said *Try me.*

I paused for a moment, rolling the words around in my mouth. "I think I feel sorry for her."

Jeremy reflected on my admission. "I get why you'd say that."

"But shouldn't I hate her? She turned my existence upside down."

"Yes, she did. And now you've recovered, and you're getting on with your life."

I settled back, chuckling cynically. "I wouldn't say I'm *completely* recovered. I've started having nightmares again. I'm sure they've got something to do with Nicola."

"What makes you think that?"

"Because when I wake up in the middle of a nightmare, I see her face?" I sighed. "Maybe I've stirred up my subconscious by tracking her down online."

"What does Aubrey say?"

"I've told her about the dreams, but I didn't tell her about the Facebook thing. Whenever I mention Nicola, she gets angry. She doesn't want me to dwell on stuff that I can't change."

"You can't ignore it if it's causing you stress, even if it's subconscious. Maybe you should see a shrink," Jeremy suggested.

Was he serious?

"Couldn't hurt — you always have had a big head," he added, smirking.

Once we'd arrived in England, successfully navigated Gatwick's security check, and worked out the three different car rental agreements, we made our way to the parking garage like a herd of turtles. As my dad loaded luggage into the trunk of his car, my mother took Jeremy's hands.

"When is your flight?" she asked, unable to conceal her apprehension.

"In a few hours." His voice was firm. Nothing was going to derail him.

"What will you do with yourself until you leave, dear?" Patty asked, her concern echoing my mother's.

Jeremy shrugged noncommittally. I leapt in.

"I'll stay for a bit. If you guys leave now, you'll be at the estate by early afternoon."

My mother nodded, comforted by this arrangement, and then she and Patty closed in on Jeremy, both of them weepy. In the twenty-three years since my aunt and uncle's accident, no one had returned to the site, and here was Jeremy, not simply choosing to visit the spot where his parents had perished, but willingly putting himself in the path of the person who'd caused their deaths.

Besides worrying about Jeremy's well-being, my mother was probably thinking about her sister, and of course Patty was remembering her beloved daughter. As they fussed over Jeremy, Penny took me aside.

"Will he be all right?" she whispered. "I wish he'd let you join him."

"He needs to do this alone, Penn. He'll be fine. I'll stay with him for as long as I can."

She nodded and patted my cheek. "Daniel, you *are* going to shave before the wedding, right?"

"I don't know," I mused, rubbing my chin, more beardy than scruffy at this point. "I kind of like it."

"It looks like a malnourished squirrel died on your face."

"Just for that, I might keep it," I teased. "What do you think, Brad? Doesn't the beard make me look debonair?"

My brother squinted at me. "If debonair means homeless, then, yeah, the beard is totally working."

With the rest of the family on their way to the estate, Jeremy and I returned to the airport and found a café. I grabbed us each a cup of coffee while he snagged a table.

"You don't have to do this," he said. "I know you were trying to calm Mom and Patty down when you said you'd stay, but I'll be fine."

"I don't mind. I'd go out of my gourd sitting in an airport alone for four hours. Are you working on a project?" I asked, pointing to his laptop bag.

"No, I finished my last job on Friday. You?"

"I brought my laptop in case inspiration strikes," I said, drumming my fingers on the table. "I'm not holding my breath. My head's a shed."

"Not surprising. I don't know why you picked such a fucked up approach for your thesis."

"Are you saying Carl Jung is fucked up?"

"Isn't he?"

"Of course he isn't."

"Not my thing. Thank God you helped me when we studied *Fifth Business* in high school."

"Jer, *Fifth Business* is Jungian paint by numbers."

"You said the same thing then." Jeremy frowned as he sipped his coffee. "Hey, what was the name of that character again? The one who threw the snowball with the stone in it at that pregnant woman when he was a kid?"

"Percy Boyd Staunton."

"Right. He didn't own up to what he'd done to her and lived with the guilt of it all his life."

"Essentially."

"And that's why he had the same stone in his mouth when he was found dead in his car, right? His guilt haunted him until the day he committed suicide."

"In the most basic sense, I suppose so."

"I guess Jung makes sense if you apply his theories to real life. No one wants to be on their deathbed with these huge regrets."

"Jeremy, is that what going to see Anita is all about? You don't want to die with a stone in your mouth?"

"No, it's not that at all." He gazed at me, a mysterious smile ghosting across his face. "I don't want to *live* with a stone in my mouth."

Aubrey

Return of Love

Let this sad interim like the ocean be
Which parts the shore, where two contracted new
Come daily to the banks, that, when they see
Return of love, more bless'd may be the view…
(Sonnet 56)

The train ride from Exeter to Bristol took about an hour. Daniel had offered to drive from Somerset to pick me up, but the journey by road would have doubled the travel time. I didn't want him making a four-hour commute the day before the wedding.

When a voice over the train's PA announced that Bristol was the next stop, my stomach fluttered. My phone buzzed in my pocket, interrupting my daydreams.

> *I'm at the station. Actually, there might be two of me here because I'm BESIDE myself with excitement.*
> *Can't wait to see you…touch you…kiss you…fuck!*
> *Hurry! -D*

The flutters migrated south where they transformed into a desperate ache. My shaking fingers flew over the phone's keyboard. Minutes. Mere minutes until we were together again!

**I can't wait to see you too (or should I say you TWO?).
Get ready to pucker up, buttercup(s). xo -A**

I rushed through the concourse of the Bristol train station, my suitcase bumping behind me. There wasn't time to admire the building's beautiful architecture—Daniel was waiting for me.

On the sidewalk outside, clusters of people milled around as cars circled. Passengers and luggage spilled onto the sidewalk from a bus at the curb. While searching for Daniel, I tried to watch where I was going. I inadvertently bruised a few shins with my suitcase as I moved through the crowd.

I finally caught sight of him about fifty feet away. He was standing with his hands on his hips, his eyes darting between the station's different entrances. My heart lurched, and my legs turned wooden.

Daniel.

I mouthed his name, but no sound came out. Regardless, he turned, squinting into the mass of people as if I'd shouted. When he spotted me, a dimpled smile transformed his features. He waved while I maneuvered through the crowd, my elbows joining in the effort. If there were a scout for the English rugby team nearby, I'd be a shoo-in.

At last, Daniel's arm snaked between two burly hikers. One of the men coaxed the bottom of my case forward with the edge of his boot, and I was through. I slipped my backpack off my shoulder, simultaneously throwing myself into Daniel's welcoming embrace. He squeezed me so hard, the air whooshed out of my lungs.

"I missed you so much," he whispered, kissing me frantically.

I was in one of those chick flicks, a cheesy song playing while the lovers reconnected after a separation, a slow-motion camera catching every detail of the reunion. Oblivious to the people around us, we stood kissing for the longest time. It wasn't until Daniel's hands slipped to my hips, pulling me against him, that I remembered we were in the middle of a crowd of people. I stepped away and looked around self-consciously.

Daniel smiled and bobbed his head. "Let's go. The car is this way."

I retrieved my backpack, and he took my suitcase, scanning my legs as we walked.

"Nice skirt. What there is of it."

"I thought you'd like it."

"My feelings are a good deal stronger than that, believe me."

His sexy accent had crept back. He squeezed my hand and swung my arm back and forth in a breezy, carefree way.

"How is everyone?" I asked.

"Great. Excited to see you. Prepare to be ambushed as soon as we arrive."

We stopped behind a car, and he popped the trunk.

"The only one I want to ambush me is *you*, sailor."

Daniel heaved my suitcase inside and slammed the trunk closed. Then he winked. "Oh, I'll ambush you—soundly and repeatedly."

"I can't wait." I stood on my toes, burrowing my nose against his neck and tickling his scruff. "What's with the facial hair?"

"You told me not to shave."

"I meant for a few days. This has to be a good week and half's growth."

"I didn't mean to let it get this long, but Penny's been nagging me about it. I'm leaving it for now, just to freak her out."

I laughed as I climbed into the car and buckled in.

"So, this worked out really well," Daniel said, backing out of his spot. "I dropped Patty and my great-aunt Gwendolyn off on my way here. They're in town having a bimble."

"A bimble?"

"A little look around. Exploring. Bimbling."

"*Bimbling*. Good word. I like it."

"It's yours to do with as you wish."

Daniel made a quick turn out of the parking lot. I gestured to the GPS. "Do you need me to put the address in for you?"

"I know where I'm going." He patted my hand. "Relax."

I took his advice, gazing out the window at the passing scenery. I occasionally shifted my position and caught Daniel gawking at my legs and gripping the steering wheel tightly. I smiled, trying not to let my imagination get carried away. I had visions of Daniel spiriting me away our room when we arrived at the estate, but it sounded as if Penny and Julie would pounce as soon as we pulled in.

"Hey, Daniel, did everything go okay for Jeremy in France? I haven't heard from Julie in a couple of days."

"He and Julie got in late last night so we haven't talked at length, but from what I gather, I'd say his only regret is that he didn't do this years ago."

"I'm happy for him."

"Me too."

Daniel threaded his fingers through mine and turned his attention back to the road, frowning and squinting at the signposts as we closed in on a roundabout. I tensed as we turned onto one of those narrow roads that didn't seem capable of carrying two-lane traffic. All of a sudden, he drove onto a grassy verge that vaguely passed for a shoulder at the side of the road.

He climbed out, walked to the front of the car, and surveyed the surrounding fields. What the hell was going on? When he ran his hand through his hair and scratched at the nape of his neck, I realized exactly what was going on—we were lost. I climbed out and joined him.

"How bad is it?"

"How bad is what?" he asked, his eyes flashing mysteriously.

"How lost are we?"

He slipped his hand around my waist. "We're not lost."

"Daniel, we're in the middle of nowhere, and you look baffled. I knew you should have used the GPS."

"We're not lost." He strode back to the car. "I know exactly where we are," he called over his shoulder.

Jesus. Typical man. When he reached the passenger door, he leaned on the side of the car, casting a rakish smile in my direction.

"Daniel, what are you up to?"

He dragged his eyes up my legs before opening the back door.

"You'd better get in, or I'll be bending you over that stile quicker than you can say '*Farmer Brown*.'"

Blindsided by what he seemed to be suggesting, I wavered for a moment, but then clambered into the car. He followed me, slamming the door soundly behind him.

"Get over here," he said, dragging me sideways onto his lap, his fingers skimming my bare thighs and coming to rest just under the hem of my skirt. "This really was an excellent choice of wardrobe."

My answering smile was lost in the soft parting of lips and the meeting of tongues.

"Are you sure about this? What if someone sees us?"

"I don't give a good farmer's fuck if someone sees us," he said, searching my neck with his lips and quickly finding the spot that always made me shiver.

"We really shouldn't do this," I breathed, but even as I spoke I was lifting my skirt and wiggling my hips, helping him pull off my panties. I moved to straddle him.

"I know," he said, his agreement accompanied by the popping of a button and the sound of his zipper peeling open.

He pushed his jeans and boxers down his thighs and steadied me over his lap. My hands were in his hair, my forehead resting against his while he gripped my hips, guiding me. I closed my eyes, focusing on the sensation of our bodies reconnecting.

"Don't move," he whispered, his ear pressed to my heart. "You feel perfect. Fuck, I missed being inside you."

I whimpered, wanting to wiggle against him, but at the same time, overcome with feeling and wanting to savor the stillness. But let's face facts. We were in a car. It was not the time for lingering love-making. His hands slipped up my legs, one coming to rest between my thighs. I dragged my T-shirt up and over my breasts and pulled my bra out of the way, gasping as his tongue moved across my skin.

Ten days seemed like an eternity to have gone without his touch. My body responded eagerly to his caresses, my hips rocking in the same steady rhythm as his teasing tongue. With my hands tangled in his hair, I held him tightly against my breast.

"That feels—God, so good…"

His lips curved into a cocky smile, and his eyes flickered up to meet mine. I was losing focus, already teetering on the edge, my eyes closing with the struggle to tip the balance in my favor.

He thrust into me hard, fingers still moving with practiced precision.

Yep. That did it.

I threw my head back, almost crying with relief as my orgasm tore through me. Daniel swore, his own movements becoming more and more purposeful. As I floated back to earth, his hands circled my waist, and he spiraled away, the tension draining from his features. Sated, he buried his face in my neck.

"Do you have any idea how much I love you?" he said.

"Abstinence makes the heart grow fonder?"

"It definitely doesn't make the sex go longer."

"Daniel, we're in the back seat of a car. A quickie was a good idea, don't you think?"

"I guess you're right. I'll make it up to you later."

"I'm game for that."

He sat back, his eyes wandering down my body. "I'm glad you wore this skirt. This couldn't have worked better if I'd planned it."

"Wait, are you saying you've done something completely spontaneous?"

"If I'd planned this, the Kleenex would be beside us instead of up front."

"Uh-oh." I grimaced, shifting my hips. I reached for my panties, and that's when I saw them—two large brown eyes peering in the back window.

"Jesus, Daniel!" I pointed.

He followed my gaze. "Huh, fancy that."

"That cow watched us have sex."

"It would appear so."

"What do we do?"

"Clean up. Quickly. I just hope we can make it into the front seat unscathed."

"Unscathed? What do you mean?" I asked, fixing my bra and tugging my T-shirt down.

"If she *has* been watching the whole time, we could be in trouble." He chuckled devilishly. "Nothing scarier than a horny Holstein."

Daniel's prediction that we'd be ambushed upon arrival was spot-on. As soon as we drove into the estate's parking lot, people arrived at the front of the property from all sides. Julie flew out the front door, nearly knocking me on my ass with her hug, while Jeremy trailed behind her. Penny hugged me next, jabbering about Daniel and dead squirrels.

As usual, I had no clue what she was talking about.

Gwen reached for my hand. "Aubrey, it's so nice to have you here."

"How was your journey?" David asked. "No problems?"

"None at all. Daniel was waiting for me when I arrived."

"We wondered if perhaps the train had been delayed," he said.

I smiled at Daniel. "We took a wrong turn on the way back and got waylaid by some cows crossing the road."

"Oh no," Penny said. "I bloody hate that. You couldn't turn around, I bet. Road was too narrow?"

"Exactly," Daniel said, picking up the thread of my fib. "All we could do was wait."

"You must be tired, Aubrey," David said. He placed his hand on Daniel's shoulder. "Why don't you take Aubrey inside and show her around? Then she can freshen up. I'm sure you two have lots to catch up on."

I caught David's stealthy wink in his son's direction.

"I *would* like to change," I said. "Traveling always makes me feel a bit grubby."

The sopping wet panties weren't helping.

Amid promises to Julie and Penny that I'd be out soon, I followed Daniel inside. He took me on a quick tour of the main floor of the eighteenth-century estate. I half expected Mr. Darcy to stride imperiously out of the library, hat and gloves in hand as he sought a servant to summon his horse. At last, Daniel led me upstairs.

"This is our room." He opened a door at the end of the hall. "The bathroom's in here."

While he washed his hands, I admired the claw-foot tub.

"I'll have to have a bubble bath at some point, but I'll settle for a quick shower right now. I wasn't lying when I said I was feeling grubby."

"Unlike when you said we were late because of a herd of cows crossing the road? Should I be concerned about your sudden ability to make up fantastic stories off the top of your head?"

"You have to admit, the story was almost true."

"One cow wandered over from the field. How does that equate to getting waylaid by some cows?"

"Come on, if you remove the 'way' from 'waylaid' and replace 'some cows' with your name, I was *totally* waylaid by some cows."

He threw his head back in laughter. "I missed you, poppet."

"I missed you too, sailor. Especially your laugh."

"I missed you making me laugh."

"Best get ready. I'm back and reporting for duty."

"I've been getting ready since the minute you left," he said, patting my butt before heading back to the main room.

I showered quickly. When I emerged from the bathroom wrapped in a fluffy white bathrobe, Daniel was lying in bed, bare-chested.

He held out his hand. "I know you're expected downstairs, but do you think you could spare a few minutes?"

I dropped my robe and slid under the covers, pressing my body against his. He closed his eyes and sighed.

"This feels better. Having sex in the back seat of a car doesn't lend itself well to the post-nookie cuddle," he said.

"Back-seat sex is also reckless. That's not like you."

"Being here this week reminds me how much I've changed. Before my life became a shambles, I was so much more easygoing. I miss feeling that way." He brushed my hair over my shoulder.

"And having sex in the back seat on a country road is the epitome of 'easygoing Daniel'?"

"I don't know. Sometimes I feel as if something's out of joint, and if I stretch myself far enough, everything will snap back into place."

"Maybe you're just a pervert," I suggested.

"You might be on to something," he said, kissing my forehead and then my lips. "You know, if you're not downstairs soon, Penny's going to phone up here looking for you."

"She can wait." I sighed, sneaking my hand under the blanket and tracing a line down his abdomen.

"I thought we were having a cuddle," he murmured, lifting his hips as my hand traveled lower.

"Actually, I'm bimbling." I ran my hand up and down his thigh.

"Bimbling?" He laughed.

"Uh-huh. It means to look around and explore, right? You said the word was mine to do with as I wish. So, this is how I'd like to use it. I'm bimbling. With my hand."

"Excellent application of new vocabulary," he said, his voice catching as I found *exactly* what I'd been looking for.

CHAPTER 28

 Ominous

My dreams will, sure, prove ominous to the day.
(*Troilus and Cressida*, Act v, Scene 3)

Forty-five minutes later, another of Daniel's predictions came true when the phone rang. He reluctantly rolled on his side to take the call. I stretched out, relaxed and ready for an afternoon nap.

"Is Penny freaking out?" I asked, once he'd hung up.

"No, just barking orders."

I sat up as he leaned over to retrieve his boxers.

"Your company is requested outside at the marquee tent," he said. "Julie and Penny are waiting for you. Gretel, the seamstress, is waiting for me downstairs."

"Gretel? Huh. She sounds Swedish. Six feet tall, blond, and buxom."

I flopped back on the bed with a sigh. Daniel moved to lie beside me again.

"You're adorable when you're jealous."

"Me? Jealous? Absurd."

"Gretel is German, approximately sixty-five years old, and about as wide around as she is tall."

"Ooh, just your type."

He ruffled my hair and pushed himself off the bed. "I'd better grab a shower."

"Absolutely. Gotta smell good for your hot date. Maybe if you're lucky, she'll check your inseam. Repeatedly."

"Get dressed and haul your cheeky ass outside, crazy legs," Daniel called back to me.

I stretched my hands above my head, closing my eyes with a contented sigh. As my hand slipped under the pillow, I encountered something silky.

I pulled my black satin nightie free. He'd brought it with him from home! What had he told me in that email?—he was sleeping with it wrapped around his left arm because its closeness to his heart kept him safe in his dreams.

Turning the garment over in my hands, I noticed a large tear in the seam. I smiled. What the hell had he been doing with it? My smile dissolved as I remembered the nights I'd come to bed late, finding Daniel with the sheets wrapped around his hands, wrestling with some unknown entity in his sleep.

Perhaps the nightie hadn't been so helpful after all.

The grounds were abuzz with activity. Julie and Penny were waiting at the entrance to a marquee tent, assessing the activity within.

"There you are," Julie said as I squeezed between them.

Penny tore her eyes away from two ladies decorating an arbor behind the head table. "Thank goodness you're here. Let's go for a walk. I'm desperate for distraction."

Julie took her by the arm. "Come on. Show us around."

Penny led us into the estate's gardens. After circling the fish pond and skirting the flower beds, she guided us to a hedged laneway, at the end of which was a fenced-in meadow full of deer.

"Oh my gosh," Julie breathed. "How cool is this? They're beautiful."

"You'd expect them to get spooked with us being so close," I said. The deer surveyed us, their heads bobbing inquisitively.

"Look at you," Penny said. "A close encounter with deer *and* cows on the same day." She wiggled her eyebrows.

"Wait, you knew I was lying? How did you—? You went along with the story and everything!"

"What was I supposed to say? '*Gwen, darling, they're actually late because they had a quick bonk on the way here.*'"

Julie giggled into her hand, and I crossed my arms defensively. "How the hell *did* you know?"

"Between the color of your face when you were telling that ridiculous story and Daniel's shit-eating grin, it was no secret to me, lovey."

"Did you go to a motel or something?" Julie asked.

"Not quite that civilized, I'm afraid."

"An obliging field?" Penny guessed.

"Not quite that *uncivilized.*" I laughed.

"Bloody Nora, you shagged in the car!" Penny gripped my arm as she cackled.

"You dirty bird," Julie said in wide-eyed wonder.

My face reddened. Penny gave me a sideways glance.

"Sounds like Daniel's feeling better."

"What? When wasn't he feeling okay?"

She tucked her hand into the crook of my elbow, directing us along a path beside the field.

"He's been a bit of a misery all week, to be honest."

"He didn't sound miserable in his emails. I thought he was having fun."

"He probably didn't want to worry you."

"Penny, don't say that. I was so concerned about him being here, after everything that happened last year."

She patted my hand. "Don't get me wrong; he didn't go off the deep end. He didn't have any anxiety attacks or anything. Not that I know of, anyway," she added.

"Frig, I hope not," I groaned. "He seemed so relaxed today. Now I don't know what to think."

"I probably ought to have kept my trap shut."

"No, I'm glad you told me." My mind flickered to my ripped nightie. "Do you think he's been having bad dreams?"

"I'm not privy to his sleep patterns, darling. Please don't tell him I said anything. He does seem better now that you're here. He missed you terribly, that's all."

GEORGINA GUTHRIE

"I missed him too, trust me."

"I know the feeling," Julie said. "I hated being away from Jer, especially knowing he was dealing with that stuff in France by himself."

"Did everything go okay?" I said.

"He said it was surreal. He stood on the exact spot where his parents died."

"Jesus. How awful would that be?"

Julie shook her head. "He said it was weird, but comforting, like he was getting a chance to say good-bye properly for the first time. He doesn't remember the funeral. He was only three."

"Oh, don't." Penny dabbed at the corner of her eye. "Poor Jeremy."

Julie looked out over the fields. "He doesn't want a pity party. He said meeting Anita and talking to her was a really positive experience."

"I'm happy for him," I said, rubbing Julie's back.

"Me too," Julie said. "Anyway, enough doom and gloom. How are your plans shaping up? What's happening next week?"

"Daniel has an itinerary planned. Bath, Stratford, Salisbury..."

"I thought you wanted to go to London," she said.

"I do. Daniel only wants to go for one night, two at the most."

"It *is* expensive," Penny pointed out.

"You know he doesn't give a crap about money, Penny," I argued.

Julie flattened her lips into a grim line. "Maybe he's stressed about going back there because of...*you know*..."

"What, that he'd be dreading being near Oxford, you mean?" Penny asked.

"Yeah, maybe he's afraid it'll bring back memories," Julie suggested.

"I'd say you're right," Penny mused. "However, Oxford isn't actually *in* London. Not even really near it at all."

"I thought it was," I said, my voice fading. I felt like such an ignoramus.

"No, silly, it's in Oxfordshire," Penny said. "About an hour and a half northwest of London."

"Okay, there goes that theory." Julie grimaced.

As we walked on, Julie quizzed Penny about their honeymoon trip, but I found myself unable to keep track of the conversation, distracted by thoughts of my ripped silk nightie and Daniel's mysterious aversion to London.

274

CHAPTER 29

Preparations

Prepare we for our marriage…
And may our oaths well kept and prosperous be!
(*Henry V,* Act V, Scene 2)

T he next morning, I had breakfast with Daniel's family and Julie in
the estate dining room while he golfed with his dad and brothers.
As Patty, Gwen, and great-aunt Gwendolyn speculated about the
weather, I squirmed uncomfortably in my seat.

After the rehearsal party the night before, Daniel had imbibed
a tad too much, and we'd ended up in our room playing a drinking
game with a tumbler of scotch. Somehow, most of it had ended up
all over me, a good deal of it between my thighs, a mess which Daniel
had kindly offered to clean up—with this tongue. At the time, it had
been fun, but now I was paying for it.

I excused myself from the table, rummaging for my phone in
my bag and finding a quiet corner in the lobby to call Daniel. After
four rings and the sound of muffled rustling, Daniel finally answered.

"Aubrey? Is everything okay?"

"Everything's fine here. How are *you?*"

"Aside from this blinding hangover and the fact that Brad has
suddenly turned into an arrogant golf pro? I'm superb."

"You're having a bad game?"

"Meh, hit and miss. You caught me mid-putt. Not that I'm particularly worried about the distraction. I don't have a chance in hell of sinking this. Hang on."

I heard him calling out to Jeremy to go ahead and take his turn first.

"So, your head's pounding?" I asked.

"Fiercely. Christ. I was a mess last night."

"Feel free to be as messy as you like as often as you please."

"I take it you enjoyed yourself?"

"Immensely. Although your scotch trick might have been a tad ill-advised. They don't call it firewater for nothing. I'm stinging a wee bit south of the border."

"I didn't even think about that. Are you okay?"

"I'm fine. A soak in the tub and a day of rest should sort everything out."

"A day of rest, huh? Sounds like I might've shot myself in the foot."

"There's nothing wrong with my *hands*—" I turned to the wall as I continued to whisper "—or my *tongue*, for that matter."

He cleared his throat. "Okay, as much as I'm enjoying imagining that, I'm about to make a spectacle of myself. Before my dad mistakes me for a flag hole marker and fires a ball at my crotch, we should change the subject."

"You could always duck behind a tree and take a few...um... handicap strokes." I giggled.

"*Aubrey...*"

"Okay, sorry," I said, tittering at my own joke.

"Is there a specific reason for your call, feisty pants?"

"Actually, yes. Do you think you could make a trip to the pharmacy on the way back? Grab some Epsom salts or something? I'd like to have a soak in the tub this afternoon."

"I should pick up some Tylenol anyway. Anything else?"

"It's not an emergency, but I'd like to paint my toenails. Can you get me a bottle of red nail polish if you see some?"

He sighed heavily. "Brad will get a kick out of me shopping for that."

"Never mind. It's not a big deal—"

"No, no, it's fine. If I see something, I'll pick it up. Listen, I should try to salvage some dignity here. We'll be back in an hour and a half or so."

"Drive carefully."

"Not easy with visions of you in that tiny skirt dancing around in my rearview mirror."

"You could send the guys off for a nature walk and take a turn in the back seat by yourself," I suggested.

"Maybe I'll try to find Harriet the Horny Holstein. I believe we have some unfinished business."

When I heard the room door open, I slid warily under the blanket of bubbles.

"Daniel? Is that you?"

A hand holding a box of Epsom salts emerged through the crack in the bathroom door.

"Of course it's me." He peered around the edge of the door. "I sure as hell hope you weren't expecting someone else."

"You're *so* adorable when you're jealous."

"Touché."

"Thanks for grabbing that," I said.

"I hope it eases the fire down below. Actually *hope* isn't a strong enough word. I'm fervently praying with every fiber of my being."

I laughed as he poured a healthy dose of the crystals into the water.

"Comfortable?" he asked, perching on the edge of the tub.

"Uh-huh. I love bubble baths."

"I hate 'em," he said, frowning at the suds. "Can't see a damn thing."

He smiled, and I gazed back at him dreamily, reaching up to link my soapy fingers with his.

"I love you, sailor."

"I love you too, poppet." He suddenly stood, reaching into his pocket. "And I endured Brad's mockery just for you." He placed a bottle of nail polish on the side of the tub. "Fire-engine red."

"Aptly named," I said, reaching for the bottle. "And a very pretty color."

He sighed, popping open the button of his pants and peeling off his shirt.

"Funny, that's exactly what Brad said." He turned on the shower and finished undressing. "You don't mind if I shower, do you?"

"Of course not. Do your thing."

Daniel did his thing. Did he ever. While he soaped up, I ogled him shamelessly, watching his muscles rippling. Such a pedestrian activity, but Daniel made showering look like an art. He stepped out and wrapped a towel around his waist, reaching over the sink to towel-dry the mirror. I slid to the other end of the tub, leaning on my hands as I watched.

"I think we should get shower doors like that at home."

"Really? Why's that?"

"Unfrosted glass is the way to go."

"You're as perverted as I am," he said. "But I confess, I've considered new shower doors a few times myself."

He smirked, squirted a dollop of shaving cream onto his palm, and lathered his chin.

"Penny will be relieved."

"She can't seriously have thought I'd go to her wedding without shaving. I'll be front and center all day."

"Are you nervous?"

He rinsed the razor, his lips pursed in contemplation. "Honestly? I'm kind of excited about emceeing."

"This sort of thing *is* right up your alley, isn't it, *Professor?*"

I gave him a saucy wink, and he shook his head, turning his attention back to the mirror. As he finally dried his face and splashed the sink clean, I perched my foot on the side of the bath.

"Can I borrow your shaving cream, sunshine?"

Daniel smiled, giving the can a shake. He sprayed a foamy blob onto his fingers and slid his hand up my leg, massaging it into my skin. He dangled my razor between his fingers.

"May I?"

"May you what? Shave my legs?"

"Sure. I'm a pro. Don't you trust me?"

"Um, of course I do."

He perched on the edge of the tub, positioning the razor at my ankle and making a slow, even sweep through the foam.

"Okay?" he asked.

"Uh-huh."

"Then why are you holding your breath?" He laughed. "I promise not to cut your leg off."

I sank under the bubbles and tried to relax. After Daniel had made several careful passes up my calf, rinsing the blade under the hot water each time, I closed my eyes and hummed contentedly.

"Do me a favor?" he said.

"Hmm?"

"Don't tell Brad about this."

"I can totally imagine him doing this for Penny."

"Really?"

"It's got a *foreplay* feel to it, don't you think?"

He chuckled as he rinsed the remaining foam from my calf, allowing his hand to travel unnecessarily up my thigh in the process.

Yep, definitely foreplay.

Gesturing for me to switch legs, he gave the shaving cream another shake and proceeded to do my other shin.

"Did you see Penny this morning?" he asked.

"No. She and the bridesmaids left for the salon early. You know, hair, manicures, pedicures…"

"Have you ever had a full beauty treatment like that?" Daniel asked as I ran my fingers up and down my legs, admiring his handiwork.

"Not for a long time. But I don't need a salon. I've got *you*," I said, wiggling my toes and reaching for the nail polish.

"*Oh, no,*" Daniel said, recoiling and waving his hands. "I don't have a clue how to polish nails."

"Please? It's easy. It's like painting."

I reached over the side of the tub for a towel and dried my feet, resting one of them on his leg.

"*Please?*"

He exhaled loudly, his expression a mixture of defeat and exasperation. He tightened the towel at his waist and knelt on the floor, taking the polish and untwisting the cap.

"I'm totally whipped, you know that?"

I ignored his comment, clapping my hands and curling my toes over the edge of the tub. He pulled the brush out of the bottle, dragging some of the excess off against the bottle's rim.

"Look at that. You're a natural," I said.

"Don't push your luck."

I closed my lips with an imaginary zipper as he went from one toe to the next. Oddly enough, he *was* very good at it.

"What a treat." I sighed.

"No guy's ever done this for you before?"

"Nope."

"For some strange reason, that makes me happy."

"I don't think it's strange knowing you're charting territory no one else has. You've been the first to do lots of things for me."

He quirked an eyebrow. "I'm listening…"

"*Fishing* is more like it."

"Call it what you will."

I pondered all the ways Daniel had been *my first*.

"No one's ever taught me to rumba. No one's put a poem to music and sung it for me before, or read me poetry in bed. I've certainly never had someone write me odes and sonnets."

"Child's play," he scoffed.

"No one else has named a boat after me."

"Yeah, that *is* pretty cool." He shrugged with a false modesty.

"Your turn." I smiled at him shyly.

"Okay." He looked up at the ceiling as he pondered. "No one's ever played Pictionary on my back before."

"That's a dumb one," I protested.

"No it's not. I love playing back-Pictionary with you."

"Think of a better one."

"No one's ever given me herself and all her stuff as a birthday gift before."

"That's strange too. Maybe I'm a weirdo."

"You're not a weirdo." He puckered his brows, his Adam's apple bobbing as he swallowed. "No woman has made me feel like my love for her is all that matters, and that regardless of what I do or say, her love will still be there at the end of it all."

My heart fluttered. What had started as a silly conversation had taken a serious turn.

"Daniel…"

"What? It's true."

"Do you think you've done something to make me want to turn my back on you?"

His eyes flickered to mine and darted down again. He hid behind a façade of concentration, as if painting my baby toenail required the utmost attention. I suppose it did.

"We all have our ups and downs," I said. "You don't always have to be at the top of your game."

"Sometimes I think I have more downs than ups."

I recalled what Penny had said the day before about his moodiness during the week. I could easily quiz him about our time apart, ask about his nightmares, dig for information to find out if he'd been hiding something, but I couldn't bring myself to drag a dark cloud over the day.

"I'm still amazed that you didn't run for the hills after you read those PDF files on the plane," he added.

"Why would you sharing your heart with me make me run? You're being too hard on yourself."

"You're very tolerant."

"No, I'm not. I'm the least tolerant person I know. I have the patience of a housefly."

"That's true," he said, screwing the top of the nail polish back on. "You win."

"It's not about winning or losing." I paused. "But you're right, I do win."

The tension broken, he dunked his hand into the tub and flicked water in my face. I was on the verge of sending a wave of soapy water into his lap when the phone rang in the other room. He leapt up, grabbing a robe as he crossed to the door.

"You're lucky, mister!" I called after him.

While Daniel talked on the phone, I surveyed my red toenails. He'd done a great job. I momentarily toyed with the idea of asking him to put on a second coat, but when he came back into the bathroom, he was wearing his jeans and pulling a shirt over his head.

"Sorry, poppet, I'm needed downstairs. Then I'll have to head to Brad's room to get ready. Maybe you can grab lunch with Julie and get ready in here."

"Don't worry about me. I'll be fine."

He leaned over and wrapped his hands around my feet, kissing each of my toes softly.

"That tickles." I giggled. "Hey, that's another one. No one's ever kissed my toes before."

I emerged from the bathroom, spinning around so Julie could see my dress from all sides.

"Holy crap, Aubrey! You look—*stunning*."

"Not too much?"

"Are you kidding? It's perfect. You're so lucky you can wear a strapless. If I wore a dress with no straps it would fall straight down to the floor." She cupped her tiny boobs for emphasis.

"Julie, your dress is gorgeous. Jeremy's gonna lose his shit when he sees you."

I sat at the dressing table, pulling my hair up and turning my face this way and that. Julie stood behind me.

"You should let me put your hair up so you can show off your shoulders."

"That would be great, if you don't mind."

"What about jewelry?"

"I don't know. I'd like to wear the bangle Daniel got me for graduation, but it's rose gold. I don't have matching earrings."

"You're sold on the bangle?" she asked, reaching for her clutch purse.

I slipped the bangle onto my wrist. "I think so. It's perfect with this dress."

"I agree. Daniel would agree too." She opened her purse and pulled out a small Tiffany box. "He wanted you to have these, but he was afraid you'd feel pressured into wearing them if you had something else in mind."

I eased open the box. Inside sat a pair of rose gold hoops, similar in style to the bangle, each with three diamonds set in the gold.

"They're gorgeous." I slipped the hoops from the velvet pad and put them on.

Julie assessed my reflection. "Beautiful," she pronounced, holding my hair in a loose ponytail.

"Isn't he the most amazing guy ever?"

She smiled at me brightly. "Next to Jeremy, he's a pretty close second."

"Do you ever pinch yourself, Julie? I still can't believe how lucky I am."

"You're *both* lucky," she said.

I turned my face back and forth so I could admire the earrings. Julie absently dragged the brush through my hair.

"Remember when he walked into that classroom the first time and you pretended you were all blasé? I knew you had it bad from day one. Talk about falling hard."

"Excuse me, what about you and Jeremy? '*I don't chase; I replace,*' my ass."

"Yeah, yeah." She giggled, twisting my hair into a spiral and clipping it into place. "I think I did know almost right away he was the one. Like, *the one…*"

"Holy shit!" I spun in the chair to look up at her. "Are you guys talking marriage?"

She shrugged. "It's sometimes implied. When we were talking about moving in together, there was a lot of, *if we're gonna be together anyway, we might as well get a place, blah blah*…that sort of thing. What about you and Daniel? Does he ever drop hints?"

"Not really. I can't even wrap my head around a wedding. Besides, we have so much to learn about each other."

"Aubrey, that's the point of marriage. You spend your life learning about each other." She rested her hands on my shoulders and looked at me in the mirror. "You know the important things. He loves you; he'd do *anything* for you. He has goals and aspirations, a decent family…"

I shook my head and grabbed one of her hands. "You're right, bun-head. I think when your parents are divorced, you tend to be a wee bit gun shy, that's all." I smiled at her in the mirror as she pushed more pins into my hair. "I've missed talking to you, Jul. I don't know what I'd do if you weren't here this weekend."

"For one thing, girl, you'd be doing your own damn hair."

Together

They are in the very wrath of love, and they will together…
(*As You Like It*, Act v, Scene 2)

I t was quarter to three. Julie and I had been standing behind the rows of assembled white chairs just long enough for my heels to sink into the grass, anchoring me in place. Julie frowned as she scanned the crowd.

"Shouldn't they be here by now? We can't take our seats without the groomsmen, right?"

Just then, a movement in the hedged laneway caught my eye. Jeremy and Daniel were striding toward us, both of them looking like they'd stepped off a runway in Paris.

Julie waved, and they spotted us, both raising a hand in greeting.

"Holy fuckballs. They look amazing," I murmured.

Daniel's eyes were focused on me, his lips curled into a smile that could charm the bra off a nun. A mere three hours ago, he'd been vulnerable and sweet, marveling at my unconditional love for him, and now here he was all debonair confidence and fuckhawt swagger.

Despite the numerous greetings awaiting them as they passed through the crowd, Jeremy and Daniel headed directly for us. As

Jeremy slipped his arm around Julie's waist, telling her how great she looked, Daniel lowered his face to my cheek, kissing me and nudging my earring gently with his nose.

"Hi, beautiful."

"Hi yourself, handsome. Thank you for the earrings. I love them."

"They look nice. You, on the other hand, look gorgeous."

"I had a feeling you'd like this dress."

He slid his hand up my arm, his eyes moving appreciatively from my waist to my chest.

"Hey, you two, quit undressing each other with your eyes," Julie said, interrupting Daniel's admiration of my cleavage.

He cleared his throat. "You're absolutely right. We should get things rolling, shouldn't we?" He offered me his arm. "Aubrey, may I have the honor of escorting you to your seat?"

Daniel led me to the front row. As we walked down the aisle, he smiled and I beamed at him, recalling what I'd told Julie earlier.

All of a sudden, a wedding didn't seem all that difficult to imagine.

One of life's little ironies is the ridiculous amount of decision-making and stress that goes into planning a wedding ceremony, an event which is often over and done with in less than half an hour.

When Penny and Brad clasped hands and walked down the aisle as husband and wife, a mere twenty-six minutes had passed. The receiving line after the ceremony looked as if it might take longer. Jeremy emerged from the crowd, telling me that Daniel was waiting for me by the fishpond. I made my way carefully across the lawn and out into the gardens to find Daniel sitting on a bench in front of the pond.

"Hey, there you are." Daniel waved me over and gestured for me to sit beside him.

He wasted no time on pleasantries, kissing me softly. "Do you know how difficult it was to pay attention with you looking so delicious in the front row?"

"You seemed attentive as far as I could tell."

"I was saying the alphabet backward in my head to stop myself from staring at your legs."

"You were not." I laughed, shoving him with my shoulder.

"I might be exaggerating slightly." He grinned and clasped my hand.

Jeremy appeared arm in arm with Julie, an attractive dark-haired man following closely behind them.

Daniel held his hand up to greet him. "Aubrey, this is Gavin, a friend of mine and Penny's. He played the piano during the ceremony."

So this was Gavin. I'd seen his pictures on Facebook. I'd thought him handsome in the photos, but he had a charisma that made him even more attractive in person. He closed in on Daniel, shaking his hand and clapping him on the shoulder.

Daniel gestured to me proudly. "Gavin, this is Aubrey."

Gavin took my hand and brought it to his lips. Yep, totally swoon-worthy.

He winked at Daniel. "*Ah, Lewis. Plus ça change, plus c'est pareil. Des jambes incroyables, mon ami.*"

"Yes, she has incredible legs. She also has a fantastic command of French, Gav. Bilingual, in fact," Daniel said.

Gavin put his hand over his mouth, feigning embarrassment. "Oh, shit. Stepped in that one, didn't I?" he said. "Sorry about that."

I waved off his apology. "*Ne t'inquiète pas. J'étais juste en train d'admirer tes bras.*"

"You cheeky monkey. Did you hear that, Lewis? Your girlfriend is ogling my arms."

"She's brazenly lecherous," Daniel said, matter-of-factly.

Gavin put his hand over his heart. "I think I'm in love."

"Unthink it. She's spoken for."

"Shame." Gavin gave me another once-over, a roguish grin dancing on his lips. Their lighthearted sparring warmed my heart.

Jeremy reluctantly interrupted the banter, bobbing his head at Daniel. "I think we have to go, man. Picture time."

Daniel sighed. "I guess you're right." He kissed my forehead. "Why don't you relax? Have a drink and some canapés. We could be a while."

I straightened his bowtie and said, "You behave yourself. If Penny wants a picture of you holding a daisy between your teeth, do as you're told."

"Yes, dear," he said resignedly. "Listen, keep an eye on Gavin, okay? Make sure he doesn't break anything or run off with anyone's wife?"

"That sounds like a lot of responsibility for just one person."

"Julie will help." He laughed.

Julie and I called good-byes over our shoulders. Jeremy and Daniel watched us leave, both of them shaking their heads.

"Ladies, I've been given strict instructions to keep you thoroughly entertained until dinner," Gavin said, gallantly holding out both elbows. "You could drink non-alcoholic punch and do a stuffy garden tour, or you could listen to a boring string quartet while drinking afternoon tea in the dining room. *Or*—and this is the option I strongly suggest—you could watch an incredibly attractive and remarkably talented fellow play the piano. It's worth noting that *I* am the aforementioned fellow, and the bar is right next door to the music room."

"Gosh, the last choice sounds pretty good," I said, smiling brightly at him. "Julie?"

"I wonder if the bartender knows how to make mojitos," Julie mused.

Gavin grinned impishly and quickened his step. "Lewis was right. This is going to be fun."

"Okay—I have to ask," I said as we reached the side entrance to the house. "What's with the nickname? Why 'Lewis'?"

He held the door open for us. "Now *that* is a fascinating story," he said. "One best told with a drink in each hand…"

Wedding receptions are predictable events, but having the inside scoop shed a different light on the events of the evening. I was aware that Daniel was concerned about becoming overly emotional during his speech, and we all knew Brad was terrified of speaking in front of a room full of strangers. Then, of course, there was Penny and Brad's nervousness about their first dance. For Julie and me, being forced to brave dinner with the Grants without Jeremy and Daniel at our sides was a minor feat compared to the anxiety brewing at the head table.

Daniel's emceeing duties kept him busy during dinner. As the dessert dishes were cleared and champagne poured, he took his place behind the podium for one last time to direct post-dinner speeches. He rested his glass on the podium and smiled at the assembled guests.

"Ladies and gentlemen, before I hand things over to the bride and groom, I'd like to say a few words. I'll be brief. I'm sure everyone is more interested in hearing what *Brad* has to say."

Brad grimaced and rubbed his face. A few people tittered.

"First of all, thanks for putting up with me all evening," Daniel said. "Emceeing this event has been one of the most stressful tasks of my life. I wanted to do a great job for Penny and Brad."

There was a unified "Aww" from the audience, and my throat tightened.

"So, what can I say about Penny?" Daniel frowned as if he were pondering the question deeply. "I've known Penny for almost ten years. She's been a great friend, a constant companion, and a trusted confidante during some difficult times. To be honest, in the time I've known her, I've come to think of her as a sister. The only difference today, I suppose, is that Brad's made it legal." He looked over at Penny and took a deep breath. "Love you, Penn."

She blew him a kiss and dabbed under her eye. How she wasn't blubbering like a fool was beyond me. I blew my nose quietly. Across the table, Gwen was sniffing up a storm. Patty held out a tissue, and Gwen snapped it up gratefully.

"As for Brad," Daniel continued, surveying his brother, "he's everything a big brother ought to be — loyal, and fiercely protective. He wasn't going to stand for anyone pushing me around. As far as he was concerned, that was *his* job."

The crowd laughed, and Brad nodded as if to say, *Yeah, that's pretty much true.*

"Bottom line, Brad, Penny, I love you both, just as everyone in this room does. We all wish you good health and happiness. Oh, and my mother has requested lots of babies ASAP."

Amid more laughter, Gwen covered her mouth and shrugged guiltily.

"Now, I can't let the day go by without sharing a brief passage to mark the occasion, if only because I know it'll drive my brother crazy. I hope Master Shakespeare will forgive me for meddling with a couple of his words to suit my purpose."

Daniel turned to Brad and Penny, and began to recite a passage from memory: *"For my brother and my new sister no sooner met but they look'd; no sooner look'd but they lov'd; no sooner lov'd but they sigh'd;*

*no sooner sigh'd but they ask'd one another the reason; no sooner knew
the reason but they sought the remedy—and in these degrees have they
made a pair of stairs to marriage... they are in the very wrath of love,
and they will together.'"*

He addressed the assembled guests to deliver the closing line:
"'*Clubs cannot part them.*'" He nodded with an air of finality, drawing
applause from around the room.

I was too busy gripping my Kleenex to clap. Not that his performance warranted concern. He was a vision of poise and self-assurance,
the Daniel I'd fallen for in the seminar room months before, cool as
a cucumber and suave as hell.

"I now have the distinct pleasure of calling upon the bride and
groom." Daniel stepped back while Brad and Penny made their way
to the podium. Brad fumbled around, adjusting the height of the
microphone and clearing his throat.

"Oh, man, I'm so nervous for him," Julie said.

I squeezed her elbow. "Think positive thoughts."

Brad put his arm around Penny's waist. She patted his chest and
whispered something. He nodded and leaned over the mic.

"Okay. First of all, thanks to everyone for coming, and a huge
thank you to Penny's family and friends for all their work while we
were four thousand miles away. Today wouldn't have been possible
without you. And thank you to my family for coming all this way
to share our day. We love you guys."

"So far so good," I said quietly.

Julie nodded and reached for my hand.

"This is kind of stressful," Brad confessed, tugging at his bowtie.
"Daniel and Jeremy are the creative ones. Public speaking isn't my thing."

Penny smiled at him supportively.

"I'm gonna put my feelings in terms that make sense to me. I'm a
business-minded guy—that's just the way I think..." He shifted his
feet and put his hand in his pocket. "So, the way I see it, marriage
is like a merger. If I was a company looking to increase my value,
Penny's assets would make her a great acquisition."

A few people snickered, and Brad frowned as Penny put her
hand to her forehead.

"That didn't sound too great, did it?" Brad asked, sneaking a look
at his bride, his eyes dropping to her chest.

She waved her hands, indicating that he should get on with things. Brad peered over his shoulder at Daniel who was patting his left lapel, his advice to his brother quite simple. *Speak from your heart.* Brad frowned and rested his hands on the podium.

"Okay, let me try that again. Um, two years ago I came to England to visit my brother, Daniel. When I got to his apartment, his roommate was packing her things to stay with a friend so I could have her room. In case you don't know, that roommate was Penny.

"The first thing I thought when I met her was '*Whoa, she's beautiful.*' After talking to her for a while, I realized she was funny, too. She stayed at the apartment for dinner, and over the next couple of hours, I saw she was gutsy and smart and pretty much everything I was looking for in a woman." Brad turned to Penny and took her hand. "What she doesn't know, is that after dinner when she grabbed her bags and headed for the door, all I could think was, '*Please don't go.*'"

"Oh my God," Julie squeaked. "*Brad…*"

Penny covered her mouth with her hand, and I found myself doing a quiet cheer in my seat.

Come on, Brad. Bring it home…

"Luckily, she did come back. She kept forgetting stuff, and had to swing by the apartment every day to grab something. I think she kept coming back because she couldn't resist my charms."

Penny rolled her eyes and slapped his arm.

"That's okay, babe," he assured her. "I couldn't resist yours, either."

I snuck a look at Daniel, who seemed to be bracing himself for Brad to start publicly lauding Penny's boobs. Happily, Brad steered clear of explicit references to his bride's ample bosom.

"Anyway, Penny and I have been a perfect match since day one. Every day is brighter because she's around," Brad said, appearing bolstered by his own heartfelt admissions. "When I screw up, Penny steps in to fix things. I hope I'm there for her when she needs me too."

He sought her confirmation, and she leaned in to kiss him, which led to a rousing chorus of *oohs* and *aahs.* Brad held up his hands, and the crowd quieted.

"So, getting back to the business side of things for a sec, when two companies merge, the goal is for the new corporation to be stronger than it was before. This is how it is for Penny and me. I *know* she makes me a better person. This is what I'd call a profitable merger."

He turned to kiss her, and the room erupted into cheers and ear-splitting glass clinking. At the Grant table, we breathed a collective sigh of relief.

Finally the speeches were over, and Penny and Brad's first dance was executed without a single crushed toe. Daniel turned things over to the DJ and pushed his way through the crowd on the dance floor. At our table, he held out his hands. He drew me onto the dance floor and held me close. "It feels good to have you in my arms. I've missed you today," he whispered.

"You did such a great job."

"It helped having you here. You always anchor me."

Nestling into his neck, I closed my eyes, perfectly content. Falling into a comfortable rhythm, we chatted as we danced.

"Have you had an okay day?" he asked. "It must have been a bit boring for you."

"Julie and I had each other. And Gavin was great."

"Ah, yes, my delightful womanizing friend."

"He was a perfect gentleman."

"Didn't try to woo your panties off with more of his dazzling French?"

"No, but that was pretty funny, him talking about my legs and thinking I wouldn't understand."

"Your comeback was spot-on. I'm sure you kept him on his toes this afternoon."

I laughed, tightening my arms around his shoulders.

"He misses you. He said he thinks you've lost weight."

"I don't drink as much beer as I used to. I'm sure that's what it comes down to."

"You don't smoke as many doobies either, I gather."

"Oh, shit." He grimaced. "I was *so* hoping he wouldn't tell you that story."

"I started it. I asked him why he called you Lewis, and he told me about your drug-induced poetry. I can imagine you giving Lewis Carroll a run for his money, but I totally can't picture you smoking pot."

"I only did it a few times. I didn't particularly enjoy the sensation. It made me too paranoid."

"How old were you?"

"Eighteen. Experimentation. Trying to fit in, I guess. You don't think I'm a total ass, do you?"

"Of course not. Can you imagine if everyone were held forever accountable for the dumbass things they did at eighteen?"

"No, I suppose not," he said, looking at me with a strange expression.

I didn't have the chance to ask him what he was thinking because, at that moment, Gavin appeared beside us.

"May I?" he asked, tapping Daniel's shoulder.

Daniel scowled at his friend's intrusion. "*Must* you?"

"Don't be a greedy sod." Gavin elbowed Daniel out of the way. "Go get a drink."

Daniel retreated, but not without raising a warning finger at his friend.

"Bloody hell," Gavin said, swinging me into the crowd as Daniel strolled off to the bar, looking over his shoulder as he walked. "Possessive bastard."

"He knows you too well." I laughed.

"Yeah, no flies on him." He grinned. "So, you and Lewis, huh?"

"It would appear that way, yes."

"Can't imagine what you see in him. Are you sure you wouldn't prefer a dashing English fellow with nimble fingers and unrivalled linguistic abilities?"

At two in the morning, Daniel and I went back to the room, both of us wiped and desperate for our pillows. Daniel tossed his tuxedo jacket onto the back of a chair, popped open the top buttons on his shirt, and sank onto the bed with a grateful groan. He held out his arms to me, and I flaked out beside him.

"What a stellar day," he said.

"It was amazing."

I rested my chin on his chest. He radiated heat, not surprising considering his dance floor escapades.

"How come I didn't know you were such a good dancer, sailor?"

"I don't like to boast."

"You *love* to boast. I never dreamed you'd have those moves. I thought Penny's aunt Flora was going to shove a five pound note down your pants when that Justin Timberlake song came on."

"I guess I wanted to surprise you," he said.

"In that case, mission accomplished. You certainly brought shmexy back."

He chuckled, and I rubbed my cheek against his chest as I pictured him popping and gliding in time to the music while Gavin hooted and clapped beside him.

"Speaking of surprises, what's that all about?" I gestured to the gift bag Daniel had dropped beside him on the bed. "Brad and Penny already gave you cufflinks as a thank-you gift, right?"

"Penny said it was an impulse. Brad wrote the card about an hour ago."

He propped himself on his elbow, reached into the bag, and found an envelope. His bemused expression became serious as he looked inside the card.

"'*Hey, D*,'" Daniel read, glancing at me briefly. "'*I'm not usually the corny type, but I wanted to thank you for everything you did today, and for bringing Penny and me together in the first place. When we started planning the wedding, we knew we wanted you to emcee. Who else would take the job so seriously? When you were born, Mom and Dad told me I had to watch out for you and be a good big brother. I guess I did okay because what comes around goes around, right? Having Penny at my side today was one thing, but knowing you had my back was a great feeling. Anyway, thanks. Love you, bro. Brad.*'"

Daniel closed the card and placed it on the bed between us.

"Wow." I reached for his hand. "Do you suppose marriage has stirred up Brad's sentimental side?"

"I don't know. I can't believe he went on the record with this. If I gave him a card like this, I'd never hear the end of it."

"He had a lot to drink. Maybe he wasn't thinking straight."

"Maybe," Daniel mused.

"Are you going to open the gift?"

He reached into the bag, ripping out reams of multi-colored tissue paper. Then he peeked inside and started laughing.

"What?"

Daniel turned the bag upside down, tipping its contents onto the comforter. A French manicure kit, a bottle of nail polish remover, a small bag of cotton balls, and two nail files tumbled onto the bed. On a sticky note attached to the nail polish kit, Brad had written:

Not judging.
Whatever turns your crank, bro.
(Consider this collateral.)

CHAPTER 31

The Tower

…thou laid'st a trap to take my life
As well at London bridge as at the Tower?
(*Henry VI, Part I*, Act III, Scene I)

Wednesday morning, I woke up alone and disoriented. Where was Daniel? And for that matter, where the hell was *I*? As my eyes adjusted to the dim lighting, I reflected on the events of the day before. We'd toured a cathedral in the morning and spent the afternoon exploring Stonehenge. Right — I was in Salisbury, which meant we were leaving for London today.

I dragged myself to the bathroom where I found a note tented over the taps.

Morning, poppet,

The fresh air yesterday must have taken it out of you. I could have paraded a marching band through here this morning and you wouldn't have woken up. I had a restless night. When I couldn't get back to sleep at six, I figured I'd pop out to fill up the car and grab some coffee and breakfast. I might try to find a car wash too. See you soon, lovely. -D

Amid thoughts of fresh coffee and food, I couldn't help reading between the lines. Daniel hadn't slept well and now he was out washing the car. Six months into our relationship, I was able to connect the dots. Daniel was anxious.

As I showered, I wondered if I was reading too much into things. Maybe Daniel's inability to sleep was a side effect of hotel bed syndrome. And the car *was* dirty. I stopped obsessing. When I stepped out of the bathroom, I was greeted with the aroma of coffee. Daniel was sitting at the desk, staring into space as he sipped a Starbucks. He snapped out of his trance and spun around in the chair, handing me my cup.

I kissed him. "You were up early."

"You got my note?"

"Yeah, thanks."

I took a sip of my coffee and perched on his lap. He tugged on my towel and peered down at my cleavage.

"What's going on under there?"

"I just got out of the shower." I giggled. "So nothing's going on under here."

He ran his lips along my shoulder, capturing a few errant beads of water with his tongue. I sighed as he tickled my thigh.

"Would you *like* to have something going on under there?"

"Don't we have to leave soon?"

His fingers wandered farther up my leg, and his lips found that sweet spot under my ear. I shivered.

"London can wait an extra fifteen minutes, don't you think?"

"Fifteen minutes?" I dropped my head back. "Is that all I get?"

"And that, crazy legs, is called a *challenge*."

Daniel carried me across the room, tossing my towel on the floor as he lowered me to the bed, not once breaking eye contact while he stood above me undressing. He then proceeded to *rise to the challenge* brilliantly.

London, it turned out, was going to have to wait an extra twenty-five minutes.

The closer our proximity to London, the quieter Daniel became and the whiter his knuckles got. When his jaw started to twitch, I rubbed his thigh comfortingly.

"You okay?"

"Sorry if I seem distracted. It's been a long time since I've driven in London. The nearer we get to the hotel, the crazier the traffic will be."

"Take your time. It's not like we have a deadline." I flinched as a car passed with what seemed like a hair's breadth between us. "I don't know how you do it. I couldn't drive over here."

He smiled and squeezed my fingers briefly before gripping the steering wheel again.

"So, when are you going to tell me where we're staying?"

"I told you, it's a surprise."

His mysterious smile fueled my curiosity. I kept quiet, though. If there was one thing I'd learned, it was that Daniel's surprises were always worth waiting for. Twenty minutes later, Daniel heaved a sigh of relief as he carefully steered through traffic. Pulling up to the curb, he pointed out the window.

"There she is. Your humble abode for the next two nights."

Holy mother of pearl! We were staying at The Ritz!

"Daniel, you've got to be kidding…"

I hugged him, both of us smiling widely through our kisses. We climbed out, moving out of the way as bellhops and a valet flew into action. Daniel rolled his shoulders and tilted his head from side to side.

"I think I need a stiff one after that drive."

"I might need a stiff one too," I said, wrapping my arms around him and nestling into his neck. "Then maybe I'll have a strong *drink*."

"You are a dirty girl." He chuckled.

"What a great way to cap off our vacation. This is amazing, Daniel. Thank you."

"It was hard keeping this a secret. It's kind of an anniversary treat. Tomorrow's the thirteenth, remember."

"I hadn't forgotten. I might have a surprise or two hidden in my luggage." My heart filled as his eyes sparkled back at me.

"In that case, I can't wait until tomorrow."

Daniel was a wonderful tour guide. He'd carefully planned an afternoon walking tour, but after hitting several of the highlights on foot, we started hopping in and out of London taxis to save our feet. As the afternoon wore on and we were finishing our time at Trafalgar Square, I cajoled Daniel into a subway ride. We descended into the Underground, emerging a few stops later at Waterloo station.

"So, what's here?" I asked, spinning around on the street corner.

Daniel pointed between two buildings. "How would you like to go on that?"

I held my hand to my eyes, blocking out the late afternoon sun. "The London Eye! Can we? That would be so cool!"

Daniel produced two tickets from his back pocket. "I pre-ordered these online. I didn't want to risk getting here and having to wait."

My enthusiasm trumped the complaints of my aching feet, and I dragged Daniel along the sidewalk toward the entrance to the riverside attraction. He laughed as I bobbed around in the line, impatient for our turn on the giant wheel that would take us into the sky over London. We were finally shepherded into our pod with fifteen or so other enthusiastic tourists. Daniel stood with his hands on my hips and his chin resting on my head as we rose skyward.

I scanned the horizon. "Hey, that's Tower Bridge, right?" I asked. "Exactly."

I peered out the window, snapping a couple of pictures.

"And that's the Tower of London on the other side of the bridge?"

"That's it."

"Maybe we can check out the Tower tomorrow," I suggested.

"We'll see," he said, with a non-committal shrug.

I continued scanning the city. "There's a great view of the Houses of Parliament and Big Ben from here."

I reached for his arm, but Daniel had stepped away, blowing gusts of air upward and wiping his forehead with his sleeve.

"Hey, are you all right?"

He grimaced and pushed his sleeves up to his elbows. "Is it warm in here?"

I pressed my hand to his forehead. The color had drained from his face.

"You're clammy. You're not afraid of heights, are you?"

He shook his head and tried to smile. "Maybe it's a touch of claustrophobia. I probably need some air."

"You're worn out. Your bad night's sleep is catching up with you. Why don't we chill at the hotel tonight? Maybe grab room service and rent a movie?"

"If you wouldn't mind, that sounds perfect. I do need some sleep. Plus, I want to be in top form for tomorrow."

"That's right," I whispered. "You'll definitely need some reserves for what I have planned for tomorrow night."

At brunch the next morning, Daniel was chatty and cheerful, but his eyes betrayed his weariness.

"Would you like another mimosa?" he asked, gesturing to my champagne glass.

"No thanks. I'm stuffed." I reached for his hand. "Are you sure you're feeling better?"

"Much better. You were right. I needed a good sleep."

I gave his fingers a quick squeeze, not altogether convinced that the rolling and tossing he'd done the night before constituted "good."

"So, what's the plan?" I asked him.

"How do you know I have one?" His wink revealed the truth. Not only did he have a plan, but he was eager to share it. He retrieved a business card from his wallet and slid it across the table.

I examined the logo: *The Ritz Salon.*

"Turn it over," Daniel prompted.

I flipped the card. My name was written at the top, and underneath were two appointment times:

30 minute pedicure ⌇ *11:45*
50 minute facial treatment ⌇ *12:15*

"This is for me?"

"You said it's been a long time since you've visited a spa. What better place to get spoiled than the Ritz?" Daniel looked at his watch. "You need to be on the seventh floor ready to be pampered in forty-five minutes."

"I've never had a facial."

"The receptionist said something about a scalp massage."

"That sounds amazing." I sighed. "Are you joining me? Is there a treatment for men? Or are you power napping while I bask in the lap of luxury?"

"Neither. There's something I need to look into — and no, I can't tell you what it is. I'm heading out for a bit. I'll be back by the time you're done, and we'll go from there."

"Another surprise? Don't you think you've done enough, sailor?"

"It's not just our anniversary; it's our last day in England." He brought my hand to his lips and traced a line of kisses across my knuckles. "I want to make it a day neither one of us will forget."

Forty-five minutes later, I was slipping my feet into my flip flops, ready to dash to the elevator, when my phone rang. I smiled as I answered, assuming Daniel would be on the other end, calling to wish me a lovely time at my spa appointments. But the voice on the other end of the line wasn't Daniel's.

"Hey, Aubrey?"

"Jeremy? Hi! Is everything okay?"

"Um, I'm not exactly sure. Are you guys in London?"

"We arrived yesterday." I glanced at my watch. I didn't have time to talk. I was already running late. "What's going on?"

"Is Daniel with you?"

"No, he's gone out for a bit."

"Shit."

"What's happened? Do you need help?"

"We're fine. It's *him* I'm worried about. Do you know where he is?"

"He wouldn't tell me. He said it was a surprise. What's this all about? You're freaking me out."

"I'm sorry. I'm not trying to scare you, but he just texted me. I replied and tried to call him, but he's not answering. Normally I wouldn't worry, but his message was weird."

"Why? What did he say?"

"He told me I was right all along and that it was *his* turn to spit out the stone."

"Am I supposed to know what that means?"

"It's a long story. We talked at the airport before I left for France. Basically, the stone thing has to do with dealing with shit that's haunting you. I think he's gone to find Nicola."

"*What?*" I sank onto the bed. "Find her? What do you mean?"

"She's in London. He knows where she works. I think maybe he's got it in his head to track her down."

"Oh no…"

"I don't mean to be dramatic, but I'm worried there's this little piece of him that's not all there when it comes to this chick after what she did to him."

"Jeremy, did he tell you that?"

"Not exactly. He said he thinks his nightmares have to do with her. Look, I'm not trying to tell you what to do…"

"But you think I should try to find him?"

"I'd do it myself if we weren't four hundred miles away."

"No, of course, I'll call him."

"He's not answering my calls. He might not answer yours either."

"Then how am I supposed to find him? I wouldn't know where to start."

"Nicola works at the Tower of London in one of the gift shops."

"How do you know that?"

"Daniel's been watching her activities on Facebook for a couple of months."

"You're kidding…"

"I wish I was. I looked her up myself. She definitely works there."

As soon as I'd mentioned touring the Tower the day before, Daniel had gone pale and broken into a cold sweat. Had he been thinking about Nicola? Had his so-called claustrophobia been the precursor to an anxiety attack?

I kicked off my flip flops and slipped on a pair of shoes.

"I'm on it, Jeremy. Don't worry, okay?"

"I might be overreacting, but I hate the thought of him being somewhere alone and having—"

"No, you're right. God knows how he'll react to seeing her."

I assured him I'd keep him in the loop, and then I hung up and sprang into action. First, I called the hotel spa and canceled my appointments. Then I dropped my phone into my purse and headed for the lobby. I needed a taxi, and I needed it now.

The Tower of London loomed in the distance, and I was stuck in traffic. There was nothing the driver could do to circumvent the gridlock, short of driving on the sidewalk. I considered getting out and running the rest of the way, but the Tower was probably a lot farther away than it looked. I tried to think rationally.

Daniel wouldn't do something like this unless he thought he could cope, would he? But Jeremy had gone out of his way to call and warn me. If he'd believed Daniel was fine, would he have interfered?

Oh God, hurry up!

Sitting helplessly in the back of the cab, I tried to phone Daniel again, and once more the call went to voice mail. I left another straightforward message, asking him to call me. When the taxi finally pulled up to the curb outside the Tower of London, I tossed some money through the front seats and clambered out. At the ticket counter, I paid and then bolted to the entrance, tourist brochure in hand as I contemplated my next move.

I didn't have to think for long. There was a souvenir shop inside the main gate. I ducked inside and approached the guy behind the cash register.

"Excuse me. Is there anyone by the name of Nicola working here?"

He shrugged and shook his head.

Helpful fellow.

I scanned the store, not sure what to do next. A girl in a blue apron approached me.

"Did you say you were looking for Nicola?"

"Yes," I said, almost leaping on her. "Do you know her?"

"Do you mean Nicola Clarke?"

"Um, I guess."

"If it's Nicola Clarke you're after, she works in the Tower Shop by the Crown Jewels exhibit."

I nodded my thanks and escaped the store, scanning the brochure's map as I jogged up the steps leading to the middle of the fortress, a square surrounded on two sides by Tudor-style buildings. A chapel was straight ahead, and the castle tower rose up on my right.

According to the brochure, the Crown Jewels display and gift shop were in the building opposite the center tower. So now what? My pulse beat in my ears, and suddenly I felt like a fool. What if Daniel was fine? What if he was in the store having a perfectly civilized discussion with the girl? I'd look ridiculous, barreling in there.

He could have told me his plans—explained that he wanted to talk to Nicola today—but not only had he failed to tell me his intentions, he'd contrived to keep me out of the way by booking me a spa treatment and then turning off his phone. For some reason, he'd wanted to do this alone. I was meddling, plain and simple. I shouldn't have come.

On the other hand, how could I have gone blithely skipping off to have a pedicure after Jeremy's worried call?

I sank onto the stone curb, wishing Daniel had been more forthright about how he was feeling, but also realizing I was partly to blame for his reticence. I'd lost track of how many times I'd said to him, "*The past is the past. I don't want to talk about her.*" After reading those files with all of his musings from the beginning of the term, I'd told him I never wanted to hear her name again.

No wonder he'd shut me out.

It wasn't too late for me to redeem myself, though. I was here now, and if he needed me, I would help him. I stood, unsure what to do, but not prepared to idly twiddle my thumbs. I spun around slowly, and that's when I saw him.

Daniel was in the middle of the square, staring at the entrance to the Crown Jewels exhibit. I resisted the urge to run to him. Instead, I hid behind the tree to watch him undetected. He turned, a bewildered expression on his face, but then he staggered to a nearby bench and sat down, bowing at the waist. As his head dropped forward and he reached up to rub his left shoulder, memories of Daniel gasping for breath in his father's office on that snowy March day flashed before my eyes.

This was *exactly* what Jeremy had been afraid of.

Daniel

Take the Current

On such a full sea are we now afloat;
And we must take the current when it serves,
Or lose our ventures.
(*Julius Caesar*, Act IV, Scene 3)

I bent forward, filling my lungs with air, trying to center myself. I was okay. I could do this. I took in another long breath, letting it out slowly.

Jesus, I was pathetic. Surely I could talk to the girl without having a meltdown. I'd been fine ten minutes ago when I'd gone into the store in the first place. And if Nicola hadn't been on her lunch break, I could've gotten it over with. Waiting for her to return was the kicker. Now I had time to second-guess myself.

A few more minutes and she'd be back. What would I say to her? She'd probably have a conniption, seeing me here. What if seeing her made *me* have a conniption? After everything she'd put me through and the trauma she'd caused in my life, could I do this without losing my shit?

I checked the time again. Aubrey would be finished with her spa treatment by one o'clock. I didn't *have* to do this alone. I could leave her a message, telling her to phone as soon as she was finished at the spa. She could hop in a cab…

Yes, that's exactly what I'd do—what I should have done in the first place, and might've if I'd given myself a chance to think. I'd leave Aubrey a message and then have an hour to compose myself while I waited for her to call back.

Satisfied with this methodical course of action, I turned my cell phone back on and stared at the screen as several alerts appeared. There was a text from Jeremy imploring me to call him. There were three unheard phone messages as well, no doubt also from Jeremy. My text to him had been brief and cryptic, but he would have understood the implications of my words. He was probably freaking out. I'd text him after leaving Aubrey a message.

Without another thought, I dialed and waited for the voice mail to kick in. It didn't. Aubrey answered after the second ring.

"Daniel?"

"I was going to leave you a message. Aren't you in the middle of your pedicure?"

"It's a long story. I ended up not going."

"Are you all right?"

"I'm fine. It's not important. Tell me what's happening with you. Are *you* all right?"

At the sound of her worried voice, all of my methodical thoughts went out the window, and a stream of doubts flooded in to take their place.

"I'm an idiot, Aubrey. Don't hate me. I don't know what possessed me to be so impulsive—"

"Daniel, it's okay—"

"No, it's not okay," I interrupted. "You'll never believe where I am." I paced in front of the bench. Christ, what would she say when she heard what I was planning? "Please don't be angry…"

"Tell me what's going on. I promise I won't be angry."

I squinted at the stone face of the building in front of me.

"I'm at the Tower of London."

"Okay…And?" she prompted.

"Nicola works in a souvenir shop here." I let a beat pass and then added, "I came here to talk to her."

"And have you already spoken to her?" she asked, strangely not sounding the least bit surprised at my confession.

"I haven't seen her. I thought I'd be okay doing this alone, but now that I'm here, I'm not so sure…"

"What do you want me to do, Daniel?"

I ran my hand through my hair, feeling like a fool, but her voice was so strong and determined. She didn't sound angry at all. I could almost feel her presence. She was holding out a lifeline, so I grabbed hold.

"I know this is a lot to ask, but can you get a taxi? I'll wait for you at the admission gate to the Tower. When you get here, I can explain why I feel like I have to talk to her."

"I was hoping you'd say that," she said. "Turn around, Daniel."

I spun around, and there she was, no more than fifty feet away from me. There was no point saying anything else. She was dashing across the pavement, and I stood, immobilized by the shock of seeing her. I couldn't pull the words together to ask how she'd known where I was. She wrapped her arms around me, and I closed my eyes, letting her comfort wash over me. She stepped back at last, looking up at me anxiously.

"Are you okay?"

"What are you doing here? How did you —"

"Jeremy called me," she said, placing her hands on my chest. "He caught me as I was heading out the door to the spa. Don't be mad at him. He was worried about you. If you wanted to talk to Nicola, you should have told me, and I would've come with you. You didn't have to contrive to keep me out of the way."

"You think I *planned* to come here today?"

"Are you saying you didn't?"

"Of course I didn't. I booked that spa treatment for you because you deserve to be spoiled. End of story. I wasn't planning this. If anything, I've been trying to avoid coming here. I didn't want to come to London at all, but I knew you had your heart set on it. Why do you think I had every minute planned yesterday? When we were at the London Eye and you said you wanted to visit the Tower —"

"You started sweating and almost blacked out."

"Because it was the last thing I wanted to do."

GEORGINA GUTHRIE

"But you suddenly decided half an hour ago that it would be a great idea to come here and talk to her?"

Exasperated, I reached for her hand, leading her to the bench.

"I told you there was an errand I needed to run and that's what I did, but on the way back to the hotel, the cabbie drove across the Tower Bridge and started babbling about Henry the Eighth and all the executions that happened here. Then he mentioned the legend about the Tower falling if the six ravens were to ever leave the fortress."

I cringed, remembering the epiphany I'd had in the back of the taxi, a moment of understanding so profound my head had snapped back with the force of what I'd realized.

"All I could see was a girl being executed, holding out her hands to me, pleading for my help, and me struggling to get through a mass of people to reach her, the crowd holding me back, and giant black birds attacking me from above so I couldn't get to her…"

"Oh my God—Daniel, your nightmares? You think they take place *here?*"

I nodded. "Over and over again I had that same dream—the crowd of people, the birds—the girl being executed was Nicola. As soon as I understood that, I had to speak to her. I texted Jeremy to put the idea out there—to force myself into action. Then I turned off my phone so he wouldn't be able to talk me out of it."

"If all you were doing was putting the idea out there, why Jeremy and not me?"

I laughed wryly. "Maybe I pictured myself coming back to the hotel after talking to her and saying, '*Guess where I've been,*' like a warrior returning from battle or something. I wanted you to be proud of me. But if I'd crumbled and changed my mind…"

"I wouldn't have known any different."

"Essentially, yes."

Aubrey lowered her eyes, gazing at our joined hands. "I want to support you, Daniel, but I don't understand why you've come. Jeremy told me you suspected your dreams were about Nicola. Now you've confirmed it. So…what? Going in there to confront her—it'll open old wounds."

"It's not about me knowing Nicola is the girl in my dream," I explained. "I think I actually *understand* the dream. She needs help. She's dropped out of school, moved out of her parents' house. She's living in some rundown apartment in the suburbs and working here full-time. Her life has gone off the rails."

"Which she brought on *herself*."

I shook my head and looked at her pointedly. "A few days ago, you said you couldn't imagine everyone being held forever accountable for the dumb things they did at the age of eighteen."

She rolled her eyes. "I was referring to stupid things like experimenting with marijuana, shoplifting lip gloss, or drinking too much at a house party—not creating life-ruining false accusations."

"The sentiment still applies. She was young, and she made a bad decision. Her behavior was appalling, but does that mean she should pay for what she did forever? Would it make a difference if I told you she feels remorseful and has thrown everything away because she can't live with her mistake?"

"What do you mean?"

"Nicola didn't have her bursary renewed, but she couldn't bring herself to use the money from my dad to pay for her second year at Oxford. Apparently her parents insisted she use the money to finance her tuition, but she refused. That's why she moved out."

"You learned all this from her Facebook wall?"

"And now I can't go back and erase what I know. When all this stuff with Jeremy going to France came up, maybe subconsciously I recognized I might be able to help Nicola the same way he's helped Anita. Maybe forgiveness is the only option I have left."

Aubrey bit the inside of her lip, mulling over my words.

"She turned my life upside down with a few words, poppet. What if I can help her with a few of my own? I have to do something before we get on that plane tomorrow. Cursing her existence isn't working for me."

After briefly scanning my face again, she sighed. "Okay. You've made up your mind. Now what?"

"She was on her lunch break the first time I went in there. She should be back by now."

"So, we walk in and demand to speak to her?"

"I guess."

"You guess?" She laughed shortly. "Figures you'd pick today to become impulsive." She stood and held out her hand. "All right, I'm ready when you are."

We entered the shop as inconspicuously as possible, standing in a corner behind a rack displaying fridge magnets. I scanned the store. I didn't see Nicola at first. In fact, I heard her before I saw her, a muffled voice coming from behind the cash register as she spoke to another employee.

As she turned around, her blond hair obscured her thin face and pale eyes. I took a quick breath, waiting for the familiar heart-pounding and spotted vision, anticipating the sensation of the ground lurching away beneath my feet and the sound of my pulse racing in my ears.

There was nothing except for a faint quickening of my heart rate — an understandable reaction — and the sweatiness of my hand. After watching my face for a moment, Aubrey finally snuck a peek across the shop.

"Is that her?" she whispered.

"That's her," I confirmed, stepping behind the safety of the spinning rack.

"Daniel, she's a kid…"

"She'd be nineteen now."

"She looks so much younger."

I stole another look across the store. Aubrey was right. Nicola had always been slender and petite, but now it seemed as if a strong wind could blow her over. Funny how our ghosts take on such mythic proportions in our tortured imaginations.

"Her appearance helped to demonize me in the eyes of the administration. She was the epitome of the helpless victim," I said.

"I guess." Aubrey drew her hand from mine, rubbing her palm on her jeans. "You're not shaky or light-headed or anything?"

"I think I'm good."

"Should I give you some space?"

"If you don't mind." I took a step, but then I hesitated, turning back. "Don't go too far, okay?"

"I'll be nearby if you need me."

With Aubrey's comforting words sustaining me, I took a few steps forward, not sure how best to approach Nicola. In the end, my decision was made for me.

Her back was turned, her attention focused on a shelf in front of her on which she was stacking books, but she spun around and looked directly across the store—straight at me. Her wide-eyed expression and backward stagger might have been comical if not for the fact that she was so obviously in shock.

I paused as she blinked and brought her hand to her heart. For a second, I wondered if *she* might have a panic attack. Then her brow furrowed, and she mouthed my name. I held up my hand, part comforting gesture and part wave. The maternal voice of Nicola's coworker, Marjorie, the same woman I'd spoken to earlier, interrupted our bizarre exchange.

"Oh, Nicola, this is the young man I was telling you about—the one who was asking after you when you were on your lunch break."

Nicola nodded and steadied herself on the counter.

"Hi, Nicola. You must be surprised to see me."

She nodded and looked vaguely at her workmate.

"Can you slip away for a few minutes?" I asked, drawing her eyes back to mine before she could speak. "I'd like to talk to you."

"I don't know," she said, her voice barely audible. "I just got back from lunch…"

"Oh, go ahead," Marjorie said as she bustled over to the cash register, eliminating Nicola's excuse, if that's what it was. "I'll be fine. Go on."

She pushed Nicola around the corner, smiling at me like some sort of co-conspirator.

"We'll go outside, shall we?" I suggested.

"Um…okay."

With Nicola walking reluctantly beside me and Aubrey tagging along behind us, we emerged into the midday sun. I gestured to the bench Aubrey and I had been sitting on a few moments earlier. Nicola perched stiffly on the edge of the seat while I sat back comfortably. Aubrey settled onto a curb stone across the courtyard.

"How did you know where to find me?" Nicola whispered, her eyes trained on her tightly clasped hands.

"Your Facebook page is quite informative."

She covered her face with her hands. "Oh, God…"

And then she started to cry. No, *cry* wasn't the right word. *Sob* was a better description. I waited for her get out whatever feelings she needed to purge. I snuck a look at Aubrey who was cringing, her hand over her mouth. But then, just as quickly as Nicola had started crying, she stopped, sniffed, and rubbed her face with her sleeves.

"I don't blame you if you want to shout at me, Daniel. Go ahead. I deserve it," she said through her sniffles.

She still hadn't looked at me. I didn't blame her. Her shame was palpable.

"I'm not here to shout at you, Nicola."

Now she looked at me—a quick sideways glance of disbelief. "You're not?"

"No."

She frowned at the ground, baffled.

"You quit school," I said.

"I had to. My bursary wasn't renewed."

"My father gave you money."

"I couldn't do it. I couldn't use the money."

"I don't see why not."

"Because I'm a horrible person. I didn't deserve to go back to Oxford. I didn't belong there in the first place. I was out of my league. But you knew that, didn't you?"

Her tone was bitter.

"A lot of first year students take a while to figure things out. You didn't give yourself time to find your footing."

"I was too busy trying to find the easy way out," she said, staring listlessly at her thin hands. "And I ruined your life in the process."

For a second, I thought she was going to cry again, but she took a deep shuddering breath and pushed herself back on the bench.

"So, if you didn't come here to give me a piece of your mind, why did you come?" she asked.

"To tell you to go home to your mother and father. Let them look after you and help you get back on your feet. Maybe Oxford isn't the right place for you, but you should look into some other schools. You don't want to work in a souvenir shop for the rest of your life."

"My parents don't want me back. I've done nothing but disappoint them. They told me as much, you know, when I wouldn't use your dad's money. They don't call me to see how I'm doing, or anything.

My brother showed them my Facebook page a few months ago, and he told me that Mum started to cry, but she didn't ring me."

I mulled this over, trying to think of the best way to move forward.

"I don't know your parents, Nicola, but I know a thing or two about parental expectations and conflict. I've been there."

"Because of me, I bet."

"I won't sugar coat it, Nicola. What you did to me was unconscionable. It hurt my whole family. In fact, the ordeal caused some bad feelings between me and my father."

"But your parents dropped everything in Canada to come over here to help you."

"My parents came over here to help me, yes, but they were also trying to protect the family. My dad is Provost at, well, a large Canadian university. Can you imagine his reaction when he heard what I'd been accused of?"

"That's what I mean," she said, her voice small and sad again. "That's why I don't deserve to have a second chance. How could I do something so awful? All you ever did was help me…"

Her voice quavered, but she bit her lip, staving off further tears.

"It's taken me a long time to be able to say this, Nicola, and it's not easy, but you made a mistake. Yes, you screwed me over something fierce, but it's over. Pick yourself up and move on. It's cowardly to use the mistake you made as an excuse to waste every opportunity that comes your way. You can do better."

"I can't believe you've come all this way to tell me this…after everything."

"I'm struggling to wrap my head around it as well, trust me. But believe it or not, I'm doing this as much for myself as for you."

After several long moments, during which she seemed to be puzzling out everything I'd said, she snuck another look at me.

"I wouldn't know where to start to pick up the pieces."

"Start with your parents. Someone has to act first, and you could wait a long time for your parents to make a move. They think they have a point to prove…They're trying to teach you something."

"But that's just it," she argued, sitting up and speaking animatedly all of a sudden. "I screwed up. Okay, I get why they'd be annoyed by that. But then when I said I wanted to send the money back to your dad, they wouldn't hear of it."

"Wait, I knew you didn't want to use the money, but you actually wanted to give the money *back?*"

"When I got home from the admin offices, I felt awful. I wanted to tell them I'd made everything up, but I couldn't figure out how to tell my parents I'd lied. Before I had a chance to do anything, your dad came over to talk to my parents. Then it looked like I'd changed my story because he'd paid us off. Things went downhill from there."

"The wheels fell off for me right around that time too, believe me."

"I'm sorry, Daniel. I know it's too late to apologize, and there's nothing I can do now—"

"Hey, it's never too late to apologize when you screw up. Don't *ever* think you shouldn't say sorry because too much time has passed." I paused, imagining my father sitting at his desk with a desperate student in the seat across from him. "And for what it's worth, I don't think my father would want the money back."

"How can you say that? That's crazy."

"I know him. He'd like to see the money used wisely. He'd want you to make something of yourself. That way, this whole mess won't have happened for nothing. It might be too late for you to start a program in September, but you could look into taking some courses in the second term."

"I don't know…"

"While you're deciding what to do, put full privacy controls on your Facebook. There's no reason for your parents to reach out to you if they can ensure you're okay with a couple of mouse clicks."

"Maybe. I'm not sure. It's a lot to think about."

"I know it is, but promise you'll give it some thought."

She shrugged dismally. "I'll try."

"Good."

I sat up with an air of finality. There was little more to say. She caught me before I could stand.

"Is everything okay with you now?" she asked. "You moved back to Canada, right?"

"I did. I've picked up my PhD and I'm doing great."

"You're here on holiday?"

"With my girlfriend," I said, pointing across the square to where Aubrey was sitting cross-legged on the curb. "We're going home tomorrow."

"She's pretty."

"She's an incredible person."

"That's good. You deserve to be happy."

"Yes." I smiled at my beautiful girl. "I guess I do."

Nicola stood and crossed her arms uncomfortably. "I should get back to work."

"We should get going too."

She rolled a small pebble around on the ground with the scuffed toe of her shoe.

"Thanks, Daniel. For coming all this way to talk to me. I promise I'll think about what you said."

I nodded, and she turned and walked back toward the shop. By the time she'd disappeared inside, Aubrey had crossed the pavement and was in front of me, holding her hands out. I stood and hugged her.

"What happened?" she whispered.

"I might need a few minutes to process everything."

"Okay, we don't have to talk about it right now. Are you glad you came, though?"

I nodded, my cheek pressed against her silky hair.

"I am. Thank you for being here. I love you so much, Aubrey."

"I love you too."

I closed my eyes, holding her close.

"So, how was your visit to the Tower of London? Everything you imagined?"

"I don't even think *my* imagination could have cooked this up." She chuckled.

As we walked toward the exit, I looked around, marveling at the irony of the setting. Nicola spent her days at the Tower of London, originally designed to house liars and thieves. She'd been both. After concocting that ridiculous story, she'd robbed me of my good name, my reputation, and my peace of mind. My name I'd salvaged, my reputation I was winning back, and with a little bit of luck, my peace of mind would soon follow.

CHAPTER 33

An Ever Fixed Mark

...Love is not love
Which alters when it alteration finds,
Or bends with the remover to remove:
O, no! it is an ever-fixed mark,
That looks on tempests and is never shaken...
(Sonnet 116)

Stepping off the Tower of London property, I felt buoyant, hope-ful, and relieved all at the same time. How could something as simple as having a conversation with someone change my outlook so profoundly? With our joined hands swinging between us, Aubrey and I strolled along the pier, eventually stopping to watch the cruise boats ferrying tourists up and down the Thames.

"I guess I should tell you what happened," I said at last.

"I understand if you'd rather not."

"No, I want to have done with it."

I rested against the railing, recounting my conversation with Nicola as briefly as I could without sacrificing the full import of what had passed between us.

"What do you think she'll do now?" she asked.

"I'm not sure. She said she'd think things over."

"You've done your part. You have to be satisfied with that."

"I am."

"So, do you think you'll be better now? The nightmares — the anxiety — do you think it'll all stop?"

"I frigging hope so."

"Me too." She hooked her fingers over my forearm. "It's funny, looking back now, it's so obvious…the changes in you. Back in May and June — after the semester had ended, but before you started checking up on Nicola — I saw glimmers of this completely carefree man. I'd love to see more of him."

"I'll do my best to find him."

I closed my eyes as she kissed me, tuning out the rest of the world, thinking only of Aubrey — her lips and sweet tongue, her gentle fingers tracing my jaw line, her perfect heart filled with unwavering love that had become one of the most important parts of my world.

"Hey," I whispered, easing away from her. "We need to talk about our plans for the rest of the day." I directed her eyes to the opposite bank of the Thames. "Look down there. That's the new Globe Playhouse. How would you like to go there tonight?"

"Can we?"

I reached into my pocket.

"I believe we can." I handed her the two tickets I'd purchased that morning. "We're going to see *The Tempest* at seven thirty this evening."

She peered down at the tickets, eyes widening with excitement.

"We are? Daniel, that's so cool!"

"I'd already made reservations for dinner in the Ritz dining room, but it occurred to me when I was lying in bed this morning — what better way to capture the spirit of our first date on our six-month anniversary than at another Shakespearean play? Anyway, that's where I went earlier…to the box office to look into last minute tickets."

"Last minute tickets? I don't believe it…"

"I know. I could hardly believe my luck either. I was sure they'd have sold out."

"I'm not talking about the availability of tickets, sailor." Her eyebrow shot up. "Two spur of the moment decisions in one day. Frankly, I'm shocked."

"Oh, *I see*. Now you're making fun of me."

"I'm just teasing you a little."

"That's fine," I conceded. "Tease away. I'll get you back. Later. When you least expect it."

As far as celebrations went, our six-month anniversary was probably the highpoint of them all. Dinner at the Ritz, a ride to the theater in the hotel's Rolls-Royce, and an evening at the Globe Theatre, revisiting the beautiful words of the man who'd brought Aubrey and me together in the first place. All of this was capped off by a sensual tumble in a king-sized bed with my beautiful girlfriend wearing a sexy black ensemble, complete with garters and stockings—a treat she'd purchased especially for the occasion. I was a lucky bastard.

We cuddled for a long time afterward, but Aubrey finally untangled herself and crawled out of bed.

"I'm going to wash up. Hey, by the way," she added, looking around the edge of the bathroom door. "I almost forgot. There's a card for you under your pillow."

A card? *Shit.*

"I'm an ass. I didn't get you a card."

"Daniel, are you clinically insane? After the evening you treated me to, I'm hardly going to think you're an ass for not getting me a card."

"I wouldn't want you to think I was getting complacent…"

With a snort, she disappeared into the bathroom. I found the card, peeled open the flap, and tossed the envelope on the nightstand.

The picture on the front was a simple one—an open pair of hands and a butterfly fluttering away against a sky-blue background. Inside, the card was blank with the exception of Aubrey's writing.

Happy Anniversary, Daniel. I love all that I've become with you, and all that we've become as a couple. Whatever trials we face, we'll face them together. Thank you for an amazing six months. I love being yours.

-Aubrey

XO

I sat up, my throat aching as I reread her words. Perhaps I was taken aback by the sentiment, or maybe I was overwhelmed by the events of the day, I don't know, but I was overcome by a rush of feeling. I closed my eyes.

"Get a fucking grip," I mumbled, propping the card on the nightstand.

I fell back onto the pillows, crossing my hands under my head. Aubrey emerged from the bathroom, shedding her wrap before rejoining me under the sheets. I waited for her to get comfortable, then I tipped her chin up and captured her lips with mine.

"I love the card. Your words were beautiful."

She snuggled against me and sighed.

"I'm glad you like it."

"I actually got a little choked up."

"Really?"

"Yes, really. You know the picture on the front of the card? Is that meant to represent us?"

"I guess."

"Which one of us is the butterfly?"

"I think we've both had our turn being the butterfly."

"What do you think I've freed you from?"

She moved her hand, idly running her fingers through my chest hair.

"I don't know. Myself, maybe. You helped me get out of my own way. Made me see that it's okay to lean on people and accept help."

"It always seems as if you're the one helping me. It's good to know I've been there for you, too."

"We're a good team."

"We sure are."

I lay there for a long time thinking about everything—all of the tension of those early weeks and the misunderstandings that followed, the misplaced jealously and the turmoil at the university, the family crises and emotional upheaval. Somehow we'd managed to get through it relatively unscathed.

I knew our ability to weather the storm had been due, in no small part, to Aubrey's strength and determination. All I wanted now was

THE TRUEST OF WORDS

to be a pillar for her—to support her unfailingly through whatever the future held, just as she'd been there for me since day one.

"Aubrey? Are you still awake?"

"Mmm. Sort of." With her face mashed against my chest, her words were little more than mumbles.

"Can you roll over for a minute?"

"Hmm?"

"Onto your tummy. Roll over."

She muttered something about being comfortable, but she flopped onto her stomach all the same, frowning at me over her shoulder. I kissed her shoulder, and then I traced a small circle in the middle of her back, swirling lines emerging from the center and flowing outward.

"Back Pictionary? Now? Isn't it a little late, sailor?"

"Humor me? Please?"

She hummed indulgently, still frowning. "I have no clue what that is. You're just tickling me."

"You have to concentrate."

"Okay, start again," she said, as I swept my hand across her back.

Once more, I drew a small circle in the center, lines flowing outward and then one long line emerging from the circle and curving down to her tailbone.

"Done. What do you think it is?" I asked.

"I think I know, but I'm not one-hundred-percent sure. Can you give me a hint?"

"Okay, how about this?"

I nibbled on her left shoulder blade, then whispered, "She loves me." Moving over to the other side, I brushed my lips across her right shoulder blade. "She loves me not…"

As I made my way downward, to feather a nibbling kiss across her side, Aubrey chuckled and propped herself up on her elbows.

"She loves you," she said.

"How can you be sure? I've only torn off two petals."

"Because I happen to know she loves you more than she's ever loved anyone."

"Did she tell you that?"

"She didn't have to. It's in her eyes when she looks at you and in her heart whenever she thinks about you."

I smiled and gently slid my nose down her spine, kissing my way backward and forward across her lower back. She flinched and laughed.

"Now what are you doing?"

"I'm weeding."

"I have weeds?"

"Not anymore."

She laughed again and rolled, pulling me up to lie beside her.

"You're crazy."

"No, I'm not. I'm fulfilling my duties. Remember, my queen, I *am* your servant. My job is to look after your flower garden."

Running her fingers through my hair, she gazed up at me affectionately. "It's been a long time since we read *The Gardener* together."

"Why don't we read it when we get home?"

"That sounds heavenly."

"You miss reading together that much?"

"I actually meant the *other* part. Home. I'm looking forward to going home. With you."

"Me too."

I kissed her tenderly and stroked her hair, and then she curled up on my chest again. Very soon, her breathing deepened. Drooling was imminent.

Wrapped in the familiar comfort of her love, I turned off the bedside lamp and closed my eyes, vaguely aware of the sounds of traffic outside. Hopefully, tonight I would sleep peacefully, and in the morning, we'd emerge onto the busy streets of London for the last time and head off to the airport. Aubrey and I would leave England behind and get on with our lives.

Together.

CHAPTER 34

Dreaming

...It's past the size of dreaming...
(*Antony and Cleopatra*, Act v, Scene 2)

The flight home was entirely different from my solo flight to England when I'd been huddled against the window in the darkness, Daniel's PDF files my sole connection to him. On the return journey, he sat beside me, our fingers loosely entwined as we crossed the Atlantic, the sun skimming the tops of the clouds and streaming through our narrow window. Our bursts of conversation were interspersed with long comfortable silences during which I didn't once worry about what was going through his mind.

After our encounter with Nicola at the Tower of London, it was impossible not to notice the energy between us shifting. Nicola had always been there—intangible, yet somehow powerfully present. It was as if Daniel and I had been on parallel paths with her shadow filling the space between us.

Then there were those times when Daniel's path had completely veered away from mine, and I'd been left scrambling to bring him back. Whether it was a conflict with his father, a crisis involving Aaron, or a recurring nightmare, Nicola's accusation had been at the root of it all.

Now that Daniel had forgiven her and unburdened himself in the process, there was something different about the way he was looking at me—something focused and centered in his expression. He'd promised he would try to find himself again. From what I'd witnessed in the course of a mere twenty-four hours, he wouldn't have to look far.

After being away for several weeks, my responsibilities at home needed attention. Several copies of the August issue of *Sidelines* were waiting for me in the mail upon our return. Still amazed that my writing was being published, I excitedly perused the articles I'd written. Then I read the note Eli had slipped inside the envelope with the magazines. He told me, in no uncertain terms, to brace myself for the late-summer and fall slate.

He wasn't kidding.

Throughout the last two weeks of August, I ran from concert to festival gig, submitting numerous reviews for Eli's blog and the October issue of the magazine. Daniel joined me at a few of the seedier venues, but ultimately he had to face reality—tagging along with me to every show wasn't a viable long-term arrangement. The notion became less horrifying every time I returned home unmolested and in one piece.

Daniel was absorbed with his thesis, working as hard as I was. I was heartened by his renewed interest in his work and encouraged by the fact that he was sleeping better and anticipating the new semester with fresh enthusiasm. By the first week of September, he'd met with Professor Brown several times to draw up plans and tutorial schedules for the year.

With the arrival of the Labor Day weekend and the school year a few days away, we finished our work on Saturday evening and made a pact to shelve our responsibilities for the rest of the weekend. Late Sunday afternoon, we made our way to Daniel's parents' house for a family barbeque. I thought we'd left ourselves plenty of time, but somehow we still arrived fashionably late.

"Here they are!" David exclaimed, standing up when he heard the garden gate swinging closed behind us. "I told your mother you'd be here any minute," he said, shaking Daniel's hand and bending to kiss my cheek.

Jeremy and Julie waved from the other side of the patio table, and I squeezed into the empty chair beside Julie.

"It's about time!" Brad complained. "Mom wouldn't bring out the appetizers till you got here. I'm starving."

"If she'd put them out earlier, we'd be doing the dishes by now," Penny quipped, smiling as Daniel gave her a kiss.

"You're one to talk, Miss Thang," Brad said, ribbing her. "You've been eating us out of house and home the last couple of weeks."

Penny slapped him on the leg, a warning look in her eyes. He chortled, leaning over to nuzzle her cheek. Marriage hadn't done anything to curb their feistiness.

Daniel dragged a chair beside mine and pulled multiple copies of the most recent issue of *Sidelines* out of a canvas bag and set them on the table.

"You did ask for a copy, right, Mom?"

"Absolutely." She smiled as Daniel handed her a magazine.

David watched over her shoulder as she flipped through to find my articles. Julie and Jeremy reached across the table at the same time, each snapping up their own copy.

"It's cool seeing your name in print," Julie said.

"I'm sure that'll never get old," I confessed, my face burning with a mixture of pride and embarrassment.

"You know," Gwen said airily, "I was talking to my friend Ralph Davidson from *The Globe and Mail* the other day. One of his free-lancers is off on maternity leave, and he's scrambling for someone to cover the Stratford Festival. I mentioned you in passing, Aubrey. He sounded interested. I think you'd be perfect."

"Oh, I don't know," I said hesitantly.

I glanced at Daniel, wondering if he'd had anything to do with his mother's suggestion. This wasn't the first time I'd heard Ralph Davidson's name.

"Don't look at me," he said, holding his hands up defensively. He pointed to his mother. "Talk to that woman right over there."

"Maybe I'll get some more information from you later, Gwen?" I said.

"Of course, dear. With your love of Shakespeare, it seemed a perfect fit." She pushed her chair back. "Anyway, let me grab some food before Brad faints. He's so delicate, you know."

Gwen and David disappeared into the house.

"Can I get you anything, babe?" Brad motioned to Penny's glass. "Another Perrier? Are you sure you're okay in that seat?"

"Stop fussing, would you?" Penny said, slapping his hands away.

"Yeah, you're her husband, not her personal care worker." Jeremy snorted.

Daniel's parents emerged with the appetizers. Gwen pointed at the plates of dip and crackers.

"That's a hot crab dip, and this one's spinach and artichoke," she said. "Dig in."

Food quickly took precedence, but as we were stuffing our faces, Penny put her hand over her mouth. Brad peered at her worriedly.

"You okay, babe?"

She jumped up, shaking her head and walking to the side of the house, fanning herself frantically. Brad followed, rubbing her back.

I turned to Daniel. "Is she all right?"

At the other end of the table, Gwen looked at the crab dip then brought her own hands to her mouth and stood.

"Gwen?" David said. "Is there something wrong with the dip?"

She shook her head, locking eyes with Brad, who was now grinning at his mother. They seemed to be silently communicating.

"Yes?" Gwen said.

Penny buried her face in Brad's neck, and Brad nodded.

Beside me, Daniel said, "Oh my God," in a reverential tone.

"What's going on?" Jeremy asked.

"I *think* we're going to be uncles," Daniel said.

With those words, Gwen shrieked. I'd never seen a less decorous display of joy from Daniel's mother. It was amazing. She dashed across the patio and hugged her son and Penny simultaneously.

David surveyed the three of them with his hands on his hips. "I don't think I'm old enough to be a grandfather."

"I suppose the truth had to come out sooner or later," Penny said, emerging from the group hug and returning to the table. "We didn't want to say anything too soon, but it's a lot easier with you all knowing."

She waved away the crab dip. Brad dutifully moved it to the end of the table, and Penny sat, the color gradually returning to her face.

"Now you know why Brad looks as pleased as a pig in mud," Penny said.

Brad leaned back in his chair with one of those cocky *my-boys-can-swim* smiles.

"So, give us some details!" Julie exclaimed. "How far along are you?"

"Just eight weeks."

"Wait, you were pregnant at the wedding?" Daniel asked, his eyebrows shooting up.

"Thanks for pointing that out, Daniel," Penny said, lancing him with an icy glare. She looked at her mother-in-law apologetically.

Gwen waved her hand dismissively. "What's the point in waiting? These days, you can never start trying too soon. I couldn't be more thrilled."

"Thanks, Mom," Brad said.

Gwen reached over to squeeze Penny's hand. "Oh my goodness, I should call my mother. Is it too soon, or is it all right for me to tell Patty?"

"Oh, why not?" Penny laughed.

"Go for it, Mom," Brad said.

Gwen clapped her hands and dashed across the patio.

"I think it's safe to say your mother's on cloud nine," David said, smirking at the proud parents-to-be. "I'd better go in and make sure she doesn't start calling everyone she knows. Best wait a few more weeks before allowing the news to go viral, yes?"

As he disappeared into the house, Jeremy gazed at Brad, a curious look on his face.

"What?" Brad said, his back stiffening defensively.

"I just had a vision of you trying to change a baby's diaper," Jeremy said.

"In the vision, did Brad look like a monkey wearing oven mitts?" Daniel asked.

Julie shook her head. "You two are awful." She turned to Penny and Brad. "I think you're going to be great parents."

"I bet Patty's going ballistic," Jeremy said. "First great-grandchild. That kid's gonna be spoiled rotten."

"No kidding," Daniel said.

"Where is Patty?" I asked. "I was looking forward to seeing her today."

"She's with Gerald," Julie said. "He sprained his ankle—possibly tore a tendon. He can hardly walk. Patty didn't want to leave him alone."

Daniel grimaced. "How'd he do that?"

"He was mowing her lawn," Brad said.

The three boys chortled, and Julie rolled her eyes. I couldn't help thinking that if Patty were here, she'd be the one turning the event into a dirty joke.

Penny tapped her nails on the table, quirking an eyebrow at Daniel and sporting her trademark cheeky smile. "So, what's up with you two? Any news to share?"

I contemplated telling everyone that Daniel's shirt closet wasn't color-coded anymore and that he no longer checked The Weather Network seventeen times before going out, but that didn't seem to be the kind of news she was digging for. Before Daniel could make some wisecrack rebuttal, David appeared at the patio door.

"Daniel, Aubrey, could you come inside for a minute? There's something I'd like to show you."

Daniel pushed back his chair and took my hand.

"What's this all about?" I asked him.

"No clue. Sorry, guys, back in a sec."

In the kitchen, Gwen was chatting excitedly on the phone. Daniel and I followed his father upstairs and into his office, where David motioned for us to sit on the leather sofa. He rooted around in his briefcase, pulling a paper free and handing it to Daniel.

"I received this letter at my office on Thursday," he said. "Read it out loud so Aubrey can hear."

After a cursory scan of the paper, Daniel's expression registered his surprise. "It's from Nicola."

"Indeed," his father said.

Daniel held the page tautly in both hands and began to read:

"*Dear Mr. Grant,*

"*You must be surprised to be hearing from me. I had a surprise, too, a couple of weeks ago, when Daniel came to see me. We had a good talk. He mentioned that you're an administrator at a Canadian university.*

*He didn't say which university, but a Google search told me what I
needed to know.*

*"I've enclosed a bank draft with this letter. Daniel said you wouldn't
want me to return the money. He said you'd prefer me to use the money
wisely. I've used a small portion to pay for some college courses starting in
January, but the rest I'm sending back. I'll continue working at my part-
time job, and since I've moved back home, I won't have living expenses to
worry about, so I'll be able to pay for the rest of my tuition. I hope you'll
be grateful to see this money returned. If you're even half as good and
kind as Daniel, I'm sure the money is better off in your hands than in
mine. I'll never be able to undo what I did to Daniel last year, but I've
learned from my mistake, and I hope he doesn't continue to suffer for it.*

"Sincerely, Nicola Clarke."

Daniel handed the letter back to his father.

"Wow," he said, shaking his head as if he'd been struck by a hard
object and he needed to collect his wits.

"I'll say. When you told me you'd gone to see her, I never imagined
this would have come out of your meeting."

"I didn't tell her to write that letter. I tried to convince her to put
her life back together," Daniel said, already on the defensive. "I'm
as surprised as you are."

David looked at his son contemplatively. Here, in black and white,
was proof that his son had been entirely innocent of the accusations
she'd leveled. *How I wished I could see inside his head.*

"Give yourself some credit, Daniel," I said, unable to hold my
tongue. "You obviously got through to her. She must have done some
serious soul-searching afterward."

"Aubrey's right," David said. "Going to see her in the first place
was decent of you, but I'm sure you put a great deal of thought into
what you said to her."

Daniel reached for my hand, taking it in both of his. "Not re-
ally. Everything happened so fast. All I did was tell her the truth."
He paused, looking down at the carpet and then back at his father.
"How do you feel about the money being returned?"

David gazed at us over his bridged hands.

"You were right. I wasn't interested in having the money back,
but she's sent it, so there's no point rejecting the gesture. I'll put it to
good use. Perhaps something philanthropic would be appropriate."

"You have a grandchild on the way," I pointed out. "You could get Penny and Brad started on a savings plan for school."

"That's a great suggestion," David said. "I'd like the money to benefit someone outside the family too." He closed his eyes. "What was that girl's name, Aubrey? The one whose family lost their house at Christmas?"

I scanned my memory, a search that took me back to a Monday morning in February when David had cobbled together a bursary with some provincially released funds — the same morning Daniel had caught me rifling through his father's filing cabinet drawer.

"Shannon Davis, wasn't it?" I said.

David snapped his fingers. "That's exactly right. I'll set her up with an anonymous bursary to help her with the upcoming term. Money well spent, I'd say." He tossed the letter into his briefcase before drawing another paper out of a folder and handing it to Daniel. "There's one more thing. This is probably a moot point, but you might be interested in seeing it anyway."

I snuck a peek at the page. There was an Oxford University crest at the top. "What's that?" I asked.

Daniel exhaled shakily. "This is the letter from Oxford, outlining the events of last year," he said. "I saw this in my file when I met with Aaron O'Connor in June. How did you get it?"

David tapped his index fingers together.

"Remember I told you I was working on something involving Aaron, and I wasn't sure if I'd be able to seal the deal? I didn't want to get your hopes up unnecessarily in June, but he came through for me in the end. This letter arrived at the office while we were in the UK."

"O'Connor gave it to you? Willingly?"

"I did give him something in exchange."

"What could he possibly want from you that would be as significant to him as this is to us?"

David shrugged. "Everything's relative. One of Aaron's greatest frustrations is Travis's difficulty finding a decent job. I wrote him a glowing letter of recommendation."

"Dad, the kid behaved appallingly," Daniel said. "What the hell did you find to glow about?"

"He had an excellent academic record. Perhaps a letter from the Provost of one of the most prestigious universities in the country will be the edge he needs to rise above the competition."

"So, Aaron helps me, and in exchange you help his son?" Daniel said.

"Essentially, yes."

Daniel frowned. "I'm surprised you'd do something like this."

"Even *my* conscience doesn't extend as far as pricking me for trying to end my son's suffering. That letter would have been expunged from your file after a year. I've merely expedited the process by two months—"

"Which ensures that whoever takes over for Aaron doesn't get an eyeful of this letter before I start the new school term."

"Precisely. I didn't want you to start another year with a black mark against your name." He paused for a moment, his lips pursed. "I suppose I felt I needed to do something significant to prove once and for all that I believe you as well."

Daniel looked meditatively at the letter. "Aubrey, would you give us a few minutes?"

"Of course." I squeezed his hand before slipping from the room, closing the door behind me.

I couldn't blame Daniel for wanting a few quiet moments with his father. After eighteen months of quibbling and suspicion, they seemed on the brink of repairing their damaged relationship. The last thing they needed was me hovering.

Downstairs, Gwen was directing traffic as Jeremy and Brad refreshed drinks. I offered to help, and Gwen gave me a couple of tomatoes to slice for a salad. Jeremy and Brad returned outside, and I got her up to speed on what was happening upstairs. She smiled as she grated Parmesan cheese for her Caesar salad.

"Things between Daniel and David have been tense for so long. It's terrible watching them snipe at each other all the time. I'm glad they're talking. This is good."

"It's fair to say they're turning a corner."

"First Penny and Brad's news, and now we're putting this Oxford business behind us." Gwen sniffed and brought her hand to her throat. "I feel like I'm dreaming. It's a little overwhelming."

Daniel's footsteps clattering down the stairs interrupted us. I spun around as he strode into the kitchen, his eyes still betraying his amazement at this sudden turn of events.

"You okay?" I asked him.

"Yeah. I'm good." He addressed his mother over my shoulder. "Is it all right if Aubrey and I sneak away for a few minutes to talk?"

"Of course," his mother said. "We won't be eating until six at the earliest. We'll wait until you're ready."

"Thanks, Mom."

Daniel took my hand and led me to the music room. He closed the door, locking it for good measure, and then he pulled me into his arms.

"The talk with your dad," I whispered. "What did he say?"

He stepped back, his hands still clasped tightly around my waist.

"The one word I've been waiting for him to say for over a year."

I searched his eyes. "What's that?"

He clenched his teeth, trying to steel himself, and then he leaned his forehead against mine. "Sorry," he said quietly. "He told me he was sorry."

I stood on my toes and stroked his hair, listening to his unsteady breaths. Gwen had been right. The talk between David and his son had been good. It had been *very* good.

"I love you so much, Aubrey," he whispered. When his lips met mine, his kisses were heavy with feeling. "I want to take you home right now."

I was suddenly overcome with a desperate, aching need, but I tried to think rationally.

"Daniel, we should get outside."

He shook his head, and this time when he kissed me, he slowly gathered the fabric at the back of my dress with his fingers.

"Everyone's waiting for us," I protested.

He walked me backward toward the built-in bookshelves.

"Didn't you hear my mom? She said to take our time. The door's locked. They can wait. I don't care."

He didn't care. Did *I* care? He nuzzled the spot on my neck that always made me tingle. At the same time, one of his hands crept under the hem of my dress and then snuck inside my panties. *Fuck, no.* I didn't care either.

He pushed me into the bookshelf. I wiggled shamelessly against his fingers while he rubbed himself just as brazenly against my leg.

"See the predicaments you get us into by being so sexy?" he breathed into my ear.

THE TRUEST OF WORDS

"Oh, God," I gasped.

He slowly slipped my panties down, making me step out of them and tucking them into his pocket with a divinely dirty laugh. Then his hands were everywhere—in my hair, feathering up and down my arms, sliding inside my dress to caress my breasts, moving down to clutch at my ass—and, God help me, I didn't stop him. On the contrary, I spurred him on, kissing him wildly, rubbing him through his pants and uttering wicked words of encouragement against his lips.

Months ago, I'd dreamed of Daniel taking me like this. My dream had been incredibly sexy, but reality with Daniel always surpassed my fantasies. He raised my hands above my head, curling my fingers around a shelf and telling me to hold on, and then he unzipped his pants and buried himself inside me. He swore and moaned, tugging on my lower lip with his teeth, and my whole body quivered. For a moment, I forgot where I was.

"Daniel...oh fuck..."

"Shh, Aubrey," he murmured, tilting his head, his lips at my ear. "Whisper..."

"This is crazy..."

"But really fucking hot..."

It was hot—and terribly reckless. But now it was too late. We were both too far gone. I was certain I could feel the ridges in the wood grain of the shelf as I gripped it, and I could definitely feel Daniel's heart beating against mine. In the silence of the room, our uneven breathing and muted moans were amplified and deliciously sensual.

I slid my hands along the shelf, imagining the scene as it would appear to an onlooker—Daniel and I, still partially clothed, but obviously in the middle of a steamy encounter. One of his hands grasped my right wrist while the other was wrapped around me, steadying us as he pinned me to the shelves with every thrust. Instead of making me tense and self-conscious, the threat of being caught created another layer of exhilarating pleasure.

I focused on the twitching muscle in Daniel's jaw as he struggled to control himself. I wanted nothing more than to let loose, but like Daniel, I held back, pressing my lips to his neck and digging the heel of my shoe into his leg, aiming my quiet whimpers toward his ear. He returned the favor, swearing through gritted teeth and sinking his fingers into my hip with his final deep thrusts. A moment later, we both laughed breathlessly at our audacity.

"I can't believe we did that," I said, hastily sliding the strap of my dress up while Daniel fixed his boxers and zipped up his pants.

"Yep. Incredibly foolish." He winked slyly. "And I'd do it again in a heartbeat."

"Me too," I said, with a mischievous smile. "Crap, we really need to get outside."

"We should wash up first, don't you think?" he asked.

"Yeah." I cringed. I definitely needed a washroom.

"We'll duck into the powder room. Come on."

We snuck out of the music room, looking around guiltily as we dashed across the hall. Daniel locked the bathroom door and washed his hands while I cleaned myself up as best I could. He was trying to tame his tousled hair when I spun around and slipped my hand into his pocket. He caught my eye in the mirror.

"Miss Price, I'm going to have to ask you to try to control your insatiable urges," he said, with a sardonic tilt of his head.

I pulled out my panties and swung them in front of his face.

"Since you just had my panties in your pocket, I'd say we're long past the days of *Miss Price*, wouldn't you?"

I slid my panties on.

"Ready?" he said.

"Ready."

He reached for the doorknob, but after wiggling it ineffectually for a few seconds, he dropped his head forward.

"Oh, shit."

"What is it?"

"The door. I can't believe it. My parents still haven't fixed the damn thing. We're locked in."

I should have panicked, or at the very least felt embarrassed by the fact that Daniel and I were about to get caught hanging out in the bathroom together, but I didn't. Instead, I started to laugh, and I couldn't seem to contain myself. Daniel rolled his eyes at me, but a smile was tugging at the corners of his mouth too. He pulled his phone from his back pocket.

"What are you doing?" I asked between giggles.

He held his finger to his mouth.

"Hey, Jeremy? It's me. Look, don't say anything, but I need you to come inside right now, and grab a coat hanger. Yep, both of us. Don't you dare, just get in here."

"Well, sailor, this is another fine mess you've gotten us into," I said, trying not to burst into gales of laughter again as he re-pocketed his phone.

He shook his head and sighed. A moment later, we heard a scratching noise and then a *pop* as the locking mechanism was freed. Daniel opened the door, and Jeremy stood on the other side holding a misshapen coat hanger, looking back and forth between the two of us. He tapped the mangled hanger against his other hand.

"I don't even want to know, do I?"

On Monday, Daniel and I set off for Toronto Island, hoping to enjoy a sail around the harbor before settling in to watch the Labor Day fireworks from the island. Lost in his thoughts, Daniel gazed out at the skyline as we crossed the harbor in the water taxi.

"How do you feel about tomorrow?" I asked him. "Are you nervous?"

"Not at all. I was actually thinking about how anxious I was in February. I feel completely different heading into this school year."

"Those freshman will love you. This is going to be an awesome year for you, sunshine."

He smiled, his fingers tightening around mine.

"No comment?" I asked.

"What can I say? Sometimes, when the person you adore says something really wonderful, it's best to just smile and nod."

He kissed me softly, and then we sat back, gazing out at the water again. Daniel bobbed his head skyward.

"Those clouds don't look promising."

"Maybe we can have a quick cruise around the island before the weather turns," I said, doing my best to be optimistic.

Arriving at the island dock, Daniel clambered out of the boat, holding his hand out to help me. We couldn't have walked more than six steps before several giant raindrops splashed around us, and then the clouds opened. We sprinted toward Daniel's slip, but by the time we'd reached the boat, we were drenched.

"Watch your step—it'll be slick," he shouted, helping me aboard.

He fumbled in his pocket for the cabin keys while I hopped around behind him, giggling and shrieking in the pelting rain. The more he hurried, the longer it took for him to juggle the right key into his fingers.

"Damn it!" he yelled, finally slipping the cabin key into the keyhole.

I took his hand and pulled him away from the door, throwing my arms around him so he couldn't move.

"What are you doing?" he exclaimed, rain streaming down his face.

"What's the big deal?" I laughed. "We're already sopping wet."

He shook his head in disbelief, but he wrapped his arms around me anyway and kissed me passionately—and soggily. He finally wrenched the cabin door open and ushered me in ahead of him. He slammed the door and threw a towel on the floor. We both stood on it, panting and dripping wet.

"*You* are a head case," he marveled, slipping my bag off my shoulder and tossing it on the counter.

"Oh, that was fun, and you know it," I said.

"You're right. As usual. And you're *soaked*."

He helped me take off my sopping T-shirt and then unclasped my bra. Pulling off his own T-shirt, he held me close and kissed me again. All wet lips and warm tongue, he chuckled as I rubbed my chest against him.

"You're also very slippery," he said.

"I bet you say that to all the girls." I looked up at him, doe-eyed.

"Nope, only the slippery ones."

I laughed, and he peeled off my soggy shorts and finished undressing himself. Then he pulled the blanket back on the cabin's tiny bed, revealing the clean sheets underneath.

"I'm really wet. Don't you think we should dry off?" I asked him.

"Uh-uh. You being really wet is pretty much perfect for what I have in mind right now."

He tugged me onto the bed with him, moving me onto my back. I reached down to squeeze his butt playfully.

"Your ass is cold, sweet-knees."

"It's your job to warm it up."

"I don't remember ass-warming being part of my job description."

"That's because I only added it ten seconds ago."

Still giggling, I reached up to comb his wet hair off his face with my fingers, wiggling underneath him and guiding his hips forward.

"What, no foreplay?" he asked, looking down at me with a dimpled smile.

"Daniel, you should know by now—just living with you is foreplay."

My hair was stuck to the side of my face, the sheets were damp under our tangled legs, and our plans had gone completely awry. Oddly enough, I wasn't irritated in the slightest. Daniel sighed, equally content as he wrapped himself around me. We lay still and silent for a long time, listening to the rain pattering on the boat, but finally he pushed himself up onto his elbow.

"Miss Price, I think that was the soggiest, slipperiest, most glorious boat romp we've had to date."

"Gah, that's it!" I laughed, rolling onto my back. "You and the Miss Price-ing. I'm strongly considering changing my name."

He looked at me with a strange expression.

"You know, I might be able to help you with that—one day."

I blinked up at him stupidly. Help me change my name? Huh? What was he saying? I swallowed thickly as he ran his finger across my collarbone.

"I'm not trying to pressure you," he said, his eyes darting anxiously across my face. "I've been thinking about us a lot the last couple of weeks…about our future. I guess I'm wondering if you'd be averse to me asking you an important question one day. I'm only running this by you because I wouldn't want to get my hopes up unnecessarily…"

I smiled, my heart too full to even try to unpack it with words.

"You've been a chatterbox all day, sweetheart. Did you really have to choose this moment to lose the power of speech?" He chuckled nervously.

"Well, you see," I said. "I've heard that when the person you adore says something really wonderful, it's sometimes best to just smile and nod."

He breathed out evenly and tucked a few wet strands of hair behind my ear.

"I love you, poppet."

"I love you, sailor. *So much*."

And that was enough. Those six words told him everything he needed to know.

EPILOGUE

Journey's End

Journeys end in lovers meeting,
Every wise man's son doth know.
(*Twelfth Night*, Act II, Scene 3)

As Daniel and I crossed the underground parking garage one Friday night in November, he stopped to pull me into his arms impulsively, his lips warm and insistent against mine. I curled my fingers around his lapels, eagerly returning his passionate kisses. What was it about Daniel in a suit that made it impossible for me to think straight? I contemplated the evening ahead. Perhaps we could have appetizers at Canoe and then call it a night.

"We're going to be late again, sailor," I whispered.

"It can't be helped. I think it's this dress. I'm not sure how I'll keep my hands to myself at the restaurant."

"You've outdone yourself, too. Incredibly swoony. I should've brought my smelling salts."

"I seem to remember a time when you gave me permission to catch you if you fall. I promise, I'll be right there with my arms ready in case your knees fail you tonight," he said.

And…commence swooning.

It had been months since we'd driven down Lakeshore Boulevard. I was reminded of the night in March when Daniel and I had traveled westward along this same road toward an unknown destination, me simmering in anger and resentment, while he'd been awash in guilt and despair, wondering if I'd be able to forgive him for falsely accusing me of messing around with Matt.

Tonight, although there was a similar chill in the air, it was a chilliness borne of the temperature alone. Instead of staring out the windows while listening to a mournful song, we had the Flaming Lips cranked, both of us bobbing our heads in time to the music. Even the brutal traffic couldn't dampen our spirits. Daniel sang along as he drove, tapping his palm against the steering wheel.

"If you don't pay attention to the road, we're going to miss the turn-off," I said. "Your family's going to think I'm a bad influence on you. We always seem to be the last ones to arrive, these days."

"The last thing my family would think is that you're a bad influence. Anyway, they can think what they please. It's not our fault the traffic sucks. We'll get there when we get there."

He continued singing, his fingers routinely squeezing mine as we crawled toward the Palais Royale. Ten minutes later, we were on our way into the dance hall, the big band music floating from inside the ballroom, carrying with it the loaded memories of our last visit. We shrugged off our coats and gave them to the girl behind the counter.

"Your family is waiting for you in the private room," she said, gesturing to the door at the end of the lobby.

Daniel slipped his arm around my waist, guiding me to the room in which we'd shared our first dance and our *almost* first kiss on March thirteenth — eight months ago to the day. Before reaching for the doorknob, he brought his fingertips to one of my earrings, his eyes dropping down to my necklace.

"Thank you for wearing the jewelry I've given you," he said, lifting my hand and kissing my wrist above the spot where the bangle sat.

"They're all beautiful pieces. I love wearing them."

His eyes clouded, and he kissed me, his lips continuing to hum against mine, even as the kiss ended.

"Do you ever feel so happy that you can't help wondering what the catch is?" he asked.

"Sometimes there's no catch. Sometimes, it's just your turn to be happy."

"You're right." A gentle smile tugged at his lips. "Come on."

We entered the room. Gerald and David were engrossed in a conversation by the bar. Penny, Brad, Jeremy, and Julie were sitting on the sofa talking in hushed voices. Penny waved, and we strolled over to join them.

"Municipal politics," Penny said, bobbing her head at her father-in-law and Gerald. "I think David's found himself a new debating partner."

"Let them get on with it." Daniel motioned for me to sit down in the remaining armchair. "Where's Mom and Patty?"

"Patty had to use the washroom. Gwen went with her," Julie said.

"So, you guys look rested," Daniel said to Penny and Brad. They were both tanned thanks to their recent southern getaway. "Did you have a good time?"

Brad rubbed Penny's back, doting on her as usual. I tried to imagine him in the delivery room. He'd either be a godsend or a menace. I was inclined to think Penny would pronounce him the latter.

"We had a fab time," Penny confirmed. "I'm glad we went away before I got any bigger. I was self-conscious enough as it was."

She patted her gently rounded tummy.

"Believe me, babe, no one was staring at your belly," Brad said.

Daniel eyed her chest. "Yeah, I didn't think it was possible for you to get more endowed, Penn. Holy shit."

"I have half a mind to get a massive breast-reduction after I've finished having children. Then what will you lot talk about, I wonder?"

"The good old days?" Jeremy suggested.

Before Penny could rebut Jeremy's comment, Daniel's mother and grandmother returned.

"Daniel, how was your week in British Columbia?" his grandmother asked, patting his hand as she moved to sit beside Penny on the sofa.

"The symposium was very enjoyable. It's good to be home, though."

"I'm sure it is. You must have missed each other?"

"Terribly," I confirmed.

"You'll have to make up for lost time," Patty whispered.

"Luckily, I have next week off," Daniel reminded his grandmother with a sly wink.

"No one wants to hear about your epic sex life, Daniel," Brad said.

Patty cast a stern look at Penny and Brad. "I hope you've all got healthy sex lives. And don't you two go paying attention to those ridiculous stories about the dangers of sex during pregnancy. That's absolute rubbish."

"Thank you, Patty," Brad said, looking at Penny as if the words *I told you so* might spill from his lips any second.

"If my baby is born with a ruddy enormous dent in its head, we'll have *you* to thank," Penny said, nodding at Patty.

Brad elbowed Daniel. "Did you hear that, bro? An *enormous* dent."

Jeremy snorted, and Daniel shook his head, sighing as he looked over his shoulder at his parents chatting by the bar.

"Mom, I don't mean to be difficult, but Aubrey and I have dinner reservations. What's the plan?"

"Of course, we shouldn't hold you up. Mother?" Gwen said, craning her neck around to see Patty. "Are you feeling up to having a dance?"

"That is why we're here, Gwen," Patty said, holding her hands out in front of her.

Daniel pulled her up as Brad gave her a helpful push from behind.

Gerald offered her his arm. "May I have the honor of escorting you to the dance floor, Henrietta?" he asked.

"My goodness, what a lot of nonsense," Patty said, trying to brush off his chivalrous advances, but blushing like a schoolgirl anyway.

We entered the ballroom, finding an empty table bordering the dance floor.

"Off you go, you two," Daniel said. "Show us how it's done."

Julie clung to my arm as we watched Patty and Gerald take their place among the rest of the fox-trotting couples.

"They're so cute," she said with a sigh. "I hope I'm that feisty when I'm older. I've never known such a pervy eighty-year-old."

"I wonder if you'll still be able to touch your foot to your ear when you're eighty," I whispered. "That would be amazing."

Julie giggle-snorted. On the other side of me, Gwen leaned over, touching my forearm lightly.

"I was talking to Ralph on Wednesday, Aubrey. He said you wrote a fabulous piece on *The Boys in the Photograph*. He's really impressed with your work."

"He's very supportive. I'm learning a lot."

"And Daniel was telling us that he's almost ready to defend his paper," she added, looking around the table. "I'm so proud of you all."

"Mom," Jeremy said, a note of warning in his voice. "Don't go getting all *verklempt*."

"I know. I'm sorry. I can't help myself."

David made his way around the table, leaning between us. "I hate to interrupt, but are we permitted a turn on the floor if we're not collecting pensions?"

Gwen held her hand out to him. "I can't imagine they'd toss us out on our ears, David. We did pay a fee for the private room."

She stood, and together they crossed to the floor.

"This place is beautiful," Julie said, surveying the room.

"Why don't you and Jeremy go and dance?" I suggested.

"Do you think we can?"

She looked at Jeremy beseechingly, and he lifted her to her feet, slipping his arm around her waist.

"Come on, fancy feet," he said.

"Try not to steal the show," I called out.

Julie beckoned us over. "You guys should come, too."

"I think I'll sit for a bit, actually," Penny said. She ruffled Brad's hair. "Not up to having my toes squashed at the moment. Daniel, you and Aubrey should go ahead."

"Are you sure?"

"Oh, go on, have a dance. We'll be fine."

Julie and Jeremy disappeared into the crowd, and we followed. Daniel took me in his arms, and after a couple of missteps, we found our groove. We'd done our fair share of dancing at clubs and concerts over the last few months, but Daniel was so versatile. He could make the switch from the bump-and-grind to the rumba without batting an eyelash. Truth be told, I was beginning to feel a lot more at home ballroom dancing, too. Daniel was an excellent teacher.

Being held close while slow-dancing was one thing, but being able to travel the floor in unison somehow seemed more intimate than plodding around in a circle. It spoke of a shared history, secret understandings. A quick double-squeeze of his hand would let me know he wanted to spin me; a slight increase in the pressure of his fingers on my lower back warned me not to move too far beyond the circle of his arms for fear of crashing into another couple.

"You're getting good at this," Daniel said, bringing me in closer. "You seem more confident."

"I'm following you, sunshine. You lead well."

"Don't get all modest."

"It's not about modesty. Being good at this kind of dancing means you have to listen to your partner's body. Communication isn't only about words — it's subtext and body language too. Dancing well together is a great indicator of compatibility, don't you think?"

"I couldn't agree more."

As we danced, I caught sight of Patty and Gerald on the other side of the floor.

"Your grandmother and Gerald look happy. I'm glad we worked this into our plans tonight. It's nice for them to have family around to enjoy these special moments after all that secrecy."

Daniel nodded and leaned his chin against my temple. As the song came to an end, he whispered a kiss on my forehead before facing the front to applaud the band. I was all set to exit the floor and rejoin Penny and Brad at the table, but when the next song started, Daniel reached for me.

"No…wait…we have to dance to this one." He drew me toward him again.

Beside us, Julie and Jeremy drifted by. Not missing a step, Julie called out to us over her shoulder, "They're playing your song."

I frowned up at Daniel. "What song is this?"

"It's 'The Way you Look Tonight.' Not quite the same as Michael Bublé's version, is it?" he said.

"Oh, right. It does sound different — especially without someone singing."

"Did you tell Julie we danced to this song the last time we were here?"

"I guess I must have. The way we're dancing right now is a hell of a lot more impressive than our first dance, don't you think?"

"I think we pulled off a pretty good Grade Nine Grope." He laughed. "It was a *quick* grope, but I'll never forget it."

I felt his smile against my temple, and then he took a deep breath, the pressure of his hand on my lower back keeping me close. I peeked over my shoulder, assuming we were on a collision course with another couple, but there was no one in our immediate vicinity. We had plenty of room. Again, I felt him take in a giant lungful of air, and then his arms seemed to tense as he breathed out. I looked up at his face.

"Are you okay, sweet-knees?"

"I'm fine. I'm wondering if I should…I mean—there's something I need to tell you."

"What is it?"

"I was going to tell you later, but I don't know. I think I should tell you now. It seems like the right time. It's kind of important."

I examined his expression. "Daniel, you're scaring me."

"I'm sorry. It's nothing bad. It's actually quite good…at least I think so." He looked at my lips, and then his eyes swept upward until they were locked with mine. "It's just—well, your dad says *hi*, and he wants you to know he might come out for a visit over Christmas."

"My *dad* says hi? When were you talking to my dad?"

"I did more than talk to him. I met him. I went out for dinner with him…"

"What are you talking about?"

In my bewilderment, I tripped over myself. Daniel led me out of the way of the other moving couples and into the middle of the floor where he took both of my hands in his.

"I told you a fib, sweetheart. I'm really sorry. I wasn't returning home from British Columbia yesterday. I was coming home from Calgary. The symposium finished on Tuesday. I flew to Calgary on Wednesday and stopped over for a night. You see, I needed to meet your father and talk to him about something important."

I shook my head. "What are you—?"

"You're going to think I've lost my mind," he said, scanning the room before turning to regard me solemnly. "I never dreamed I'd do this here, in the middle of a crowded room, but what you said before about Patty and Gerald…it's true. *We've* spent too much time hiding in the shadows, as well. I don't want to hide. This wasn't how I'd planned things, but God help me, I've chosen now to do something completely spontaneous."

He squeezed my hand, and then he stepped back and dropped down to one knee.

I was so completely unprepared for what was happening that I drew my hands up to cover my enflamed cheeks. The elderly couples around us smiled and moved to the edge of the dance floor.

On the other side of the floor, Patty's mouth dropped open, and Gerald put his arm around her waist to steady her. Even the bandleader looked over his shoulder, perhaps sensing something unusual was happening behind him.

All of this happened in the space of ten seconds, the time it took for Daniel to lower himself to his knee and reach into his jacket pocket to pull free a small velvet pouch.

"Your father gave me his blessing, Aubrey, so I'm going to ask you a really important question," he said. "Are you ready?"

I nodded, my eyes stinging and my hand over my mouth as I swallowed my tears. If only he'd given me a hint, I could've prepared myself. I could have been articulate and composed instead of idiotically mute. He gazed up at me, still clutching my fingers. I tried to breathe evenly, willing myself to stay upright, although my kneecaps were threatening to jump out of their sockets. Daniel swallowed hard.

"Aubrey Price, over the past nine months, you've been my muse, my jester, my favorite sparring partner, and my best friend. You've shared everything with me. Your intellect, your heart, your body, and your soul.

"I feel like I could spend all night making a list, describing the ways you touch my life, and still not be able to adequately explain what you mean to me. Perhaps with enough time, I can give it my best shot. If you do me the honor of becoming my wife, I'll prove to you every day how important you are. Knowing you'll be beside me for whatever my life holds would make me the happiest man alive."

He released my fingers long enough to withdraw the ring from the small pouch and place it tentatively at the end of my ring finger.

"Please say you'll marry me."

"Yes," I said, laughing and crying at the same time. "Yes, of course! Of course I'll marry you."

He took my shaking left hand and slipped the ring on. I suppose I should have held the ring up to look at it, but I was too preoccupied with the happiness on Daniel's face and the adoration shining in his eyes as he stood up, hugged me, and whispered, "I love you, Aubrey."

"I love you too, Daniel. I think I'm going to burst."

He laughed and kissed me, and the couples around us applauded. As he held me tightly, his lips found my ear.

"That was the most singularly nerve-racking moment of my life."

We stood, gently rocking until the song came to an end. I grabbed his shoulders.

"My knees are jumping. I swear I'm going to fall over. Don't you dare let me go."

"Don't worry. I'm not letting you go. Like it or not, you're stuck with me. Forever."

"Promise?"

"I promise."

Julie squealed and hugged us from behind, dragging us off the floor with Jeremy following close on her heels. Penny was making a beeline for us with Brad in tow.

"Bloody hell! Brad just told me what happened. I missed everything," Penny exclaimed, throwing up her arms in frustration. "I was in the damn loo!"

"Sorry, Penn." Daniel shrugged. "Should I have sent around a bulletin beforehand?"

"I can't believe you proposed in the middle of the dance floor." She took his face in her hands, slapping his cheeks lightly and scrutinizing his eyes. "Is that really you, Daniel?"

He removed her hands and grimaced. "Stop being so dramatic."

She whirled around, her eyebrows shooting upward. "Did you hear that, Brad? Daniel told *me* to stop being dramatic."

"You guys. Enough," Julie said, taking my left hand and bringing it close to her face. "Oh my gosh, the ring turned out perfectly…"

Before I even had a chance to inspect my own engagement ring, Patty and Gerald emerged from the dance floor, with Gwen and David in hot pursuit. Everyone crowded around us, talking over each other, enthusiastic hugs and kisses and handshakes coming at us from all sides. My head spun.

Daniel drew me close to his side.

"I'm so sorry," he murmured against my cheek. "What the hell was I thinking?"

In the private room, Daniel and I stood by the French doors, and I finally took the opportunity to examine my ring. Across the room, David was pouring champagne, and everyone else was speaking in hushed voices, giving us a moment to collect ourselves.

"Are you all right?" Daniel asked.

"Of course. A little overwhelmed. I wasn't expecting this tonight."

"We'll have a few sips of champagne, let everyone make a fuss, and then we'll head to Canoe, okay?"

I nodded, holding my hand out and tilting my fingers from side to side.

"Daniel, I love the ring. It's beautiful. It's so…*me*."

"Your mother helped me design it."

I gaped up at him. "My *mother?*"

"We've been emailing each other since Labor Day weekend. I told her my ideas and explained what I was working with, and she started sending me sketches and pictures."

"I had no idea."

"Of course not. Your mom's a great secret keeper. Julie was the one who said you tend to wear silver, and suggested white gold, but see this?" He pointed to the delicate thread of rose gold running through the center of the band. "It's from Patty's engagement ring."

"What? Are you kidding?"

"The night she met you in March, she took me aside after dinner. I think you were in the washroom. She told me that when I was ready, she wanted me to have the ring—she said she really hoped it would be for you."

I looked across the room at Daniel's grandmother. I recalled the moment he'd just described. I'd come out of the bathroom at Patty's house to find Daniel kneeling beside her chair as she spoke to him quietly. I'd retreated to let them finish. How had she known I was the one, and that, eight months later, Daniel and I would be planning a future together?

"There wasn't much to her engagement ring," he said, drawing me from my reverie. "My grandfather didn't have a lot of money. In those days, rose gold was quite reasonable. He got her another ring on their fifth anniversary, but she kept that first one, and when she gave it to me, she said I could do whatever I wanted with the band and the diamond. I wanted to incorporate both. That's what inspired me to buy you the rose gold jewelry in the first place."

I touched the pendant at my neck.

"Daniel, you bought this necklace *months* ago. Did you know, even then, you'd be proposing to me one day?"

"I knew we weren't ready, but I guess I quietly hoped. Even now, there's no rush. We can have a long engagement if that's what you want."

He gently squeezed my fingers and pointed to the band again. "These small diamonds are cuts from Patty's solitaire. There are six on each side, plus the one in the middle. That diamond is new, of course…"

"Thirteen diamonds…"

"Exactly. Thirteen *is* my lucky number."

Could he be more adorable?

"You've planned everything so carefully."

"I've had lots of help. Julie's been scouting for me since the summer, picking your brain, making sure you weren't completely averse to the concept of marriage."

"Everything makes sense now."

"Everything's always made sense, poppet. We just didn't know it."

I'd told him earlier I thought I was going to burst, but now I truly thought I might. My feelings were impossible to contain — my body was simply incapable of holding in all of that love. Even my face ached from the effort of keeping myself together. I finally had to move, sniffling and rubbing under my eyes.

"Here, try this," Daniel said, pinching the bridge of my nose.

I laughed, feeling ridiculous. Batting his hand away, I stepped into his arms, hugging him tightly.

"Hey," he said, his voice low against my ear. "How does it feel knowing you're going to be Mrs. Shmexy?"

Brad was the one who finally decided we'd had enough quiet time.

"You guys can smooch later," he called across to us. "We can't drink this champagne without you, you know."

Julie joined us. "Here you go," she said, giving us each a flute glass.

I hugged her. "Thanks, bun-head. And thanks for giving Daniel such stellar insider information about what kind of ring I'd like. You know me so well. It's important for a maid of honor to be completely in touch with what the bride likes, don't you think?" I looked at her hopefully.

"Are you serious?" she squeaked.

"Of course I'm serious. Is that a yes?"

"Well, duh," she said.

"This is so touching," Daniel said, pretending to dab his eyes with his tie.

Again, Brad waved impatiently. Daniel guided me across the room, and I reached for Patty and hugged her.

"Thank you," I whispered. "I love my ring."

I wanted to say more, but my throat tightened again. She squeezed my hand.

"Thank *you* for giving a weary old artifact a new lease on life."

"How did you know, Patty?" I asked her. "When I came over for dinner in March—how did you know?"

"I watched you two interacting. Daniel's a tough nut to crack. When someone spends so much time trapped in his own head, it can be terribly challenging to reach him, but you seemed to have such lovely *long arms*," she said, squeezing my elbow for emphasis.

Daniel chuckled and kissed his grandmother's cheek, and then he turned to thank everyone for their support over the past couple of months. Daniel's family—soon to be mine. I could hardly believe it was possible.

Penny tapped her nails dramatically against her Perrier glass. "I'm just so blasted relieved it's out in the open. I hate keeping secrets like that."

"You should all apply for jobs with CSIS because I didn't have a clue," I said.

"Years and years of practice," Gwen said, giving David a wry smile. "I believe it's hardwired into our DNA."

"There certainly do seem to have been fenceposts around every corner over the last couple of months," David agreed. "But I think we can all relax now."

"I thought you were going to propose over dinner, dude," Jeremy said. "What happened?"

Daniel gazed down at me. "I think I got caught up in the moment."

"And almost gave your grandmother the vapors in the process," Gerald pointed out.

"Sorry, Patty," Daniel said.

Patty waved her hanky at him. "Don't apologize. What a treat to share such a wonderful moment, spontaneous or otherwise."

With his glass held high, Gerald said, "Here's to getting caught up in the moment."

"Thanks everyone," Daniel said, holding me close and tapping his glass against mine before taking another quick sip.

"Now, we're certainly not trying to get rid of you," David interjected, "but you have a dinner reservation. Don't let us keep you."

Gwen nodded. "Your father's right, especially with the roads being wet and goodness knows what's happening with the traffic. It was terrible earlier."

As we commenced the round of parting hugs and kisses, Gwen made us promise to look at a calendar as soon as possible. Daniel rolled his eyes and assured her we'd get right on that.

I never thought I'd say it, but I *did* want to get right on it. Neither planning our wedding nor living within the confines of a marriage seemed at all worrisome. My mother had been right in June when she'd told me I mustn't allow the shadow of her and my father's failed marriage to cast a pall over my attitude toward a lifelong commitment to one person. *My* one person was Daniel, a man who loved and supported me unequivocally.

"See you soon!" Penny called out as we escaped the room, a chorus of good-byes ringing out as we closed the door.

Daniel expelled a long, relieved breath. "Jesus, you do realize what you're getting yourself into, right?" he asked as we crossed the lobby. "Planning this wedding is going to be insane. Why do I feel like I should've written an escape clause into the proposal?"

"It's gonna take more than a few overzealous wedding planners to scare me away."

"You may live to regret those words."

"How about if I need a break, I get to bring you with me? Deal?"

"Deal. Shake on it?"

We laughed and shook hands, and then we collected our coats and made our way out to the parking lot arm-in-arm, the faint strains of the orchestra floating out the door behind us.

"Alone, at last." Daniel sighed as we buckled ourselves in. "Come here. I want to give my fiancée a proper kiss."

"*Fiancée.* Wow, I love the sound of that."

"I think *wife* sounds incredible too, but one thing at a time, yes?"

I nodded, melting into his kiss.

"Tell me something?" he said.

"Hmm?"

"Was there any hesitation? When I proposed…did you waver?"

"Not in the slightest."

"Honestly?"

"How you can doubt it? You know how much I love you."

"I defy any man putting his heart on the line like that *not* to feel a flicker of doubt, Aubrey."

"Well, to quote your favorite troubled young hero, '*Doubt thou the stars are fire; Doubt that the sun doth move; Doubt truth to be a liar; But never doubt I love.*'"

"Look at you, stealing my tricks. I'm supposed to make *you* swoon."

"I've been swooning all night. You don't need Shakespearean sonnets to bowl me over. Your own words were pretty damn amazing."

"I meant every one. I hope you know that."

He kissed me again, and I cursed our plans for the second time that evening.

"Hey, sweet-knees? I know this is going to sound crazy, but how would you feel about skipping dinner and going home?"

"You don't want to go to Canoe?"

"I think I'd rather get cozy and flake out on the couch. We could order a pizza and have a few drinks without worrying about driving."

"I don't think that sounds crazy at all. Can I make a request?"

"Sure."

"Would you wear your Bard to the Bone T-shirt with some white panties and a pair of sweat socks?"

"I'll wear that if you'll wear your holey jeans and a black T-shirt."

Daniel pulled out his phone and called Canoe, canceling our reservation amid profuse apologies.

"There," he said as he ended the call. "Easy as that."

"Thanks, sunshine. I don't mean to seem ungrateful."

"Hey, I threw you for a loop tonight. I'm not surprised that you need some time to digest what's going on."

"It's not that. I'd kind of like to dive into planning right away. It would be a good idea to pick a date so I can give my parents and Jo and Matt lots of notice."

He smiled as he rubbed his thumb across my knuckle. "When you imagine our wedding day, what does it look like?"

"I'm not sure. I wasn't one of those girls who spent her teenage years dreaming about her big day."

"How would you feel about an evening wedding?"

"That sounds romantic."

"I'm glad you think so. I've been looking at next year's calendar," he said, his eyes lit with enthusiasm. "How about a ceremony in midsummer, maybe on a Friday evening?" He held out his phone, opening the calendar app. "Look at this. Friday, July thirteenth."

"Huh. I like it. It sounds *right*."

"Yeah?"

"Absolutely. I think we just set a date."

He gaped at me. "Jesus, that was easy. Why did I think this was going to be painful?"

"I'm not sure. Maybe I'm still in shock."

Daniel's hand enclosed mine, his thumb curling around to touch the ring.

"Hey, can I make one *small* change in the wardrobe for tonight, sailor?"

"What's that, my poppet?"

"No sweat socks. My feet aren't even *remotely* cold."

Daniel grinned and pulled out of the parking space. While he focused on driving, I reveled in my happiness, gazing out at the road ahead. Traffic may have been crazy earlier, but now the boulevard lay before us, virtually clear of cars. Our journey home would be an easy one.

Smooth sailing ahead.

Acknowledgments

So here we are, at the conclusion of Poppet and Sailor's journey! It's been a thrill sharing this story with all of you. When I started writing *The Weight of Words* in September of 2009, I never dreamed I'd see my words in print. What an incredible year!

To Elizabeth and the Omnific team, I'm so grateful for your hard work in bringing my books to life. To the editorial team — Sarah and Cindy, in particular — thanks for taking such good care of my words. Special props to Micha for designing three stunning covers and to Cory for the impeccable work on the interior design.

Enn, amazing publicist and genuinely wonderful friend, thank you for everything you do, not just for me, but for all of the authors you cheer on. You are a tireless champion for the stories you love. I'm so grateful that you fell in love with mine. I'll never forget your first review. (In case you've forgotten, it was this: "Agh"). Thank you from the bottom of my heart for your never-ending (though oftentimes inarticulate) support.

Once again, I must thank the readers who take the time to write reviews on Goodreads or Amazon, or simply write a post on their Facebook wall. Word of mouth recommendations are so important to authors. I also owe a huge debt of gratitude to the bloggers who spread the word about the books they love. Your efforts are so appreciated.

To my fellow authors, and especially the Omnific family, it's wonderful to be a part of a community in which everyone respects and helps each other.

Thank you to Jenn and Dee and all the friends who've stayed by my side throughout this adventure, and a huge shout-out to my T-dot gals for always having my back.

To my family, I'm so lucky to have your love and support. Thanks, Mum, for saying "well done, you." You have no idea how much I needed to hear that. And the biggest hug ever to B, my life-long bestie, for taking this crazy turn in my life in stride and rooting for me every step of the way.

To my husband, thank you for holding my hand and nodding, regardless of how crazy the words coming out of my mouth must seem sometimes. I don't know where I'd be without your unfailing love and support.

~GG

About the Author

Georgina Guthrie is a self-professed book hugger and compulsive diarist. Though GG now resides in Canada, she was born across the pond and still considers herself a Brit through and through, which may explain her frequent visits to her favorite local British import shop.

GG is often happiest when reading and writing, but she's just as likely to be found hanging out with friends and family, almost certainly with a glass of red wine in one hand a bag of cheese and onion crisps in the other.

Join Georgina on Twitter @georgey_girl

New Adult Romance

Three Daves by Nicki Elson
Streamline by Jennifer Lane
The Shades series: *Shades of Atlantis* & *Shades of Avalon* by Carol Oates
The Heart series: *Beside Your Heart, Disclosure of the Heart* & *Forever Your Heart*
by Mary Whitney
Romancing the Bookworm by Kate Evangelista
Flirting with Chaos by Kenya Wright
The Vice, Virtue & Video series: *Revealed, Captured, Desired* & *Devoted*
by Bianca Giovanni
Granton University series: *Loving Lies* by Linda Kage

Paranormal Romance

The Light series: *Seers of Light, Whisper of Light* & *Circle of Light* by Jennifer DeLucy
The Hanaford Park series: *Eve of Samhain* & *Pleasures Untold* by Lisa Sanchez
Immortal Awakening by KC Randall
The Seraphim series: *Crushed Seraphim* & *Bittersweet Seraphim* by Debra Anastasia
The Guardian's Wild Child by Feather Stone
Grave Refrain by Sarah M. Glover
The Divinity series: *Divinity* & *Entity* by Patricia Leever
The Blood Vine series: *Blood Vine, Blood Entangled* & *Blood Reunited*
by Amber Belldene
Divine Temptation by Nicki Elson
The Dead Rapture series: *Love in the Time of the Dead* & *Love at the End of Days*
by Tera Shanley

Romantic Suspense

Whirlwind by Robin DeJarnett
The CONduct series: *With Good Behavior, Bad Behavior* & *On Best Behavior*
by Jennifer Lane
Indivisible by Jessica McQuinn
Between the Lies by Alison Oburia
Blind Man's Bargain by Tracy Winegar

Erotic Romance

The Keyhole series: *Becoming sage* (book 1) by Kasi Alexander
The Keyhole series: *Saving sunni* (book 2) by Kasi & Reggie Alexander
The Winemaker's Dinner: *Appetizers* & *Entrée* by Dr. Ivan Rusilko &
Everly Drummond
The Winemaker's Dinner: *Dessert* by Dr. Ivan Rusilko
Client N° 5 by Joy Fulcher

Historical Romance

Cat O' Nine Tails by Patricia Leever
Burning Embers by Hannah Fielding
Seven for a Secret by Rumer Haven

Anthologies

A Valentine Anthology including short stories by
Alice Clayton ("With a Double Oven"),
Jennifer DeLucy ("Magnus of Pfelt, Conquering Viking Lord"),
Nicki Elson ("I Don't Do Valentine's Day"),
Jessica McQuinn ("Better Than One Dead Rose and a Monkey Card"),
Victoria Michaels ("Home to Jackson"), and
Alison Oburia ("The Bridge")

Taking Liberties including an introduction by Tiffany Reisz and short stories by
Mina Vaughn ("John Hancock-Blocked"),
Linda Cunningham ("A Boston Marriage"),
Joy Fulcher ("Tea for Two"),
KC Holly ("The British Are Coming!"),
Kimberly Jensen & Scott Stark ("E. Pluribus Threesome"), and
Vivian Rider ("M'Lady's Secret Service")

Sets

The Heart Series Box Set (*Beside Your Heart, Disclosure of the Heart* &
Forever Your Heart) by Mary Whitney
The CONduct Series Box Set (*With Good Behavior, Bad Behavior* &
On Best Behavior) by Jennifer Lane
The Light Series Box Set (*Seers of Light, Whisper of Light, Circle of Light* &
Glimpse of Light) by Jennifer DeLucy
The Blood Vine Series Box Set (*Blood Vine, Blood Entangled, Blood Reunited* &
Blood Eternal) by Amber Belldene

Singles, Novellas & Special Editions

It's Only Kinky the First Time (A Keyhole series single) by Kasi Alexander
Learning the Ropes (A Keyhole series single) by Kasi & Reggie Alexander
The Winemaker's Dinner: RSVP by Dr. Ivan Rusilko
The Winemaker's Dinner: No Reservations by Everly Drummond
Big Guns by Jessica McQuinn
Concessions by Robin DeJarnett
Starstruck by Lisa Sanchez
New Flame by BJ Thornton

Shackled by Debra Anastasia
Swim Recruit by Jennifer Lane
Sway by Nicki Elson
Full Speed Ahead by Susan Kaye Quinn
The Second Sunrise by Hannah Downing
The Summer Prince by Carol Oates
Whatever it Takes by Sarah M. Glover
Clarity (A *Divinity* prequel single) by Patricia Leever
A Christmas Wish (A *Cocktails & Dreams* single) by Autumn Markus
Late Night with Andres by Debra Anastasia
Poughkeepsie (enhanced iPad app collector's edition) by Debra Anastasia
Poughkeepsie (audio book edition) by Debra Anastasia
Blood Eternal (A Blood Vine series single, epilogue to series) by Amber Belldene
Carnaval de Amor (The Winemaker's Dinner, Spanish edition)
by Dr. Ivan Rusilko & Everly Drummond

coming soon from
OMNIFIC PUBLISHING

The Poughkeepsie Brotherhood series: *Saving Poughkeepsie* (book 3)
by Debra Anastasia
The Hidden Races series: *Incandescent* (book 1) by M.V. Freeman
The Legendary Saga: *Claiming Excalibur* (book 2) by LH Nicole
The Runaway series: *The Runaway Ex* (book 2) by Shani Struthers
The Forever series: *Forever Autumn* (book 1) by Christopher Scott Wagner
Something Wicked by Carol Oates
Going the Distance by Julianna Keyes

www.ingramcontent.com/pod-product-compliance
Lightning Source LLC
Chambersburg PA
CBHW020254120726
47904CB00001B/200